Praise for

"Heartfelt, heartwarming, joyful, and uplifting. You can't go wrong with a Rachel Linden book."
—Debbie Macomber, #1 *New York Times* bestselling author of *One Night*

"A poignant, hopeful must read for anyone who has ever wondered about a different path. Rachel Linden creates unforgettable characters that will work their way into your heart and a compulsively readable story that will keep the pages turning late into the night. Five huge stars!"
—Kristy Woodson Harvey, *New York Times* bestselling author of *The Summer of Songbirds*

"A magical novel about second chances! Warm, witty, and wise, I loved it! Linden is a master at creating loveable characters! *The Magic of Lemon Drop Pie* is escapist reading at its best!"
—Jill Shalvis, *New York Times* bestselling author of *The Summer Deal*

"An enchanting tale about the one thing we've all imagined: a magical second chance. Rachel Linden expertly mixes romance, mystery, and family drama into a delicious recipe of a story. With her trademark warmth, Linden delivers a captivating story with a magical heartbeat at its center."
—Patti Callahan, *New York Times* bestselling author of *Surviving Savannah*

"Magic, sweet treats, heartfelt charm . . . this dreamy tale has it all!"
—*Woman's World*

"*Recipe for a Charmed Life* is actually a recipe for a magically marvelous read about expectations, second chances, and following your heart. Rachel Linden writes complicated and compelling characters that are as relatable as they are likeable. I enjoyed every bit of this delightful novel."
—Jenn McKinlay, *New York Times* bestselling author of *Summer Reading*

"The perfect mix of delicious backdrop details, family secrets, and the quest for purpose and lasting love. Enchantingly delightful from first page to last."
—Susan Meissner, *USA Today* bestselling author of *Only the Beautiful*

"Rachel Linden whips up an irresistible family drama oozing with charm and magic! *The Magic of Lemon Drop Pie* is a must read for anyone who longs for second chances. A gem of a novel that charmed me from [the] get-go, perfect for fans of Sarah Addison Allen and Alice Hoffman."
—Lori Nelson Spielman, *New York Times* bestselling author of *The Star-Crossed Sisters of Tuscany*

"A delicious read, down to the very last lemon drop! Rachel Linden delivers a delightful escape, wonderful characters, and a magical experience that will leave readers hungry for her next book."
—Julie Cantrell, *New York Times* and *USA Today* bestselling author of *Perennials*

"A delightful tale of food, family, and sweet romance. This story is an absolute feast!"
—Lauren K. Denton, *USA Today* bestselling author of *The Summer House*

"Completely charming! Take a spunky heroine, add a swoonworthy, orange-rubber-overall-wearing oyster farmer, throw in a dash of the real-life messiness we all understand, and sprinkle a dusting of Linden's signature magical realism, and you've got the recipe for a delightful story you can't put down."
—Katherine Reay, bestselling author of *A Shadow in Moscow*

"A deliciously sweet tale about refusing to give up on your dreams and finding your bliss against all odds. Linden gives readers so much to enjoy—romance, family drama, and bittersweet second chances—all served up with the perfect dash of magic."
—Kate Bromley, author of *Here for the Drama* and *Talk Bookish to Me*

BERKLEY TITLES BY RACHEL LINDEN

THE MAGIC OF LEMON DROP PIE

RECIPE FOR A CHARMED LIFE

THE SECRET OF ORANGE BLOSSOM CAKE

The Secret of Orange Blossom Cake

RACHEL LINDEN

BERKLEY

NEW YORK

BERKLEY
An imprint of Penguin Random House LLC
1745 Broadway, New York, NY 10019
penguinrandomhouse.com

Copyright © 2025 by Rachel Linden
Readers guide copyright © 2025 by Rachel Linden
Penguin Random House values and supports copyright. Copyright fuels creativity, encourages diverse voices, promotes free speech, and creates a vibrant culture. Thank you for buying an authorized edition of this book and for complying with copyright laws by not reproducing, scanning, or distributing any part of it in any form without permission. You are supporting writers and allowing Penguin Random House to continue to publish books for every reader. Please note that no part of this book may be used or reproduced in any manner for the purpose of training artificial intelligence technologies or systems.

BERKLEY and the BERKLEY & B colophon are registered trademarks of Penguin Random House LLC.

Book design by Jenni Surasky
Title page and interior illustrations by Jyotirmayee Patra

Library of Congress Cataloging-in-Publication Data
Names: Linden, Rachel author
Title: The secret of orange blossom cake / Rachel Linden.
Description: First edition. | New York: Berkley, 2025.
Identifiers: LCCN 2025012980 (print) | LCCN 2025012981 (ebook) | ISBN 9780593816639 trade paperback | ISBN 9780593816646 ebook
Subjects: LCSH: Women cooks—Fiction | Cookbooks—Fiction | Families—Fiction | Self-realization in women—Fiction |
LCGFT: Magic realist fiction | Novels
Classification: LCC PS3612.I5327426 S43 2025 (print) | LCC PS3612.I5327426 (ebook) | DDC 813/.6—dc23/eng/20250408
LC record available at https://lccn.loc.gov/2025012980
LC ebook record available at https://lccn.loc.gov/2025012981

First Edition: September 2025

Printed in the United States of America
1st Printing

The authorized representative in the EU for product safety and compliance is Penguin Random House Ireland, Morrison Chambers, 32 Nassau Street, Dublin D02 YH68, Ireland, https://eu-contact.penguin.ie.

For Sarah,
my best friend forever because you know all the good stuff.

And for my father, Stan,
thanks for being half Italian and a wholly good man.

The Secret of Orange Blossom Cake

Chapter 1

The summer that changes my life begins with a bright orange molded Jell-O salad.

"A Jell-O salad just feels perfect for June, don't you think?" I chatter breezily to my roommate and cohost Drew as I set out grated carrots, crushed pineapple, and a big box of lemon Jell-O on the kitchen counter of our apartment, arranging all the ingredients in a pleasingly photogenic way. "Now that we're finally getting some sunshine, I think a molded gelatin salad is just the thing for this last segment." Only this week did it finally feel like summer in Seattle after months of gray drizzle.

Drew adjusts the lights and recording equipment, fine-tuning before we start shooting. It's late afternoon on a Sunday in mid-June, and we're getting ready to record the last of the short cooking show segments we release each week on Instagram. We're using our day off to film an entire month's worth of segments for our show *The Bygone Kitchen*, just as we have once a month for the past five years.

"I just don't get the appeal of Jell-O salad," Drew admits. "It feels like old lady at a church potluck type of food." He shoots me a wry, dimpled grin. "I'd go for a craft brew IPA and some cheese curds over Jell-O any day." (Drew is from Wisconsin, a state in which cheese features prominently in the comfort food category.)

"Scandalous!" I gasp in mock outrage, rearranging a few ingredients on the counter so I can grab everything easily as we are filming. "Clearly, you don't understand the positive power of Jell-O salad. I'm convinced any sadness or disappointment in life can be helped by a nice big scoop. And there are so many to choose from. Sunshine Salad, Cherry Cola Salad, Strawberry Pretzel Salad, Orange Sherbet Salad, Broken Glass Salad . . ."

Drew pulls a face. "Nothing people eat should be named 'broken glass,'" he says, giving me a playful smirk. He fiddles with the sound levels, his sandy blond head bent over our fancy new recording equipment.

"Okay, you might be right. But our followers are going to love this, you watch. Ethel especially," I promise, brushing a wisp of dark hair from my cheek, smoothing it back into my short, wavy bob and untying my flour sack apron—red polka dots with a bluebird on the front, made from an actual Blue Bird Flour sack. I wore it for the episode we just shot where I made a peach pandowdy. Now I'm doing a quick costume change. Underneath the apron I'm wearing a 1960s orange, yellow, and green floral polyester shift with a white Peter Pan collar, my outfit for the Sunshine Salad segment. Usually, I thrift my outfits for the show, but this one came from my own closet. I love everything with a '60s vibe.

"Did you see the comment Ethel left on the johnnycake recipe segment from last week?" Drew asks with a raised eyebrow and a grin. Ethel is one of our most ardent followers, a spunky eighty-nine-year-old great-grandmother from Pennsylvania who leaves detailed comments in all capitals on every segment we post but hasn't quite mastered the nuances of emojis.

"You mean when she posted heart eyes and three eggplant emojis after the word 'tasty' in all caps?" I smooth the Peter Pan collar.

"That's the one." Drew laughs. "She's lethal with those emojis. Okay, we're all set. Give me a sec and I'll go get changed." He disappears down the hall toward his room.

I slick on a little Burt's Bees lip balm over my orangey-red lipstick and take a deep breath. I always feel a touch nervous before we start shooting, wanting everything to go to plan. I like things to go according to plan. I try to tamp down my anxiety, then remember the advice of Dr. Dana, the therapist I started seeing after the accident that claimed my dad's life. *Acknowledge, embrace, release.*

"It's okay to feel anxious," I murmur to myself, naming the emotion. "Just remember, if something gets messed up, we can always rerecord it." I take a second deep breath, hold it for four beats, breathe out through my nose. Right now the kitchen smells deliciously like freshly baked peach pandowdy. That could definitely be worse. Last month we made liver mush for an episode and the rank smell lingered for days. I still sometimes catch a ghostly whiff of it wafting from the stiff brown carpet near the kitchen doorway. I take another deep breath, hold it, then exhale slowly. Better. I still feel a flutter of anxiety in the center of my chest, but as soon as the camera clicks on and I read the first ingredient aloud, I know from experience that my nerves will dissipate and I'll be in my happy place once more.

I glance around in satisfaction. I love this basic little kitchen in the apartment we've called home for the past five years. The plain oak cupboards are brimming with my vintage kitchen gadgets and bakeware—glass-lidded pastel Pyrex dishes with their pretty snowflake pattern, a tall stack of aluminum Jell-O molds in pleasing shapes. In this simple little space I take such delight in sharing vintage recipes with viewers. These recipes helped me make it through the very darkest days of my life and helped me navigate overwhelming loss and grief. Now I want to share their strength with others.

People like Ethel are the reason I keep making these fifteen-minute segments each week. I do it for Ethel—who is widowed and can no longer drive—and many others who are disabled, retired, lonely, or simply needing an escape for a few minutes from the hard things in life. I love knowing that, for those few minutes, I'm giving our followers something useful and happy, filling people's lives with encouraging, informative, and hopefully entertaining content to make their day a little brighter.

This show is the most valuable thing in my life, the reason I get up every day. Which is why the thought of the meeting scheduled for later tonight causes my stomach to flip over with a new wave of anxiety mixed with a wild dash of hope. Tonight could change everything in the best way possible.

"Ready to roll?" Drew pops back into the kitchen wearing a gray suit, white shirt, and slim black tie and matching fedora he found at Goodwill. It's a very Frank Sinatra vibe. He doffs the fedora, a quick little trick of the wrist as he rolls it down his toned arm and flips it back onto his head. "Do you fancy the Twist, the Mashed Potato, or the Swim to go with your Jell-O salad?" He pushes a button on his phone, and the unmistakable notes of a doo-wop song swell through the kitchen. He demonstrates the dance steps, his movements quick and lively. I've never known someone who could move their body like Drew. He was born dancing, his mother told me once.

"Um . . . how about the Swim?" I pick one at random, not entirely sure what the dance move is. Jell-O salads shot to popularity in the 1950s and '60s, so Drew is leaning into the era with a little song-and-dance routine for the segment. It's the special sauce that he brings to the show. When I first began filming the cooking segments during the long, monotonous early days of the pandemic lockdowns in

Seattle, Drew was solely behind the camera. He was a good friend and supportive roommate who generously helped me record my little hobby. It was a way to connect with other people and break up the stifling boredom and anxiety of those seemingly endless months, and we thought it was fun. Then one day after a few months of filming a new segment every week, on a whim Drew popped on-screen and performed a little soft-shoe dance routine wearing a straw boater while I was cleaning up an accidental soup spill. Viewer numbers spiked noticeably.

Realizing we'd stumbled upon a good thing, we capitalized on it. In the ensuing five years, I've remained the mainstay of the cooking segments, giving a little history of the dish and showing step-by-step instructions on how to make each vintage recipe, but Drew has become my invaluable sidekick, the goofy show-off that makes the segments funny and fun. By day Drew is a music teacher at an exclusive private school in Seattle, but he's always loved to dance, and his big dream is to move to LA someday and try to make a career in the entertainment industry. I'm trying as hard as I can to keep him here. Without him, I'm pretty sure I won't have a show worth watching. Realistically, I figure at least half of our viewers tune in each episode just to see Drew. Maybe more if I'm honest. He's charming and cute and a little zany, a good counterpoint to my more calm and studious on-screen presence. Together we make the magic that keeps this show going. If I lose him, I'm afraid it will spell the end of everything.

Which is why I have to convince Drew to stay. He's been getting restless lately, talking about possibly doing a scouting trip to LA. Hopefully, the meeting tonight will provide just the right incentive for him to stick around. I've managed to cobble together a life again after losing almost everything fifteen years ago. I honestly don't know what I'll do if he leaves. I don't think I could handle losing him and the show both. They're the two most important parts of my life now.

"The Swim it is." Drew claps his hands together. "You ready?"

I nod, glancing at the clock. The meeting starts at nine. Plenty of time to film the segment and walk over to Needle & Thread, the trendy speakeasy near our apartment in the Capitol Hill neighborhood where Keith has arranged to meet us.

Keith Garvey is a TV series developer who stumbled upon our show on Instagram a few months ago and contacted us, saying he was interested in potentially helping us turn our segments into something far bigger. We've been in conversation since then about possibilities, and tonight he's meeting us because he says he has news to share. Now standing at the kitchen counter, I cross myself and kiss my thumb for luck, just as my Italian Nonna Bruna taught me when I was a little girl.

"Please let it be good news," I murmur a quick prayer, then firmly push the thought of the impending meeting away. Right now, I have a Sunshine Salad to teach viewers how to make. I don't have room to worry and fret.

"I'm ready." I give Drew a nod, turn to the camera, and grab the box of lemon Jell-O, offering my brightest, most welcoming smile as he starts the recording. "Good morning, friends, and welcome to *The Bygone Kitchen*. Today I'm going to show you how to make the perfect summery treat from yesteryear..."

And just like that I'm once again doing the thing I love the most. The anxiety and worry melt away under the glow of the lights and the eye of the camera, just as they always do. I am in my happy place, and I'll do everything I can to stay here.

Chapter 2

"*Drew, Juliana, thank* you for meeting with me tonight. As I said in my call, I have some news." Keith leans forward in a navy crushed velvet club chair amid the Art Deco elegance of Needle & Thread and smiles professionally.

"Good news, I hope?" I wiggle nervously in a ridiculously tall and not very comfortable linen balloon chair and take a sip of my bespoke cocktail, trying to look cool and sophisticated, not sweaty and antsy, which is how I actually feel. I can't believe that just thirty minutes ago I was washing off lemon Jell-O as we wrapped filming for the day. Now here we are in a business meeting that could change our futures.

Next to me in a matching balloon chair, Drew clears his throat nervously. Keith, Drew, and I are crowded around a tiny table in the glamorous, narrow speakeasy hidden above Tavern Law, a popular bar near our apartment. Currently, I am drinking a St-Germain—a deliciously bubbly twenty-dollar champagne and elderflower liqueur cocktail. Thank goodness Keith is paying. My job at Trader

Joe's and my half of the modest amount we make through the show do not allow for such luxuries in a city as expensive as Seattle.

All around us there's a low hum of conversation. The dim lighting and muted jazz soundtrack make the small space seem exclusive and very posh. Beside me, Drew is sipping a fancy French gin cocktail. Outwardly, he looks calm and affable, but his knee is jiggling, a sure sign that he's as agitated as I am. He's seemed a little off today, to be honest. When I asked him on the way over if he thought it would be good news, he hesitated and didn't meet my eyes, which isn't like Drew. Usually, he's Mr. Enthusiasm. Maybe he's just nervous too. We both want this to go well. There's a lot riding on it.

"Well, that depends on how you look at it, I guess." Keith smiles coolly. He isn't drinking a cocktail, which for some reason makes me even more nervous. Actually, Keith makes me nervous period. He's very well-groomed for a man in his fifties, tanned with wavy blond hair and shockingly white teeth. His smooth, blank face gives away nothing. He must be a great poker player. I can never tell what he is really thinking, and I have this sneaking suspicion for some reason that he doesn't really like me. He's a successful talent scout for TV series and has turned more than one YouTube sensation into a genuine star. As the brains behind *Nailed It!* and *Snack vs. Chef* among other shows, he has a nose for winners, he's told us more than once. Somehow when he looks at me, though, I get the niggling feeling that I am being measured and found wanting. I never feel like a winner around Keith. And yet, here we are. I sip my cocktail, the elderflower liqueur and champagne tickling my nose.

"So what's the news?" Drew asks with a strained smile. I draw a quick breath, equal parts anxiety and anticipation. What we are hoping for, what Keith has been working toward, is getting a contract for a limited series on one of the streaming networks like Peacock or Max. Netflix would be a dream come true, although Keith says that's a long shot. Any deal with a network would mean significantly more money and viewership reach than anything we've done before. And it would allow us to keep filming together. We'd have to move to LA, but that's a price I'm willing to pay. Seattle has always been my home, but since my dad passed away and my older sister Aurora got married and relocated to the East Coast, it's also felt lonely. Maybe something new could be good. I take a gulp of my cocktail for courage.

Keith picks up his glass of water and takes a small sip. "Look, I know we were hoping for a limited-run series for *The Bygone Kitchen*." He glances at both of us dispassionately and sets his glass down with a clink. "Let me be frank. That's not going to happen. I presented the idea to several streaming services, and unfortunately, none of them were interested in picking up your show."

"Oh." My hopes deflate as suddenly as a popped birthday balloon. No LA. No TV deal. "Why not?" I ask hesitantly.

"They don't see the current format resonating with audiences. They're looking for something more . . . on trend," Keith says carefully.

"On trend." I swallow the words and taste disappointment, as bitter as flat champagne. I take a moment to absorb the news. Honestly, I'm crushed. But then I try to look for the positives, another Dr. Dana trick. True, it's not what I was hoping for, but it isn't the worst news in the world. Drew and I can keep doing what we've been doing, keep building the brand, and maybe something good will happen soon. We have seventy-five thousand viewers. We're growing slowly, but it could potentially turn into more . . .

I realize Keith is still talking.

"There is some interest from another angle," he says.

Beside me, Drew leans forward curiously. "What angle?" he asks.

My heart skips a beat. Maybe there's good news after all?

"Peacock has decided to test out a new show with a different format," Keith explains. "They want to offer a limited-run series of six episodes, to see how it does with audiences." He pauses. "They're interested in a show that hosts a themed dance contest in local iconic dining spots around the US."

"What?" I stammer in surprise just as Drew blurts out, "Cool!"

I'm baffled. How is this going to be a good fit for us? Drew is the dancer. I have no rhythm. "I don't understand. They want us to host this new show?" I'm trying to imagine myself hosting this. I think I'd be a disaster.

Keith holds up one well-manicured hand and smiles regretfully. "I'm sorry, Jules, but unfortunately, they only want Drew."

"Only Drew?" I stare at Keith as an icy feeling of comprehension trickles through me.

"Hey, that's not what we discussed," Drew protests. I glance over at him in surprise. His expression is mingled confusion and disbelief as he looks at Keith. "You said you were going to find something for Jules too," he says.

"You knew about this?" I whisper in disbelief, the feeling of betrayal cutting sharp and quick.

Drew squirms in his seat. "Keith called me a couple of days ago and asked me to submit an audition recording, but he said he was working on finding something for both of us in LA," he tells me, looking guilty. "It was supposed to be for both of us." He shoots a helpless glance at Keith, who is watching us impassively.

"I tried to find something for you both, but unfortunately, right now there's only interest in you, Drew," Keith explains. "I'm sorry, Jules." He frowns sympathetically in my direction.

I stare at Keith, then Drew in bewilderment. Drew submitted an audition tape and didn't tell me? I thought we had no secrets from each other. Confused and hurt, I look down into my glass. The champagne bubbles are still rising lazily from the bottom in a beautiful golden stream, like anticipation, like hope. They only want Drew. The rejection stings so badly. I swallow hard and look up at Keith.

"Why don't they want our show?" I'm trying to control my voice so it doesn't tremble, although I can feel a hard knot of disappointment and embarrassment tightening in my chest. I feel so small in his eyes, the one who wasn't wanted. I hate this feeling. I'm failing all over again. I'm losing the thing that is most precious to me. I bite my inner cheek hard. *Keep it together, Jules. Just a little longer.*

Keith sets down his water glass. "The producers want the new show to appeal to a certain young demographic, and they feel both the show and your hosting style just doesn't set the right tone." He steeples his fingers and waits, his pale eyes on me, impassive. "If you had a bigger following or a fresh concept, that would be one thing, but as it stands now . . ." He spreads his hands, implying there is nothing he can do. I am simply not enough. No one wants me.

I nod numbly, the hard knot unfurling into a familiar feeling of shame and grief. I'm going to cry. Suddenly, I can't stand to stay here a moment longer. Setting my half-empty champagne coupe on the table, I rise abruptly, fumbling for my vintage flower power patterned handbag. I turn to Keith. "Thank you for this opportunity," I say with as much dignity as I can muster. I'm fighting hard to quell the hot tears pricking the backs of my eyelids. Keith stands and shakes my hand firmly. His look of dispassionate sympathy almost wrecks me.

"Good luck, Jules," he says. "And if you come up with a really fresh, new concept or if you get those numbers up, feel free to contact me, okay?"

I nod silently and whirl toward the stairs, deliberately not looking in Drew's direction.

"Jules," Drew calls to me, but I don't stop, stumbling down the narrow stairs, my chunky penny loafers making a clunky racket with each step. I can't quite seem to breathe.

Chapter 3

"**Jules!**" **I've reached** the bottom of the stairs when Drew catches up to me. Ignoring him, I push through the heavy bank vault door, shouldering my way through the packed pub and finally making it outside into the misty cool of the night. Reaching the sidewalk, I take a gasping breath, catching a whiff of pot smoke and rain-slick pavement in the chilly air.

"Jules, wait!" Drew grabs for my arm, and I whirl on him in the spill of light from Tavern Law's front windows.

"Why didn't you tell me he'd asked for an audition tape?" I demand, hurt by his omission. Several pedestrians skirt us on the sidewalk, giving whatever is going on between us a wide berth.

Drew looks baffled and distressed. "Keith said it was to make sure I was a good fit. He said there might be options, but I thought he'd find something for you too." His tone is pleading for understanding. "He said he'd try to find something for both of us."

"Did he tell you about the other show?" I cross my arms and fix him with a hard stare. I'm not generally big on confrontation, but this feels like a betrayal of our friendship. I can't just meekly accept it. A soft rain is misting down around us, and the sidewalk is crowded with passersby hurrying to get inside one of the many nightlife spots nearby. I shiver with cold and shock. I feel blindsided by Keith's revelations. In all my imaginings of what he might say, I just didn't see this coming.

Drew hesitates, confirming my suspicions. "He said he thought he could get both of us a spot, but maybe not together on the same show," he admits. "Keith mentioned something about this other one, yeah." He scuffs the toe of his sneaker against the pavement.

I can't believe he didn't tell me. Why didn't he tell me?

"Who's the other cohost? Did he say?" I try to ask it coolly, like it doesn't matter much to me.

Drew's shoulders slump. He takes off his driving cap and runs a hand through his hair so it sticks up on end. He looks like a chastised little boy.

"Desiree Reyes," he says finally.

My mouth falls open. "Desiree Reyes? *The* Desiree Reyes?"

Unless you've been living under a rock, you've at least heard the name Desiree Reyes. A super popular social media influencer, she combines normal kitchen activities with acrobatic hip-hop dance routines. Her million plus followers on TikTok love to watch her shimmy and grind her way through making a smoothie or pouring colorful kids' cereal to peppy dance beats. She's gorgeous, lithe, and confident. They want to pair Drew with *her*? I try to imagine it. Sweet, cute, goofy Drew with that sexy sun-bronzed dance goddess? Horribly, I can see it. The thought makes my stomach curdle. He is going to take this job. There is no way he says no. No one says no to Desiree Reyes and her huge following.

"You're going to say yes." It's not really a question. Drew opens his mouth. He looks torn and a little guilty and my hopes plummet. Of course he's going to say yes. How could he not? It's a huge opportunity, a once-in-a-lifetime chance. We've talked about getting a break like this for years, but it was supposed to be both of us, together. Now I'm the one who's going to be left behind.

"I told him I'd think about it," Drew says finally, reluctantly. "Nothing's decided yet." He glances back toward the door. He wants to go back to Keith, I realize. Of course, they have more to discuss. This is so much worse than just a simple "no thanks" from the studios. This is the end of all my dreams for *The Bygone Kitchen*.

"Go," I tell him wearily. "I get it. It's an amazing opportunity." And it is, for Drew, but it feels so unfair that this golden opportunity for Drew comes at such a cost to me and to our show.

Drew looks torn. "Jules," he says, "I'm so sorry." His forehead is creased with worry.

I nod. "I know." I believe him, but it doesn't lessen the sting of disappointment. "I've got to go," I say, although he knows as well as I do that I have nothing I need to go do. I back up until I step off the curb into a puddle. Instantly, my shoes are soaked through.

"Jules, wait." He stares at me unhappily. "Don't give up, okay? We can still make this work."

"You heard Keith," I respond dully. "They don't want me. They want someone with more followers, someone 'on trend.'" I'm only thirty, but right now I feel ancient.

"You still have a chance," Drew challenges. "Keith said he'd reconsider if you had a fresh concept or grew the viewership of the show."

"Drew, there is no show without you," I point out.

His face falls and he nods. He knows it's true. "You can't give up, Jules," he urges. "You're really good at this. You're smart and super cute. You've got a great sense of style. You sparkle on camera and you're kind. People love you. They . . . they feel understood, like you care about them, even when they've never met you. So maybe these bonehead producers don't want you. Someone else will. You just have to show them who you are." He looks at me pleadingly. Easy words for someone who's just been given his dream job.

"And how would I do that?" I challenge. "If you say yes to Keith and move to LA, I have no show and no way to prove anything."

Drew worries his lip, thinking. I can tell he wants to make this better, but there is no way to do that now, not unless he says no to Keith, and I would never ask that of him. This is his chance to live his dream. I'm hurt he didn't tell me, but it's not his fault the producers don't want me or the show. I'm just not what they're looking for and Drew is. It's the hard, sad truth.

"What about the cookbook?" Drew asks suddenly, face brightening.

"What about it?" I squint at him in confusion. Six months ago I signed a cookbook deal with a boutique publisher in New York for a *The Bygone Kitchen* cookbook of my favorite recipes. The deal was a longtime dream of mine come true. A few months ago I sent them samples of vintage recipes, all ones I've used on *The Bygone Kitchen*. Now I'm waiting to hear back about what they think so far.

"That's how you get noticed," Drew enthuses. "You already have the contract. That's going to get you some good publicity, get your name out there. Think about all the famous TV chefs with cookbooks. Giada. Gordon Ramsay. Your secret chef crush, Nigella." He ticks off all the celebrity chefs I like to binge-watch on rainy nights when we're staying in. He seems genuinely excited by this idea. "The cookbook is how you can prove to Keith and the producers that you and the show are more popular than they think. All they care about is numbers anyway. If you can prove you've got a bigger audience, if you could get your numbers up and get some buzz around the cookbook, I bet it would make them take notice."

I hesitate, turning the notion over in my mind. Could a successful cookbook really generate enough publicity to make Keith rethink turning *The Bygone Kitchen* into a show? Frankly, it seems like a long shot, but I want it to be true so badly.

"Even if that were true and Keith changed his mind," I challenge, "you're half the show. I can't do it alone."

Drew frowns his thinking frown. It's raining a little harder now, droplets beading on the shining blond of his hair, dappling my forehead and bare arms.

"This show with Desiree is just a limited six-episode series," Drew says slowly. "If people like it, Keith says the network will renew it for more episodes. But even if it gets picked up for another season, we won't be filming all the time. It's a few months of filming and then some off time. Maybe if things went well I could . . . do both?" He sounds hopeful and hesitant. "It's worth a shot, right? You shouldn't give up on the show, Jules. Not when you've come this far. It's your dream. At least see if you can turn this cookbook into something."

At Drew's words, my heart gives a little sputter of life. Is it possible that we could still find a way to make this work? My head is spinning with questions and possibilities. I'm afraid to hope too hard. And yet . . . and yet . . . if there's a chance, isn't it worth a try? What have I got to lose?

"I'll think about it," I tell Drew. I need a hot bath and a strong espresso with two cubes of sugar and space to process this roller coaster of an evening. I need to think this through carefully and make a plan. I love a good plan. Drew hesitates, clearly torn.

"I'll see you later." I start down the sidewalk, soggy leather squelching with every step. "Go talk to Keith," I call over my shoulder. A couple skirts me, side-eyeing my wet, bedraggled appearance. My hair is now plastered to my forehead and I'm starting to shiver, but I am also feeling a small stirring of hope. Maybe, just maybe, I can redeem this night.

"Am I forgiven?" Drew yells after me.

"Not even close," I yell back. "But if this works and we actually save the show, I'll consider us even." Then I turn in the direction of our apartment. I have an early shift at Trader Joe's in the morning and a lot of strategizing to do before then.

Chapter 4

11:09 p.m. from vintagegirlcooks@gmail.com to Michelle@harrisliteraryagency.com

Hi Michelle,

Just checking in to see how the editor at Epicure Press liked the sample recipe pages I sent? I have all the recipes and photos ready to go. I'm just waiting to make sure they like what I sent them. With the deadline coming up in September, I'd love to know what they think so I have enough time to make changes if they want me to tweak anything. Also, out of curiosity, how much does having a cookbook usually help an author grow their platform and reach? Is it a lot?

Thanks!
Jules

9:22 a.m. from Michelle@harrisliteraryagency.com to vintagegirlcooks@gmail.com

Jules,

Thank you for reaching out. I've just heard back from the editor at Epicure. I think it's best if we talk on the phone about this. Can we chat this afternoon?

Thanks,
Michelle

My phone rings as I'm climbing the stairs to my apartment after my shift at Trader Joe's. Arms laden with groceries I grabbed at the store after I clocked out, I set the heavy bags on our welcome mat and check my phone. It's Michelle. My heart skips a beat.

"Juliana, Michelle here. So glad I caught you." Her tone is warm yet brusque. She is a woman with no time to waste on chitchat. I picture her in her office in New York City. We've never met in person, but her photo on her website shows a tall Black woman in her forties in a no-nonsense navy business suit holding a stack of bestselling nonfiction books from clients she represents. When she agreed to take me on as a client a year ago, I felt like I was floating on a cloud for a week. It still thrills me to say "my literary agent." I'm hoping she has good news for me. I'm so ready for some good news. This is step one of the plan I concocted late last night in the bath, fueled by espresso, sugar, and a daring, desperate hope.

I need this cookbook to be a winner if I'm going to pursue Drew's idea and use the cookbook to widen my audience and prove the viability of *The Bygone Kitchen*. Currently, everything is hinging on it. Keith may not think the show and I have enough star power, but

Epicure Press seems to believe in me. If I can prove that the publisher is right, that I do have what it takes to succeed with this cookbook, maybe it will convince Keith too. It's worth a shot, at least. I stayed up until one a.m. last night trying to brainstorm other ideas, but finally concluded that Drew's idea is the only plan that makes any sense. I think it's my best bet even if it feels like a long shot. I'm not ready to give up hope. I'll do anything to keep this dream alive.

"I got your email," Michelle tells me, "and thought we should talk. I checked in with your editor at Epicure about the sample recipes you sent and she had some feedback." Michelle pauses. "Frankly, Jules, Claire says they're looking for something quite different."

My stomach does a strange little flip-flop. "Different how? What did they not like?" I ask in confusion. I'd sent them a collection of my best vintage recipes, complete with a brief history of each dish. It's what I do on the show, and the show is why they offered me a contract in the first place, right? How could they not like it? I stare down at the scrubby courtyard in the middle of our building, waiting with a growing sense of trepidation. The sky is a heavy gray, and the air smells like green budding things and impending rain.

Michelle sighs. "Claire says they like the idea of using vintage recipes, but they really want to showcase you personally. You're the reason they wanted a cookbook, not the recipes themselves. They're looking for a warmer, more personal, connective feeling to the cookbook. Less dry history lesson and more intimate. Claire is a big fan of *The Bygone Kitchen*, and they want a cookbook that reflects that friendly, positive tone you set in the show. Anyone can pull the recipes you sent off the Internet. They want something that is uniquely *you*."

Uniquely me? I don't know what to say. I'm trying to tamp down the panic rising in my throat. "This is what I do," I stammer. "I find old recipes and introduce people to them. That's me. I don't know how to do anything else." The truth is that I *can't* do anything else.

Thinking about what Claire is asking me to do makes me feel physically ill.

I press back against my apartment door to make room for my heavily pierced neighbor as he wheels his bike past me in the hall. He gives me a nod and his tiny, mostly toothless chihuahua runs up, tongue lolling, and turns in circles barking until I fish a soft dog jerky treat out of my pocket and give it to him. I might be the only girl in Seattle who smells like Trader Joe's smoked chicken tenders, but it's worth it. All the dogs in the neighborhood love me.

"There you go, Lester," I whisper, scratching the spot behind his huge batwing ears. I'm trying not to panic and Lester helps calm me momentarily.

Michelle sighs again. "Look, Jules, I understand what you're saying, but the problem is that Epicure paid an advance and you've signed a contract for a cookbook, and they need a book they can sell. They're within the terms of the contract to request that you set a more personal tone. They want fifty recipes from you that have personal history or backstory. They don't need to be original recipes that you create. They can be vintage recipes, old family recipes, something—but they need to showcase who *you* are. There needs to be a personal theme tying them all together. And photos. Good photos of the finished product. Can you do that?"

"Um." I swallow hard, mind racing. It's starting to rain, and I shiver in the chilly breeze. I'm wearing a sleeveless lime-green short-sleeved mod dress that might, upon reflection, have been too optimistic for today's weather. It was sunny when I got dressed this morning, but the weather has turned. An apt metaphor for my life right now. Everything has suddenly gone an ominous gray.

Michelle's words are an unexpected blow. I was so sure that what I sent was what Epicure was looking for. But now they want fifty recipes with a personal touch? How in the world am I going to come up with all of those by the September deadline? I don't even know where to start. It feels impossible.

"Jules?" Michelle prompts. "Can you do that?"

I sag against the door, calculating the remaining time before my deadline in my head. It's the middle of June now. That leaves roughly ten weeks. How can I possibly have everything ready by September? Across the courtyard someone is listening to the Backstreet Boys turned up high. I can hear "I Want It That Way" vibrating through their wall. I wrap my arms around myself. "What happens if I can't deliver by September?" I ask in a small voice.

Michelle pauses. "Jules, if you don't deliver fifty recipes and photos that they're happy with by the submission date, they have the right to cancel the contract, and you'll need to repay your whole advance."

Suddenly, I can't breathe. Repay the ten-thousand-dollar advance? I've already spent it. I invested in some better recording equipment and a professionally crafted website for the show. I told myself I was investing in my professional future. Now that future looks increasingly precarious, and I'm suddenly wishing I had squirreled the money away instead. If I can't deliver those recipes, I have no way to pay back the money. My paycheck from Trader Joe's barely covers the basics like rent and utilities.

The reality of my situation sinks in slowly. I'm trapped. I have to deliver what they ask for. I don't have another choice. I rest the back of my head against the cool, painted wood of our front door and try to breathe around the tight band of panic squeezing my chest. This is a disaster. The issue of the ten-thousand-dollar advance aside, if I don't deliver what Epicure wants, my chance to change Keith's mind will vanish. If I don't manage to pull this off, I can kiss all my dreams for the future goodbye. I think of the show, of Ethel and our other followers, of saying goodbye to them, of losing the one place where it feels like I contribute something good to the world. The thought is so bleak.

"Okay," I tell Michelle, trying to sound confident and pushing down the panic. "I'll have the recipes by the deadline." Right now it feels utterly impossible, but I'm just going to have to make it work. I have no choice but to figure out how to come up with fifty recipes with personal stories and accompanying high-quality photos in two and a half months. No big deal. I close my eyes and try not to hyperventilate.

"Jules, are you okay?" Michelle pauses on the other end of the call. She sounds concerned. Maybe she can hear my shallow breathing all the way in New York.

"Absolutely," I lie. I struggle to sound calm and nonchalant.

"Okay, good." Michelle sounds relieved. "I'll let Claire know you'll have everything to her on time. And send me some samples as soon as you have something, just to make sure we're on the right track."

"Of course," I assure Michelle, trying to sound breezy, but the words come out squeaky, like someone is pressing a thumb against my larynx. I hang up quickly and grab my groceries, pushing through the door and slamming it behind me. Sinking down onto the worn brown carpet, back against the door, I put my head in my hands. I try to breathe in through my nose and out through my mouth, counting silently. Nothing is helping my anxiety right now. It's through the roof, heading straight to the moon.

Because what Michelle doesn't know, what no one knows, is that I haven't made a recipe that has a personal connection to me in over a decade, not since the accident. I haven't been able to. In the beginning after Dad's death, I tried to make familiar dishes, but over and over my mind would go blank and I could not, no matter how hard I concentrated, remember the ingredients or steps. It was like all the recipes I knew by heart had been replaced by a fuzzy sort of static, a white blankness that blocked out everything. And frankly, even thinking of making the recipes hurt too much. They reminded me of all I had lost, who I had lost, and so after a few times of trying, when my mind would start to go blank and my heart would ache with grief, I just . . . stopped. I haven't made a chocolate zucchini cake (my sister Aurora's favorite) or my dad's famous pizza dip or Nonna's almond and olive oil biscotti in well over a decade. Now I only make recipes that have no connection to my history, no connection to Dad or my family, nothing that might remind me of that terrible summer I lost everything. Yet now I'm being asked to delve into the most painful parts of my life once more and it is terrifying me. What choice do I have, though? Everything hinges on this cookbook being a success. Somehow I have to make this work, though I have no idea how. I need a miracle and quickly.

Chapter 5

"Come on, Jules. You can do this! What's a recipe that means something to you?" A half hour later I'm standing in front of the open refrigerator staring at the ingredients I bought at Trader Joe's and giving myself a pep talk. To be honest, when I picked up groceries after my shift, I was looking forward to coming home, putting on an episode of my favorite guilty pleasure—the Pasta Grannies YouTube channel—and letting an eighty-something-year-old Italian woman teach me how to make some carb-heavy and yummy type of pasta. But now I have big work to do.

Unfortunately, I've been standing in front of the refrigerator for the past twenty minutes, completely stuck. Everywhere I turn I see ingredients for vintage recipes I've made for the show, but I'm drawing a blank on anything more personal to me. I close the refrigerator and move to pantry staples. Maybe they'll be more inspiring.

"Do beans mean anything to me?" I ask, eyeing some dried fava beans. I try to picture my dad. Did he ever make anything with beans? All I can summon is a memory of him teaching Aurora and me to make farting noises with our armpits and the three of us doubled over laughing hysterically in our kitchen in Beacon Hill. A fond memory, but not particularly useful right now.

Drew pokes his head into the kitchen. "Did I hear something about beans?" He's wearing faded basketball shorts and a University of Wisconsin Mead Witter School of Music sweatshirt. He's been holed up in his room listening to Danish death metal and packing for LA since I got home. He said yes to Keith and signed the contract this morning. Keith and the production company want him in LA before the end of the week. This is really happening. Apparently, things move quickly in the TV production world. Every time I think of him leaving, my heart breaks a little more.

"Ugh, I talked to Michelle earlier." I explain about needing fifty personal recipes for the cookbook. I don't mention how stuck I am, or how much I cannot seem to make any recipes that have an emotional connection for me. I haven't told anyone that, not even Drew. Not even my older sister Aurora, and she knows practically everything about me.

"Can you think of any recipes that are meaningful to me?" I ask hopefully.

"Hmm . . ." Drew frowns and opens the fridge, grabbing a loaf of bread and a wedge of cheddar. He sets about making himself a cheese sandwich slathered with mayo and garnished with half a jar of fancy homemade pickles he picked up at the farmer's market. "Well, what makes a recipe personal to you? What do you love about the vintage recipes you make on the show?" he asks. "I mean, there must be a reason you choose the ones you do, right?"

"I don't know why I choose the recipes I do," I admit to Drew. "Maybe I just find making them soothing."

I purse my lips, mulling over his question. I've never really thought about it before. Why *do* I love making vintage recipes? Maybe it stems from cooking with Nonna Bruna every summer when I visited her in Italy, using her cherished leather-bound book of Italian family recipes passed down through generations. Maybe for me these vintage recipes are a substitution.

After my dad's death, when I stopped being able to cook the recipes from our family, I found solace in trying out classic recipes I discovered online or in vintage cookbooks I gleaned from thrift stores.

I cooked late at night, long after my mother and stepfather Ted were asleep in the gleaming New York apartment I was now forced to call home. I'd had to move in with them after Dad passed away. In that awful year, when my anxiety was running high and I couldn't sleep, I'd lie in bed night after night with my thoughts whirring at a hundred miles an hour, feeling panicky and out of control and crushed by the grief. I'd get up, find a recipe that appealed to me, and cook until the wee hours of the morning. When I was done, I'd feel calm again. I'd clean up all traces of the tomato soup spice cake or vinegar pie I'd made, dumping everything in the trash can and hiding it away under layers of paper towels. I didn't need to eat what I'd made. It was the act of cooking that gave me comfort. Afterward, I'd carefully clean up the kitchen and fall into bed exhausted and heartsore but peaceful and at ease.

Those recipes from the Great Depression, from WWI and WWII, from the Vietnam War, saved me in a way. They made me feel safe. They grounded me, reminding me that generations of people had lived through hardship and fear and uncertainty, and with the power of prune pudding and potato peel soup, they'd survived. I could too. Years later, in the dark lockdown days of 2020, I'd taken those same recipes and—with Drew's encouragement and help—created *The Bygone Kitchen* as a way to comfort and strengthen others as we weathered a global catastrophe together.

Now, however, I'm being asked to leave my cooking comfort zone. What do I do?

"Hey," Drew interrupts, spearing a pickle and crunching it. "Can I talk to you for a minute?"

Grateful for the interruption, I steal one of his pickles and listen with a sinking heart as he explains uncomfortably that he's going to have to sublet his room for the summer while he's filming in LA. Rent is sky-high both here in Seattle and in LA, and he can't afford to pay double rent. Our apartment is affordable, probably because our 1970s-era building has all the charm of a square of Spam, but it's still pricey. Everything in Seattle is. I understand his predicament, but I'm nervous at the thought of a new roommate. Drew and I have been roommates for over five years.

"I hate this," I tell him glumly. I'm going to miss Drew, and don't relish the thought of having to get acclimated to someone new. But I can't afford our entire rent on my own, and our lease isn't up until December. It looks like I'm stuck with whoever Drew finds, at least until the fall. Maybe Drew will come back then, but who knows. It all depends on how his show goes.

I crunch the pickle and glower at him. "I'll never find a roommate that cleans toilets as well as you."

Drew laughs. "We're the best," he agrees. "I'm going to miss you too, Jules. You and your amazing pasta." He pulls me into a one-armed hug, and I briefly wrap my arms around his torso, grieved at the thought of losing him. He gives me a comforting squeeze and releases me to grab his sandwich.

"I'll find somebody good, I promise," he assures me, looking guilty to be putting me in this position.

Our cohabitation started somewhat accidentally. Drew had just started subletting the other bedroom in my apartment from my old roommate while she did a postdoc research trip to Rome in the early spring of 2020. But what was supposed to be a few months turned into far longer when Drew and I suddenly found ourselves in lockdown together in a small apartment in the midst of a global pandemic. Almost overnight we became each other's lifeline. We suddenly went from practically strangers to each other's sole source of company in a scenario no one could have imagined. It was a little uncomfortable at first, but we quickly discovered that we had a lot in common and were surprisingly compatible as roommates. Gradually, as the months wore on, we became good friends.

Pro tip: If you have to be in lockdown with a virtual stranger, try to pick a good-natured music teacher from Wisconsin who can play the piano, soft-shoe like Fred Astaire, and break into song at a moment's notice. And who likes to do dishes. That's always a plus. With Drew as my roommate, our little shared apartment in the Capitol Hill neighborhood of Seattle has never been dull or dirty.

By the time the lockdowns lifted, we were comfortably broken in together, like an old pair of slippers. Sometimes we joke that we're like an old married couple, weathering the pandemic, breakups and broken hearts, employment ups and downs. But now this. Now he's leaving, and I don't know if he's ever coming back. He's going to LA for the summer to shoot the new series, then he'll reassess. He may not come back if things go well. I can tell he's hoping they do.

Drew cuts his sandwich in half. "I already have a few leads for someone to sublet, a couple of teachers from school," he tells me. "I'm hoping to find somebody before I leave."

He fishes another pickle from the jar and proffers it to me, a peace offering. Usually, Drew is very stingy about these pickles. He's really feeling bad about getting the job and moving and leaving me in the lurch, I can tell. And I am still feeling the sting of his decision. I know in my head it's the best choice for him, and I'm trying to be excited for him, but it still hurts that he is leaving me and the show like this. And now I have to acclimate to a new roommate. Ugh.

The thought of a new roommate being one of Drew's posh private school teacher buddies is a little cheering, though. Maybe it will be one of the hot, single ones. I've seen more than my fair share of cheesy rom-coms. Who knows? Maybe this is destiny.

It's always been platonic between Drew and me. There was one ill-advised night early on during a *Buffy the Vampire Slayer* marathon—a sloppy midnight kiss fueled by cheap margaritas. Both of us recoiled instantly. It felt like kissing a brother or a cousin. Good friends, we'd agreed hastily. Nothing more. And we'd been that for each other for five years, but now that he's leaving maybe I could get a roommate with a little more romantic potential. It's been a dry spell for a while now since I stopped dating Krish, one of my coworkers at Trader Joe's. He relocated to Phoenix and we didn't survive long distance.

"Can I request a hot, single teacher as a new roommate?" I call down the hall as Drew takes his sandwich and heads back to his room to pack. "How about Conor?" Conor is a teacher buddy of Drew's. He's originally from Galway and has dimples. It's not fair how cute he is.

"What about Conor?" Drew yells back.

"Can I please have Conor as a roommate?" I wheedle. "I want to fall asleep listening to him lecture me on the Etruscans." I'd listen to anything if it's in a delicious Irish accent. I'd listen to Conor read the warning label off a pack of light bulbs. I'm a sucker for a good accent.

Drew pokes his head out of his room and blinks at me. "Sometimes I worry there's something wrong with you," he says. Then, "I'll see what I can do." He lifts his sandwich plate in a little salute and disappears back into his room.

A moment later, the Danish death metal starts up again, pulsing dully through the hall. I go back into the kitchen to face down the refrigerator once more. I stand by the open fridge door savoring the last tangy bite of pickle, trying not to worry about this new roommate situation. It's only for the summer and then Drew might be back. Even if he stays in LA, it's just six months until the lease is up. I can deal with almost anything for three to six months, right? What's the worst that can happen?

Chapter 6

As it turns out, I've significantly underestimated the worst-case scenario.

> They're coming up! Early!

I get the text from Drew just as I'm frantically trying to fluff the pillows on the couch and make sure our apartment looks as inviting as possible. I abandon the pillows and settle for fluffing my bangs instead. It's been three days since Drew told me he was looking for a subletter, and he's found one. Two, actually. Solomon and Sandra both work on staff at Drew's school. Apparently, they've been living in a yurt on Vashon Island, but the ferry commute was getting to be a headache. Drew tells me they're running intensive summer camps in art and theater at the school until the fall term starts, so they want a place near the school right away. I'm disappointed that it is not sexy history teacher Conor, but maybe they'll be great. Art and theater people could be really fun. I refresh my lipstick, take a deep breath to try (and fail) to calm my nerves, and hope for the best.

Five minutes later, my hopes are deflating like a leaky birthday balloon.

"So this is it then?" Solomon demands heartily, standing in the dining room and looking around in expectation. "Low ceilings, aren't they?"

A portly, bearded man wearing what appears to be a patchwork velvet cape, he has round black-rimmed glasses and an overly firm handshake. I dart a look at his partner, Sandra, who is very tall and heavy boned, with long brunette hair swept back in a loose braid. She is wearing a pumpkin-colored smock smeared with clay and holding a large white cat with a squished face, some sort of Persian, maybe? I was not prepared for the cat.

"You have a cat?" I ask faintly, trying to hide my surprise. Drew definitely did not mention a cat. I love animals. I volunteered with an animal rescue in Seattle every Saturday all through college, helping frightened and abused dogs learn to trust humans again. For my birthday every year, I ask my friends to donate to the Humane Society. However, I'm pretty sure our building has a strict no-pets policy. And I think I'm slightly allergic to cats.

"This is Ophelia," Sandra says indulgently.

"Hi, Ophelia." I reach toward the cat, trying to be friendly. The cat hisses.

"She doesn't like strangers," Sandra tells me, moving away slightly.

I smile weakly, trying to cover the sinking sensation in my stomach. This is going to be a very different summer than I envisioned. And is it my imagination or are my eyes starting to itch?

"Come on back and I'll show you the bedroom." Drew ushers them down the hall. His room is empty now. He's leaving early tomorrow morning for LA. I stare at their backs, worrying my lip. When Drew mentioned the English teacher and art instructor from his old school would be subletting his room, I pictured quiet school librarian types. I was not prepared for . . . this.

"Is she clean and quiet?" I can hear Solomon's voice booming through the wall. I think they're talking about me. This is humiliating. Even with two bathrooms, it is going to be uncomfortably tight in this apartment with three humans and a grouchy cat. I can already tell they don't love the idea of living here with me. Ditto.

Sandra comes back into the dining room and looks around critically.

"I'll need to sage the space," she announces. She doesn't wait for an answer, just lets the cat slide from her arms, and Ophelia promptly darts under the couch and hides. "She can sense bad energy," Sandra tells me. She draws a bundle of dried sage from her large quilted bag and holds up a lighter, not waiting for my reply before she lights the sage. I stare at her in bewilderment. Bad energy?

"I don't think our apartment building allows pets," I tell her.

She ignores me and starts wandering around the apartment, methodically waving the smoking sage and opening windows, then pokes her head into the kitchen and frowns. "We're strictly macrobiotic vegans, and we can't cross-contaminate our bodies with food that's been poisoned by pesticides, is out of season, from any animal, or grown more than twenty miles away." She looks pointedly at the dirty dishes I've left sitting by the sink, specifically the remains of an egg salad sandwich and an empty cup of yogurt I had for lunch. She waves the sage over it. "We can set up a kitchen schedule so we keep our cooking hours separate," she tells me. "We like to eat late, at a more Mediterranean hour."

I stand there numbly, not sure what to do. There's a sick sort of feeling of apprehension in my gut when I picture sharing my apartment with these people for the next few months. I don't think I can do this. How in the world am I supposed to quickly come up with fifty recipes this summer if I'm sharing an apartment with people so vastly different from me and a cat I think I might be allergic to? From down the hall I can hear Solomon peppering Drew with questions about everything from parking ordinances to recycling options to requesting measurements for the bathtub and the width of the hallway. I take another look at Sandra. She is saging the inside of our refrigerator with a look of distaste.

I sink down on the couch, seeing a vision of the summer stretching out before me. It is bleak. From underneath the couch comes a loud hiss and a mew of protest. Ophelia is definitely not happy. And my eyes are absolutely feeling itchy.

"Me too, Ophelia," I whisper. Clearly, this is not going to work. I need a plan B and quickly.

Chapter 7

"Che cacchio!"

It's nine p.m. and I'm giving up. I'm standing at the kitchen counter which is littered with failed recipe attempts. So far I've used up all my swears in English and have moved on to the Italian ones I learned from Nonna. All evening I've been trying and failing to resurrect personal family recipes with no luck. I spent years cooking with Nonna and now I can't manage to make one half-decent replica of a dish from my childhood. I simply cannot recall any of the recipes. It's like I've blocked everything out subconsciously, my mind a blank white sheet of paper. Try as I might, I cannot pull up even a single simple pasta recipe Nonna taught me. And now I've wasted an evening and a lot of ingredients for nothing. How frustrating!

"Che palle," I mutter. I started with the mild swears and am gradually working my way up.

To make matters worse, Solomon and Sandra agreed to sublet the apartment after their tour today, which is not helping my mood any. So now I'm watching an episode of Pasta Grannies on YouTube and making myself comfort food.

"You take the flour like this and make a little hill and then a hole," adorably wrinkled ninety-six-year-old Isolina instructs in Italian. The narrator on the video translates her instructions into English, but I can follow Isolina's Italian if I concentrate. Tonight we are making homemade gnocchi with basil pesto. Pasta Grannies is my guilty pleasure. I love watching the elderly Italian women give tutorials on how to make their favorite pasta dishes from scratch. The grannies remind me of Italy, of Nonna, of everything I've missed so much in the past fifteen years. For a few moments I can capture a fleeting echo of what I felt with Nonna in her kitchen every summer—the grounded happiness, the sense of history and place.

Just as I am poking a hole in my flour hill, my phone rings. I swipe to answer before I fully register who it is.

"Juliana!" My mother, Lisa, peers at me through the screen of the video call.

Instantly I regret my hasty pickup and look around to find an excuse to get off the phone. But there is no one to save me. I'm alone in the apartment tonight. Drew is out at a bar in Georgetown with his teacher buddies. They're throwing him a teachers-only send-off before he leaves super early in the morning for LA. He and I already had our own little bittersweet send-off last night on the rooftop deck, sharing a bottle of soju in a light drizzle. I cried. So did he.

"Lisa." I sigh in resignation. I haven't called her Mom since high school. She's been Lisa to me for years now for good reason. Tonight she is in a dimly lit, packed room with a swing band playing behind her.

"You look tired, sweetie!" she tells me. She's holding a martini glass with a toothpick skewering three olives and is sporting a jet beaded headband around her smoothly immobile, Botoxed forehead. Also, what on earth is she wearing?

"Is that a silver sequined leotard?" I ask, poking a hole in the mound of flour and pouring in a healthy glug of olive oil and some tepid water. I don't really need to watch Isolina's video to make the recipe. I've seen it enough times to know it by heart. Behind me on the stove, half a dozen potatoes are bubbling away in a pot of boiling water. I mix the flour/oil/water by hand a little. Talking to my mother always makes me anxious. She's a vortex that swirls everything and everyone into her orbit whether you are willing or not, and she has an uncanny ability to get things her way. I wonder what she's calling about. She never calls for no reason. Lisa always has an angle.

"Ted and I are at a benefit cocktail party. It's circus themed. We're fighting children with diabetes," she says airily, taking a sip of her martini.

"You mean helping children fight diabetes?" I observe dryly.

She pulls a face, missing my point entirely. "Or maybe it's children with scoliosis? What's the one where they're in a wheelchair and have trouble controlling their arms and legs?"

"Cerebral palsy?" I hazard a guess, removing the potatoes from the boiling water and dropping them in the sink.

"Whatever it is, we're being very generous. It's a very serious condition. The poor children." She waves a hand dismissively. She and Ted attend a lot of charity events. The details don't seem to really matter as much as being seen attending. "Ted is bidding on a hunting lodge trip to Sweden in the auction right now, but since I already bought a spa package for Telluride, I stepped out."

I try to imagine my oral and maxillofacial surgeon stepfather Ted dressed in hunting attire. Ted is an okay enough human, although he has about as much personality as a boiled potato. I can't picture him on a hunting trip. Ted is benign, very pliable, and very affluent. My parents divorced when I was ten, and Ted and my mother married suspiciously soon afterward. They are, in many ways, a perfect pair. Ted makes a lot of money and does whatever my mother tells him to do. She spends the money and makes their lives comfortable and their social circle exclusive. They live in New York City with my fifteen-year-old half sister Alessandra. After Dad died, I lived with them for my junior and senior years of high school, but hightailed it back to Seattle as soon after graduation as I could. I haven't been back to visit in almost five years.

Lisa glances around cautiously and lowers her voice a notch. "I just can't enjoy anything right now. I'm *so* concerned about Alessandra." She pauses significantly. I'm supposed to ask her what she is concerned about. I know the script. I stall peeling the warm skin from a potato, deciding if I'm going to play along.

"What's going on with Alessandra?" I ask finally, reluctantly, reaching for another potato. I'm not close to my half sister, but I do want to know if something is wrong. Often, Lisa gets dramatic about things, though. She catastrophizes.

"My incompetent personal assistant forgot to register her for camp!" Lisa announces indignantly. I think she's trying to look outraged, but her face is frozen in a fixed expression of mild surprise. "So now your sister has nowhere to go for the summer. And school is out next week!"

"Half sister," I reply automatically. Camp is a huge deal with Lisa and Ted's crowd. Not getting a kid a spot at the favored handful of exorbitantly expensive summer camps in the Adirondacks would be disastrous for any parent who tries hard to make sure that having offspring doesn't unduly impact their own social schedules. Every kid in Alex's orbit is packed off to summer camp on the East Coast as soon as school lets out. Some of them stay at camp for the whole summer. Alex is one of those. She has spent every summer at Camp Champlain since she was old enough to button her own camp uniform shorts. I don't envy her. I was sent there for one awful summer between my junior and senior years of high school. I don't wish anyone a summer of snobbery, tennis elbow, and bug bites.

"Can't she just go to the Hamptons with you?" I ask, grabbing my hefty vintage metal ricer and plopping a peeled potato into it.

"Of course not." Lisa looks scandalized. "Ted is working in the city. And I need time to focus on my art. I can't get inspired creatively if I have to take care of your sister."

All of a sudden I feel an unexpected stab of sympathy for my half sister. Poor Alex. I know how awful it is to be seen as an inconvenience. There is a reason my older sister Aurora was like a surrogate mother to me all growing up. Lisa sees parenting as a lot of inconvenient work.

"Plus," Lisa adds, "Alessandra is having . . . issues at school. She needs to be around other teenagers her own age this summer. She needs to make some friends." She pulls the phone close and glances around, then murmurs conspiratorially, "The school counselor says she's 'self-isolating.' She says she's been bullied this year."

"She's been bullied?" That doesn't sound good. I squeeze the handles of the ricer, and long, hot ribbons of potato fall onto the flour mixture.

Lisa waves her hand. "When I was in school, it was just teenagers being mean. It's a hard age. We all survived. Now everyone is so dramatic about it. All this talk about mental health. It's so stressful." She takes a gulp of her martini. Behind her, catering staff in tails glide by with appetizers, weaving among the guests who are dressed like ringmasters with top hats and circus performers in glittering leotards. I think I see someone in a tiger costume. This is a weird fundraiser.

A server pauses and offers Lisa a tray of canapés, which she refuses. She prefers to drink her calories. I can hear the auction faintly in the background. It sounds like they are now auctioning off a unicorn-themed birthday party where live ponies dyed pastel colors and sporting glittering horns come to your home.

"Alessandra is miserable at school," Lisa continues. "I told her she should try out for cheerleading. That would put her in the same circles as the popular kids who she says are bullying her, but she said she'd rather drink lye." Lisa frowns. At least I think she's trying to frown. Her forehead doesn't really move under the beaded headband. "I don't know where she gets these disturbing ideas. Maybe all those Japanese comics she reads. So depressing. And they all have such big creepy eyes." Lisa shudders.

I rice the rest of my potatoes over the well of flour and knead the ingredients together with long, slow motions until they form a soft dough. "Wow, drink lye, huh?"

What exactly is lye? Aurora would know. She probably makes it by hand. But whatever it is, why is Alex threatening to drink it? That sounds concerning. I wonder if she really is in some sort of trouble.

I have very little relationship with my half sister. She was still a toddler when I graduated high school and headed back to Seattle. Since then I've seen her only a handful of times. She's always struck me as a smart, sober child who generally looks like she's enduring rather than enjoying life. Given that she's grown up living with Lisa and Ted, I imagine that's not far from the truth. I haven't seen her since I was last in New York. She was about nine or ten. I remember her huge gray eyes peering at me over the rim of a book. She seemed so serious, observant, and a little standoffish. I tried to befriend her each time I saw her, but she never warmed up. Last time I don't think she said two words to me the entire visit.

"So what are you going to do with Alex this summer if she's not at camp?" I cut the soft potato dough into chunks and form the first chunk into a thick rope. I am still trying to figure out where this call is going, what it is that Lisa wants. I start cutting the rope into small bite-sized pieces and then roll each piece down the tines of a fork to create the signature gnocchi ridges.

"Well . . ." Lisa pauses. "That's why I called you. We think you can help Alessandra."

I pause and brace myself. And here it is, ladies and gentlemen, the real reason for this call.

Chapter 8

"**You've got to** be kidding." The fork slips from my hand and clatters to the floor. I bend to pick it up, sure I've misheard my mother. She can't possibly have just suggested that.

"You want me to take Alex to Italy for the summer? To stay with Bruna?" I stare at her in astonishment.

She nods, sipping her martini and looking satisfied. "Exactly," she says, as though it's the most reasonable thing in the world. "Ted and I think it could help Alessandra."

I seriously doubt Ted thinks anything of the sort. This feels like classic Lisa. "Help her how?" I ask cautiously, cutting another rope of dough into bite-sized, pillowy gnocchi.

"It would be so good for Alessandra to have some time in the homeland. You and Aurora always seemed to enjoy your visits, at least until your father . . . you know." Lisa sips her martini.

"I can't just up and go to Italy for two months," I protest. "I have a life here, a job, a show." Okay, maybe not a show anymore. Or much of a life, come to think of it. But still . . . I balk at the idea. I can't go to Italy. End of discussion.

"But it would be so good for Alessandra to get in touch with her roots, to spend time with family," Lisa urges me. Her tone is overly bright and sparkly. She's trying hard to sell me on this idea.

"She could spend time with you, her actual parents," I point out dryly. "Besides, Alex isn't even Italian. Nonna isn't related to her at all."

Nonna Bruna is my dad's mother, so she shares no blood with Alex. To the best of my knowledge, Nonna and Alex have never even spoken to each other. Lisa ignores this observation entirely. She seems determined to convince me that this is a marvelous idea. She really must be desperate because she and Nonna Bruna loathe each other. Nonna apparently made no bones about the fact that she thought her only son made a poor choice when he married Lisa after she got pregnant with Aurora just a few months into dating. And Lisa has never forgiven her former mother-in-law for it.

"It's been so long since you saw your grandmother," Lisa presses a little harder. "She's not getting any younger, you know. This could be your last chance." She gives me as meaningful a look as she can through the Botox. That part is true. I wince. Nonna Bruna is eighty-two now. We don't talk often on the phone, but I send her cards on her birthday and at Christmas, and she sends me letters a few times a year, written in a mixture of Italian and English. In the past few years I've noticed her handwriting has gotten a little frail looking, though; spindly where it used to be bold. She sounds as feisty as ever in her letters, but the reality is that she is getting older. She can't live forever. I hesitate.

"That's a low blow." I grab my mortar and pestle and throw in one clove of garlic and two handfuls of pine nuts, pounding them with a little more force than is strictly necessary.

I haven't been back to Italy since I was fifteen. Not since that terrible, fateful summer. After the accident, when Lisa flew in to take me back to New York to live with her and Ted and finish high school, she insisted I not go back to Italy until after I graduated. She said it would be too traumatic for me to go back, but I suspect she just wanted to get me away from Nonna's influence since they dislike each other so much. Whatever the reason, I didn't go back to Italy the next summer, and in some way I felt relieved.

After graduation, I moved back to Seattle for college, and every year there was a new good reason not to return to Italy. A summer internship for my marketing degree, a job that wouldn't give me time off. Then after graduation I struggled to find my footing in an expensive city. There was never enough time, never enough money; at least that's what I told myself.

Next summer, I'd promise myself. But next summer somehow never came. I planned each year to return but never actually bought the ticket. And now here I am, fifteen years later, and I have yet to set foot in what used to be my favorite place in the world.

I don't quite know how it happened that all these years slipped by. I think I was reluctant to return to a place that held such painful memories for me. I lost the two great loves of my life in one terrible summer, and now Italy holds the best and the worst memories for me.

"I can't go to Italy," I growl, throwing a bunch of fragrant basil into the mortar and grinding a touch savagely. "I have things to do here this summer." Which is a lie. My summer is going to consist of trying to recall fuzzy family recipes while avoiding my opinionated new roommates and their temperamental cat. Ugh.

"Just consider it," Lisa urges breezily. She moves across the room to the bar and motions for another martini. "Ted and I would pay for everything—your tickets, all expenses, and even throw in a stipend to make up for the time you'd take off work."

They must really be in a pinch if they're sweetening the deal like this. I add a generous heap of grated aged Parmigiano-Reggiano cheese and grind it into the mix. The aroma of the pesto is heavenly. In Italian cooking, there is a correct way to pair ingredients and types of pasta, and this is a very traditional dish for good reason. It's absolutely delicious.

"I think this could be so good for you both," Lisa says confidently, picking up the toothpick from her martini and sliding an olive into her mouth with her teeth. "You and Alessandra can get to know each other better, have a little sister bonding, and spend some time with your grandmother. You could teach Alessandra to cook, just like Bruna taught you."

I close my eyes briefly and I'm suddenly transported back into the warm kitchen of the old farmhouse with its barrel-vaulted ceiling with dark wood beams, the whitewashed walls and deep stone fireplace, the scarred dark olive wood table. The air is redolent with the aromas of uncooked flour and egg from freshly made pasta and the rich unctuousness of basil and garlic frying in olive oil. And there is Nonna, handing me her ancient book of family recipes, letting me carefully open it at random. Whatever recipe it opened to was the one we made together. I loved the surprise of it every time. Every recipe somehow seemed like the perfect one, exactly what I wanted without even knowing it. It felt like magic in that kitchen every day.

Suddenly, I am struck with a flash of inspiration that hits me with blinding clarity. That's it! The recipe book! Nonna's thick book of family recipes, passed down from generation to generation. Recipes with a story, a sense of place, recipes that I have grown up making. Recipes that I could use for my own cookbook, recipes that could perhaps make it possible for me to meet my September deadline . . . My eyes pop open. Is there really a way I could still finish this cookbook in time? If I went to Italy, could I make it happen?

I glance up to find Lisa watching me narrowly. She can smell my resolve weakening.

"I'll think about it," I concede, dumping the uncooked gnocchi into a waiting pot of boiling salted water and giving the little pillows a stir. I don't want to agree too hastily. I have to consider this carefully before I commit. The thought of actually going back to Italy is weighty for a lot of reasons. But then I remember Solomon and Sandra and Ophelia. If I went to Italy for the summer, I would not have to share the apartment with them. A definite bonus. They're moving in tomorrow as soon as Drew leaves. I waffle for a moment.

"Of course," Lisa says with a satisfied smile, like she's already gotten what she wanted. Around her flow the glitterati of Upper Manhattan, chicly thin women dressed as lion tamers and trapeze artists. A man in a leopard-print unitard holding a giant fake barbell wanders by. The band is really swinging now. "But don't take too long," she warns. "You'll need to fly here to pick up Alessandra in the next week or so, as soon as school is out. We'll need to make arrangements."

"I said I'll think about it," I tell her again, firmly, as I fish the gnocchi out of the water with a big metal ladle when they bob to the surface. They glisten on the ladle, plump and delicious looking. I hang up with Lisa and heap the gnocchi into a bowl. As I spoon the fresh pesto over the bowl, I can't stop thinking about the invitation to go to Italy for the summer. I think of Sandra saging our refrigerator. I think of all those delicious family recipes waiting for me in Italy. Maybe being there will jog my memory, and even if it doesn't, there's a whole book of time-tested family recipes I can consult. A cheat sheet of sorts. It's so tempting, so very, very tempting to say yes. But it makes my heart race to even consider returning to Italy.

Fifteen years ago my entire world fell apart on the shores of Lake Garda. In some ways I've never recovered. Now here I am, with an urgent reason to return, but I am deeply torn. There is a swell of longing in my chest when I think of going back, and yet, and yet. I remember the utter devastation of that still, hot afternoon. The pebbled lakeshore, the big-boned figure splayed on the damp grass. His swarthy skin was too pale, his thinning dark hair plastered wet across his forehead like duckweed, those kind eyes closed forever. The day my father drowned in Lake Garda ripped my world apart. Little by little, I've been trying to stitch it back together again ever since. But that was not the only loss I suffered that summer. My heart broke twice.

When I close my eyes, I see his face. Nicolo. Those beautiful dark eyes with their sooty lashes. His earnest, tender expression. When he gazed at me, I felt the warmth of his adoration like the sun. In his eyes I was the most beautiful girl in the world. *Meraviglia*, he called me. *La mia stellina*, he'd whisper when he pressed his eager mouth to the pulse point of my neck. My little star, the one who shone so brightly. I was fifteen and he was sixteen, young and foolish and as star-crossed as Romeo and Juliet. No one has ever looked at me like that since. Nicolo. I haven't thought of him in years. I let out a sharp breath. I've been holding it without realizing it, as though I'm underwater with these memories.

If I'm honest, I'm scared to go back. Plain and simple. I'm scared I'll find it nothing like I remember it, scared I'll feel like a stranger in the only place I've ever really felt at home. But I already feel like a stranger, cut adrift on an unfamiliar sea. I've felt that way in every place I've ever lived since that fateful summer. Maybe it would be different if I returned. What if Italy still feels like home? My heart constricts painfully at the thought. I can taste my longing for a place to belong, bittersweet as the candied lemon rinds Nonna simmers long and slow each Christmas. I want it so badly.

I think of all the reasons to go to Italy. I think of all the reasons to stay. For a long while I waver. I never thought I'd actually return, but now going back may be the only way to save my dream and my career. Am I really brave enough to board a plane to Italy? Closing my eyes, I offer up a little prayer to Saint Sebastian, patron saint of courage, strength, and perseverance, then cross myself and kiss my thumb for luck. Feeling as though I am breaking through the surface, coming up for air after a long deep dive, I text Lisa.

Okay. I'll go.

Chapter 9

"**You're going where?**" My older sister Aurora stares at me through the phone screen, her mouth a perfect pink O of astonishment. It's just past eight a.m. in Seattle, but in the Blue Ridge Mountains of Virginia, Aurora's six kids are already hours into their daily chores around the historic manor house and hobby farm Aurora and her husband Will run together. Today she's in the henhouse, and she's propped me up in an empty nesting box while she gathers fresh eggs with two of my nieces. All around them I can hear the soft clucking of the brood as she and the girls gather eggs and gently tuck them into a basket she wove by hand. She's dressed in a flowing muslin peasant dress that looks vaguely like a Jane Austen–era nightgown. On her it looks strangely amazing, though. Everything does. She even somehow manages to rock the elaborate ruffle around the neck. Her flaxen hair is in two braids wrapped around her head like a crown, Heidi-style. The girls are wearing matching ruffled pinafores and pigtails. They look darling.

"I'm going to Italy for two months with Alex," I confirm. "We leave in a week." I wedge the refrigerator door open with my hip and grab the entire bowl of leftover Sunshine Salad. Sometimes you just need the whole bowl. Drew left before dawn this morning for his flight to LA, and the apartment feels empty and lonely without him. Solomon and Sandra are moving in this afternoon. Hence the Jell-O salad. Breakfast of champions. I imagine what Sandra would say if she could see the Jell-O salad in all its jiggling, processed glory. I grab a spoon. Today is . . . a lot.

"How are you feeling about going back?" Aurora asks, watching me carefully. We text each other every day or two, so I've already filled her in on the disastrous meeting with Keith, the Solomon and Sandra debacle, Drew leaving, and the cookbook conundrum. However, my conversation with Lisa last night and my snap decision to go to Italy have caught her by surprise.

"I don't know," I tell her honestly. "I'm really torn."

Older by three years, Aurora has always been something of a substitute mother to me, filling the gaps when Lisa left our family to marry Ted. Even after she went away to college, Aurora cared for me as best she could from out of state. I had always secretly hoped she'd come back to Seattle, but after getting her degree in business at the University of Virginia, she surprised everyone by marrying Will, a gentle giant of a man who'd made a fortune selling a game app when he was twenty-three. After making millions on the sale, Will promptly renounced technology and entered an apprenticeship to train as a blacksmith. Who knew that was even a profession anymore? Apparently it is, and Will seems very happy.

After the wedding, Aurora and Will purchased and spent five years renovating a historic manor house in the mountains of Virginia and now live there with their flock of six children, homeschooling, churning their own butter, and generally living a slow pace of life like they've time traveled back to 1890. It is a somewhat mystifying life that seems deeply satisfying for them. I'm glad for my sister, but every time I visit or call and she is rendering her own tallow (I'm still not entirely sure what tallow is or what you do with it) or the children are learning to falcon hunt or hammering their own leather quivers for their handmade arrows for archery, I am reminded of how different our lives are turning out to be.

I'm not envious of her. No part of me wants to homeschool a brood of children and hand dip candles, but I find myself sometimes longing for the stability and sense of purpose and place she's found, the serenity of knowing you are exactly where you belong. I haven't had that in so long. I'd give anything to have it again. The only place I feel that sense of purpose is when I'm filming the show. It has become my safe place. That's why I'll do anything to save it.

"I'm nervous to go back to Italy," I admit. I head out the apartment door, bowl of Jell-O and spoon in hand, and climb up the few flights of stairs to the rooftop deck of our building, settling into a rickety vinyl lounger with a view over Capitol Hill. It's sunny today, and seagulls wheel and cry above me on the cool breeze. I have the entire rooftop to myself, a luxury. I take a big bite of Jell-O salad, instantly soothed by its sweet creaminess.

On the video call, Aurora has moved out of the henhouse to the barn where the children are taking turns milking their placid Jersey cow Sadie.

"I think it's a wonderful idea," Aurora announces as she shows her youngest daughter Meadow how to firmly grab the cow's teat and pull and squirt. She pauses and gazes at me speculatively. That look makes me nervous, like she's planning my life for me. "Italy could be good for you," she muses, leaning down to adjust Meadow's grip on Sadie's teat. "And I think it's a good idea for one of us to check on Nonna. The last time I talked to her she seemed . . ." She hesitates.

"Seemed what?" I ask, instantly alert to anything amiss. Is something wrong with Nonna? We haven't exchanged letters in a few months. Has something happened?

Aurora purses her lips and frowns. "It's probably nothing. Just a comment she made about the farm, about not being sure how much longer she could keep going. I'm sure she's fine, but she sounded . . . tired. She's getting older, you know. It is probably good to have one of us see her in person, just to make sure she's okay."

I nod in agreement. All this time I've imagined Nonna and the farm existing in some sort of stasis, frozen peacefully in time until I return. But I realize now how foolish I've been. Nonna is in her eighties now. I have been gone a long time. I have no idea about her health or the condition of the farm. How is she managing to keep up the workload of running it as she ages? The thought of something going wrong instantly twists my stomach into a knot of anxiety. I need to see with my own eyes that everything is okay.

"And who knows, you might see Nicolo!" Aurora exclaims, clasping her hands in delight at the thought. I scoff but my heart skips a beat unexpectedly. How strange that I am thinking of him again, now twice in two days. It's been years since I thought of him more than in passing.

"That sweet boy was so head over heels for you," Aurora muses. "As soon as he laid eyes on you. Do you remember how you two used to write each other sonnets and hide them in that old olive tree?"

I wince at the memory. We would leave each other secret love notes in the cleft of the oldest olive tree on the farm. I still have one somewhere, crumpled and cringy, but sweet. I'd fancied us a modern-day Romeo and Juliet, destined to be together but torn apart by fate and cruel circumstances. More accurately, we were two headstrong, hormonal teenagers who got carried away in the intoxication of first love. When Nonna Bruna and her next-door neighbor, Nicolo's grandmother Violetta, discovered our secret romance, they promptly put an end to it. Nothing can stand up to two stubborn old Italian women who have been locked in a feud for fifty years, not even the strength of young love.

"What a dreamboat he was," Aurora says with a wistful little sigh. "I wonder what ever happened to him?" Like me, Aurora spent her summers in Italy, at least until she went to college. It was our summer tradition every year. Dad was a teacher, and as soon as school was out, we three promptly headed it back to Italy and spent the entire summer basking in the sun, stuffing ourselves with Nonna's cooking, swimming, and eating gelato. It was heaven.

"Nicolo's probably fat and bald and married with a dozen kids by now," I grouse uncharitably, mainly because I'm not feeling so hot about my life and don't want to think of my first love driving around Italy in a red Ferrari with a gorgeous olive-skinned Italian goddess by his side. I take a big bite of Sunshine Salad.

Aurora shakes her head, patting Sadie's flank. "No, Italian men just seem to get more handsome as they age," she says. "And Nicolo was always handsome, even as a skinny teenager. Plus, the Fiore family is wealthy. I bet he's doing just fine."

I think of Nicolo the first time we saw him. It was the summer I was twelve and he was thirteen. All of a sudden there he was that first morning of our annual visit. He was sitting on the wall separating our two properties, looking like he'd been waiting for us all his life. His pants were too short and his hair a little too long, curling at the ends, and his eyes were melancholy and beautiful. He'd picked oranges for us, and he offered one to me, warm from his hand. I took it, fingers brushing, and our eyes met. I felt a shiver run through me. It seemed like destiny.

Within a week it was like we had always known him. Every

chance he got, Nicolo would slip away after his chores were done to come spend time with us. Nonna would stuff him with biscotti and sweets. We would play board games and hide-and-seek. Dad would take us swimming in the lake. Simple things, but he seemed to soak in the joy of family life like a dry sponge.

He was a year old than me, but we were in the same grade in school. He'd spent years flitting from place to place around Europe with his unstable mother and a string of her boyfriends. He spoke five languages but struggled with math due to missing so much school. When his mom left with a Dutch boat captain for a year of working on a luxury yacht in the Mediterranean, she dumped Nicolo with her parents who owned the villa and olive farm next to ours. It was supposed to be for only a year, but she never came back.

It was not an easy transition for a boy of thirteen; Nicolo had traded an unstable vagabond lifestyle for one of stern rigidity, duty, and hard work with his grandparents, Violetta and Alberto. It was a toss-up as to which of his grandparents smiled less. My money was on Violetta, although Alberto's stern countenance always intimidated me.

Nicolo never complained and seldom spoke of his mother or his life before. He just worked hard and did his best to please his grandparents, a seemingly impossible task. He was quick to grin and laugh, but underneath he had an air of melancholy about him. He struggled to believe he was ever worthy enough, good enough. When he was with us, he would try so hard to do everything right, and apologize profusely if he even messed up a little—spilling a glass of water or missing a turn on a game. It broke my heart. I wanted him to know how special he was, how good and kind and smart.

I can still picture him so clearly—those dark eyes like melted chocolate; those bee-stung lips; his crooked, almost shy smile; his earnest, good-natured charm. The sweet intensity of his ardor. He was my first kiss, my first everything. Even Nonna Bruna, who *hated* Violetta, had adored him. I adored him too. I had given him my heart at fifteen, and even now, all these years later, I wonder if he still has a tiny piece of it.

Enough reminiscing, I scold myself, shaking off the memories and focusing on the task at hand.

"I'm just going back for the recipes," I tell Aurora. "That's why I said yes. I don't have time for romance. I've got a cookbook to finish!"

Aurora quirks a brow at me. "Never say never!" she says cheerfully. "Pack your good lace bra, just in case."

I open my mouth to respond when my nephew Dante, clad in a pair of sand-colored dungarees, comes barreling into the barn yelling, "Mummy, Mummy, Doris is eating your gardening gloves!" Behind him, Doris, a brown-and-white Nubian goat with long ears, tiptoes into the barn. She is brazenly chewing on what is left of a gardening glove. When she sees Aurora, she stops and backs up, employing evasive maneuvers. Doris is one wily goat.

"Quick, go get the Twinkies," Aurora urges Dante, who sprints off.

"What are the Twinkies for?" I scrape the last bite of Sunshine Salad from the bowl. Twinkies seem very un-Aurora. She doesn't keep refined sugar in the house.

"It's the only thing Doris likes better than all the inedible things she tries to eat," Aurora tells me, rolling her eyes. "Last week she ate a basket of begonias. Not the flowers . . . the entire wicker basket! We have to bribe her with Twinkies to get her to do anything. I swear, if she didn't produce such delicious goat's milk . . ." She falls silent for a moment, eyeing the goat in exasperation. Doris chews off the cuff of the glove with relish.

"So you think me going to Italy is a good idea?" I ask Aurora nervously.

She narrows her eyes and peers at me through the phone screen. "I think it's time you stopped playing it safe and let your life get messy," she replies frankly. "I think you need a wild fling this summer, or an adventure, or . . . I don't know . . . but you need to do something risky to make you feel alive. I think you should do the thing that scares you. And who knows what will happen? You may get way more than what you're looking for in Italy. I'm glad you're going. I have a feeling this might be the best thing that ever happens to you." She beams at me.

I process this for a moment. I don't agree. I don't need a wild fling or a grand adventure. I just need fifty good recipes and a chance to salvage my dream.

I drop the spoon in the empty bowl, resolving not to let anything distract me this summer. My goals are clear. Convince Nonna to let me use her recipe book to find fifty good recipes with personal ties, make sure everything is okay at the farm, and then return to Seattle ready to make this cookbook a success and hopefully convince Keith our show is worth it. Nothing else matters. I will steer clear of anything that gets in the way, even handsome, dark-eyed Italian men. Especially them. I have to keep my eye on the prize.

When Dante returns with the Twinkies, I say goodbye to Aurora and disconnect the call, but I linger on the rooftop deck for a few minutes more, picturing our family's serene olive groves on the shore of Lake Garda, Italy's largest lake. I can almost hear the whisper of the olive trees' long, silvery leaves rustling in the breeze off the water. It is the sound of utter peace to me, the place my heart has always felt most at home. I've never loved a place more. I've never been so scared to return. Lisa's assistant has already booked me a ticket to New York, leaving in a week, and then two round-trip tickets to Italy from JFK the following day. We will return to New York at the end of August, right before Alex's school starts. This is really happening.

My phone dings with a text from Drew. **Made it to LA. My apartment smells like old burritos.** He includes a frowny-face emoji.

Probably still beats the smell of liver mush, I text back with a vomit emoji.

I think about Drew unpacking and getting settled in LA. I think about getting on that plane in seven days, and suddenly, I can't breathe. What if I'm making a huge mistake? What if this is all a terrible idea? I scrabble for my phone, suddenly needing reassurance, to hear confirmation with my own ears that going back to Italy is a good idea. I need to know before I get on that plane. I punch in the +39 country code for Italy and the familiar number, heart pounding.

One ring . . . two . . .

"Pronto." It's her voice, brusque and earthy and a little impatient, as though the call is interrupting her.

I take a deep breath. "Nonna?"

"Juliana?" Instantly, her tone melts into warmth. "Mia cara, are you okay? Are you eating, sleeping? How is your health?" She peppers me with questions, talking in a jumble of English and Italian. I don't respond, just squeeze my eyes shut, feeling the prickle of tears. It's been too long. Now that I'm choosing to go back, I feel the weight of all those years, the distance. Cards and letters and a few calls at holidays and birthdays have not been enough to bridge the distance of an ocean and so much time. I feel the distance now more acutely than ever, those lost years that have slipped by faster than I realized. All of a sudden, I can't wait to hug her again, to step onto the soil of the farm, to be there once more. How I've missed her. I need to see that she is okay, that everything is okay.

"Nonna, I . . ." I plan to ask her if it truly is all right that we're coming to visit for the summer, to double-check even though Lisa assured me she'd already talked to Nonna and she was happy for us to come. Instead I just say simply, "I'm coming home." The words tumble out, surprising me.

There is silence on the other end of the line, then a murmured "Meno male," which translates roughly to "Thank goodness."

"I know," she says. "When your mother called me to ask if you and Alessandra could come for the summer, of course I said yes. You do not need to ask to come home, Juliana. You are always welcome here. It will be so good to have you back," she says, and there is such joy and relief in her tone that I feel guilty but also flooded with relief too. A weight lifts from my shoulders. This is a good idea after all.

"I've missed you," I tell her honestly.

"Come home to us, Nipotina," she says finally, using the diminutive Italian word for "granddaughter." "Our arms are open wide. We have been waiting for you."

Chapter 10

Ding!

"Ladies and gentlemen, the captain has turned off the seat belt sign. It is now safe to move about the cabin," a flight attendant announces in a smooth British accent.

Soaring above the clouds at about 35,000 feet somewhere over the Atlantic, it finally sinks in that this is real. I am on my way to Italy.

It's been a whirlwind of a week getting ready to leave for two months, although to be honest in the end there wasn't that much to arrange, which seems a little sad. I didn't leave much behind. Solomon and Sandra are watering my plants while I'm gone and gathering the mail. Truthfully, I'm not sure who was more relieved when I told them I'd be gone for the summer, them or me. It's a toss-up.

My job is a question mark. I talked to my captain at Trader Joe's and got approval for an unpaid leave of absence for the summer to "take care of family matters." Hopefully, I can get back on the schedule for enough hours when I return, but he warned me there's no guarantee. My friends and colleagues from work gave me a little break room send-off party after my last shift yesterday. With any luck it's not a permanent send-off. And now here I am, headed for Italy. And I am not alone.

Sipping my ginger ale, I sneak a furtive glance at my half sister sitting in the window seat beside me. Alex has an enormous pair of Beats headphones on and is concentrating hard on a documentary about Supreme Court Justice Ruth Bader Ginsburg. Except to go through security, she hasn't taken the headphones off since I picked her up in a taxi to head to the airport hours ago. Nor has she said more than six words to me total. I survey her with a sideways look, but she doesn't seem to notice. At five foot three, I'm pretty petite, but Alex is even smaller boned, waifish in a baggy black sweater that I suspect cost a fortune and looks like it's from Goodwill. Along with the sweater, she's wearing acid-washed jeans and chunky black loafers, rocking the casual rich kid NYC prep school look. I know that look. I spent a miserable junior and senior year not fitting in to one of those schools where all the kids dressed like that.

I reach over and tap her shoulder. She slides one headphone off her ear and glances at me briefly. "Yes?" Her face is impassive, waiting. On the screen, the Notorious R.B.G. is giving a dissent wearing her black Supreme Court justice robes and a fancy bejeweled beaded collar.

"Hey, are you excited to be going to Italy for the summer?" I ask, giving her a friendly, encouraging smile.

She shrugs, glancing back to the documentary. "Not really."

I survey her a little more boldly. In the years since I've seen her, Alex has grown into a pretty young woman. She looks like a character from the manga graphic novels she has stuffed in her backpack, all huge cool gray eyes and a Cupid's bow mouth. We have the same mouth, I realize with a start of recognition, although I favor bold lipsticks and she is barefaced. Her shoulder-length hair is pulled back in a sleek ponytail. While my hair is a dark, burnished brown with a decided wave to it, hers is more of a light ash-brown shade and pin straight. She resembles Ted more than she looks like any of the rest of us, but still when I look at her now, I see parts of my face in a stranger. It is a little disconcerting.

"Are you sad to miss camp?" I try again.

She pauses the documentary, then gives me a narrow look and snorts. "No."

"Yeah, me neither. I hated that place."

For a brief moment, a look of surprise flits across her face, replaced almost instantly by a slightly skeptical expression. "You went to Camp Champlain?" she asks.

"For one horrible summer the first year I lived with you guys in the city. I don't think you'd remember, though. You were a baby. I hated camp," I tell her. "I'm pretty sure I still have bug bites. And I'm terrible at tennis. I got put with the elementary kids when I was going to be a junior in high school. The third graders beat me."

Alex looks at me with a flicker of interest and maybe a touch of amusement, then shrugs again. "Tennis is okay. It's the other kids who are the worst."

I nod. I know what she means by that too. A lot of the kids there come from families who have tons of money and little time to spare on them, raised by a revolving door of au pairs. Many of them have spent their lives being shuttled from prep schools to enrichment activities to camps that run all summer. By the time they reach high school, they've had to socially and emotionally fend for themselves for years. It's a tough, privileged crowd with an often brutal pecking order. I never broke in, nor did I want to. I wasn't rich enough, connected enough, or interested enough to try. And the fact that I had just lost my dad and was still sort of a mess and also had a Seattle offbeat sense of style made me hopelessly uncool.

"Well, this summer is going to be great," I tell her. "Nonna Bruna is my favorite person in the universe, and the olive farm has been in our family for seven generations. It's the most beautiful place in the world, and it's right on Lake Garda. You're going to love it."

She looks at me and shrugs unenthusiastically. "Okay."

She un-pauses the documentary and puts her headphone back on. I'm a little taken aback. Clearly, she does not want to be here doing this. I blow out a breath, wondering just how I'm going to handle a prickly teen for two whole months.

The reality is that my half sister is virtually a stranger. I know so little about her. Maybe I should have tried harder when she was younger, but her presence always stung. If I'm honest, she's always been a constant reminder that Lisa abandoned Dad, Aurora, and me for Ted and a new life and family.

I've given up trying to understand my mother's choices, yet I'm still dealing with the fallout. And now here I am, in charge of Alex for the summer, a responsibility I haven't fully grasped until now. I wonder what she thinks of this trip. Did she even want to go? It doesn't seem like it. I frown, considering the situation. Like it or not, she's going to be with me in Italy for the rest of the summer. How are we going to relate to each other? How will this all pan out? I sigh and take a sip of my ginger ale, mulling things over.

Just then the flight attendant leans over my seat. "I have a vegetarian meal for 13C?" She holds out a tray.

"Oh, sorry, I think there must be some mistake. I'm not a vegetarian," I tell her.

Alex pulls her headphone away from her ear again. "It's mine."

I stare at her in surprise. "You're a vegetarian?" I ask. When did that happen? And we're going to spend the summer in *Italy*? Oh boy. It's going to be tough to bond over cooking. I don't remember Nonna's recipes being super vegetarian friendly. The flight attendant hands her the meal and offers me chicken or pasta. I take the chicken, peeling back the foil and staring at the naked little shriveled white chicken breast on a bed of mashed potatoes.

"How long have you been a vegetarian?" I ask Alex, still trying to connect with her.

Alex rolls her eyes and stirs her rice and grilled vegetables. "Since seventh grade. I think eating meat is cruel, unethical, and environmentally irresponsible," she informs me coolly. She shoots a pointed look at my tray, then spears a slice of her eggplant and turns back to the documentary.

I stare down at my little dry oval of chicken, at a loss for words. This could be a very long summer.

Chapter 11

"*Ciao, ragazze!*" **my** great-uncle Lorenzo cries as he peels into the arrivals area of the Verona airport in a rusty old red Fiat Panda. He slams to a halt at the curb and peers at Alex and me through the open passenger window, breaking into a huge grin. I grin back. I'm feeling equal parts nervous, antsy, and excited now that we've landed. I'm finally back in Italy. Lorenzo allays a little of my anxiety with his jovial welcome.

"Ciao, Zio Lorenzo. Thanks for the ride," I call through the open window.

He looks as though he has not aged a bit, his hair as thick and white as ever, his weathered, tanned face and sharp blue-eyed gaze moving from Alex to me. Technically Lorenzo isn't quite a great-uncle, although we've always referred to him as such. He is my grandfather Carlo's cousin, and after Carlo had a heart attack and passed away when I was young, he started helping Nonna Bruna around the farm. He has his own cozy little apartment in the upper level of the old stone stables and has been a fixture around the farm for as long as I can remember. He hops out of the car spryly.

"Welcome home, mia bella Juliana." He engulfs me in a hug, kissing both my cheeks soundly. He smells like sun and sweat, garlic and good olive oil, and maybe a little red wine. That hug makes me hungry and homesick all at once. He pulls back, and I introduce him to Alex. He gives a little bow and shakes her hand solemnly, engulfing her tiny hand in his big, work-roughened paw.

"You look like sisters," he tells us, glancing from one to the other, twinkling eyes narrowed shrewdly. Neither of us say anything. We may look like sisters, but to me we feel more like strangers. When I glance up, Alex is looking down at her clunky loafers. She looks uncomfortable. Maybe she feels the same.

Gesturing for us to get into the car, Lorenzo grabs our bags and stows one suitcase in the miniscule trunk and the other in the back seat. Alex clambers silently into the back seat next to her suitcase and I take the passenger seat, holding on for dear life as we roar north along Lake Garda toward the farm. It is only about thirty minutes away, but Lorenzo does it in twenty, keeping a lead foot on the pedal as the ancient Fiat stutters alarmingly at every turn.

We don't speak much. His English is limited and my Italian is a little rusty. I drink in the scenery as we pass the places I know so well, although my stomach is writhing with nerves and excitement as each kilometer brings us closer to the farm and to Nonna. Lorenzo drives us along the lake, the sparkling deep blue of the water winking enticingly from the driver's side, and I avert my eyes hastily. The lake holds such conflicting memories for me. It is painful to look at it, shimmering placidly in the sun. I can't see it without remembering my father, the terrible shock of losing him there.

I feel my gut clench with a memory. Lorenzo sprinting up the farmhouse drive shouting for Nonna. I will never forget the stricken look on his weathered face as he told us my father had been found floating in the lake. Lorenzo had seen rescuers pulling his body from the water. When she heard the news, Nonna gave a strangled cry and crumpled to the floor in a faint, hitting her head so hard she had a lump the size of a quail egg on her forehead. In that moment, my entire safe and happy world shattered. And since that day, all of this—the family olive groves, Lake Garda, and Nonna Bruna—has been sour, tinged with the tragic loss. Yet here I am again.

I focus on the view out my window, keeping my eyes firmly turned away from the lake. On my side of the road the rolling hills are blanketed with vineyards and a scattering of olive farms as well as dozens of small hotels and pensions. Everything is peaceful and sleepy in the late-afternoon sunshine. The air-conditioning in the Panda hasn't worked as long as I've been alive, so I keep my window rolled down, taking deep lungfuls of the warm air. The lake and the hills here create a unique, sunny microclimate that mimics the Mediterranean southern regions of Italy. Although it should be too far north, the special topography of the lake has allowed farmers to cultivate olives and citrus fruit here for centuries. This place is like nowhere else in Italy. I glance back and find Alex with her headphones on, pensively gazing out the window at the lake. I wonder what she's thinking about, how she feels about her first glimpse of this special part of Italy.

We pass the small, charming ancient walled town of Lazise, and my heart speeds up a little faster. We are getting close now. There are tourist attractions advertised everywhere along the road—wine tastings, olive oil tastings, panoramic viewpoints overlooking Lake Garda. Nearby Lake Como is more famous and draws more American tourists and the glitterati (thank you, George Clooney), but Lake Garda is the biggest lake in Italy and very popular with Italian, German, and Swiss tourists. Signs for gelato make my stomach rumble. That tiny square of desiccated chicken was a long time and a layover in London ago.

Lorenzo turns to me and grins. "Hai fame?" he asks. Are you hungry?

I nod ruefully. "Always," I tell him.

He beams, satisfied. "Soon," he says in English. I know what he means. Soon we will be at the farm, and Nonna has never let someone go hungry a day in her life. I think it's the solemn duty of every Italian nonna to feed anyone who crosses their kitchen door, stuffing them so full they have to roll out the way they came. I will not be hungry for long.

A few minutes later, we turn off the road and wind up the hillside along a familiar graveled drive. My pulse picks up. Through the silvery scrim of olive trees covering the gentle slope, I catch a glimpse of the red tiled roof and white stucco walls of the farmhouse. We're here.

"Welcome home," Lorenzo announces in English as we pull into the flat graveled parking area that sits between the farmhouse and the low-slung stone-walled stable that houses Lorenzo's apartment and all the equipment and supplies for the farm. I drink it all in. I've been away for fifteen years, but in that time little seems to have changed. The place has a timeless quality, nestled into the hillside of olive groves with a panoramic view of the lake far below. The stone farmhouse is two stories tall. The walls are thick stone overlaid with stucco, some of which has fallen off in places, showing the gray stone beneath. The windows have wooden shutters painted a dark green. It all seems a little smaller and shabbier than in my memory, but still, the familiarity of it makes my chest ache. I hop out of the car as soon as Lorenzo stops, and draw a deep breath as I look around. The warm air is redolent of sunbaked earth, a tinge of lake water, and the scent of lavender and herbs from the tidy herb bed that runs along one side of the house. I have missed this place so much. I didn't realize how much until this moment. I blink back tears, overcome with a confusing sense of homecoming mixed with grief.

"This is it?"

I almost forgot Alex. She's standing behind me looking around, clearly unimpressed.

I clear my throat, trying to dispel the lump of emotion lodged there. "It's amazing, you'll see," I assure her.

She sighs and grabs her backpack from the seat. "Whatever. I guess anything beats Camp Complain," she mutters.

Lorenzo and I exchange a look. He raises a thick white eyebrow and I shrug, then grab my carry-on bag and follow him across the courtyard. As we approach the farmhouse I hang back a bit, feeling suddenly a little shy and unsure.

"Mia bella nipotina!" Nonna Bruna flings open the heavy wooden kitchen door and rushes out before we can knock. She throws her arms around me and squashes me against her ample bosom, kissing me on the cheeks soundly, then holds me at arm's length and looks me up and down. To my relief I see that Nonna is as tiny and stocky and dynamic as ever, her dyed dark brown hair caught up in its signature tight bun, her quick black eyes flashing with joy.

"Santo cielo!" she exclaims in amazement, then switches to English. "Look at you, so beautiful and all grown-up." She reaches up and pinches my cheek like I am a child. "You have your father's eyes." She puts one hand to her bosom and her gaze turns sad. "May he rest in peace." She crosses herself and I follow suit by instinct, feeling the warm spread of joy in my chest at the effusive welcome, at how normal it all feels. She wants me here. This was a good idea to come. Then Nonna turns to Alex.

"Alessandra." For a moment she pauses, taking Alex's measure. I wonder briefly how this will go. After all, Alex is no blood relation to her. Instead Alex is a stark reminder that Nonna's ex-daughter-in-law left Nonna's beloved only son to raise their two girls alone while she swanned off and created a new life and new family. Nonna would have every right to hold no fondness for Alex. But an instant later her face relaxes into a smile. "Welcome," she says warmly. "You are welcome in my home." Then she embraces Alex and kisses her on the cheek. Alex stands rigid, looking slightly shocked. Nonna seems not to notice. She gestures to us both. "Come inside," she directs. "You must be hungry." She issues a stream of rapid-fire instructions to Lorenzo and shoos him back toward the car.

"Lorenzo will get your suitcases." She waves us forward, into the kitchen. "Now we eat. You are both too thin and pale. But don't worry, we will fatten you up in no time."

Chapter 12

"**Come, it's time** for a merenda," Nonna announces as we follow her through the door from the courtyard and into the kitchen.

Alex gives me a quick, uncertain glance. "What's that?"

"She's giving us a snack," I explain in a half whisper. My favorite room of the house, the kitchen is large and spacious with a low ceiling, white plaster walls, heavy wood beams, and a chipped tile floor. Everything looks exactly the same as it has for as long as I can remember.

At one end sits a huge open hearth, the inside blackened from decades of fires. In the middle of the room stands a heavy scarred table made from olive wood. My grandfather Carlo crafted it for Nonna as an engagement present and she uses it as her prep table for cooking. There is a smaller round table nestled at the back of the kitchen where the family gathers to eat. No one uses the formal dining room or parlor, which lie down a hallway toward the front of the house. All of life happens here in this kitchen.

Nonna directs us to be seated at the round table and sets tall, sweating glasses in front of us. I take a sip, instantly transported back to childhood. It is Nonna's lemonade, a delicious concoction of soda water, fresh-squeezed lemons, and honey. I happily drink the refreshingly cold beverage, watching Nonna bustle around the kitchen, soaking in the serene normalcy of the moment. I can't quite believe I'm really here again.

I focus on Nonna, watching her closely. How has she changed in the years since I've seen her in person? Nonna claims she's five feet tall, but I don't think she's ever actually reached five feet. She turned eighty-two in February, and she wears the years well. Small and stocky, with thick dark hair she dyes religiously every two weeks and sharp black eyes that miss nothing, she is still vigorous. She is all movement in the kitchen, her strong hands chopping and arranging as she stomps around in her sensible black pumps.

She has aged in the fifteen years since I last saw her, though. I can see it now. Her shoulders are a little more stooped, and she moves more slowly. But she is still vibrant and proud, with her strong Roman nose and thin mouth that belies the tender expansiveness of her heart. She is firm and unyielding, warm and nurturing, all at the same time. She will badger you with love and stuff you with good things to eat. Like every Italian nonna, food is love to her.

"Mangiate, mangiate." She slides two small plates in front of us, urging us to eat, eat. On each plate sits a thick slice of crusty bread drizzled with olive oil, a wide smear of creamy goat cheese, and two quartered figs. I devour the bread first, the unctuous olive oil coating my tongue, cut with a sharp sprinkle of sea salt. I utter an involuntary groan of appreciation, and Nonna's mouth curves up in a satisfied smile. Alex holds up her bread and sniffs it suspiciously.

"Try it," I urge her. "The olive oil is from our farm." Nonna doesn't use anything else in her cooking.

Alex takes a tentative bite and sets it back down quickly, making a face. She sips her lemonade and looks down at her plate with a frown. I can see Nonna Bruna watching us both from the corner of her eye as she arranges a plate for Lorenzo at the prep table. When Alex hesitantly asks to use the bathroom and disappears up the stairs to the only bathroom in the house, Nonna marches over to the table and interrogates me, hands on her hips. "What? She don't like the food?" Her lips are pursed in dismay.

"I don't know what she likes," I admit honestly. "She's practically a stranger."

"But she's your sister." Nonna looks shocked.

"Half sister," I correct. "And I barely know her."

Nonna frowns. "There is no half family," she tells me firmly.

Lorenzo comes in from outside, carrying our suitcases, and hauls them up the stairs to our rooms. There are a total of five bedrooms upstairs, along with the sole bathroom. Nonna's room is at the far end of the house. On either side of her are two generously sized bedrooms that have only ever been used as storage rooms and are full of old furniture and boxes of yellowing books and odds and ends. They were a treasure trove to explore when we were kids. Aurora and I always shared the biggest, brightest room at the top of the stairs. It faces the courtyard and has a lovely lake view. Dad's room was directly across the hall from ours, looking up the hill and over the olive groves behind the house.

Alex has not reappeared yet. Nonna is bustling around, and I take the opportunity to glance around the kitchen, looking for the cookbook. If I remember right, Nonna always kept it in a nook built into the wall, along with a statue of the Blessed Virgin Mary, and an extra pair of reading glasses because she was forever misplacing hers. The nook still contains the Blessed Virgin presiding over not one but two pairs of reading glasses, but there is no cookbook in sight.

"Nonna, where's your cookbook, the one we cooked from all the time when I was younger?" I crane my neck, searching for it. "I'd love to see it again."

Nonna pauses, and a strange expression flits across her face for a brief second. She looks almost... furtive. She slices into a fig firmly. "That old thing? I don't know. It's probably around here somewhere." She brushes away the question. "If you want good recipes, Maria Azzano from Garda just published a recipe book last year, all local recipes they use in their family restaurant. Good food and not hard to make."

"Oh." I settle back in the chair, disappointed and a little worried. I need that cookbook. How am I going to gather all the recipes I need if I don't have it? I was counting on it for those fifty recipes in one convenient, easy-to-access place. "I was just hoping to look through that specific cookbook again. I have such fond memories of it."

Nonna hurries over with a plate for Lorenzo as he comes back down the stairs and settles himself with a loud sigh in a chair opposite me. "I don't know where it is," she says dismissively, "but we can cook together while you're here. We'll make those almond biscotti you always loved. They were your favorite as a child."

"Sure, that sounds great." I nibble a quarter of a fig, mind racing with worry. This is an unexpected problem. I need to locate the cookbook as soon as possible. I'm going to have to poke around and see if I can find it. My entire plan hinges on it.

Alex still has not reappeared.

"You think your sister is okay?" Nonna asks, brow furrowed with concern.

"She wanted to know where her room was," Lorenzo says. "So I showed her and put the suitcase in there. You too." He nods to me. "I put your suitcase in your room."

I thank him. My room. All these years later, and it is still my room.

"Do you think she wants something more to eat?" Nonna asks, brow furrowed in concern. "She looks as skinny as a chicken bone." She snaps her fingers. "Maybe some pork sausage?"

"Um." Gently, I break the news of Alex's vegetarianism.

Nonna looks shocked. "But what's wrong with the meats, the goat cheese?" she asks in horror. "What about the pasta? The pasta is made with eggs!"

I shrug. "I think it's a personal conviction. Eggs should be okay. I think most vegetarians eat eggs. And I think the goat cheese is fine. You'll have to ask her."

Nonna frowns and I can see her struggling to translate the words in her head and wrap her mind around the concept of vegetarianism. Then her face clears and she makes a dismissive gesture. "It's okay," she announces. "Tonight I make fish. And pasta."

I glance at Lorenzo, who shrugs and pops a whole fig into his mouth. "I don't argue anymore," he tells me in Italian, throwing a knowing grin toward my grandmother's small but mighty figure. "I learned many years ago. There is no point in arguing with Bruna."

"That's right," Nonna says firmly in English, pouring herself a glass of lemonade and sitting down heavily across from me. "You're a smart man despite having such a thick skull, Lorenzo."

It's been this way with them for as long as I can remember, this good-natured bickering and ribbing. I think they do it for entertainment. Lorenzo has never married and Nonna never remarried after my grandfather Carlo died. They run the farm together, just the two of them, squabbling and managing everything themselves, getting older and grayer every year.

"You should be on Pasta Grannies," I tell Nonna spontaneously. "They'd love you. You can show the world your special pasta recipes."

"What is this Pasta Grannies?" She looks mystified and a little suspicious.

I smile. "It's nonnas like you from all over Italy showing people how to make pasta through videos on the Internet." I whip out my phone and show her. She watches for a moment, then quirks a brow at me, bemused.

"And these women make money from putting these videos on the Internet?"

"Yes. People love them."

She waves a hand dismissively. "She's making the tagliatelle wrong. I know a better way."

"Of course you do." I exchange an amused glance with Lorenzo, who shrugs dismissively.

"See, I don't argue," he mutters.

I slip my phone back in my pocket and concentrate on my snack. Nonna takes a sip of lemonade, then sighs and fixes me with a searching gaze.

"We missed you, bambina mia," she says softly. She reaches out and takes my hand in hers—big-knuckled and a little cold. Her fingers are twisted from arthritis but her grip is still surprisingly strong. "It is good to have you home."

I feel a lump rise in my throat and look down at my plate. "I missed you too, so much," I whisper, feeling ashamed that it has been so many years. Aurora is right: I let fear keep me from a good thing. I see that now. I could have come back, should have come back. I let my conflicted emotions keep me away for so long.

"Juliana, look at me." Nonna interrupts my thoughts.

I do. She gives me a searching look as though she can see all those thoughts going through my head, then nods once, firmly. "You are here now," she pronounces, squeezing my fingers with her own. "You are home. And that is all that matters."

At her words, Lorenzo clears his throat and she glances at him, a brief flash of warning in her eyes.

"Not now, Lorenzo," she mutters in Italian, so low I almost can't catch the words. Lorenzo holds up his hands, a gesture of surrender. I take note, thinking of what Aurora said. I feel like there is something I'm missing, something they are not saying. I wonder what it is. The not knowing makes me uneasy. I hope it's not bad news. I squeeze Nonna's hand, vowing to somehow make up for lost time. I'm here now, and I'll do whatever I can to atone for all the years I've stayed away. At the same time, I have to find that cookbook pronto. All my hopes are pinned on it. I have a lot of work to do.

Chapter 13

"*Buongiorno, sleeping head.*" Nonna greets me cheerfully as I stumble downstairs late the next morning, still in my pajamas. I blink blearily, feeling groggy and very jet-lagged, as Nonna bustles about the kitchen. Alex is already sitting at the table with a cup of milky coffee and a half-eaten brioche in front of her. She glances up as I enter the room but doesn't say anything. She looks haggard and wan. Jet lag must be hitting her pretty hard.

The room smells heavenly, like strong, dark coffee and warm, sweet bread. The enticing aroma of a true Italian breakfast perks me up instantly. I give Nonna a peck on the cheek and greet Alex, who gives me a muted, "Hey," in return. I slide into a chair across from her, eager to start my day the typical Italian way, with caffeine and a little something sweet. Then I'm determined to figure out where the recipe book is. That's the first and most important order of business for the day. Without that book, I'm completely stuck.

"You want a caffellatte, Nipotina?" Nonna asks me, and I gratefully accept. She brings it over along with a fresh brioche on a plate.

"How did you sleep?" she asks, and before I can answer she looks at me critically and clucks. "You look tired. And thin. Eat something."

I happily oblige. I am tired. And I feel worn thin. After I went to my room last night, I gave Aurora a quick call to let her know we'd arrived safely. Then Solomon texted me three times. First to ask if we had any borax powder. The answer is no. What is borax powder anyway? He texted again to ask if Ophelia could sleep on my bed as she "likes her own space." The answer was also no, and then he texted to ask if they could use my Italian espresso maker. That one I agreed to, so I don't seem unreasonable.

Right before I drifted off to sleep, I texted Drew a photo of the farmhouse and the lake. He texted back a photo of him and Desiree at a retro burger joint somewhere with the caption "Rehearsal." Desiree was looking lithe, fit, and cute in a sports bra and leggings, her standard outfit. She was puckering up for the camera. And next to her, arm in arm with her, was Drew. His hair was styled differently and he was wearing a fitted bowling shirt. I think they might have bleached his teeth. He looked a little like a Ken doll. Seeing him made me sad. He is getting his golden chance. I still have to try to earn mine.

The thought spurs me into action. This morning I have no time to waste. After breakfast I'm going to do a thorough search for the cookbook. I take a bite of brioche and my resolve weakens. I'll search right after I have a second caffellatte and maybe another brioche. I forgot how much better everything tastes in Italy.

"Where's Zio Lorenzo?" I ask around a big bite of brioche.

"Out in the courtyard. Nicolo is helping him fix something on the car this morning."

The brioche sticks in my throat. "Nicolo?" I cough. Surely, not the same Nicolo. Not my Nicolo. There are thousands of Nicolos in Italy. The last time I saw him, my Nicolo was being packed off to a great-aunt in Genoa after our romantic tryst came to a miserable and wet end.

"Yes, yes, Nicolo Fiore. You remember him. He was always such a sweet boy. Now he is all grown-up and what a fine piece of man." Nonna clicks her tongue appreciatively. "He's back now, running the farm like they always wanted him to. That Violetta doesn't deserve him. Che vecchia strega!" Nonna pretends to spit on the ground for emphasis, her mouth puckering like she is tasting something bitter, the exact same expression she wears every time she says her next-door neighbor's name.

Alex pauses, her brioche halfway to her mouth. "What did she say?" she whispers, looking confused and cautious.

"Nonna and her neighbor Violetta don't get along," I explain in a low voice. "They've got this feud that's been going on for like sixty years." I don't translate the Italian phrase Nonna just used, although I'm pretty sure she called Violetta an old hag. Or a witch, depending on the context. Regardless, nothing complimentary.

The property next door belongs to the Fiore family, Nicolo's grandparents. With a sprawling olive farm and a large, elegant villa, the estate is far bigger and more prosperous that ours. The matriarch of the Fiores, a tall, formidable woman named Violetta, is Nonna's archnemesis. I've never been able to find out what exactly went sour between them so long ago, but they've been locked in a feud for over sixty years, or so Dad told me. He had no idea what happened between them either. No one seems to know except Nonna and Violetta, and neither of them are telling. It's a long-standing family mystery.

But now I focus on the most surprising news. Nicolo is back home? And he's currently in our courtyard? My heart gives a quick little flutter of excitement.

"Violetta is still alive?" I ask. She's over eighty now. Her husband Alberto died years ago. "And Nicolo is living next door?"

Nonna turns and looks at me narrowly. "Yes and yes, but we do not speak of that woman here," she says in a tone as sharp as vinegar. "She stole something of great value from me many years ago. I have never forgiven her." She speaks with such an air of gravity that I shiver a little, wondering again what in the world happened when they were young to produce such lifelong ire.

"Wow," Alex murmurs, chewing her brioche and watching Nonna wide-eyed. "Remind me not to get on her bad side."

A moment later, the kitchen door flies open and Lorenzo bursts in, stomping his feet and talking to someone behind him in rapid-fire Italian.

"Come in, come in," Lorenzo calls, gesturing. I catch a glimpse of curly dark hair behind him and my heart stops for a second. Then I glance down at my stretched-out and ever so slightly sheer Hello Kitty sleep tee in horror. No. Please don't let this be Nicolo. I can't see my first love looking like I just rolled out of bed except . . .

"Juliana?" That familiar voice. I haven't heard it in fifteen years. Oooh, I want to sink through the tiled floor. I glance up. It's him.

"Nicolo!"

He's standing in the doorway, morning light streaming behind him, illuminating him like the archangel Gabriel painted by an Italian master. I stare for a moment as he steps inside. In the fifteen years since I last saw him, he's grown from a sweet, slightly awkward boy into a gorgeous, self-assured man. Gone is the faint hint of a mustache over his upper lip, the gangly limbs of his youth. He stands a few inches shy of six feet. Not tall, but he's filled out beautifully. His curls are cropped close to his head at the sides but long enough in the front to fall just slightly over his brow, and his olive skin, straight nose with the slightest bump at the bridge, and full, almost sulky mouth give him an effortless Mediterranean appeal. And those dimples and dark eyes. I'd kill for those eyelashes, inky smudges like he's wearing eyeliner. It isn't fair.

He's dressed in a pair of dark work pants and a white cotton shirt rolled up at the sleeves. Like so many Italian men, he looks ridiculously stylish, even if his shirt is smudged with what appears to be axle grease. I'm achingly aware of my dishevelment and groan silently in despair. I have a very cute pair of pajamas upstairs. Of all the days to choose comfort over style . . . I try to pull the T-shirt down over more of my exposed thighs. Did I even touch my hair this morning? Oooh, this is unbearably humiliating.

"Nicolo, you must eat something. You want a caffellatte?" Nonna buzzes around him, clearly adoring.

"I already ate, but thank you, Bruna," Nicolo says, not taking his eyes from me.

There is a warm familiarity between the two of them that surprises me. It feels almost like they're family. I wonder what I've missed in the years I've been gone. How much time does Nicolo spend with Nonna and Lorenzo? Just how long has he been back home? I realize I don't know much of anything at all.

While Nonna bustles around cutting large wedges from an almond cake, Nicolo leans against the counter and crosses his arms (tanned forearms, leanly muscled, I notice). He meets my eyes. His are so dark you can't tell the pupil from the iris, and filled with a warm curiosity.

"Nicolo!" I decide to brazen out this excruciating reunion. There's no help for it. It's that or try to sink through the floor. "You're all grown-up," I say, trying to sound confident and a little flippant. It just sounds cheesy, or maybe a bit creepy. This is not my best effort. I am giving this interaction a solid one star. Do not recommend.

His smile is slow and a little teasing. "So are you, and as beautiful as ever," he tells me in perfect, slightly accented English. Across from me I can see Alex watching our exchange in puzzlement.

"I didn't know you were back," I plow on, trying to salvage this awkward conversation. What I wouldn't give for five minutes with a blow-dryer and a mascara wand. Heck, I'd even settle for a toothbrush and my decent pajamas. I tuck my hands under my thighs so I don't reach up to try to tame my hair. It's a lost cause.

Nicolo eyes me and his mouth, that lush mouth, quirks up at the corner. "Eventually, we all return home, right?"

I have a feeling he's enjoying the situation. He's always had a mischievous way about him, and that has not changed. I swallow hard, trying not to remember the last time we saw each other. The wool blanket we'd spread over the fragrant straw in the stall of the Fiores' unused stable had been scratchy against the bare skin of my back, but Nicolo's lips on my neck had blazed a trail that felt like fire. We'd been caught up in the moment, in the heady passion of young love and lust, unaware of anything except our desire for each other . . . until Nonna and Violetta turned a garden hose of icy water on us accompanied by a stream of Italian invectives that still make my ears burn thinking about it. The pope had been referenced, and all our dead relatives. And the Blessed Virgin Mary.

I thought I would die of embarrassment when they sat us down like two sodden, scolded children and confronted us about our secret romance. And I was convinced I'd die of a broken heart when Nicolo was promptly sent away. Oh, the euphoria and heartbreak of young love.

Flushing at the memory, I glance at Nicolo's hands, those big, square, capable hands, recalling with a visceral thrill what they felt like wrapped around my rib cage, pulling me closer, tangling his fingers in my hair as he kissed me clumsily, earnestly. What he'd lacked in experience he'd made up for in sheer enthusiasm. We had been so young.

I clear my throat and look hastily away, gulping more of the rapidly cooling caffellatte. I am thirty years old, not fifteen. I need to get my thoughts under control. I feel like my face is on fire.

"And this is Alessandra," Bruna says by way of introduction. "Juliana's little sister."

I see Alex stiffen, but I can't tell if she's objecting to being called little, or my sister, or both. "Alex," she corrects. "My name is Alex."

Nicolo tips his head to her. "Molto piacere, Alex." Nice to meet you.

Alex blushes furiously and buries her face in her caffellatte.

"Nicolo? Let's go," Lorenzo says in English, clapping him heartily on the back and stepping out the door, carrying a big wedge of cake in one hand.

"So nice to see you again," I call after Nicolo as brightly as I can, relieved he is leaving. I catch Alex staring furtively at Nicolo, a dull blush staining her cheeks.

"Nicolo, here is a little something sweet for later. I worry you are not being fed enough at home." Nonna catches him at the door and presses a paper-wrapped packet of cake in his hands. "Have lunch with us," she urges. "Anytime you are here working, you must eat with us, yes? You need good food, a big strong man like you." She pats his cheek indulgently.

"You are too kind, Bruna," Nicolo says, giving her a fond look and a quick peck on the cheek.

"Ciao, Jules, Alex." He glances over his shoulder, catching my eyes. Something crackles between us. I wonder what he remembers of our brief summer of love. He nods farewell and follows Lorenzo outside, Nonna at their heels. I take a little gasp of air.

Chapter 14

"**Who was that . . . ?**" Alex says in a slightly awed tone. She's gazing after Nicolo like she's just seen the Second Coming of Christ. It's the first time she hasn't looked either bored or skeptical since I picked her up in New York.

"That's Violetta's grandson. We were . . . friends when we were younger," I tell her. It's a pitifully inadequate explanation for the boy who was once the center of my world.

"Are all Italian guys that hot?" she asks, a note of grudging admiration in her voice.

"Ew, Nicolo's almost old enough to be your father," I scold her.

"So?" She rolls her eyes and goes back to her brioche. "Everyone I know has an old dad. Dad is fifteen years older than Mom. It's, like, not uncommon."

"Maybe, but at your age it's also illegal," I tell her.

She rolls her eyes and unzips the backpack sitting by her chair, pulling out her headphones and phone and retreating into her own world.

I hastily down my caffellatte, deciding to go get dressed before anything else unexpected happens. I make a solemn vow not to ever again come downstairs unless I'm wearing appropriately cute clothes and have at least looked at myself in the mirror, front *and* back. Then I firmly put Nicolo from my mind. I've wasted enough time this morning. I can't just sit around all morning drinking delicious coffee and mooning over an old flame who has matured into an extremely hot olive farmer. I can't forget why I'm here. I have work to do. First things first . . . I have to find Nonna's cookbook.

Nonna is still outside. I can hear her in the courtyard, bossing the men around in rapid-fire Italian. I take my dishes to the sink and decide to do a quick search for the cookbook before I get dressed, just for a minute. I peruse the built-in cubbies and open shelves. Nothing. There's a heavy old buffet under the window on one side of the kitchen. I remember its drawers were always filled with a fascinating jumble of items. When I was a child, I loved to sift through them, poring over the huge iron keys, spools of twine, nubs of pencils, and bits and pieces of farm life inside. I pull open a few drawers now, finding a stack of linen napkins in one, a mixture of junk in another. Then I pull open the top drawer, where I remember Nonna kept some of her more treasured and often-used possessions. And there, under the mother-of-pearl rosary Nonna's mother had gifted her, I spy a familiar caramel-colored cover. My heart leaps in recognition and relief. I've found the cookbook.

I ease it out of the drawer, smoothing my fingers over the calfskin cover worn soft and buttery with handling. It is spotted with grease stains and heavy in my hand, though not particularly big, about the size of a hardcover novel. I heave a sigh of relief. This is the book that is going to save everything.

But then I pause. Nonna told me last night she didn't know where the cookbook was, but it's here, in the drawer of her most treasured possessions. She prays the rosary every morning and night using those special rosary beads from her mother. So how could she not have known the cookbook was in this drawer? It makes no sense. I frown, puzzled. Why would she not tell me where it was? Is she growing forgetful?

I file the question away to ponder later, and turn back to the book. It's been so long since I held it in my hands. There are so many delicious recipes inside. I can't wait to see them all again. Where should I start? I think of our special choosing game. Every morning Nonna would hand me the book after breakfast, and I would close my eyes and flip to a page without peeking. When I opened my eyes, we would make whatever recipe I'd turned to. It had been our little shared ritual. I always got to choose, but only at random, and with my eyes closed. Every time I played, the result would surprise and delight me.

No matter the recipe, it always seemed to be exactly what we needed for the day. On the day I flipped the book open to a recipe for anicini, we made dozens and dozens of the anise-flavored cookies. They reminded me of a very thin, crunchy, flat waffle, and I loved using the anicini maker to imprint a beautiful pattern on each one. We made over a hundred cookies, and just when we were done, a neighbor stopped by to invite us to an impromptu neighborhood party. We boxed up the anicini and took them to the party, pleased to have something to contribute. On the day Aurora came down with the flu one summer, I opened to a recipe for a simple chicken soup. The recipes always seemed to show up at the perfect time, as though the book was somehow offering us just what we needed every time we opened it. To my young heart it felt magical.

I decide to play the game again now, just for old times' sake. I glance over at Alex, but she's absorbed in her phone and has her headphones on. I almost interrupt her to show her the book, but she doesn't look like she would welcome the intrusion. I close my eyes and flip the book open to somewhere in the middle. Then I focus on the page, eager to see what recipe I've turned to. But there is no recipe. The page is blank. Puzzled, I turn to the next page and the next, but they are blank too.

"What in the world?" I frown in confusion. This is Nonna's recipe book. I can still see the charcoal smudges of my childish fingerprints on the spine from the time I touched the inside of the cold fireplace and then picked up the book without washing my hands. But where are all the recipes? It has always been brimming with recipes. I riffle through all the pages, but each one is the same, completely blank.

"Juliana, what are you doing?" I glance up with a start. Nonna is standing in the doorway from the courtyard, watching me with a questioning gaze. Her tone is a little sharp.

"Trying to find the recipes we used to make together," I say, fanning the pages again to see if I somehow missed something. "But it's all blank. What happened to them?"

Nonna looks surprised. "Show me." She hurries over and I show her. "See?"

She blinks in astonishment. "How could this be?" she murmurs to herself. "Try another page," she commands. I do. That page is blank too.

"Try another," she tells me. Obediently, I flip to another page. Same result.

"They're all blank," I tell her. "Where are the recipes?" There is an edge of panic in my voice.

Nonna leans forward and looks from the book to me and back again, ignoring my question. She makes a *hmm*ing noise in her throat. "Very peculiar," she murmurs, frowning.

I'm thoroughly confused and more than a little perturbed. "What's going on? What's peculiar?"

"Nothing." Nonna reaches for the book, and I hand it to her. Except when I glance down at the book in her hand, the page that was completely blank a moment before is no longer empty. Instead it now holds half of a recipe, with ingredients and instructions written in an ornate script. I can see the torn edge running right down the middle of the recipe, cutting it in two and showing only half the ingredients and instructions. The other half of the page is just blank white paper. I stare at it in astonishment. Where did that come from? I could have sworn the entire page was completely blank, just a moment before. Am I seeing things? I squint at the page in confusion.

"You don't want this old thing," Nonna says firmly, starting to shut the book. "Let me find you something better."

I put out a hand to stop her. "What's this recipe?" I point to the writing on the page. It is in Italian, and I can just read the recipe title, scrawled in large cursive above the incomplete ingredients list. Torta Fioritura Degli Aranci. I translate it in my head. Orange Blossom Cake. That sounds yummy . . . and intriguing.

Nonna shuts the book with a firm snap. "That is nothing," she says, avoiding my eyes.

"What's Orange Blossom Cake?" I ask.

Nonna presses her lips together and replaces the cookbook in the drawer, shutting it with a little more force than seems necessary. "An old recipe from the past that has brought enough trouble for a lifetime." But she does not meet my eyes. I have the distinct feeling there is a lot she isn't saying.

"Nonna, where are all the recipes we used to make together?" I ask in consternation. "I thought they were all in that book."

She hesitates.

"They are not there, mia cara," she tells me gently. "They are gone."

"Gone?" My hope sinks like a stone. "What do you mean, gone?" I need those recipes. So much is depending on them. There is a looming deadline, a waiting publisher, and a fairly large sum of money at stake. Not to mention any chance I have of saving my show. So basically everything.

Chapter 15

Nonna shrugs and bustles around, cleaning up crumbs and dishes from breakfast as I try to absorb her words. "It was an old book, Juliana," she explains. "Nothing lasts forever. Ink fades. Moths eat paper. Perhaps it's better this way. Now you can make something new instead of using those old recipes. You can cook from your heart."

Which is exactly what I can't seem to do. I slump into the nearest chair, stunned. It makes no sense. The book is here but the recipes are all gone? How did that happen? Humidity? Age? Would the ink fade like that? Whatever the reason, the recipes are obviously not in the book. This is a catastrophe. What am I going to do now?

As the reality of my predicament sinks in, I can feel my anxiety kicking into high gear. I shake out my hands, like I'm shaking water off them, trying to calm down. It's a Dr. Dana trick to regulate emotion. Nonna is there in an instant. "What's wrong, Juliana?" She puts her hand to my forehead. "Do you feel sick? Did you get caught in a draft? I can crush some garlic for you to eat. Or maybe you want some hot wine?"

I brush off her concern, embarrassed. "I'm okay. It's nothing."

She fixes me with a disapproving stare. "This is not nothing, Juliana. What is it?"

I gust out a loud sigh. Now I am going to have to tell her what's really going on. Nonna is as stubborn as a rock. If she thinks I am withholding something, she'll badger me gently but persistently until she gets the truth. Believe me, I know this from experience.

I glance over at Alex, but she seems absorbed in her phone at the table.

I close my eyes and concentrate on breathing deeply for a moment, holding and counting. "Nonna, I'm in trouble." And then I tell her about my predicament—about the cookbook deal, about what they want from me, and about how little time I have to come up with fifty recipes that feel personal. I do not tell her about the blankness, about how I cannot seem to remember a single recipe she taught me or any recipe that I have emotional ties to. I can't admit that to anyone, not even Nonna. It feels so personal, shameful even.

Nonna listens intently, eyes narrowed in thought. "So you must come up with these recipes, these dishes from your heart in such a short time?" she says at last.

I nod miserably. "And I have no idea how I'm going to do it."

"Hmm..." Nonna tilts her head and fixes me with a beady, considering gaze. "Why did you want that old recipe book?"

I hang my head. "Because I thought I could use the recipes for my cookbook," I admit. "The recipes in your cookbook are the ones that have meant something to me. But now that the recipes are gone..."

"You are in trouble," she finishes my sentence. "Yes, I see." She gazes at me thoughtfully for a moment, then sits back and slaps her hands on her knees. "Juliana, those old recipes are gone, but do not despair, mia cara. They live on in here"—she taps my forehead—"and in here." She touches my chest right above my heart. "You can do this. You must do this," she announces. "I will help you."

"But how?" I protest, lifting my hands in a gesture of helplessness. "I don't even know where to start."

"Ah." She holds one finger up in the air. "We stop and listen until we understand. There is magic in this kitchen, Juliana, whether you know it or not, and the magic never lies. It is always right, and it is trying to tell you something now. We just have to hear what it is saying. It will lead us to the answer."

"Listen to what?" I'm confused. Italian nonnas are a naturally superstitious bunch, armed with a staunch Catholic faith supplemented by old wives' tales and folk remedies. Is that what Nonna is talking about when she speaks about kitchen magic? Some folktale from the past?

"The kitchen magic," Nonna says mysteriously. "It will show us how to make these recipes you need."

I deflate instantly. "Right. Good luck with that."

Nonna reaches out and lightly cups my cheek. Her palm is tough and leathery from years of hard work. "What happened to you, mia cara?" she asks. "You were always my brave girl, full of laughter and life, full of light. When did that light go out? When did you get so full of doubt? What are you afraid of?"

I open my mouth but find I have no answer. What *am* I afraid of? Failure? Loss? Feeling like the rug keeps getting pulled out from under me over and over in my life? It started the day they dragged my father's lifeless body from the lake. Or maybe it had started even before that, when Nicolo was sent away and broke my heart, or even earlier, when Lisa left us to begin a new life and a new family. There has been so much loss in my life. It has made me afraid to hold on to anything too closely, because I know in the end I will probably lose the things I love the most.

I glance over at Alex, who's tapping on her phone and doesn't look up, but I have a feeling she is listening to everything. One of her headphones seems to be partly off her ear.

"Juliana!" Nonna stands and gestures to me impatiently. "Come, there is no time to waste. We start now."

I stand reluctantly too. "Okay, but I'm going to get dressed first." I am determined to at least brush my teeth and put on a touch of mascara, just in case Nicolo reappears. And to immediately throw away this embarrassingly skimpy Hello Kitty sleep shirt.

I have very little confidence that Nonna is going to be able to unlock my culinary creativity using her kitchen magic powers, but at least if I am going to fail again, I want to look as cute as possible while doing it. I head upstairs, bracing myself for whatever the day may hold.

Chapter 16

Fifteen minutes later, I come downstairs dressed smartly in my favorite '60s-style high-waisted white shorts and yellow blouse, hair tamed, and a flick of mascara on my lashes. I hope I look casual and effortlessly cute, not like I'm trying too hard.

Nonna is standing at the big old work table, chopping herbs. Alex is nowhere to be seen. Her backpack is gone too. Upstairs, the bedroom door where she is staying, right across the hall from mine, was closed when I walked by, so I figure she's retreated to her room.

With a flutter of nerves, I present myself to Nonna, curious to know if she has a plan. I sure hope so. I wipe my sweaty palms on my shorts. I'm so nervous I feel a little nauseated.

"Okay, I'm ready."

Nonna glances up at me. "Good. I am sending you to the market."

"The market?" I raise my eyebrows. It's Tuesday. There's an outdoor market in Bardolino that's popular with tourists, but that's on Thursdays, which means she's probably sending us to the smaller, less well-known market in Garda Town. It's been running since long before I can remember. I love that market. My dad loved it too.

"You're going to take Alex with you," Nonna adds, chopping a large bunch of basil. "She needs to get out, see something. And eat something. She's too thin, like a little twig. I can see all her bones." She tuts in concern. Being too thin is a major concern for nonnas.

"Okay." I hesitate, wondering what Alex will think of the market and Garda Town. She seems unimpressed by just about everything so far with the exception of Nicolo. I feel a little reluctant to go back for the first time to the market with her. I have so many memories there.

"I sent her upstairs to get ready," Nonna says. "It will be good for you to spend time together."

"I don't think Alex really wants to spend time with me," I tell Nonna honestly. I don't add that I pretty much feel the same way, but Nonna is no fool. She knows what I'm not saying. She pauses and fixes me with a stern look. "That sad, lonely child is your sister," she states firmly. "And you don't even know each other. Everyone with eyes can see that both of you are lost. Why don't you try to find each other?"

I bite my lip. "I don't think Alex and I have much in common," I say finally. "I don't think she even likes me."

Nonna shoots me a withering look. "What does that matter? You're blood. That ties you together whether you like it or not. You should try harder with your sister." She goes back to chopping vigorously.

I heave a sigh. I know she's probably right, but if I'm honest, I'm tired of trying. Alex has never warmed to me, even when I was living with them finishing high school. She was a clingy baby and toddler who was suspicious of strangers, and I seemed to always be in the stranger category, even though I lived in that house for two years. I got the sense that she saw me as an interloper, and frankly I felt the same about her. She was a painful, constant reminder that somehow

I was not enough for my mother, that Lisa had left me behind. She had not wanted me in her new life. It still stings, all these years later.

I hear a sound behind me and turn to see Alex standing in the doorway leading to the hallway. Did she hear us talking about her?

I glance at her face; her expression is guarded and a touch defiant. So basically exactly like it always is. I have no idea if she heard us or not.

"Ready to go?" I ask lightly.

She nods, gripping the black backpack she carries everywhere with her. She's changed from her sleep outfit of sweatpants and a hoodie and is now wearing a plaid miniskirt and a black mesh top and her chunky black Doc Marten combat boots. She's lined her huge gray eyes with thick black liner, and they stand out from her pale face, luminous and so serious. She looks so young—wary, stubborn, and a little vulnerable. I blink, struck by how alone she seems.

It dawns on me once more, looking at her, that I'm in charge of her welfare. When I agreed to accompany her for the summer, I saw the assignment as a ticket to get me to Italy. I honestly didn't think much about how it would go once we got here, how we would navigate an entire summer together. But it's becoming clear to me that I'm going to have to embrace her presence in my life, make more of an effort. She's my responsibility. I want her to be happy here, or at least content. Otherwise this is going to be a long, tough two months.

"Are you excited for your first Italian market?" I ask, adopting a cheerful tone.

Alex shrugs indifferently. "I guess."

Nonna waves her knife at us. "Lorenzo will drive you. Alessandra, I need you to choose something sweet for tomorrow's breakfast and also some fruit. Juliana, I want you to get whatever you need to make our merenda for today, a little snack you will like. Whatever you want to make, but something you loved as a child, something you remember eating from your summers here with us. And while you are there, please enjoy a little something for lunch. We will have a big dinner later tonight." She pulls some euros out of the pocket of her polyester skirt and counts off twenty. I try to protest, but she waves away my concern.

"You are my family and my guests," she says. "Let me feed you. I am old now, and I have few joys in life. Don't rob me of this one."

Resigned, I take the money, determining to pay her back later from the plump stipend Lisa and Ted are forking over to me. I'm guessing twenty euros might be better used for something else around here rather than feeding us lunch and buying snacks. The more I poke around, the more I see how shabby things are getting. Everywhere I look are signs of decay, age, and wear. The sheets I slept in last night were threadbare and mended several times with Nonna's neat, even stitches. And I noticed this morning that some of the tiles in the bathroom are cracked along the base of the wall. The water pressure isn't great either, and the water comes out of the tap a bit rusty colored. The farm seems tired and a little sad. It concerns me.

Alex and I pile into the Fiat Panda, Lorenzo at the wheel, and head toward Garda Town along the winding road that hugs the curves of the lake. The drive is beautiful with the lake on one side and the mountains sloping up on the other. Villas, olive groves, and picturesque vistas dot the landscape everywhere you look. The sun pours down like liquid gold over everything, making a drowsy, dreamy panorama.

Lorenzo drops us off in Garda with a promise to return in an hour. I glance around. Everything is exactly as I remember it.

"Come on. Let's look around." I gesture for Alex to follow. The market is comprised of a few dozen stalls lining the street for a handful of blocks around the harbor, their white awnings fluttering in the warm breeze. I look around, drinking it all in. I've missed this market. Dad used to bring me here every week in the summer to try various local delicacies. He loved a good market. He would purchase bottles of limoncello at a stall here to take back as gifts for friends in the US. The limoncello was delicious, made with lemons grown on the shores of Lake Garda. I love limoncello. Nicolo and I used to sneak shots from the bottle on Nonna's seldom-used liquor shelf, We'd replace what we'd consumed with vodka, diluting the strong lemon flavor little by little until it tasted more like lemonade mixed with rubbing alcohol. I pull my mind firmly from Nicolo and concentrate on the task at hand. I have one hour to introduce Alex to an authentic Italian market, complete our shopping, and find a little lunch. There is no time to waste.

Chapter 17

"Whoa," Alex says, surveying the market stalls with surprise. "I thought we were going to, like, a Whole Foods or something."

"Really?" I almost roll my eyes, then catch myself. How would she know? She's never been to Italy. Ted and Lisa tend toward St. Barts and Aspen for vacations. I glance sideways at her. She is wearing her usual bored expression, but underneath I can see a flicker of curiosity and also uncertainty.

"This is a local outdoor market where people from the area bring all sorts of things to sell," I explain. "It's all grown or made around here. Let's go this way." I gesture for her to follow me. "There used to be a stall that sold the best homemade biscotti. Let's see if it's still here." We weave our way along the cobblestone street, passing stalls brimming with rainbows of fresh blooms in metal buckets, a man selling carpets, several clothing stands, and a vendor selling Lake Garda–grown fruit. We pause there.

"I thought you said this was all local," Alex says, eyeing a pile of perfect lemons, each one carefully swaddled in white paper. There are kiwis too, and oranges and limes.

"Lake Garda has a very unique, mild climate," I explain. "It's the most northern area in the world where citrus fruits can grow, particularly lemons like those." I point to the lemons. "It's the same for the olive groves at the farm."

"What are those?" Alex points to a fruit that looks like a huge, rough lemon with a thick knobby rind. Each fruit is about three times the size of a normal lemon. There are only two sitting on the shelf and the price is shockingly high. "They look like giant mutant lemons."

"They're citron, the ancient relative to every other kind of citrus fruit we have. They've been grown here for generations but they're really rare and expensive." I lean closer to inspect the citron but don't touch it. Touching the fruit is frowned upon until you've paid for it. "My dad told me that citrus fruit was first introduced to this region by St. Francis of Assisi. His friars grew the first lemons in a monastery on the western shore of the lake," I tell her, remembering the history lesson. Dad loved history and loved to teach it to his students and his girls.

"Weird. I've never seen anything like these," Alex admits. She pulls out her phone and snaps a few photos of the citrons. "I've never been anywhere where they actually grow citrus fruit before."

"Really? I figured Lisa and Ted must have taken you everywhere with them." I survey the selection of fruit. "Didn't they go to the British Virgin Islands last year?"

Alex hesitates. "Yeah, and Bermuda the year before that, and Switzerland at Christmas for skiing, and the Bahamas the winter before that . . . but they never take me with them. I always stay home with the nanny, although now they think I'm old enough to stay home alone," Alex says with a shrug. She focuses her phone camera on a large citron carefully nestled in white tissue paper and takes a close-up.

I stare at her in shock. "You're kidding. You don't go on any of those trips with them?"

She examines the photo on her phone screen and takes another shot from a different angle. "No, I stay in the city if they're gone during school, and I'm at camp all summer. I went to Niagara Falls once on a field trip, so I guess technically I've been to Canada, but that's about it." She frowns. There's something a little forlorn in her expression.

I feel an unexpected stab of pity for her. I always imagined she was the child who got everything, but it looks like maybe I was wrong. At least I had Dad and Aurora. We were a tight-knit threesome. There wasn't much money, but I always knew I was loved, that they had my back. I wonder if Alex can say the same. I suspect that her life has been lonelier than I thought.

We buy some candied citron peel and two expensive lemons and continue on our way. I narrate as we go along, and as we wander through the market, my enthusiasm grows. I want her to see and experience everything here, just like my dad helped me to do as a child. I want her to taste and touch and smell the Italy I remember from my youth. I want her to fall in love with this wonderful place. And to my surprise, she goes along with it. She's still a teenager, rolling her eyes and acting unimpressed. But she tries persicata, a local treat made of ripe peaches boiled with sugar (her verdict: pretty good) and candied citron peel, which she rates as just okay. She documents everything on her cell phone as we stroll.

Unexpectedly, I realize how good it feels to be back here again. Everywhere I look there are reminders of my dad, and though it's bittersweet, I find that somehow it's easier to be here with Alex, showing her everything with fresh eyes. My stomach gurgles as we pass a bakery stall, its table piled high with crusty loaves of artisanal bread, rounds of focaccia, brioche, and the almond crumb cake famous in the nearby Lombardy region. When I catch Alex looking longingly over her shoulder, we make a U-turn and go back.

I purchase some focaccia for our lunch, and Alex chooses two varieties of biscotti for breakfast tomorrow. I translate the options for her so she knows the choices. She repeats the biscotti flavors quietly to herself after I've said them, haltingly stumbling over the pronunciation of the Italian words. I order from the vendor in Italian, enjoying the feel of the words rolling off my tongue. I'm out of practice, but I'm loving speaking the language again. I was never completely fluent, although when I was younger I came close. Now the Italian words are coming back to me, and the sensation of them bubbling up in my throat brings an unexpected burst of joy and relief.

"Grazie mille." After I've paid and thanked the baker, I turn to find Alex watching me thoughtfully.

"What's it like to speak a different language?" she asks as we walk away.

The personal question and her nonhostile tone take me by surprise. I have to think for a minute. I've never really considered the mechanics of speaking Italian. It's always just been a part of my life.

"Italian is a beautiful language," I tell her. "My dad always said Italian is a language with a soul. And when I speak it, I feel different . . . more relaxed maybe? If that makes sense? It makes me feel like I belong here, like I'm a part of this place, like the rocks and olive trees."

A fleeting smile brushes Alex's lips. "Must be nice to feel that way," she says. There's something plaintive in her tone.

"You could learn Italian if you wanted to," I tell her, handing her a square of focaccia and taking a big bite of my own. "It's a pretty easy language for an English speaker to learn. There are a lot of free programs online now."

"I'm learning German in school but I don't like it much." She shrugs and says nothing more.

Munching our focaccia, we wander through the rest of the stalls, sampling the region's prized olives preserved in brine, and even tasting a tiny shaving of truffle that makes Alex gag a little. I enjoy a drizzle of acacia honey on a paper-thin slice of local cheese while Alex gulps some mineral water from a glass bottle and tries to get the taste of the truffle out of her mouth.

The sun is warm, the water of the lake a glittering cobalt at the end of the street. The scents of salted meat, ripe fruits, pungent cheeses, and briny olives mingle into a delicious mélange. To my surprise, I realize I'm enjoying myself and I think Alex is too. If Nonna sent us here for some sisterly bonding, it's going unexpectedly well. I don't mind Alex's company when she's like this. Sure, she's prickly and critical, with a dry, ironic sense of humor, but she's smart and I can tell that she's interested in everything we're seeing, even if she's trying to play it cool. It's actually sort of fun to show her new things. I like seeing her eyes light up with interest, her curiosity come peeking out from beneath that jaded shell she usually hides behind.

The market isn't crowded, just a few nonnas perusing the stalls with baskets on their arms, some moms with young kids in tow, and a handful of tourists. There's a dreamy sense of contentment over the afternoon. Everything just moves slower in Italy. I forgot this unhurried pace, the warmth of the sun on my skin, the sense of peace that comes with a lack of push.

On impulse, I buy a bottle of the locally crafted limoncello liqueur my dad always favored. It's expensive, but I have such fond memories of it, I can't resist. As I tuck the bottle into my bag, I suddenly remember what I'm supposed to be doing at the market, making a favorite merenda from childhood. I wander the stalls with

Alex, trying to keep up friendly chatter while my mind races frantically. I'm quietly panicking a little. What were my favorite snacks? What did I make with Nonna when I was younger? I cannot remember. I'm drawing a blank and running out of time. When I try to recall something, it's like running into a wall in my mind, a blockage that keeps me from accessing those memories. Just like all the other times I've tried to remember. It's so frustrating and thwarting. I don't know how to fix it.

I check my phone. It's almost time to return to Lorenzo and the car and I still haven't managed to come up with anything.

We pause at a large stand selling cured sliced meats and sausages. Alex seems intrigued by how many varieties there are. She pulls out her phone to take some photos, and I step away for a moment. I'm starting to sweat in the warmth of the sun. I slip under the shade of a tree and gaze out at the lake. I have so many memories here. Surely, something will spark a recollection of a snack I enjoyed.

I close my eyes, breathing slowly, thinking of my dad—all the times he took me here, the joy of discovery as we tried everything—the crunch of local walnuts, licking the viscous stickiness of orange blossom honey from my fingers, the cold silky sweetness of a scoop of pistachio gelato. As I let myself sink into the memories, I relax into the moment. I'm not trying to wrestle information from my brain; I'm just remembering the joy of being here with him. And just like that a memory rises. I can picture it clearly. My dad and I sitting just a few yards away on the lakefront, sharing a snack of ripe figs stuffed with goat cheese and wrapped in a local salted, cured meat, a sort of prosciutto. I was probably twelve or thirteen. Dad was using his pocket knife to slit the figs and stuff them with gobs of the creamy goat cheese, his big fingers surprisingly dexterous. I open my eyes and glance to the right, seeing us sitting there side by side, dangling our legs in the cool water. I can almost taste again the gritty sweetness of the figs, the rich creamy funk of the goat cheese, the salty umami of the dried meat. It was a simple, perfect snack on a simple, perfect day.

"There it is," I murmur. I'm so relieved I could cry. It's not much, not even really cooking, but it's a snack with a fond memory attached. It's mine and it counts.

"Alex, we've got to go." I say, pausing to purchase a dozen slices of a local salted, cured meat. We have only a few minutes until we need to meet Lorenzo.

At a fruit stand I stop and buy ripe figs. The owner is there, a broad-hipped woman with wavy, dark hair. A young man in his mid-teens who has the same wavy hair takes our order. He chooses the figs carefully, darting quick, appreciative glances in Alex's direction. He's very tall, gangly, and cute, and Alex seems to notice him too. She's concentrating hard on the display of fruit, but I can see her watching him out of the corner of her eye. I hand her the euros and ask her to pay. Surprised, she does. The boy blushes a dusky red when he takes the money and hands her the punnet of figs, their fingers brushing. He murmurs his thanks in Italian and she looks down at her boots. It's sort of endearing, how flustered she is. For a moment, I recall the almost painful euphoria of adolescent crushes and first love, the heightened awareness of the other person, the self-consciousness mixed with anticipation. I haven't felt that way in years. Sometimes being an adult is boring. It's fun to see a little romance unfolding before my eyes.

We stop at a cheese stall to purchase a soft goat cheese with a rind of ash. I also pick up a small jar of orange blossom honey. I check my phone. It's time to meet Lorenzo. As we head up the street, I glance back at the lake. I see us sitting shoulder to shoulder, my father's broad form bent toward me, listening to my words. He always listened gravely, intently, as though what you said was the most important thing in the world. In my mind he hands me a fig bursting with goat cheese.

"Here you go, my little farfallina."

I was his little butterfly. Aurora was his coccinella, his ladybug. I see us there, savoring that sweet, unhurried moment in the sun, blissfully unaware that a few short years later our time together would be cut brutally short.

"Un bel pomeriggio," I murmur, pausing for a moment, feeling wistful and a little sad. I wish I had held tighter to those fleeting moments. I wish I had known.

"What does that mean?" Alex asks, coming to a stop next to me.

"It means 'a good afternoon,'" I tell her, turning away from the water. "It's something my dad would say every day we were here in Italy. He'd watch the sun set over the lake every evening and say it before the night fell. He loved it here."

"Oh." She pauses, sounding a little hesitant. "That's really nice."

It's so rare I talk about my dad. It feels good to speak of him to someone else.

"We should get going," I tell Alex, and we head back the way we came. Lorenzo will be waiting with the car. I glance back once more over my shoulder at the lake. That afternoon with my dad was a good one, a happy memory clouded by what came too soon after. But here I am again, so many years later, making a new good memory. It's unexpected, but I find it is not unwelcome.

"Un bel pomeriggio," I whisper again. And this time I am not thinking of the past but of today.

Chapter 18

"*Va bene,*" **Nonna** says approvingly, standing at the kitchen prep table and surveying the snack I've made. "You remembered something special then?"

"I did." After getting home from the market, I set to work on the merenda while Alex disappeared upstairs and Nonna went outside to putter in her herb garden. Now it's time for us to try what I made.

Nonna scrutinizes the plate. "That looks good," she says approvingly.

"I hope so." I feel inordinately proud; such a small accomplishment, but it means something big to me. One down, forty-nine to go. At this rate I'm going to reach fifty recipes far too late, but one is better than none, I remind myself. One is a good start. I think wistfully of Nonna's book of recipes. I still can't quite believe they're simply all gone. It makes me a little sick to think of it, to think of what that means for me now. How easy this process would be if I had them. No reason to walk back down memory lane in search of recipes. They would just be at my fingertips. I sigh with regret. I guess

I'm going to have to do this the hard way. One recipe at a time, trying to dredge them from my memory.

I'm almost tempted to go look at the book again, just to be sure the recipes have truly vanished. I know what I saw—the pages all blank—but I still can't quite believe it. And what about that strange moment when Nonna grabbed the book from my hand? The page wasn't blank then. I picture the torn recipe for Orange Blossom Cake, and recall what Nonna shared about this kitchen, the magic that she insists is here. I wonder if everything is connected. I wonder if I'm missing something important.

"Let's eat." Nonna interrupts my train of thought. I shake off my thoughts and carry the plate to the table. I need to concentrate on the one recipe I do have and not spend time pining for the ones I don't.

It is a simple dish, just figs stuffed with goat cheese, wrapped in the salted meat, and drizzled with a little honey. Simple but delicious, and most importantly, meaningful. I already know how I'll introduce this recipe for the book, talking about that day at the market with my dad. As soon as we're done, I plan to pop upstairs and write out the recipe and the accompanying story. It feels good to have made at least some progress.

"Alessandra!" Nonna calls up to the ceiling. She grabs a broom from the corner and bangs the top of the handle against the ceiling a few times. There is a distant, irritable "Okay, okay," and a few minutes later Alex clatters down the stairs and into the kitchen, looking sleepy and a little out of sorts.

"I guess I fell asleep." She yawns. "What time is it?"

"It's the jet lag," I tell her. "It gets you." I should feel just as tired, but weirdly, I feel energized by my little victory.

"Just past three in the afternoon," Nonna tells her, replacing the broom in the corner. "Time for the delicious snack your sister prepared."

I don't correct her about the sister / half sister distinction. I just let it go. Alex slides into a chair and pulls out her phone, immediately scrolling and tapping away. She's always on that thing. I wonder what she's doing. Nonna makes lemonade and sets a glass in front of each of us. "Now we try your creation," she says, sitting and reaching for a fig.

"Wait!" I put out a hand. "I just remembered, I have to take a photo of each completed dish for the cookbook." I scowl at the plate of food. This is going to be a problem. I'm not good at staging or taking photographs. Michelle specified that I have to submit photographs with the recipes. High-quality photographs. Originally, I planned to use photos Drew took of dishes I made for the show. He always took a few good still shots of any recipes I made when we were filming the segments, and I was going to include them with the vintage recipes. But now all those recipes and accompanying photos are useless. What do I do?

I try to arrange a few things on the table to make it look like a still life—a few whole figs and a drizzle of honey on the plate, the goat cheese with a knife slicing through the rind behind it. It feels corny and staged. I snap a few photos and they look . . . okay. Not great.

"This isn't working," I admit finally. I step back and survey my handiwork in exasperation, biting my lip, trying to think. Now what?

"Maybe if you turned the plate like this?" Nonna suggests. It doesn't help.

"It's the light. Your lighting's wrong."

Nonna and I both look up in surprise. Alex is still looking at her phone as though she hadn't spoken.

"What?" I ask.

Alex glances up and frowns critically at the still life I'm trying to create on the table.

"You can't have the light coming down from above like that. It makes shadows."

"Oh." I step back and survey the scene. "Um, okay. How do I fix it then?"

She makes a *tsk*ing sound and stands up. "Okay, fine. I'll show you."

She goes and grabs the lamp from the sideboard in the hall, plugging it in near the table and angling the light so it illuminates the dish. Instantly, the snack looks a hundred times better. The figs look plump and luminous, bursting with the creamy goat cheese. Cocking her head, Alex studies the dish from different angles, circling the table. Then with quick, hesitant movements, she adjusts a few things, changes the angle of the plate, moves the cheese, and removes the knife. Satisfied, she raises her phone and starts snapping. A few seconds later she shows me what she's got.

"Wow, those look great. Like professional level." I'm impressed. "How did you know to do that?"

"I took a couple of photography electives." Alex shrugs, deft fingers adjusting the plate minutely, nudging the figs slightly into a different arrangement. "And I spent all winter break at a photography camp in upstate New York last year while Mom and Dad were skiing in Tahoe."

She lifts the phone again, moving slightly, squinting, assessing. She's got the newest, fanciest iPhone, the one with a camera that can practically take a photo of the surface of Mars. Of course it's the newest one. Money can't buy your parents' love, but it can buy really expensive electronics. She shows me the photos.

"Those are amazing," I tell her honestly. "You're really good."

She ignores the compliment, but I think she's secretly pleased. She glances down. "It's no big deal."

"Are you done yet?" Nonna asks. "I'm hungry." She scoops up a fig and pops it into her mouth without waiting for a reply. "Buonissimi!" She beams at me. "Delicious." She eats another one.

I try a fig too. Yep, delicious.

Alex is looking longingly at the snack, which is not vegetarian-friendly since it's wrapped in salted meat. I set out a small plate I made just for her, all the yummy things sans the meat.

"Oh," she says in a small, surprised voice. "Thanks."

"Thanks for helping with the photos," I tell her, taking a chair across the table.

She nibbles one of the figs, brow furrowed into an assessing scowl. A moment later she takes a bigger bite. "Pretty good," she admits. Her faint praise makes me feel a little gleeful. Even Alex likes it.

"One down, forty-nine to go," I announce to no one in particular.

Alex pauses. "Forty-nine what?"

I explain about the cookbook and needing fifty good, personal recipes. I don't tell her everything. I don't mention Drew or Keith or my plan to save the show. I just explain about my contract and deadline. When I'm done, she's quiet for a moment, then offers, "I can take photos of each of the recipes you make, if you want me to." She says it in an offhanded way, like she couldn't care less either way.

"Really?" I hear the eagerness in my own voice. "Are you sure?" I try not to appear desperate, but I am. For the first time since finding that the recipe book is completely blank, I feel a small spark of hope. Maybe all is not lost. With Nonna and Alex's help, I might have a chance, even without the recipe book. Could we really meet the deadline if we work together?

"I mean, it's not like I've got anything else to do this summer," Alex says dryly.

"That would be amazing." I sit back in relief. Her photos are really good. "How about I pay you in vegetarian-friendly snacks?"

She gazes at me for a moment with those cool gray eyes, then pops a whole fig in her mouth. "Deal," she says, cheeks bulging. We shake on it.

Chapter 19

"**Lorenzo and Nicolo** are working hard all day pruning the olive trees," Nonna says the next morning after breakfast as she and I clear the dishes. Alex cleared her own plate and headed outside with her phone as soon as we were done eating. "We should take them a little something sweet." She wraps up a few of the biscotti we picked up at the market yesterday in squares of brown paper.

"Oh, sure." I'm busy washing the dishes and don't register the calculated expression on her face until it's too late. She makes two caffellattes and pours them into two glass bottles, then hands the packet to me along with the bottles.

"They're working in the upper groves," she announces.

Apparently, I am supposed to deliver the snack. I hesitate for a moment. The thought of seeing Nicolo again makes me feel flushed and bothered . . . and a little eager.

Stop it! Eyes on the prize. You don't have time to go mooning after old flames. I try to scold myself into compliance. It doesn't entirely work. At least I'm wearing mascara this morning and my hair is cute, wavy in the heat and pulled back in a cherry-red headband.

"Go before the caffellattes grow cold." Nonna shoos me out the door. I narrow my eyes at her, trying to figure out if she's got some ulterior motive, but she doesn't meet my gaze. She looks away, her face the picture of innocence, and busies herself wiping down the table with a cloth. She's humming to herself. I take the bottles and the packet with a sigh. I'll deliver the snack, chat for a minute, and get back here to the kitchen. I need to get cracking on more recipes if I have a prayer of being ready by September. I slick on some lip balm, smooth my hair, and go in search of the men.

Outside, the morning sun is growing warmer. Up a short flight of stone steps, I skirt the flagstone patio tucked to the right of the house with its ancient olive tree spreading gnarled branches over a long table and eight chairs. A low stone wall separates it from the olive grove below, and the patio has a commanding view of the lake far down the hill. There is a dark-clad figure sitting in one of the chairs. Alex. She has her headphones on and glances up, acknowledging me with a brief lift of her chin before she turns back to her phone. It looks like she's talking to someone. She's staring intently at the screen and her lips are moving. I pass by and head up the hill.

The sun filters through the silvery leaves of the olive trees as I make my way to the upper field, following the grassy track big enough for Lorenzo's little farm work truck to get through. Along either side of the track are olive trees, spreading their branches out over the hills. Our olive grove is old, and the trees are spaced widely but not uniformly apart. The newest groves in many olive farms have trees planted much closer together and spaced exactly right for mechanical harvesting. Our olives are still harvested by hand. Everything in this grove is done by hand. It's time-consuming, but there's something so satisfying about working with your hands here. I remember summers helping Lorenzo in the grove, caring for the trees, looking out for diseased limbs, tramping behind him inspecting and tending and fussing over each one. Lorenzo treats them as tenderly as babies.

Once, the year Lisa left us, Dad flew Aurora and me back here in late October to take part in the olive harvest. We relished the week off of school and the chance to be part of the family harvest time. It was hard work, but fascinating to learn how to handpick the olives, using a little plastic olive rake to gently pull the olives from the lowest branches. Dad and Lorenzo operated the electric olive-harvesting rakes, setting up wooden ladders against the trees and spreading big tarps beneath each tree to catch the falling fruits. Nonna harvested by hand with us, showing us girls how to do it without breaking the branches. I smile at the memory.

Our trees are the Casaliva olive variety, a special type of olive unique to our northern region. The Casaliva olives produce a beautifully clear, pale green olive oil with the aroma of almonds and a light, fruity taste with hints of herbs and grass. The oil is rare and highly prized for its delicate flavor and gorgeous hue. In Italy, olive oil is used for everything—cooking, illnesses, beauty treatments. Most nonnas, Nonna Bruna included, firmly believe that there is almost nothing that cannot be solved or at least improved with the application of a little good-quality olive oil. We all grow up with this philosophy. Our veins all run with the precious, pale gold.

I'm sweating a little by the time I get to the end of the track, from the heat and the uphill climb. When I reach the upper field, Lorenzo is nowhere to be found, but I spy a stack of tools underneath an olive tree by the edge of the track, and I can hear a rustling noise coming from somewhere farther into the grove. Wandering between the olive trees, I try to locate the source of the sound.

"Hello?" There is no answer.

Suddenly, right in front of me a figure drops from one of the trees, landing on his feet like a cat. Dark curly hair, laughing eyes. Startled, I jump back with a muffled shriek.

"Juliana." Nicolo looks surprised by my appearance. His face breaks into a wide smile. Those dimples! Gaah! It's not fair.

"Oh gosh, you startled me." I put a hand to my chest, trying to regain my composure, laughing nervously. "I'm looking for Zio Lorenzo. Nonna sent a snack." I hold out the bundle as proof.

"Ah yes, I see. Thank you. Lorenzo has gone into Bardolino to get a tool repaired," Nicolo explains easily. He's holding a pair of pruning clippers. "He'll be back soon. We're pruning diseased limbs today." He brushes bits of bark and olive leaves off his pants and closes the pruning clippers. His English is excellent, I notice. Yesterday I was too flustered to realize how flawless it is. When we were young he didn't speak any English at all. We muddled through with my almost-fluent-enough Italian. But now he speaks fluidly, no hesitations. His accent is still there though, as rich and delicious as espresso.

"Here." I thrust the package into his hands, feeling self-conscious. My heart is beating a little faster than normal. *Come on, Juliana, get a grip on yourself*, I scold. *You are just running an errand for Nonna. Get it over with and get back to work.* I don't move an inch.

Nicolo takes the package, grinning. "I think it's Bruna's secret goal in life to fatten me up. She thinks my grandmother doesn't feed me. Want to join me?" He settles down at the base of one of the olive trees, sets the pruning clippers beside him, and leans back against the trunk. He makes a gesture of invitation for me to sit. I hesitate, but curiosity wins out over my duties in the kitchen, so I gingerly lower myself down next to him, and sit cross-legged on the grass beneath the tree, hoping I don't get grass stains on my cute flower-patterned romper.

Chapter 20

The day is warm and sunny, filled with the scent of living things, of the lake and the lush green grass and gnarled olive trees. Everything is still and yet so alive. Side by side, Nicolo and I gaze down the hillside through the olive groves to the lake winking blue below. It's peaceful up here under the sun-dappled olive branches, beneath the gnarled trunks with just the dry whisper of the breeze through the leaves. I'd forgotten how quiet it is.

"Isn't it late to be pruning?" I ask. If I remember right, the trees are usually pruned in the spring.

Nicolo shrugs. "A little late this year, but I was not free to help Lorenzo until now. So he waited."

"Do you help out around here a lot?" It's something I've been wondering about.

Nicolo unscrews the cap on the bottle of caffellatte. "Lorenzo is getting older. He can use an extra pair of hands to help him, not that he'll admit it." He chuckles and takes a drink of his caffellatte, then offers the bottle to me. I hesitate, but it's hot and I'm thirsty. I accept the bottle and take a sip, aware that his lips have just been where mine now are. The intimacy of it gives me a little thrill.

"Thanks." I hand the bottle back. "That's really nice of you to help him," I say, wondering why Nicolo is spending time aiding a rival olive farm and not on his own farm. Doesn't he have enough to do on his own family's property? It's so much bigger than ours. They grow a few different types of olives over there. No Casalivas, but a few other varieties, like Leccino and Pendolino.

"I don't mind," Nicolo says, taking another drink and wiping his mouth with the back of his hand. "Bruna and Lorenzo have been good to me. Now it's my turn to help them. Besides, we have workers, hired hands, to help at the villa. I oversee things there, but much of the work is done by others. Here it's just Lorenzo trying to manage this whole farm. It's too much for one man, even a much younger man."

I frown at his words. Is this why everything is looking a little rundown and shabby? Is it just too much for Zio Lorenzo and Nonna to handle now? That makes sense. Running this place must take a lot of work.

Nicolo interrupts my thoughts. "When Bruna told me you were coming back, I didn't quite believe it." He looks at me with open curiosity. "So tell me, Juliana Costa, famous Internet cook, what brings you back to Italy?" His tone is light, almost playful, but I catch the fact that he knows about my show. Has he been keeping tabs on me? More likely Nonna has been filling him in. She loves to brag about her granddaughters.

"I'm here babysitting my teenage half sister and trying to save my cooking show," I tell him baldly. I surprise myself with how readily I volunteer that information. There's a familiarity I feel with Nicolo that is disarming. We have such a shared history it doesn't feel right to try to put on a pretense. I feel I can be honest with him, that

I *should* be honest with him. After all, no other boy has ever shared a first kiss with me. A first everything.

"How is your visit going so far?" he asks, unwrapping the package and selecting two biscotti. His eyes are steady as he watches me and crunches a cookie. His mouth is turned up in a warm half smile, but those lively dark eyes are sharp, missing nothing. I feel strangely comfortable with him and at the same time a little unnerved. I feel like he sees me, really sees me, maybe more than I even want him to. I want him to see me as all grown-up, successful and poised and in control, but I think he might be able to see beneath that façade to the real me, the messy, scared parts. The girl who has no idea what she's doing.

"It's good to be back," I say honestly. "But things in my life are a little complicated. What about you? What are you doing back here? I lost track of you after . . . after you got sent to Genoa."

"Ah, Genoa," he murmurs. His tone is gently ironic. He offers me the package and I choose two biscotti. They're small and Nonna packed lots.

"So what happened when you were sent away?" I ask, biting off the end of a crunchy cookie and trying to put out of my mind the memory of what we'd been doing together that got him sent to Genoa in the first place. *Focus, Jules, focus*, I scold silently, willing myself not to glance at his mouth. Too late. Now I'm totally ogling him. It's that full lower lip. I've always been a sucker for it. It would look pouty on anyone else, but instead it gives him a hint of vulnerability beneath the self-controlled exterior. He carries himself now as an adult with a mixture of duty and determination, as though he balances weighty responsibility easily on those broad shoulders. I feel a little twinge of nostalgia looking at the full, firm mouth of this gorgeous man. Where has that sad, sweet boy gone? What have the years held for him?

He rests his forearms on his knees, the half-full bottle of caffellatte clasped between his fingers. "I finished high school in Genoa, and hated every minute of it," he says frankly. "I resented that we hadn't even gotten to say goodbye, that Bruna and Nonna V. had managed to keep us apart like that. And it haunted me when I heard about your dad's passing. For years I've wanted to say I'm sorry. Tony was a good man." He lifts his bottle in acknowledgment.

I drop my eyes and murmur my thanks. Grief spikes through my heart unexpectedly. Nicolo knew my father well, and in the aftermath of his death, it was doubly hard not to have his comfort as I struggled through the loss. "It was . . . a horrible time," I admit, meeting his gaze.

He looks at me, dark eyes unexpectedly tender. "I wanted to find you, Jules," he tells me. "For two years I planned to come after you when I was done with school. I was even saving money for a plane ticket, but then Bruna told me you had moved back to Seattle, that you were starting university and had a boyfriend. She told me you were happy, so I figured you had forgotten me. And I decided to try to forget you too." He gives a little shrug of one shoulder.

"I didn't forget you . . ." I tell him hastily. "I wanted to find you too. But no one would tell me where you were. I had no way to contact you. I tried a couple of times in the years after Dad died, but you weren't on social media. I had no idea how to get in touch."

Plus, if I am being honest, I was reluctant to come back to Italy. My grief and sense of guilt outweighed even my tender feelings for Nicolo. I feel ashamed to admit it, but it's true.

"And now here we both are," Nicolo says with a wry smile. "What a twist of fate." He shakes his head in disbelief.

"What happened after Genoa?" I ask, curious about those years in between then and now.

"I went to university and law school in Rome, at Sapienza University."

Sapienza University is an excellent school, sort of the Italian version of an Ivy League college. That's impressive. "You're an attorney?" I ask, surprised, trying to reconcile my vision of the young boy I knew with this self-assured, grown man sitting next to me.

"Is that so hard to believe?" He grins. "I spent seven years practicing law for international clients and living all over—Singapore, Switzerland, Australia."

"Really?" So this tanned, work clothes–clad olive farmer next to me is actually an international lawyer? Curiouser and curiouser. What is a hotshot international attorney doing clambering around in our olive trees?

"What brought you back here?"

"What calls any Italian back home?" He spread his hands wide. "Family. The land. We come back because we are needed."

"Did Violetta ask you to come home?" I'm surprised. Italians are family oriented, but still, leaving a successful career to farm olives is a huge sacrifice.

He chuckles dryly. "I doubt my grandmother would ask for help even if she had fallen down a well and it was her dying breath," he admits ruefully. "It was more what she didn't say. My grandfather died about five years ago, and she's been struggling ever since. Running the farm is a big operation, and things had been let go for many years, even before his death. I'm trying to get the farm back into shape, and then we will decide how to proceed. I want to see if I can make it profitable enough to survive before we just give in and sell."

"Sell it? Really? Are you considering that?"

"It's the reality for many small farmers in this region right now," he explains with a grimace. "Many are finding they cannot survive, and those that can are having to modernize, sometimes against the will of the older generations. It's the nature of progress. They have to adapt to the times if they want to keep their land." He frowns. "Your farm is no different than ours in that way," he adds.

I pause. "What do you mean?"

He meets my eyes, his own serious. "You've been gone a long time, Jules. Bruna and Lorenzo are growing older. They're strong, but they're tired. I don't know how long they can keep this place going." He pauses. "I think they're in more trouble than they let on."

My heart constricts. Is this what Aurora was picking up on? "What sort of trouble?"

Nicolo's gaze is compassionate and clear. "They don't complain, but Lorenzo has told me a little. They aren't making enough money to keep the farm solvent. I think they've just barely been scraping by for a while now. I think they've been waiting, hoping they can hold out long enough."

"Long enough for what?" I ask with a twinge of apprehension.

Nicolo takes a long drink of caffellatte and looks at me frankly. "Long enough for you to come back."

Chapter 21

"*I don't understand . . .*" I stammer, gazing at Nicolo in confusion. Why are they waiting for me? What good am I to the farm? I know very little about olive farming. But before I can question him further, we're interrupted by a tinny growl heralding Lorenzo's return. He bumps up the grassy track in his baby blue Piaggio Ape. It's a ridiculous vehicle, equal parts cute and absurd, with its improbable three wheels, a tiny cab barely big enough for Lorenzo to squeeze inside, and a small bed for tools and hauling things. It looks like a cross between a Vespa and a pickup truck, almost like a toy. Lorenzo, broad shoulders and stout belly straining his work shirt, hunches over the steering wheel as he drives up to us and cuts the engine. The silence is abrupt.

I open my mouth. I have so many questions, but I glance at Lorenzo as he gets out of the cab with a grunt. This is not the time. Instead, I spring to my feet, brushing grass from my romper. "I'd better get back to the kitchen," I tell Nicolo. "It was nice to catch up with you."

He looks up at me intently, then glances at Lorenzo and nods. "It's good to see you again, Jules. I'm glad you're back."

I give a stiff little nod and turn to leave. On my way past, I hand Lorenzo his packet of biscotti and the second bottle of now-tepid caffellatte, then head back down to the farmhouse.

As I walk down the lane between the olive trees, I mull over my conversation with Nicolo. It has unsettled me. Is what he said about the farm, about Nonna and Lorenzo true?

As I approach the farmyard, my steps slow and I gaze around with new eyes. The old stone farmhouse is looking tired. The green paint is peeling from the shutters and doors. Across the courtyard the low-slung stone barn is sagging at one end.

I see it more clearly now. What I initially saw as charming and rustically aged, in the bright glare of the mid-morning sun and Nicolo's observations, looks more like neglect. Is Nicolo right? Is the farm in trouble?

I think of Aurora's comment before I left, her hesitation and her sense that something is amiss here. I think of the unspoken thing between Nonna and Lorenzo when I first arrived, the sense I have that there's something they're not saying. Combined with what Nicolo said, it ratchets up my concern. I need to find out what is really going on. What secrets is this place hiding?

As I head toward the kitchen, one thought is still niggling at me. Nicolo's words about how they've been waiting for me. Waiting for what? Are they hoping I can save them somehow? Because if so, I'm afraid I'm going to sadly disappoint them. I adore Nonna, Lorenzo, and this slice of land that is so close to my heart, but I'm not even sure I can save myself, much less an entire farm and a hefty family legacy. They need someone braver, stronger, more capable. Someone who knows how to run a farm. Someone who has their life in order. Someone who isn't going to fail them. If this place needs saving, I am not that girl.

☙

Early the next morning, a metallic crash wakes me from a light sleep. It sounds like it came from downstairs. I check my phone. It's just past six thirty in the morning, but already my bedroom is filled with the mouthwatering aroma of simmering meat sauce and pasta. That's weird. Why is Nonna cooking hearty dinner foods at the crack of dawn? I pause, listening. Several unfamiliar voices drift up from the kitchen along with Nonna's voice. She's telling someone to stir, stir with gusto. What in the world is going on down there?

Curious, I slip out of bed and tiptoe to the window, cracking open a wooden shutter and peeking out. There are several cars in the driveway—a shiny Audi and two less flashy hatchbacks. Who is here at this early hour? I yawn and stifle a groan.

Softly, I creep downstairs, intending to just take a peek. I can hear women talking animatedly in Italian. Wary of repeating the Nicolo disaster, I am cautious not to be seen. I'm wearing my cute pajamas, but still prefer not to meet strangers at this hour and in my sleepwear. I peep around the corner into the kitchen. Three young Italian women are clustered around Nonna, wearing aprons over what looks like smart office attire. They are all gathered around the heavy table in the center of the room, dishing up pasta. Their hands and aprons are dusted with flour, and the room is a mess. They've clearly been cooking for a while. I sniff. The enticing scent of fresh pasta and savory sauce hits my nose. One of the young women, a slim girl with her long brown hair in a chignon, ladles what looks like gnocchi into a takeaway container. "I hope this works," the girl declares in Italian, giving a nervous laugh. "I like him so much, but I think he sees me only as a friend, just the girl in the next office."

"After today, that may change," Nonna says with a small, mysterious smile. "Feed him the pasta and see what happens. This recipe is powerful for love."

"Two years we've been dating and no engagement yet," another girl with a jet-black bob says to Nonna. She's spooning a different pasta and sauce, maybe rigatoni, into a plastic carton. "My cousin told me about you. She had a very nasty boss at work, and you made fish soup with her and the next week he had taken a job in Shanghai. If anyone can make that boy set a date for the wedding, it is Bruna, she told me, so I came to see you."

"My mother is despairing of me ever finding a boyfriend, so she sent me here. Bruna will make it happen, she assured me." This from a petite, curvy girl with chunky glasses. She's carefully sliding cooked tortellini into a container. They are each boxing up a different type of pasta. What is going on? An early-morning cooking class? I'm so confused.

"No, no, I don't make it happen at all." Nonna looks satisfied. "The cookbook shows us what we need to do. All will come out as it should with each of these dishes. Mark my words. But remember, you must serve this food today, while it is still fresh. That's important if it's all going to work correctly." She grabs a spoon and carefully ladles some sauce from a pan into the curvy girl's container of tortellini. I can smell the butter and sage from here. "Offer a taste of this to anyone who catches your eye today. Whoever is destined to be your first love is going to adore this pasta," Nonna says.

My stomach rumbles, and I shrink back into the shadows of the hallway. Which cookbook is Nonna talking about? What is happening? The young women take off their aprons and grab their containers of pasta. Each kisses Nonna's cheek, pressing a wad of euros into her hand as they file out the door. A moment later I hear their cars drive away. And then I sneeze.

"Ciao?" Nonna hurries across the kitchen and comes into the hallway, tucking the euros into the pocket of her apron. I spring back, hopping back up on the bottom step so it looks like I'm just coming down the stairs. Nonna peers into the dimness at me. "Juliana?"

"I thought I heard voices," I tell her, trying to sound sleepy and nonchalant. I yawn. I'm a terrible liar. "What's happening?" I brush past her and head into the kitchen, curious.

Nonna hesitates. "Just a little cooking class I offer sometimes," she says finally, reluctantly. "A few office girls wanting to impress their men with homemade pasta."

"It smells amazing." I go over to the leftover pasta and glance into the bowl. I recognize it instantly. Tortellini nodo d'amore, love-knot tortellini, a specialty of the region, dripping with butter and sage. Another pot holds gnocchi. A third contains Rigatoni alla Bolognese.

And then I see it, the blank recipe book. Except it isn't blank. It is lying open on the table beside a bag of flour. A handwritten recipe for Tortellini nodo d'amore is clearly visible on the open page.

"Where did this recipe come from?" Puzzled, I lean forward, trying to make sense of what I'm seeing. I know this entire book was blank, but before I can read more, Nonna snaps the cookbook shut.

"I need to tidy up before Lorenzo wakes up and wants breakfast," she mutters, not meeting my eyes and making a shooing motion, urging me back upstairs. "Go back to sleep, and when you come down we can make those almond biscotti you loved as a girl. It's a good recipe for your collection."

Absently, she pats the wad of euros in her pocket and busies herself cleaning up. Clearly, I am dismissed. Reluctantly, I head back upstairs, but I don't fall asleep. My mind is racing, trying to make sense of what I just saw. I am obviously missing something and it seems to center around the cookbook. And why is Nonna being so secretive? What is she hiding and why? Wide-awake, I lie there as the sun rises, determined to do whatever I have to do to peel back the layers of secrets wrapped around the cookbook and figure out what is really going on.

Chapter 22

"*Chop, chop, Juliana.* Put your strength into it." Nonna hovers at my shoulder later that afternoon, instructing me in the fine art of making almond biscotti. This was my favorite treat when I was growing up, a few biscotti dipped in a cup of hot cocoa. I'd devour three or four in a sitting. I want to include the recipe in my cookbook, so Nonna is giving me a refresher course on how to make biscotti properly. I lean down and redouble my efforts to chop the roasted almonds to just the right coarse consistency.

"There, good. Stop now, and add your flour mixture to your bowl of eggs," Nonna instructs. I obey, adding the flour, baking powder, and sugar to the bowl containing a beaten mixture of eggs, good olive oil, vanilla, and the zest of a lemon. My mouth waters at the aroma. I glance at Alex, who is sitting at the table with her headphones on, listening to something and mouthing the words as she taps on her phone.

"Bruna!" Lorenzo bangs on the window over the sink, startling us. "Come outside." He's holding a shovel that is grimy with dirt.

"You scemo," Nonna snaps, putting her hand on her heart. "One day you will give me a heart attack doing that." She rolls her eyes and heads for the door. "Shape the dough into two logs," she reminds me. I have other ideas, however. As soon as she's out the door, I wash my hands and make a dash for the drawer where I saw her stash the cookbook earlier this morning. I slide it out, fingers caressing the worn buttery-soft leather cover, and flip it open to roughly the spot where I saw the tortellini recipe. There is nothing there. Every page is blank.

"What in the world? This is crazy." Keeping one ear tuned for Nonna's return, I carefully look through the entire book twice. Every single page is now blank, but I know what I saw this morning. There are recipes that show up in this book, just not when I am looking for them. There's something strange going on, something I don't understand. I think about what Nonna said about kitchen magic. Maybe she's right. I have a sudden inspiration.

"Alex," I hiss, waving my hand to draw her attention. She's concentrating on her phone, but glances up and takes off one headphone reluctantly.

"Yeah?"

I hand the cookbook to her. "Can you do me a favor and flip through this? Stop if you see anything written on any of the pages."

She takes the book warily. "Okay . . . why are we doing this?" She shoots me a skeptical look.

"Just . . . please? And hurry." I glance at the kitchen door. Nonna could be back at any moment. I have a feeling she's not going to like it if she sees me with the cookbook again. She seems to want to keep it away from me for some reason.

Alex sighs and opens the book to somewhere near the front, then holds it out for me to see. There is a recipe written on the page, plain as day. It's for pizza brushed with olive oil and garlic and covered in basil, mushrooms, artichokes, and fresh mozzarella. I skim the recipe in surprise. I've never seen a pizza recipe in this cookbook.

"What's it for?" she asks, frowning at the Italian words. I translate for her.

"Vegetarian pizza?" Alex murmurs.

I glance over the ingredients. She's right. "Let me see that." I reach out and take the book, holding my place at the pizza recipe with my finger and flipping to another page. The new page is blank. Of course it is. I flip back to the pizza recipe. It is blank now too.

Alex looks up from the empty page and our eyes meet. Hers are wide and puzzled.

"Did you just see that?" I whisper.

She nods slowly. "What's going on?" she asks, looking unnerved.

"I don't have any idea..."

"Juliana, Alessandra, what are you doing?" Nonna is standing in the doorway to the kitchen, hands on her hips. We didn't hear her come in. We both scramble to attention like guilty children.

"Nonna, what is happening with this book?" I hold the cookbook out to her. "Alex just opened it and there was a recipe for vegetarian pizza, but when I open it, everything is blank."

"Juliana." Nonna marches across the room and grabs the book from my hand, attempting to close it, but I hold on. We both glance down. Where my hand is, the page is blank. But on the other side, where Nonna's fingers grip it, the torn recipe for Orange Blossom Cake has suddenly appeared on the paper.

"Nonna," I say softly. "Please tell me: What is going on?"

Nonna glances up at me, then at Alex.

"Why is the book blank for me but not for Alex?" I press. "And what in the world is Orange Blossom Cake?"

"Something weird is going on around here," Alex pipes up

unexpectedly. Nonna looks from one to the other of us and her shoulders sag. She lets go of the book. I stumble back a little, then sit down hard in a chair and clutch the cookbook to my chest protectively.

"You want to know what is happening?" she says heavily. "Okay, I will tell you what you want to know. First, though, we must finish the biscotti. I'll explain all to you as it bakes." She goes over to the prep table and gestures for me to follow. I obey, setting the cookbook on the table. Alex gets up and joins us, taking a couple of quick photos with her phone as Nonna and I shape the dough into two long logs on a baking tray. Nonna slides the tray into the oven, sets a timer, and sinks down in a chair at the table, gesturing for us to follow.

"This book," she says, patting the cookbook's grease-spotted leather cover, "has been in our family for many generations. It has been passed down through the women in our family, both the book and the special ability it contains." She glances from Alex to me.

We are both silent, waiting. "It first belonged to my great-great-grandmother Angelica," Nonna says. "She saved a religious pilgrim who was on her way to Venice. The pilgrim, a noblewoman named Margaret, was traveling disguised as a man, heading to Venice to fulfill a vow to pray at the Basilica di San Marco." Nonna pauses, takes a drink of water, and continues. "Margaret was a pious woman, a mystic from a convent in England. Near Verona she fell into the hands of robbers who took all she had of value and abused her quite badly. By the time Margaret came across our farm, she was desperate for help—sick and hungry and weak. It was a time of great poverty and conflict and suffering in the region." Nonna looks grave, glancing between us. Neither of us moves a muscle. She continues. "Yet my great-great-grandmother Angelica took compassion on this needy stranger. She killed a chicken, a rare luxury in those days, and made soup from a recipe in this very cookbook, feeding Margaret and offering her shelter, binding her wounds. In return, when Margaret recovered and left our farm, she gave Angelica a blessing." Nonna smiles softly, her fingers caressing the cookbook reverently. "The story goes that the saintly Margaret placed her hand on this cookbook and anointed it with holy olive oil from Jerusalem, from the Mount of Olives. She proclaimed that from that day on, anyone seeking aid or wisdom could turn to the book for help. And from that moment, this cookbook has given just that." Nonna Bruna pauses, fixing us with a firm look. "You see, this book is special. It does not have many recipes filling its pages like most cookbooks. When someone opens it, the book shows just one recipe at a time, the recipe that person needs most. And if the person makes that recipe, they find help in unexpected ways."

She pauses expectantly. Alex and I exchange a dubious glance.

"What sort of ways?" I ask.

Nonna purses her lips and thinks for a moment. "Last year a woman from Riva del Garda came to me. She had been longing for a baby for many months. She opened the cookbook and there was a recipe for Risotto with Amarone wine. That night her husband, who had been very busy with work matters, took the time to eat the delicious risotto she made. And after dinner, they made passionate love. Nine months later, she sent me a photo of their beautiful little daughter."

"Maybe that wasn't the recipe, though," I counter. "Maybe it just worked out that way?"

"Or it was the wine," Alex murmurs skeptically.

Nonna gives a small shrug. "Perhaps you're right," she says, looking completely unconcerned. "But it happens over and over. I don't know how. I don't need to know how. It just works."

"The young women this morning . . ."

"Are all looking for love. One is single, one longs for a man she works with, and one wants her boyfriend of two years to propose.

We made the recipes the cookbook showed us for each girl. Now we wait and see." Nonna smiles with satisfaction. "And already it is working. Look." She pulls out an ancient cell phone and shows me a text. It's a photo of the young woman with the long brown hair. She's standing smiling with a cute Italian guy in a suit.

> Ciao, Bruna. I shared the gnocchi with my coworker Edoardo at lunch. He asked me to a concert in Bardolino next week!!! Grazie mille!

I stare at the text on the screen. My mind is reeling. There is no way this is true, except I've seen the cookbook change with my own eyes. Could it really be? "Nonna, do you really think this is a magic cookbook?"

Nonna shakes her head. "Not hocus-pocus magic, not witchcraft." She makes a spitting gesture and the sign of the cross, warding off evil. "You should know better than that," she scolds gently. "The mystic Margaret offered a beautiful gift to Angelica, and each generation of women in our family has been sharing this gift with those who need it ever since. It is a blessed book, a wise book that knows exactly what each person who seeks its help needs. It is a gift from above."

"So it thinks I need pizza?" Alex pipes up skeptically. She looks unconvinced.

Nonna tips her head. "Alessandra, do you know what pizza symbolizes in Italian cooking? The circle of the pizza represents unity and togetherness. A pizza means you have others to share your table. Maybe it is not the pizza you need but someone to share it with." She gives Alex a meaningful look.

Alex stares down at the table. She fiddles with her phone and says nothing.

"But what about me?" I challenge. "I desperately need to come up with a bunch of recipes, but the entire book is blank. Every page. How is that helpful?"

Nonna nods sagely. "This surprises me too. But mia cara, sometimes the book does not give us what we think we want. It gives us something deeper, what our heart really needs. You think you need fifty recipes, but perhaps that is not all you need. Perhaps the blank page holds the key."

This is annoyingly unhelpful.

"Why is there half a torn recipe for Orange Blossom Cake when you open the book?" I ask.

At that question Nonna's face shutters, and she stands abruptly, picking up the book. "That's enough for today," she says curtly. The timer rings, and she looks relieved. "Come, your biscotti is done. We must slice it now while it is still warm." She carefully tucks the cookbook back into the drawer and goes to the oven to pull out the biscotti.

As I carefully slice the biscotti into even sections, I reflect on Nonna's revelation about the cookbook. Of course it is absurd. There is simply no way our family has a magic cookbook that knows what each person needs and provides just the right recipe. Her story is just a myth, a family fable, right?

But I cannot quite convince myself of that as I transfer the crescent-shaped biscotti back to the baking sheet and slide it into the hot oven. As I set the kitchen timer for ten minutes, I think about all those summer mornings growing up, me flipping the cookbook open at random, and how Nonna and I would make the recipe that I flipped to. How it always seemed to be just the right thing for that day. In light of what Nonna shared, I wonder if every day little Juliana was flipping open the cookbook and it was giving me exactly what I needed. No wonder it felt so magical! And now as an adult I've seen it with my own eyes. I saw the recipes on the page transform—completely blank for me, the pasta from this morning for the young women, half a recipe for Orange Blossom Cake for Nonna, vegetarian pizza for Alex. I don't understand it, but I know it's true.

I glance over at Alex, who has her headphones back on and is absorbed in something on her phone. She looks so young, sitting there all by herself. I envision a pizza cut into slices, how it's meant to be shared around a table, shared with family and friends. I think about how alone she must feel in the world. How it seems she's already grown used to being on her own. How sad that is for anyone, let alone someone so young. And again I feel a little ashamed for my own distance, for keeping her at arm's length and in some small way holding her responsible for Lisa's poor decisions.

Then I think about my own blank page of the cookbook. If the cookbook knows what I need, why is it not giving me recipes? It is withholding the exact thing I most desperately need. How is that helpful? It feels just the opposite.

The timer rings, and I take the baking sheet out of the oven. Carefully, I transfer the biscotti to a big plate to cool and start to tidy up. But my mind wanders back to Nonna and that torn half a recipe for Orange Blossom Cake, and I can't help but wonder: What does all of this mean? I shake my head, feeling more thwarted and more confused than ever.

Chapter 23

> The garbage disposal is making a strange grating noise. It is disturbing Ophelia.

I receive the text from Solomon as I'm cuddled up in bed very late that night, writing up the recipe for the biscotti.

> She is hiding under the couch and cannot be coaxed out even with wild salmon.

I send him a frowny-face emoji and the number of the apartment repair line, then dash off a quick, hopeful email to Michelle with the two recipes I have so far – the merenda recipe and the biscotti recipe I just finished. I attach the gorgeous photos Alex took of both dishes, along with short personal anecdotes about sharing the merenda with my dad and how I loved to bake biscotti with Nonna every summer.

Is this what Epicure Press is looking for? I ask, then cross myself and kiss my thumb for luck, and hit send.

It's getting late, but I'm wired. Instead of going to sleep, I type out another recipe from today, a simple yet delicious pasta dish called agnolotti (which translates to "priest hats" for their crimped, square shape) that Nonna and I made for dinner. As we were baking the biscotti, I remembered making this dish with Nonna when I was younger, the pasta stuffed with a savory meat filling and served with shaved local white truffles on top. It's one of Nonna's favorites, and she was happy to show me how she prepares it. Tonight we ate it on the patio under the olive trees strung with café lights. It was magical.

Next, I text Lisa, who has (unsurprisingly) not checked in with me since I let her know we'd arrived safely. Maybe she's in communication with Alex, but I kind of doubt it.

> Buongiorno! We're enjoying delicious Italy.

I include a photo I snapped at the market of Alex and me eating focaccia, the lake a deep blue behind us, our smiles wide and happy.

My last task is to post the week's *The Bygone Kitchen* cooking segment, the peach pandowdy episode, and I spend a few minutes responding to all the likes and comments on last week's segment. Ethel has posted a comment about the green tomato pie, telling us it was the perfect cure for morning sickness when she was a young wife. Then she ends her comment with a line of fourteen tomato emojis interspersed with hearts and baby bottles.

I take my time responding to everyone. I really do love this community. There's a Vietnam vet in a wheelchair, Marv, who makes the featured recipe every week, then posts a photo and his honest opinion on the dish. He hates most of them, but I think he's lonely and likes to feel a part of something. And of course Ethel, and so many others. I have come to care about these people. It feels like a real little community we've built over these past five years. It's hard to think about what comes next. There are only two prerecorded segments left, and soon I'm going to have to figure out what to do about the show. I'm not ready to think about that or make any decisions yet, though, so I put it off another week. Instead I call Aurora.

"Tell me everything!" Aurora demands when she picks up the video call. "I need all the details."

I sigh and snuggle down in the big heavy double bed, ready to oblige her. It's the bedroom Aurora and I shared when we would visit during the summers, and now I feel nostalgic talking with my sister while sitting here alone.

It's late afternoon in Virginia, and she's in the garden with the children. They're scattered down the rows of vegetables behind her, wearing straw sun hats and picking various types of lettuces. Aurora is wearing a straw sun hat with a floral ribbon, her golden hair in a thick braid over her shoulder. It's giving off big Anne of Green Gables vibes. I grab a few biscotti from the plate on my nightstand and fill her in on the juicy details of our trip so far, including my excruciatingly humiliating reunion with Nicolo, the horrid sleep shirt, and introducing Alex to the market.

"Wait a minute, let me get this straight," Aurora says when I'm finished. "Your first love has moved back next door, is always around helping Zio Lorenzo, and is a superhot international attorney?" She looks delighted. "I absolutely love this for you!"

She bends over a row to help two of the boys with their lettuce-harvesting technique, showing them how to cut the lettuce correctly. "Remember, Atticus and Dante, cut no more than one third of the butter lettuce leaves," she instructs, then straightens and says to me, "I need a picture of Nicolo instantly."

"I'm not going to snap a sneaky photo of him," I protest indignantly. "That's creepy." But already I'm trying to figure out how to get a photo of him. Maybe I could google him? Surely, there's some photo of him on the Internet if he was working as some hotshot attorney?

"Meadow, start on the snap peas, honey," Aurora instructs. "The rest of you keep cutting the lettuce. Remember, take the lower outside leaves first." She floats to the other end of the huge garden where she can oversee the children but have a bit of privacy. "Now, tell me everything. I want all of the juicy details." She leans forward and confesses, "Will has been gone for three days at a farrier's convention and I am desperate for adult conversation. I almost turned on the television last night after the kids went to bed." She looks guilty since they've all committed to a no-screen-time summer. "I came this close to caving and watching *The Real Housewives of Salt Lake City*."

"Well here's something that's worthy of reality TV," I tell her, then share the family legend of Margaret and Angelica and the cookbook, about how it is blank for me but shows Nonna half a recipe for Orange Blossom Cake. I tell her about the three women cooking pasta super early this morning, and Nonna's explanation about the cookbook's abilities. When I'm done, Aurora's eyes are round and blue as Delft saucers. "No, this is way *better* than reality TV," she breathes.

"I know it sounds crazy," I tell her, sure she's going to say I'm imagining things. But she surprises me.

"Maybe it sounds crazy, but it also makes so much sense," Aurora muses. "When we used to stay there in the summer, sometimes I'd come downstairs for a drink of water and there'd just be a random person in the kitchen cooking with Nonna late at night or early in the morning. And once I went with her to Mass and a woman came up as we were leaving. She was crying and she told Nonna the recipe had worked, that her husband had come back to her and that the other woman had moved to Naples. Nonna hugged her and they were both beaming. When I asked Nonna about it later, she just brushed my question away."

"Do you really think all this could be true?" I ask, voicing my own inner skepticism. I can't quite admit that I'm pretty sure it actually is true.

Aurora tips her head thoughtfully, considering. "Whether it's true or not, I think people believe it's true. Did you ever notice how people treat Nonna in the community? She's revered. Everyone knows who she is."

"You're right." I'm surprised. I hadn't thought of it before, but Nonna does seem to know everyone and to be held in pretty high esteem. People greet her on the street, defer to her in line at the post office; vendors offer her the best of everything at the outdoor markets . . . I honestly just thought it was because Nonna is Nonna, but now I wonder. Maybe it's the cookbook's reputation. Maybe everyone knows this open secret about our family but us.

"I'd think the whole magic cookbook thing was completely crazy except I saw it with my own eyes," I admit. "I think it might actually be true. But if so, why isn't it working for me? The book is totally blank." It's so frustrating. The book helps everyone but me? It feels so unfair.

Aurora taps her finger against her lips and frowns. "What if the blank page *is* the help you need?" she asks. "What if that is your answer?"

I don't like this line of thought. I want the book to deliver fifty great recipes in time for September. I don't want to do this all on my own. "That's what Nonna said too," I admit reluctantly. "But I don't know how I'm going to make the deadline without the cookbook's help."

"How many recipes do you have so far?" Aurora asks.

"Three," I admit, feeling a little deflated. "But before I came to Italy, I had zero. I've been . . . having trouble remembering recipes that have ties to our family. It's been happening for a while, since Dad died, actually. It's like I've blocked out the memories of those recipes. I try to remember and it's just a big blank. It's weird. I can't remember any of them. Well, until now."

"Oh Jules!" Aurora looks stricken. "Oh honey, I had no idea. I'm so sorry. That must be so scary for you." She pauses, thinking. "I'll text you all the dishes I remember you making with Nonna and see if that helps jog your memory."

"Thanks." I'm glad I finally told her. Maybe her recollections will help.

Suddenly, I remember what else I was calling to tell her about. "Hey, I think you might be right about something going on with Nonna and the farm." I lower my voice and relay my conversation with Nicolo, ignoring how Aurora grins and wiggles her eyebrows suggestively every time I say Nicolo's name. By the end she looks concerned, though.

"Do you think it's as bad as Nicolo says?" she asks.

"I hope not." I shiver a little, from the cool night air slipping through my window and from thinking about the future of this place if Nicolo is right. I don't want him to be right.

From the garden beds I hear one of the children calling for Aurora. I think it's her oldest, Louisa. "Mom, Doris is out of her pen again."

Aurora glances over her shoulder with a frown. "Doris!" she shouts, then turns to me. "She's in the radishes. Jules, I've got to go."

"No problem," I tell her hurriedly. "I'll let you know more when I figure out what's going on."

"Send me that picture of Nicolo," she demands as she blows me a quick air-kiss. "Don't forget." I hear her calling for Atticus to run into the house for a box of Twinkies as she hangs up.

As soon as we disconnect the call, I google Nicolo. Sure enough, I quickly find a very professional-looking headshot from a fancy law firm based in Sydney. Nicolo's hair is shorter, no curls, and he's in a navy suit and red power tie, but the dimples and those deep brown, sooty-lashed eyes are the same. I send Aurora a screenshot. A moment later she responds with five heart-eye emojis.

For the record I think you should make sweet, sweet love to him under the olive trees and have lots of deliciously plump Italian babies, she texts back. I blush and don't reply. It would not be the first time Nicolo Fiore and I engaged in amorous activities under the olive trees. I send her an eye-roll emoji.

For a moment, I gaze at the photo of Nicolo and think about everything that has happened in the short time I've been here. The mysteriously blank magical cookbook, Nicolo's unexpected reappearance next door, my burgeoning relationship with Alex, those forty-seven recipes I still need, not to mention Nonna and the questions and secrets surrounding the farm. I agreed to this trip thinking it could be a tidy way to solve my pressing problems, but now it's becoming clear that I'm going to need every ounce of fortitude, courage, and cunning I possess to navigate all of these challenges before we head home at the end of August. One thing is for certain. This summer is shaping up to be a lot more complicated than I could ever have imagined.

Chapter 24

"**How is this?** Like this? Make sure my nose doesn't look so big."

The next morning, I come downstairs, tired from my late-night chat with Aurora but ready to get started on cooking only to find the kitchen empty. The kitchen door is standing open, however, and I hear Nonna's voice coming from outside. Yawning, I wander out into the morning sunshine to find Nonna and Alex in the courtyard. Nonna is dressed in her usual knee-length skirt and blouse, with her hair scraped back in its severe bun. But she's wearing burgundy lipstick and her one good strand of pearls, like she's going to Mass. Alex is holding her phone up and appears to be filming her.

"What's going on?" I squint in the bright sunshine. It's already warm and growing hotter by the minute. The air is alive with twittering birds and the scent of sun-warmed rocks and green living things and crumbly earth. No sign of Lorenzo or Nicolo, although I am wearing a cute lime-green shirtwaist dress just in case.

"We are making a video to share the beauty of our farm and this region with people on the Internet," Nonna says, never taking her eyes from the camera. "Alessandra is going to put the videos on the TikTok."

The TikTok? "What's happening?" I'm confused. Nonna is making TikTok videos with Alex? The woman doesn't even own a computer.

Alex shrugs. "We're making videos so people can see how a real Italian olive farm works. It's cool. People love this kind of stuff."

I'm surprised. Just a few days ago Alex seemed to think nothing was cool, this farm included, so this is an interesting shift.

Bemused, I head back inside in search of coffee. Maybe this day will make more sense with caffeine. Then I need to start brainstorming more recipes. I've managed to make three recipes so far, which is encouraging, but now I've got no idea what to make next. I need help. Hopefully, Nonna has some bright ideas. Aurora texted me some dishes she remembers making, but I skimmed the short list and nothing stood out to me.

However, there was a hopeful email from Michelle waiting for me when I woke up.

This is exactly what Epicure is looking for, she wrote. Keep up the good work. Send more when you have it.

So that's positive. At least now I know what they want and I can theoretically provide it. Time to get cooking! I make myself an espresso and head back outside to see if Nonna can help me. They seem to be wrapping up their video shoot.

"So why are you doing these videos?" I pause in the doorway and lean against the heavy wood frame, sipping my espresso.

"To share the beauty of our home and this land." Nonna sweeps her hand across the horizon, across the gray-green flutter of olive leaves rustling in the breeze, down toward the blue shimmer of the lake. "We are blessed to live in such a place. Seven generations have cared for these groves. I want others to understand why it is important to us, what is so special about the place we call home."

Alex is reviewing the video footage she shot, hunched over her phone. She looks up from the screen. "I think that's good for now," she says. "We got what we need for the first video. We can show them the inside of the house tomorrow. I'll create the account today and do the first post."

"Come, it's time to eat." Nonna herds us into the kitchen.

"Nonna is going to have a TikTok account?" I ask Alex quietly as we head back inside.

She shrugs. "She asked me to. She said she wants to show people what life is like here on the farm before it's gone."

"Gone?" That's a worrisome word.

Alex shrugs again. "Don't ask me. I just told her I'd help her post the videos."

I sit down at the round table, catty-corner from Alex, trying to puzzle out what Nonna could mean. There is no sign of Lorenzo or Nicolo. I wonder where they are. Probably already in the groves working. Or maybe Nicolo is at the Fiore estate today. Nonna told me he comes by when he has time to spare. Nonna sets breakfast in front of us, waving away my attempts to help. "I've waited many years to have you sitting again at this table, Nipote. Give me the satisfaction of feeding you, yes?"

I acquiesce and munch a couple of our homemade biscotti dipped in my espresso, the hard almond cookies softening slightly in the bitter brew. I watch Nonna carefully, mulling over Nicolo's words about the state of the farm. Across from me, Alex is working her way through a few biscotti, crunching so loudly it sounds like she's chewing gravel. I can't tell if she likes them. Her face looks pinched but she keeps chewing. Since our trip to the market that first day here, she seems to be more open to trying new things. I think she might be enjoying her time in Italy more than she cares to admit.

Nonna sits down heavily with a gusty sigh. "Today is the day, Juliana," she announces, taking a sip of her espresso.

"For what?" I ask.

"For you to find your creativity again. I can feel it, in here." She taps her broad bosom. "It is a day for miracles."

I frown. "I wish it were that easy."

She gives me a look of surprise and disapproval. "Who said anything about easy?" she asks with a wave of her hand, dismissing my words. "Few things in life are easy, not if they're worth anything. You should know this by now, mia cara. Life isn't easy, but we don't just roll over and give up. We struggle and persevere. Sometimes we lose and sometimes we triumph. But you can never win a fight you don't show up for in the first place." She looks down her nose sternly at me.

I nod, chastened. She's right. It may be hard, but yesterday I proved it was possible. I take a deep breath. "Okay then, let's do this." Three down. Forty-seven recipes to go.

She holds up a hand, waving me back down into my seat. "First we finish our espresso, then we make a miracle."

※

A half hour later, I'm standing at the heavy prep table in the middle of the kitchen, staring once more at an array of ingredients spread before me—rice, a wedge of Parmesan, fresh tomatoes, a bunch of basil. I'm trying to tamp down my panic and summon some creative juices by sheer force of will, but nothing is coming to me. I even checked the recipe book again this morning, hoping something had changed. Still blank. I guess I'm on my own. I was so hopeful after the success of the past couple of days that I was going to be able to unlock so many more memories, but currently, I feel like I'm back to square one. I rub fragrant basil from Nonna's herb garden between my fingers, inhaling the aroma rising from the crushed leaf.

I look around the kitchen, desperate for inspiration. I spent years in this kitchen cooking with Nonna, but now those memories have all deserted me. When I try to concentrate, I run up against the blankness again. Can you have selective amnesia? Is that a real thing? I try hard to focus on dinners Dad liked, but attempting to corral my thoughts and recall those specific memories makes me feel itchy and a little panicky inside, like my brain is shying away from them. I don't know what to do.

Alex has disappeared upstairs with her phone in hand. It's just me and Nonna now. She's standing at the sink watching me from the corner of her eye. She comes over to me and places her hand gently over mine. "Mia cara, what is the matter?" she asks. "What are you so afraid of?"

I shake my head, trying to formulate my answer. "I don't know how to explain it."

Her forehead creases and she gazes at me in sympathy. "I remember you, from the time you were small, standing at this table, your eager little face looking up at me so expectantly. You couldn't wait to help me. Every day we cooked together, all those years. You were not afraid then. What changed?"

How do I explain what I don't entirely understand myself?

"I think it might have something to do with Dad," I blurt out. "It all changed when Dad died."

Nonna's face wrinkles in confusion. "My Tony? What does his passing have to do with your cooking?"

I take a deep breath and try to trace this panicky, itchy feeling all the way back. Where had it first started? After Dad's death, I know that. Reluctantly, I think back to the afternoon my father drowned. I close my eyes and concentrate, forcing myself to remember every painful detail.

That day I was making La Torta de Fregoloti for the first time by myself. A local cake made with almonds, grappa, and a *lot* of butter, it was my dad's favorite dessert. I was making it as a surprise for his birthday. He was turning fifty the next day. He'd invited me to go swimming down at the lake, our almost daily tradition, but I'd declined, wanting to make the cake instead. It was a decision I'll regret for the rest of my life.

I was whipping the butter and egg yolks together, adding the salt and grappa under Nonna's watchful eye. She gave occasional instructions, but mostly let me do it myself. It was late afternoon and the kitchen was hot, the shutters and windows open. Everything felt slow and golden and perfect. I was so excited to make my dad something he liked so much and proud that I was making it all myself. I planned on serving it with whipped cream and a sprinkle of toasted hazelnuts. It was my gift to him. After all, he was my favorite person in the world.

I was holding the mixing bowl over the buttered cake pan, scooping the batter into the pan in big plops, when the door crashed open. Lorenzo stood there in the doorway, breathing heavily. His face was ashen, his eyes panicked. I'd never seen him look like that. "It's Tony," he gasped. "Hurry."

And just like that, my world collapsed.

Late that night, when we came back from the hospital, numb and in shock, we found the raw batter still waiting in the pan. Wordlessly, Nonna scraped the batter into the trash can. I never made that cake again. The smell of grappa still makes me feel a little sick.

"That birthday cake was the last thing I made that was connected to Dad," I confess to Nonna, feeling puzzled, as though an answer is sitting just beyond my fingertips. I feel like I'm just starting to put the pieces together. "I think . . . I think after he was gone it was just too painful to think about him, about losing him. Cooking a recipe that reminded me of him brought all those feelings back up." I had not been able to articulate this before now, but when I say the words, they feel true.

Nonna frowns. "But don't you want to remember him?" she asks gently. "Cooking those recipes can help us feel close to those we've loved and lost. They connect us to the past, to the generations that came before us, to those who have gone on ahead. The recipes we make together, Juliana, they help us honor and remember. I still cook Carlo's favorite pasta every year on our anniversary. It helps me celebrate him and the love we shared. Your father loved you, Juliana, so very much. You had many happy years together here, so many meals, so much joy. Why do you want to block all that from your mind?" Her brow is furrowed in puzzlement. She really doesn't understand.

I clear my throat trying to swallow the aching knot stuck there. "Yes, but Carlo died of a heart attack. It wasn't your fault." It's hard to get the words out.

Nonna looks confused for a long moment, then her face clears with understanding. "You think Tony's death was your fault?" she murmurs. "But why?"

I hang my head, not looking at her. "He asked me to go swimming with him that day, but I said no." I murmur the confession, soft enough she has to lean forward to hear me. "I wanted to surprise him with the cake I made." I clear my throat again. All these years later, it's still so painful to recall that afternoon. All these years I've never spoken the words aloud, but I've felt the shame of them, the crush of guilt, since the day he died.

"I remember that cake," Nonna says, her gaze far away. "His favorite. You were going to surprise him."

I sniff. "He never even got to taste it. I chose a stupid cake over time with him, over the last time with him. And maybe if I'd been there with him, if I'd said yes and gone swimming with him, I could have saved him . . . but I didn't. It was more important to me to finish that cake than to spend time with my dad, and now he's gone." My voice cracks.

Nonna is staring at me in consternation. "Juliana, you think if you had not made the cake your father would still be here? You think you could have saved him if you had gone swimming with him?" She looks astonished.

I nod, eyes brimming with hot tears. Even now, even after all these years, it is still agonizing to think of that day. I miss my father every day, living with the ache low in the center of my chest, the space where once I'd felt his love and presence, where I'd felt safe and strong. Now it just feels cold and dead, hollowed out with guilt and grief. I'd give anything to go back and make a different choice.

"Oh, Juliana." Nonna reaches up and cups my cheek in her gnarled hand. "Nothing could have stopped what happened. Your father had a massive heart attack while he was swimming. Nothing could have saved him."

"What?" I step back, shaking my head. "No, that was Carlo. Carlo had the heart attack. Dad drowned in the lake. I saw him after they pulled him out of the water."

Nonna looks surprised. "That's what it looked like at first, yes," she says patiently, "but the medical report after his death said that was not true. He had a heart attack while he was swimming and died instantly. Just like Carlo."

Chapter 25

"**Tony was dead** before he slipped beneath the water," Nonna says gently. "There was nothing anyone could have done, the doctors told me. Not even if you or I had been right there. It was his time to go."

Astonished, I let this news sink in. At the time of his death, everyone assumed a drowning. No one told me my father had suffered a massive, fatal heart attack. After the funeral, when I flew back to New York with Lisa, we didn't talk about Dad's death. She wanted to "put the sadness behind us." I'm not sure she even knew he hadn't drowned. She and Nonna did not talk after the funeral that I knew of.

"Thank goodness you were making the cake, Juliana," Nonna adds. "Otherwise you would have watched your father die and had to run to get help yourself. He would not have wanted that for you, mia cara. He would have wanted to spare you that memory. Your last memory of him is a good one. He knew you were making something special for him. He knew you loved him, and he loved you and Aurora more than anyone in the world. He died a happy man in the place he loved best, with his girls safe nearby. There are much worse ways to go."

"He was so young, though," I protest, as though pointing this out can somehow undo his death, as though it were a clerical error, a glitch in the system, that a man one day shy of fifty would drop dead under a clear blue summer sky.

"Young, old." Nonna shrugs, her face sorrowful yet philosophical. "Death comes for all of us, Nipotina. Did my Tony die too young? Of course, but none of us could have changed the outcome, not even you." Her gaze is pure compassion. "I miss him too, mia cara. So much. Every day. That's the way it is to love someone and lose them. We must remember all the good times, even as we grieve the emptiness of the world without them." She gazes into the distance for a moment, and I'm guessing she is thinking of Carlo. I remember only the scent of his tobacco, and that he was a tall, quiet man, so tall to my toddler self that he seemed to block out the sun. How has she carried on with life after burying her husband and her son?

"Everything here reminds me of Dad," I admit. "That's why I... didn't come back for so long. I just didn't know how to face this place without him in it." My voice is barely a whisper. "And I blamed myself for his death. I felt responsible."

Nonna squeezes my hand. "Oh, Juliana," she says with a sigh. "I wish I had known you felt this way. You have carried this regret and responsibility for so long, but you must lay it down. Let yourself embrace all of the past now. Memory is bittersweet. We must remember the sweet times too, not just the bitterness at the end." She rubs my cheek with her thumb, swiping away the tears leaking from the corners of my eyes. "Ah, mia cara, he would not want you to be so sad, carrying such a heavy burden of regret. He would want to see you alive, filled with joy, free."

"I miss him so much," I whisper, leaning into Nonna's touch. I picture him in my mind's eye. He was the most vital man I've ever known, barrel-chested, robust, with a big grin and an easy way about him. Thick dark hair, receding slightly, and warm brown eyes. He taught middle school history at a public school in Seattle. After Lisa left us, he was the pillar of our family, raising two girls by himself. He bungled things at times, sure, but he tried his best and was always there for us, always steady and safe. I adored him.

"I miss him too." Nonna nods. "Every day."

I'm crying openly now, my shoulders shaking, from grief and from relief. I feel like I've just put down a crushing load I've been carrying for years. I am not responsible for my father's death. I could not have changed anything. That revelation makes me feel like I'm floating. It also breaks my heart.

I could not change his death. That was always going to be his last day on earth. So many times in life there are lasts, and we don't realize it. If we knew, we could savor them, hold them close, cherish them. Instead we breeze through them carelessly. The last times so often pass by unnoticed. Only in retrospect do we glance behind us and realize what is gone.

Nonna embraces me, pulling my head down against her shoulder. She smells like rosemary and laundry soap and a faint hint of garlic. I feel like a little girl again, the grief as fresh as it was fifteen years ago. Nonna is patting me on the back like she's burping a baby. She's murmuring things in Italian too low for me to hear, but the sound is comforting.

I picture my father splayed out limply on the pebbled shore of the lake. Someone driving by had seen him floating face down and called the emergency services. When I saw his body, he was dripping, clad in his swim trunks, his black thatch of hair falling over his brow, his warm, dark eyes closed forever. He looked like he was sleeping, lying there, except that his limbs were too slack and his barrel chest did not rise and fall. I refused to believe he was really gone until I knelt beside him and laid my head on his bare chest, his curly dark chest hair still slick with lake water, my ear pressed frantically right over the heart that had gone silent. And in that moment I felt my own heart crack right in two.

Now I pull back, wiping my tears on my sleeve, and gaze at Nonna with new eyes, seeing the deepening wrinkles at the corners of her eyelids, the stripe of silver showing at the roots of her hair. I lost a father that day, but she lost her only child, her son. And then she lost me when Lisa swooped in and insisted I fly back to New York and move in with her and Ted immediately after the funeral. Aurora was in college, already dating Will and although she grieved Dad immensely, she did not experience his loss quite the same way I did. His death almost destroyed me.

For years, every time I thought of Italy, all I could see was my father's body laid out on that pebbled strip of beach, his eyes closed, face peaceful and slack, as though he had lain down and drifted off for a nap from which he would never wake. And I believed it was my fault.

"So there really was nothing we could have done to save him?" I clarify.

"Nothing," Nonna says firmly. "Only the good Lord knows when it's our time to go, and it was Tony's time." She crosses herself and murmurs a little prayer under her breath.

I sniff and wipe my tears away with my sleeve. "I blamed myself for so long," I confess, still trying to come to grips with this bombshell. For years my grief and guilt have been entwined with every memory of my dad and this place. I don't know how to feel. "What do I do now that I know the truth?"

"Now you figure out how to live again," Nonna says gently. "For so long you've been avoiding and blaming yourself, but now that you know the truth, you are free. Your father would not have wanted you to live this way—trapped in guilt and fear. To live bound by fear is to live a small life, a pinched life." She pinches her fingers together to illustrate. "So often people think that fear keeps them safe, that it protects them, but that is a lie. So often fear is a prison, not a salvation. Fear is a ball and chain. It makes you imagine the worst that can happen and then forces you to live in the shadow of that terrible imagined thing. Fear can rob you of the life you were meant to live. It does not keep you safe, it keeps you small. You were made for bigger things, Nipotina, starting with a life set free by the truth, by reality. What is here. What is now. That is what matters." Nonna raps the table firmly.

"A life set free." I roll the words around in my mouth. They send a little shiver right through me. "I'd settle for fifty good recipes," I grumble, shooting Nonna a shy half grin.

She chuckles. "How about today you try for just one. One good recipe that means something to you." She pats my hand. "You made a wonderful merenda and pretty good biscotti. And the pasta was not bad either. Now for the next step, how about you make us lunch?"

"Okay." I nod, still sniffling but feeling much lighter and more hopeful. I try to think about all the meals from this region that my father loved to eat. All the recipes I made over the many summers spent in this kitchen cooking with Nonna. I was so small when I started helping her in the kitchen. Every summer I spent many happy hours here, learning the dishes of my heritage. Nonna is right. Surely, I can make one good dish. A simple lunch. What should I make? I concentrate, thinking of Dad, not straining to remember but letting a memory rise to meet me. And to my surprise, it does.

"Risotto con la tinca," I declare aloud. "Dad always loved that dish." The risotto with the sweet, firm flesh of the freshwater fish from Lake Garda had been one of his favorites. I remember that now, how his eyes would light up, how he'd always have seconds and scrape his dish clean. It hurts a little to recall how much he enjoyed that dish, but it makes me happy too. He always ate with gusto; he lived with gusto too. I could use a little more gusto in my life. Less fear, more gusto. I like the sound of that.

Nonna nods, looking satisfied. "First we go to the fish market. Then you cook for us."

Chapter 26

"*Delizioso!*" Lorenzo declares enthusiastically, scooping up another spoonful of my freshly prepared Risotto con la tinca. Everyone is enjoying a late lunch on the flagstone patio under the olive trees, seated at one end of the long wooden table. Today I've made two risotto recipes, and I dish up a plate of the second one, Risotto all'Amarone, for Nicolo. Much to my surprise, he has joined us for the meal. Alex is snapping photos of the dishes, and trying to capture the ambiance of the patio with candid shots of us at the table, all the while sneaking little glances at Nicolo. Nicolo pours wine for all of us, then holds the bottle aloft and raises an eyebrow, tipping his head toward Alex.

"A little wine for everyone?" he asks.

I hesitate, then nod. I started drinking a little wine at family meals when I was younger than Alex. "Sure, when in Italy..."

Alex shoots me a grateful glance, which I appreciate. I've never gotten to feel like the cool older sister before. I like the sensation.

Nicolo pours a very modest portion of wine into a glass and hands it to Alex, who blushes beet red. She appears to have momentarily lost the ability to speak. She scurries to her chair and buries her nose in her glass.

Nicolo pours a generous glug of white wine into my glass and Nonna's too. I sit across from him and take a sip, letting the delicious, cold, crisp liquid slide down my throat. It is perfect with the risotto. Everything in this moment is perfect, actually. After my conversation with Nonna about my dad's death, I'm feeling more relaxed than I've felt in forever. No, not relaxed. Relieved. I'm feeling relieved of the secret burden of guilt I've carried for so many years. It's a gloriously light feeling, and I'm savoring everything about this moment. The lemony sunlight filtering through the olive branches, the call of birds and hum of insects, the unhurried pace of an Italian meal. I gaze around in satisfaction.

After the kitchen, the patio has always been my favorite part of the farm. A century ago some enterprising ancestor carved a picturesque entertaining area out of the hillside next to the house and laid a somewhat level flagstone floor. The patio sits slightly above and to the right of the farmhouse, nestled among the olive trees and overlooking the lake below. It is accessed by a short flight of stairs from the gravel courtyard. Surrounded by a low stone wall, the patio has a long weathered wooden table under ancient, gnarled olive trees strung with café lights. Sitting at the table, you feel as though you are at the edge of the world—so high above everything in the most tranquil, serene spot. Meals here are never hurried. Time moves more slowly.

Beside me Alex is poking at the plate of risotto. For a picky eater she's been fairly adventurous, but red wine–soaked risotto seems to be testing her limits.

Nonna samples both types of risotto, pursing her lips, assessing. "Ottimi!" she declares finally. "These are both very good."

That is high praise coming from her. I beam, satisfied. Five recipes down, forty-five to go. I'm feeling hopeful. Even while I was making the risotto, a few more snatches of memory came back to me, along with a handful of dishes that were special to me from childhood. Nonna stirred the risotto while I hastily scribbled a list—a few sentences describing the memory and the name of the corresponding dish. It's a good start.

I take a bite of my risotto and am startled by the flavor. Nonna is right, it *is* delicious! The prized, intensely flavored Amarone della Valpolicella wine combined with the local Monte Veronese cheese makes a richly satisfying risotto. It's simple and perfectly balanced.

"Dad would have loved everything about this lunch," I say wistfully. "He loved risotto and he loved eating on this patio."

Nonna nods. "Tony always loved it out here, even as a small boy, even when it was cold or raining. He liked to always keep one eye on the water. He loved the lake." She takes another spoonful of risotto, her expression a little distant and sad, as though she's seeing memories all around her.

"Tony and I used to play briscolone out here in the evenings after the work was done," Lorenzo mused, holding his plate out for more Risotto con la tinca. I oblige, giving him another heaping spoonful serving.

"Sometimes you were out here playing before the work was done," Nonna comments dryly. Nicolo chokes on a sip of wine, casting an amused look at me.

Lorenzo gives Nonna a slow smile. "I miss those days," he says. "Those were good days."

"They were," she says simply. "And now we have good days once more."

He nods, not taking his eyes from her. There's some sort of message passing between them that I'm not privy to. I take a sip of wine, watching them, trying to decode their cryptic communication.

"Not now." She shakes her head, her words so quiet I almost don't catch them. "This is not the time."

I translate the Italian in my head. What can she mean? Time for what? Nonna looks away after a second, but Lorenzo's eyes are still fixed on her. A brief expression crosses his face, so fleeting I almost think I've imagined it. It surprises me, the tender, raw emotion in his gaze. It looks an awful lot like longing. Startled, I glance at Nonna, then around the table. No one else seems to have noticed anything. I turn my focus back to my plate, but still I wonder. Could Lorenzo have feelings for Nonna? The thought is intriguing yet perhaps not all that surprising. They've been living here for so long, just the two of them. If it is indeed true, how long has he felt like this? Why has he never done anything about it? And what is the secret they are harboring between them? I am determined to figure it out before I leave Italy.

Chapter 27

"Nicolo, you must try some of Juliana's Torta delle Rose," Nonna urges, cornering Nicolo as he and Lorenzo stop into the kitchen for a drink of water late one morning a few days after our leisurely lunch on the patio. "It is still warm, fresh from the oven."

Nicolo, who looks unreasonably attractive even clad in grimy work clothes, glances at Lorenzo behind him. Lorenzo shrugs from the doorway. "I never say no to cake," he tells Nicolo. "The wall can wait."

"And maybe a little espresso with the torta?" Nonna says, with a calculated gleam in her eye. "Juliana will serve it on the patio. We will join you." She's up to something, I can tell, but I'm not sure what.

Nonna makes espressos for all of us while I grab plates. The sweet, golden brown pastry reminds me a little of cinnamon rolls, minus the cinnamon. Made of individual portions of brioche dough rolled up around a rich filling of sugar and butter and nestled in a pan, the dessert resembles a basket of roses, hence the name. The aroma is delectable and my mouth waters. Alex comes downstairs from her room just in time to join us.

"Wow, that smells good," she observes, stopping to capture a few candid photos with her phone. She already got a quality photo of the finished dessert for the cookbook a little earlier right after I pulled the torta from the oven. I take off my flour-dusted apron, glad I've stuck to my policy of trying to look cute at all times in case Nicolo pops up. Today I'm wearing a tangerine-colored sundress with a halter neck that ties in a bow at the back.

I've scarcely seen Nicolo or Lorenzo since the risotto lunch. They've been busy repairing a stone wall that runs between our two properties, and I've barely left the kitchen. Since Nonna's revelation about my dad, I've been remembering more and more things from the past. Throughout the day I'm jotting down memories and recipes as they come to me, keeping a note open on my phone to quickly capture whatever springs to mind. It's going well and my list of ideas and memories is getting longer each day.

Nonna and I have also made categories for my cookbook—dividing the fifty recipes between appetizers, main courses, merendas, drinks, and desserts. Nonna is acting as my sous-chef and recipe adviser. Alex has been hanging around to take photos and shoot video of our cooking and the finished dishes. It's working well. Now, however, instead of starting on another sweet bread recipe, apparently we are taking a break with the men on the patio. I should be annoyed by the delay but I'm not. Alex and I follow Nonna out the door, laden with tiny cups of espresso, plates and forks, and the pan of Torta delle Rose.

When we are seated on the patio, I serve everyone generous portions of the torta.

"Isn't it delicious? Our Juliana is so good in the kitchen," Nonna says as Nicolo samples his. She casts a sly glance in my direction, and I narrow my eyes at her. When we were teenagers, Nonna tried her best to keep Nicolo and me apart. Now I'm starting to suspect that she is deliberately trying to bring us together. I'm not sure what her agenda is, but I'm getting the feeling she has one.

"Delicious," Nicolo assures Nonna, glancing in my direction. "And how can I say no to such good company?" He winks at me, just the slightest dip of an eyelid. He sees it too, whatever Nonna is trying to do. I grin down at my espresso, enjoying the sensation of being on the inside of a joke with him. I suspect he sees right through Nonna, but he humors her anyway.

"And your grandmother doesn't mind you being here every day?" Nonna sniffs, looking pleased. I'm pretty sure that she sees feeding Nicolo as a win against Violetta. She likes to win, even if the winning is just feeding Nicolo sweets.

"She knows I am working to repair the fence between our two properties," he admits with a grin. "I don't mention how much good food it takes to mend the fence."

"It's a long fence," Lorenzo interjects heartily, mouth full of pastry.

"To long fences," Nicolo says soberly, raising his espresso cup in a toast. It looks absurdly small in his big hands.

"And old friends," I add spontaneously.

He tips his head in my direction and shoots me a lingering look I don't quite know how to decipher. "To old friends," he agrees. I sip my espresso.

I hear the click of a camera and glance up to find Alex taking photos of us.

"Sorry," she murmurs, concentrating on her phone. "Just taking some footage for the account." She gets up and wanders around the patio, stopping every few feet to snap a photo. I think she's filming some of this too.

Alex launched their TikTok account a few days ago under the name @OlivesandAmore. It's a great name, and what she's posted so far is quality content. She's got a good eye and seems to know how to build a brand. I watched her first post, the video she'd taken of Nonna introducing the farm. She spliced a few takes together and added a cool indie soundtrack. I'm impressed. Since then she's posted a few times each day. Every time I turn around she has her phone in hand and is filming or photographing something. It seems second nature to her.

"Tell Nicolo how many followers we have now on the TikTok," Nonna says, sounding eager.

Alex checks her phone. "Um, a little over two thousand," she says.

"You have two thousand followers already?" I ask, incredulous. "In like three days? That's really fast."

She shrugs. "Yeah, I guess people just really like Italy."

"Of course they do." Nonna sniffs, slicing another generous portion of torta and giving it to Nicolo without asking. "What's not to like?"

We're interrupted by the sound of tires crunching on gravel. A sleek silver Mercedes appears at the mouth of the driveway. Nicolo makes a little choking sound and sets down his espresso cup hard. It clinks in the saucer.

"Porca vacca," he mutters.

It translates to "pig cow" and is a mild swear of consternation. The car grinds to a halt in the courtyard and the driver's side door snaps open. A tall, spare figure emerges. I recognize her instantly and my mouth goes dry.

"What's that strega doing here?" Nonna splutters.

Silently, we all watch the woman advance. Nonna is wearing an expression like she's just bitten into a lemon. She crosses herself and kisses her thumb, muttering something darkly.

Violetta Fiore, grandmother to Nicolo and Nonna Bruna's sworn enemy, strides slowly toward us at a stately pace. Her handsome face is sober, her dark eyes narrowed with displeasure. She is wearing an all-black dress with a high collar, and her silver hair is pulled back in a high, tight bun. She is a striking woman, and she carries herself with a gravity and elegance, but the lines of her face are set harshly, her mouth pressed in a grim line. I'm not sure I've ever seen her smile. She's certainly not smiling now.

"Who's that?" Alex breathes.

"Violetta Fiore," I whisper out of the corner of my mouth. "Nicolo's grandmother and one of the most intimidating women alive."

"Nicolo, what is the meaning of this?" Violetta demands sharply in Italian as she slowly makes her way up the stairs. "I thought you were repairing a wall?"

"We took a break to eat. It's very hard work." Lorenzo waves his fork at Violetta. He seems unbothered by her appearance.

Violetta reaches the patio table and shoots Lorenzo a dismissive look. She repeats her question to Nicolo. Nonna stands. Violetta must have six inches on her at least, maybe more, but Nonna refuses to give an inch.

"Your grandson is enjoying a good homemade treat for once," she says stoutly to Violetta. Oooh, Nonna Bruna is throwing shade. This is getting juicy. Alex and I exchange a glance. Violetta gives Nonna a disdainful look, but then catches sight of me and does a double take. Her nostrils flare in surprise. She stares at me for a long moment.

"You," she says in English. "So you have come back." Her tone is flat and frostbitten with an icy disdain. Then she turns away. Her silence speaks volumes. I haven't seen her in years, but all of a sudden I am fifteen again, flushed and chastened and shivered next to Nicolo in the Fiores' unused stable, wet and half-naked in the cool evening air, facing two feuding nonnas filled with righteous indignation.

"There is a problem with the irrigation system for the citron trees," Violetta tells Nicolo briskly. "The workers have been looking for you. It's urgent. We could lose the crop."

He stands immediately. "Of course. I'll come back with you." Violetta turns and heads back to the car without another word. It's like a little black thundercloud moving away from us as she goes. I sigh with relief.

"I'm sorry." Nicolo meets my eyes, his mouth twisting with a rueful smile of regret. "The torta was delicious." He glances at Lorenzo. "I'll be back to help with the wall as soon as I can," he says.

Lorenzo waves him away with a fork, chewing philosophically. "A man has to do what a man has to do."

We watch as the Mercedes disappears down the long drive.

"Wow." Alex whistles. "She's terrifying."

Nonna snorts. "That woman's heart is as black and ugly as her dress," she scoffs.

Alex and I exchange another glance. "Nonna, why do you hate Violetta so much?" I ask, emboldened to ask the question I've wondered about for years.

Nonna shakes her head. She puts her hands on her hips and frowns. "It was too long ago. I don't remember."

I don't believe her for one minute. Nonna's mind is as sharp as a newly honed paring knife. She just doesn't want to talk about it.

"Can't let a good pastry go to waste." Lorenzo reaches over to Nicolo's plate and spears his uneaten torta.

"Let's get back to work," I tell Nonna and Alex. We are on a roll, and I can't let anything slow me down. With every day that passes, every memory I recall, every recipe we create, the tightness in my chest eases just a little. Even without the help of the magical cookbook, I'm beginning to believe that there's a good chance we will be able to pull this off.

"Eye on the prize, Juliana," I tell myself, then turn to the kitchen to get back to cooking.

Chapter 28

Less than a week later, everything starts to fall apart.

I stay up late one night working, writing the personal reflections for the recipes I created with Nonna. Polenta Carbonara was the clear winner of the dishes we made this afternoon. Rich with unctuous olive oil and three different local cheeses, this is the ultimate comfort food. It's a local specialty, and was Aurora's favorite dish growing up. I write about a humorous incident when I was six, helping Aurora grate the cheese for the dish and accidentally grating part of my thumb and having to start all over.

Then, reluctantly, I post the second-to-last segment for *The Bygone Kitchen*, a recipe for Easy Bread and Butter Refrigerator Pickles. It makes me sad to see Drew with me on the screen. I only have one final post left and then I'm going to have to come clean to our followers about the future of the show. There won't be any more segments to post. I'll have to bid them farewell and go inactive. I don't see any way around it. I can't do the show without Drew. I spend a few minutes replying to dozens of comments from followers. Turns out the peach pandowdy recipe was very popular. Ethel loved it, commenting,

"LIFE'S A PEACH!" with an accompanying string of emojis including five peaches, a flamenco dancer, and three fire symbols. I write back, "Thanks, Ethel!" and add about a dozen heart emojis in a variety of colors. Even Marv liked the recipe. He rated it as "okay." Which is high praise coming from him.

Right before bed, I close my computer and tiptoe to the kitchen for a snack. It's after ten, but the light is still on in Alex's room when I pass by on my way downstairs. At the foot of the stair I start to head to the kitchen but stop, catching the murmur of voices coming from the rarely used front part of the house. Curious, I reverse course and head away from the kitchen and down the long hallway. There are two voices and golden light spilling from the formal dining room. This is strange. The door is open a crack, and I peer in to find Lorenzo and Nonna sitting at the long, heavy dining table, a thick black ledger and papers strewn around the tabletop and two empty espresso cups in front of them.

Lorenzo leans forward, his thick white eyebrows pinched together in concern. "Bruna, we cannot go on," he says in Italian.

"It's been bad before," Nonna replies with a dismissive wave of her hand. "We'll figure something out. We always do." She sounds so weary. "Maybe there is something else we can sell? Anything of value left in the stables?"

Lorenzo shakes his head. "No. Nothing. We've sold everything we do not absolutely need."

I shrink back in the shadows in the darkened hallway with a gasp. I know I shouldn't eavesdrop, but the concern tightening their voices makes the hair on the back of my neck prickle in alarm. Something is very wrong. I have a feeling this is what they've been hiding from me. And now here's my chance to find out what is really happening. I lean in a little to catch their conversation, concentrating hard to follow their rapid Italian.

"So we manage to pay this bill," Lorenzo is saying. "What then? There is always another bill, another tax, and the repairs on this place should have been done years ago. We're slowly letting it fall down around our heads waiting for something that may never come." He sounds discouraged. I've never heard him sound defeated about anything in my life. It worries me.

"Something will work out," Nonna tells him, placing her sturdy little hand over his big, work-worn one. "She could still decide to stay."

My ears perk up. Who are they talking about?

Lorenzo shakes his head. "For what? What then? She stays but still there is no money to keep this place running. What do we have to offer her? There are so few jobs here for young people like Juliana."

I freeze. They're talking about me.

Lorenzo is still speaking. "We cannot saddle her with this place. It would be like giving her a problem to solve and no way to solve it. Bruna, together you and I have managed and struggled for so many years, but I think we need to be realistic. I think we need to consider selling."

I cover my mouth with my hand, stifling a gasp. They're thinking of selling the farm?

"Vicenzo told me last week they're selling their farm to one of the big olive oil companies from the south," Lorenzo says, his voice heavy. "The price is fair, and the trees will be cared for, not cut down like some of those foreign investment buyers are doing, making room for hotels and holiday houses."

"Never." Nonna spits out the word, her voice rising as she speaks in rapid-fire Italian. I struggle to keep up with her pace. "You will have to pry this place from my cold, dead hands. What are you saying, you cretino? This is our home, our family legacy. I will never stop fighting for it. You want one of those big farming companies to buy our farm? They may not cut down the trees, but they'll cut out the heart of this home, this family. This is our land, our history. If we don't stand for it, it will be lost like so many others. It's happening all over Italy, even here around the lake. You know as well as I do. We cannot let it happen to us. We have to save it, not just for our family, but for our community, our legacy, for the future. It's bigger than just us."

Lorenzo spreads his hands. "I agree, but our plan is not going to work. We waited years for Juliana to come home, hoping that if she did she would see a future here, that those happy summers would be enough to draw her back, but I don't see that happening. She wants to save this show of hers, and she has a cookbook to write. She has a different life, Bruna, one that is not here."

Nonna nods, toying with the handle of her espresso cup. She frowns, making a deep furrow between her brows. "You may be right," she says finally. "But if not Juliana, then who? Who else is there? You and I have given our lives for this place, for this family and its legacy. But I'm old now. You too, even if you want to ignore your creaking knees."

Lorenzo looks at her with weary resignation. "Time is not on our side, Bruna," he says gently. "We can keep it going for a few more years, two or three if we're lucky, but after that . . ." He spreads his hands helplessly. "There is no one else. We must face the fact that without Juliana, this farm and its legacy will end."

They go on to talk about the particulars of paying the upcoming tax and bills, shuffling papers and stacks of euros around the table, trying to make their meager savings stretch further than humanly possible. I slowly back away, feeling heartsick. In the dark warmth of the kitchen I pour myself a glass of water and drink it standing at the sink, looking out at the olive trees, silent and silver in the moonlight. My hands are trembling so much I have trouble bringing the glass to my lips. My mind is racing and I'm stunned by what I've just heard. It's true. What Nicolo told me is true. They've been waiting for me to come back, hoping I'll stay and save the farm. The weight of their hopes and expectations feels suffocating. I didn't come back to stay. I came back to get what I needed and go on with my life's plan.

"This is only for the summer," I murmur aloud. "It has always only been for the summer."

It breaks my heart to hear the resignation in Nonna's voice, her weariness. The realization that we might lose the farm hits me like a punch in the gut. It has been in our family for generations. Who are we without it? Who am I?

Standing at the sink in the darkness that still smells like the cheesy polenta I made for dinner, I realize for the first time just how much this place truly means to me. It has always been the center of my universe. To think of losing it feels like losing gravity itself. I would spin out into space, lost and unmoored. It is unthinkable.

Yet what is the alternative? I stay and try to save the farm? The thought curdles my stomach with anxiety. What do I know about olive farming or keeping up a property that is hundreds of years old? Next to nothing. I have no savings, no income, very little skill outside of the kitchen, and limited Italian. I'm not the right one to do this. I can't do this. I will almost certainly fail, and the loss of our homeland and generations of our history will rest firmly on my shoulders.

But if not me, then who? With sudden cold clarity I see the choice before me. If I stay and try to rescue the farm from financial ruin, I give up all hope of saving my show and resign myself to almost certain failure. If I go back to Seattle and try to save the show with Drew, I ensure we will lose our land and home, and bid farewell to the heart and legacy of our family. It feels like there is no way to win. How can I possibly choose?

Chapter 29

"*Juliana, where is* your head? In the clouds?" Nonna thumps the prep table in exasperation. She looks remarkably alert after her late-night meeting with Lorenzo. I do not. I feel like I'm walking around with my head wrapped in cotton wool. Everything is fuzzy. I tossed and turned for hours last night, thoughts going round and round in a fretful, helpless loop.

"Sorry!" I snap to attention to find that I can't remember how much salt I've added to the brioche dough. Guiltily, I pinch a piece of the dough off and taste it, then add a bit more salt before mixing in the softened butter. This morning I'm a mess. I'm spacey and forgetful and distracted. I keep thinking of the conversation last night. There's a hard knot of worry clenched in the pit of my stomach that will not ease.

We are attempting to make the two most iconic Northern Italian pastries this morning, brioche and cornetto. They are the cornerstone of Italian breakfasts, along with a caffellatte. Espresso is usually reserved for later in the day, drunk black and accompanied by a glass of water to cleanse the palate. Creamy, sweet caffellattes are just for the morning, the perfect accompaniment to a fresh pastry. Italians love a sweet breakfast.

I am supposed to be mixing up the brioche dough, but I'm having trouble concentrating on it. It should be easy. Aurora loved making these for breakfast, and she and I have helped Nonna a dozen times or more, but I'm forgetting everything today. I try to focus on the dough. It will rest for an hour or so and then we'll form the brioche into little bun shapes with a knob of dough on top. The buns will be filled with apricot jam in a nod to Aurora. It's her favorite flavor of jam. There are few better ways to start a day in Italy than with a caffellatte and a freshly baked round of this sweet, buttery pastry bread.

As soon as the brioche dough is resting, Nonna mixes up a batch of fresh, cold lemonade and pours it into small glass jars.

"Take this to the men while we wait for the dough to be ready to shape," she urges me, handing me the jars. "They're working on rebuilding the wall today, a hard job. They need a little refreshment."

There doesn't seem to be any room to demur, so I slip on my sandals, slick on some tinted rose-scented lip balm, and set off to find the men. I'm wearing a red dotted sundress, and I realize after I'm already out the door that I forgot to take off my apron. Oh well.

It's midmorning but promises to be a hot day. Already, the air is filled with the buzzing of bees, and the sun feels strong on the top of my head. By the time I reach the crest of the hill, I've sweated through the underarms of my sundress.

Nicolo is alone when I find him at the far end of the property, rebuilding a partly collapsed section of the ancient drystone wall that separates our land from that of the Fiores. Lorenzo and his little truck are nowhere to be seen.

"Ciao, Juliana." Nicolo waves to me as I approach, wiping sweat from his brow with one gloved hand. He's shirtless, which takes me by surprise, dressed only in work pants and heavy boots. He's tanned a beautiful olive golden color, slick with sweat, with broad shoulders and a compact, muscular frame. I look away from the faint V of dark hair that trails down his chest toward his navel, feeling embarrassed by how drawn to him I am. I lick my lips and stare over his left shoulder as I hand him a lemonade.

"Nonna sent this for you," I tell the space over the top of his shoulder. "Where's Zio Lorenzo?"

"Gone into town. He'll be back soon." Nicolo strips off his gloves. "Grazie mille."

He gulps the cold lemonade and makes a low sound of satisfaction that catches me off guard. I've heard that sound from him before, and it had nothing to do with a fizzy drink. I feel my cheeks flush.

"This is delicious." He holds up the glass bottle gratefully, then reaches down and picks up his shirt. To my equal parts dismay and relief, he slides it on and buttons it smoothly. The hair on his forearms is lightly dusted with a fine layer of soil.

"How's the wall coming along?" I ask, eyeing the progress. They are painstakingly restoring the crumbled section, rebuilding it with the age-old traditional method that uses small stones and dirt instead of mortar, hence the term "drystone wall." These types of walls dot the hills and fields of Italy, an integral part of the landscape.

"Slow, but we are getting there. This kind of repair cannot be rushed. It takes the time it takes." Nicolo slips his gloves on again and surveys the wall. They've built the smaller inner wall that stabilizes the entire structure and are starting to build the outer wall. I wander over to the piles of repurposed materials they've gathered and sorted from the collapsed sections—dirt, small stones, and a big pile of large stones dotted with lichen. Nothing is wasted in this process.

"You were right," I tell Nicolo abruptly, suddenly needing to share the weight of the information I've been carrying all morning. "When you said they were waiting for me to come back." I briefly tell him what I overheard last night.

He listens carefully. "I'm not surprised," he says with a sigh. "It's impressive that they've managed to keep it running this long. They're strong and stubborn—their entire generation is." He leans down and sifts a few pebbles from the dirt at his feet, tossing them on the tall pile of similarly sized pebbles. "So are you going to stay?"

I'm already shaking my head before he's done asking the blunt question.

"I'm only here for the summer," I tell him, feeling a little defensive. "That was always the plan. I can't stay. I'm trying to save my show, and if I stay, I give up on that dream and five years of work. Besides, I'm not like you. I don't know anything about olive farming." I gently stub the toe of my sandal into the mound of pebbles, and a handful fall in a little avalanche. Guiltily, I scoop them up again. "Violetta and Alberto trained you to run your family's business. I wasn't raised for that. I think the plan was that my dad would take over someday, but then . . ." I lift my hands helplessly. When he died, that plan obviously ended too. The only problem was that apparently the plan B, me, had been whisked away by Lisa and never returned.

Nicolo laughs but it's humorless, dry as dust. "They may have trained me to run the farm," he concedes, "but Nonna V. won't let me change anything. She wants my help, but only on her terms. She maintains full control. She won't listen to a word I say, and it's slowly choking the business to death."

"That sounds really frustrating," I empathize, waiting to see if he wants to share more.

"Tremendously," he agrees with a sigh. He stands back and surveys the pile of large stones, then chooses a big flattened one and hefts it aloft, muscles straining with the effort. "I left a high-powered career I liked to come home and be treated like an overgrown child," he tells me, carefully fitting the stone into a space in the wall with a grunt. "And the worst part is, the farm is in trouble and it doesn't need to be. It's big enough that if it were properly managed, it could be profitable. But she won't mess with tradition or allow anything new." He eyes the stone he just set, nudging it more firmly into place. He looks thoroughly exasperated.

"Well, my family wants me to take over a job I don't want and am not qualified for," I chime in glumly. I come to stand beside him, surveying the foundations of the wall. I helped Lorenzo rebuild a small portion of one of these walls when I was younger. I still remember the painstaking process. I eye an empty space, trying to picture what sort of stone it needs to fill it.

"I have a feeling you could do anything you put your mind to," Nicolo counters with a half smile. "Remember the tree house we built that first summer we met?"

I squint, trying to remember.

"You got the idea from an old American movie," he prompts.

"*Swiss Family Robinson*," I say in surprise. I'd forgotten all about that.

"You were tireless, scouring the neighborhood for scrap wood and pulling rusty nails out and pounding them straight. By the end of summer you'd managed to collect enough for us to build a tree house."

"Which was about four feet long by four feet wide if I remember right," I say with a laugh. "We could barely both fit inside once it was all built. I'd forgotten about that." I choose a long, flat stone from the pile and wedge it carefully between two larger stones in the wall. It's a good fit, I note with satisfaction.

"You've always been good at that, making something out of very little," Nicolo responds, and there's a fondness and admiration in his gaze that surprises me. He sees something in me I forgot was even there.

"You were the one who worked tirelessly putting it together," I remind him. "By the time we were done, I think you had smashed both thumbs trying to hammer in those old bent nails, but you didn't give up. You were tenacious."

He chuckles. "I did it for you," he confesses, crossing his arms and shaking his head. "I would have done anything for you, Juliana Costa."

I clear my throat and glance down, feeling self-conscious. "I wish I had that kind of confidence now," I confess. "If only succeeding at life were as easy as building a tree house."

Nicolo raises an eyebrow. "Building that tree house wasn't easy," he says, looking surprised. "I had two smashed black thumbnails by the time we were finished. Life isn't easy, now or then. You have to pick the hard that means the most to you. Pick the right hard thing."

I consider his words for a moment. "Is this your right hard thing?" I gesture to the Fiores' land. "Even with the challenges?"

Nicolo nods thoughtfully. "I think so. My right hard thing is trying to save my family's olive farm. Is it difficult? Almost always. Is it worth it?" He shrugs. "Time will tell. But I know it is worth the risk. I have to try." He walks over to the pile of stones and picks up a medium-sized dark gray rock with a white vein running through it, then carefully nestles it between two other stones in the wall. It's a perfect fit.

"What is your right hard thing, Jules?" Nicolo asks, standing back from the wall and watching me, his eyes alight with curiosity.

I hesitate, thinking back on my string of failures. Right out of high school I'd applied for and gotten into a culinary school in Seattle only to drop out after two quarters. I just couldn't seem to muster any joy for cooking that soon after my dad's death. Then there had been a handful of waitressing jobs. I'd done okay at those, but had finally settled on Trader Joe's for the better hours. I felt like a horse that had stumbled at the first turn and somehow never managed to find her feet again. The only thing I had was my show. That was the only thing I'd managed to build and keep going. I love it, and I'm proud of it. There is very little else in my life I feel proud of.

"My show," I tell him at last. "That's my right hard thing. It's the only thing I've managed to succeed at, the only thing that's mine, but recently I've . . . had some setbacks." I blow out a breath, trying not to think of Drew off on location with Desiree Reyes, of the last remaining segment waiting for me to post it, and then what? "Right now there's a slim chance I can keep it going if I can finish my cookbook in time and it sells well. That's why I'm here. I'm trying to save the show and preserve what I've worked so hard for."

Nicolo looks at me searchingly, then nods. I'm not sure why, but it feels like he's taken a step back, even though he hasn't moved a muscle. "I'm sure you'll succeed, Jules," he says, his voice a little flat. "You can do anything you set your mind to." Then he claps his hands briskly, a puff of dust rising from his gloves. "Thank you for the drink, but I'd better get back to work."

Clearly, I've been dismissed. I get the sneaking feeling I've disappointed him in some way. I brush dust and crumbles of lichen from my apron, leave the other jar of lemonade for Lorenzo, and start toward the farmhouse. When I glance behind me, Nicolo is shirtless once again, muscles straining as he hauls a large rock into place. I walk back to the house feeling vaguely disquieted. This is what I want, right? I am accomplishing the thing I came to do. One by one I'm getting the recipes I need. Everything is going in the right direction. I should be jubilant. So why do I suddenly wonder if I'm making a mistake?

Chapter 30

"I think I got some good shots," Alex steps back from an artfully arranged plate of freshly baked brioche and cornetto. She flips through the photographs she's just taken on her phone, scrutinizing them critically, and then nods. "These are good enough to use."

She's been with Nonna and me since I got back from delivering lemonade and has been filming and photographing us filling the brioche with apricot jam and shaping the cornetto into the familiar croissant shape. Cornettos are the Italian cousin of the French croissant. Not as buttery and flaky as a croissant due to the use of eggs in the dough, they are an iconic Italian pastry and utterly delicious. While brioche are usually eaten only for breakfast in Northern Italy, cornetto are considered appropriate for anytime. Sometimes they are filled with custard or chocolate. The jam-filled ones are my favorite.

"What's for lunch?" Alex asks, her stomach making a loud gurgling noise. It's early afternoon and I realize we've been busy and worked through lunch.

"What about that pizza recipe the cookbook showed you?" I pull the cookbook from the drawer and hand it to Alex. There is no use in me opening it. I know what I'll see. I've opened the book a dozen times over the past days, hoping that I might finally see a recipe now that I am recalling memories and recipes from my past. Apparently not. It's still showing me just a blank page. Alex opens the cookbook.

"It's still the vegetarian pizza recipe," she announces.

Nonna peers over her shoulder at the recipe. "That's an easy one to make," she says. "We have all the ingredients." She taps the list of ingredients on the page. When her finger touches the page the words change. For a brief instant I see an unfamiliar list of ingredients where the pizza toppings just were. Olive oil. Sugar. Orange blossom extract. Nonna pulls her hand back sharply and the words instantly disappear, replaced by the vegetarian pizza recipe once more. I glance at her. She is carefully not looking at me. I don't say anything about what I saw. She is so obviously hiding something about that recipe. I'm burning with curiosity.

"Let's make this pizza for lunch." I scan the pizza recipe, careful not to touch the book.

Together we tackle the recipe. Nonna expertly rolls out the pizza dough, and Alex chops the vegetables. She's clumsy and admits that she doesn't know anything about cooking. "I don't think I've ever chopped vegetables before," she says shyly. I show her how to hold the knife, and Nonna lets her sprinkle the toppings on the pizza. Alex pauses now and then to shoot video footage and take photos for TikTok. She films Nonna and me teasing each other, and Nonna's strong, gnarled hands rolling out the pizza dough, capturing the feeling of warmth and productivity in the kitchen. I've never seen Alex look so happy. I put music on my phone, some Lady Gaga, whom Alex bashfully admits she likes. Nonna is scandalized by the music until I tell her Lady Gaga is Italian, which seems to mollify her.

When it comes out of the oven, we carry the pizza outside to the patio. It smells heavenly, the yeasty fresh crust brushed with olive oil and garlic and covered in basil, mushrooms, artichokes, and fresh mozzarella. We sit at the shady end of the table, glasses of cold lemonade sweating in front of us. The afternoon sun is fierce. The men are still working on the wall. Nonna had Alex deliver sandwiches to them while the pizza was baking. Now it's the height of the afternoon heat, and all around us the air is filled with the sound of bees drunkenly buzzing in the fragrant lavender planted around the perimeter of the low patio wall. There is no breeze and everything is still and drowsy.

"This smells amazing," Alex comments, leaning forward to grab a slice. "I've never had homemade pizza before."

For a few moments, the only sound is the humming of the bees and our contented chewing. After a little while, I boldly broach the question that's been on my mind since the first time I saw Nonna touch the recipe book.

"Nonna, what is Orange Blossom Cake?"

She doesn't answer for a long moment. She darts a look at me, then sighs and sets down her pizza. "A recipe that leads only to misery."

"What do you mean?" She's been evasive before, but this time I press the issue.

"I mean the recipe doesn't work," she says shortly.

"What's it supposed to do?" Alex takes another slice of pizza and chews, watching Nonna curiously.

For a moment Nonna balks, then she looks from me to Alex and sighs heavily. "Every recipe in this book has the potential to help someone in need. The recipes work in many different ways, depending on the individual's circumstances," she explains, "but the recipe for Orange Blossom Cake is special. The person who takes the first bite of the cake will see a vision of the sweetest moment of happiness that awaits them in life."

"Whoa, what?" Alex says, wide-eyed. We exchange a skeptical look.

"They see a vision of the happiest moment of their lives?" I clarify. It seems so fantastical.

Nonna nods. "The cookbook has offered this recipe to dozens of people over the years, and each time the vision they see comes true. It is a powerful thing, to catch a glimpse of your future, of the happiness that awaits you."

For once Alex isn't on her phone. She's listening intently, a slice of pizza forgotten in her hand, looking rapt but a little doubtful. I feel the same way, but the idea of a cake that shows you the happiest moment of your future is tantalizing. What could it reveal? Who you will love and possibly marry? If you'll have children? Or something else entirely. A major accomplishment in your career? A moment of pure bliss on a dream vacation? The possibilities are endless. If you could see the happiest moment of your life, wouldn't you want to?

"Did you ever make the recipe?" I ask, intrigued. "What did you see?"

Nonna sits back. "I saw nothing," she says, her mouth twisting as though she's bitten into something bitter. "I did not make the cake. You cannot make the cake with half a recipe."

"What happened to the other half?" I sense that we're getting close to the heart of the mystery.

"The other half is in the possession of Violetta Fiore," Nonna says grimly.

My jaw drops open. "Nicolo's grandmother? She has the other half of the recipe? Why?"

Nonna scowls. "She was once my best friend," she says, her lips thinning with contempt, "but then she betrayed our promise to each other and our friendship."

"What did she do?" I hold my breath. This feels like two secrets in one—the mystery of the torn cake recipe and the reason for

Violetta and Nonna's decades-long feud. I am eager to know the answer to both.

"She destroyed my life and my chance at happiness. I have never forgiven her." Nonna slaps her hands on the table and says the words with such quiet ferocity that it sends a shiver up my spine. Alex and I exchange a dumbfounded look. What did Violetta do that betrayed Nonna and destroyed her life? But when I ask her about it, Nonna refuses to say more.

"It's time to get back to work, girls," she says, getting to her feet with a little groan. She's so short that standing up she's only a little taller than I am sitting down. "We have more baking to do. This afternoon we are tackling desserts, are we not?" Frowning, she stumps off wordlessly down the stairs toward the house.

Across the table, Alex gazes at me, wide-eyed. "Do you think it's true?" she asks. "Could a cake actually show you the happiest moment of your life?"

I shrug. "I don't know what's possible anymore," I tell her honestly, "but I guess it doesn't matter if there's only half a recipe. We'll never know if it's true or not."

I think of Nicolo then, wondering if he knows anything about the recipe for Orange Blossom Cake. Is it possible Violetta still has the other half?

When I glance over, Alex is already on her phone again, tapping away. "I just want to finish this post," she murmurs. I clear away the pizza mess from the table, stacking the plates and gathering the glasses, warm now and sticky with lemonade. Alex finally pushes her chair back. "There. Done."

"What did you post?" I ask, my hands full of our dishes.

"Us." She holds out her phone to show me. It's a thirty-second montage of us making the pizza, laughing and working in fast forward, then a slow shot of our hands all reaching for the freshly baked slices. She's set it to a poignant soundtrack. The montage captures the sense of family and togetherness, but there's a sense of the fleetingness of time too. She really has a knack for this. She's got good instincts artistically and she's also good at capturing the emotion of a moment. I note that the @OlivesandAmore account already has almost five thousand followers. That's very fast growth.

"You're really talented at this," I tell her honestly, handing her the phone back.

Alex blushes and shrugs off the compliment. "People just like Italy, I guess. It probably wouldn't matter who was holding the camera."

I shake my head. "That's not true. Anyone can take a picture or shoot a video, but you're showing viewers Italy in a way that's really engaging. You're making it beautiful but also meaningful. It feels like real life."

Alex looks embarrassed. "Thanks." She tucks the phone in her pocket and hesitates for a moment. "And thanks for making the pizza," she says finally. "No one's ever made a recipe just for me."

"Oh yeah?" I sense she wants to say more. Lisa isn't really much of a cook, or much of an eater for that matter.

"It was . . . nice," she says. "To do it together." She lingers for a moment.

"You're welcome," I tell her. "We can make pizza together anytime."

I recall what Nonna said about pizza, that it helps bring people together. The pizza did exactly that tonight. Somehow it has bridged a little more of the gap between us.

Alex gives me a quick, ironic little smile. "Anytime until the end of summer, though, right?" she says. She sounds a little wistful.

"Right, until the end of summer," I tell her. "So let's make the most of it."

Alex shoots me a cryptic look, then grabs her backpack and a stack of sticky glasses and goes down the steps and into the house. I watch her go, feeling somehow like I failed to answer a question I didn't know she was asking. I think I've disappointed her, but I'm not quite sure how.

Turning my attention away from the puzzle of teenagers, I clear the rest of the table and wash the dishes. Hands in a sink of warm, soapy water, I think about what Nonna told us, about the supposed magic of the Orange Blossom Cake recipe. What if it really were true? If I took a bite of that cake, what would I see?

I close my eyes and try to picture the happiest day of my life. Maybe my wedding day—walking down the aisle in a tea-length white dress with a bouquet of poppies to meet a hazy (but definitely handsome) man? Or getting Keith to reconsider and finally give us a limited-run series on Netflix?

Unbidden, my mind flashes to an image—me tucked up in bed in a whitewashed room on a rainy Saturday morning, cuddling under a fluffy duvet with someone, warm and safe in our little pocket of comfort. The man beside me in bed is shirtless, with golden olive skin and warm, dark eyes. He reaches for me with a languid half smile of amusement and I see that it's Nicolo. I jump back, eyes flying open, splashing soapy water onto the floor and almost dropping a wet plate. I'm blushing furiously.

"Get yourself together, Juliana," I scold myself. "Stop it."

I fan myself, opening the window above the sink. Is it hot in here? Great, just great. I'm going to have to look at him over the lunch table tomorrow and try not to think about him nibbling my earlobe like a plump, ripe apricot.

I dry my hands and pull out my phone, checking my texts in an attempt to distract myself and simmer down. There's a text from Aurora with a picture of Doris standing placidly in the middle of their kitchen, chewing on what looks like a hand-spun linen dish towel.

> How's the Italian hottie? Has he seen
> your cute lace bra yet?

I drop my phone back in my pocket and focus on the dishes, vigorously scrubbing the melted cheese from the plates. I came to Italy with very clear goals. I need to refocus on those. I can't afford any more distractions, even if those distractions have adorable dimples and dark curls and smell like sun-ripened olives and good coffee. I cannot afford to forget why I came back to Italy in the first place. Firmly putting all the thoughts of Nicolo and the Orange Blossom Cake out of my mind, I get back to work.

Chapter 31

The next few weeks pass in enjoyable productivity. Each day after a light breakfast of pastries and caffellatte, Nonna and I brainstorm the day's recipes, then shop for and make one to three dishes, depending on their complexity. We break for a leisurely lunch or dinner to enjoy the fruits of our labors. In the evenings, I stay in my room writing up the recipes and the personal reflections to go with each one. It is a lovely, predictable, gentle pace of life. Until Nonna goes and throws a wrench into the plan.

It starts one morning when I find Nonna and Lorenzo drinking espressos on the patio, heads together, deep in conversation. They look like they're plotting something. Alex is nowhere to be seen. Probably still sleeping. Lorenzo greets me heartily and Nonna rises and kisses me on both cheeks, announcing, "Buongiorno, Juliana. I hope you are ready for a challenge today."

"A challenge?" I raise an eyebrow. I need a lot of things but a challenge is not one of them. I've got enough of those.

Nonna nods firmly. "To help you strengthen your courage and face your fears." She sips her espresso and eyes me in a satisfied way.

"What do you have in mind?" I ask warily, sinking into a chair across from her. I have a bad feeling about this. There is already a caffellatte waiting for me along with a custard-filled cornetto. I take a hesitant sip of the coffee.

"You remember the Luce del Sole festival in Lazise?" Nonna asks casually. "Tony used to take you when you were little. It is a festival to celebrate the summertime."

The light of the sun festival. I close my eyes briefly, memories flooding back. Me riding on Dad's shoulders as he wove his way through crowds of Italians eating and drinking local delicacies on the beautiful shores of Lazise, a tiny, historic walled city on the lake just south of Bardolino. I remember contentedly sitting in the hot sun next to Dad as he hummed along to a local band. We'd share a plate of misto, a mixture of battered and fried pieces of lake fish, served with polenta. Afterward Dad would sip a glass of light red wine from Bardolino, and I would devour a cup of granita made with local peaches, deliciously icy and cold on a hot summer day. But most of all I remember how happy I felt at the festival, everyone crowded together, celebrating summer, celebrating the joy of being alive in such a beautiful place.

"I loved that festival," I murmur.

Nonna nods, looking pleased. "You did. Your father loved it too. Do you remember the cooking contest they have every year as part of the festival, to determine the best local dish?"

"Didn't you win that one year?" I interject.

"Two years in a row," Nonna says airily. "But now I have retired from contests. I am too old. It is time for another Costa to carry on the tradition."

I have a sudden suspicion I know where this is going.

"It is a highly sought-after competition, with only a few dozen spots. Just this morning someone had to drop out because of a family emergency. She offered her spot to me," Nonna says. "But since I am retired"—she shrugs nonchalantly—"I told told them you would do it."

I almost spew a mouthful of caffellatte across the table. "You want me to compete in the cooking contest?" I gasp. "I can't go up against all the local Italian grandmas. They're incredible cooks. I'll get creamed!"

Nonna shrugs, unconcerned. "It will be good for you. Maybe you need a little push, hmm? Remember, a life free of fear? You can make the recipe you're most proud of, and see what happens. Who knows, maybe you will win?"

I highly doubt that. "I don't have time to enter a contest!" I argue, feeling panicked at the thought of trying to come up with a winning dish. "I've got enough on my plate already."

"You can't back out now," Nonna argues calmly. "I already gave them your name. Everyone knows about your Internet cooking show. If you turn down the invitation, you'll bring shame upon our family."

Oooh, she's sneaky, playing the "shame the family" card. I glare at her. Nonna sips her espresso placidly. She missed a career as a high-stakes negotiator somewhere along the line. She could have excelled at hostage negotiations. I hesitate, feeling neatly trapped. I think of Aurora telling me I needed to shake up my life. Right now my life feels like a soda bottle that's been dropped down several flights of stairs. I certainly don't need anything else to shake it up.

"Maybe the competition will give you good ideas," Lorenzo interjects. "Lots of cooks, lots of local food." He gives me a sympathetic look.

I sigh. He's got a point. So does Nonna. I am trying to be courageous, to embrace opportunities and not close myself off because I'm afraid. And I have so many happy memories at that festival with my dad. Maybe I'll get some good inspiration. I still need more recipes for the cookbook. I waver for a moment. Maybe this is a good opportunity, even if it seems intimidating. Am I brave enough to do something so far outside my comfort zone?

"Okay," I agree, deciding to be bold. "I have a few recipes I was already planning to make in the next couple of days anyway. I guess I can just make one of them for the contest but"—I hold up a finger warningly—"I am not responsible if I bring shame upon the family by coming in last place."

Nonna nods in satisfaction. "Good. And you will not bring shame on us. I have faith in you."

"When is the festival?" I ask, nibbling the corner of my cornetto. "How long do I have to prepare?"

"You'd better get started," Nonna advises me. "The contest is in two days."

Chapter 32

"Follow Lorenzo so you are not crushed in the crowd," Nonna calls back over her shoulder to Alex and me as we squeeze down another narrow street in the old town center of Lazise early in the afternoon on the day of the festival. "He is making a path for us."

Together with Nonna, Alex, and Lorenzo, I weave my way through the narrow, winding streets. The tiny walled town is packed with revelers celebrating the Luce del Sole festival. It seems as though everyone around Lake Garda has turned up today. Lorenzo had to park the Fiat Panda ten blocks away, and now we are making our way to the cooking contest pavilion that's been erected in a square near the lakefront.

"Are you okay?" Alex asks, eyeing me as I struggle to keep hold of a large pot of Strangolapreti, a local gnocchi-like dumpling dish that is one of Nonna's specialties. Yesterday she taught me how to make her specific recipe, which she swears is the best in Italy. Today I made the recipe again on my own to comply with the competition rules.

"So far so good." I nod and grip the pot more tightly. Created by blending stale breadcrumbs, spinach, and Grana Padano cheese, these oddly yummy little dumplings are boiled in salted water and then coated in a browned butter and crispy sage sauce. The smell coming from the pot is mouthwatering. No wonder the name translates roughly to "priest-choker," an allusion to a dish so tasty the local clergy would indulge in it until they choked.

I'm feeling tentatively optimistic about my entry. It's the one pasta dish Dad made every year on his birthday without fail. Nonna told me it was what he requested every year for his birthday dinner when he was growing up. After he moved to the US and had us, he still tried to recreate it on that special day. I think he'd be proud of my efforts today.

Nicolo is supposed to meet us here, but there is no sign of him yet. I find I'm keeping an eye out for him. *Stop it!* I scold myself silently as I follow Lorenzo, who is shouldering his beefy way through the crowd. I concentrate on not dropping my entry for the contest as we squeeze through narrow passageways. So what if Nicolo is hot? A hot Italian neighbor with great hair who used to be a boy I loved fiercely. So what if he is funny and intelligent and kind? So what if he makes my heart stutter in my chest? It doesn't mean anything. I'm not staying in Italy past the summer. There could never be anything between us. It's a lost cause with an old flame. I make myself focus on something else, but I keep craning my neck looking for that familiar broad-shouldered figure.

"Che palle, so crowded," Nonna complains, coming to a stop when a group of young men jostle in front of her rudely. I halt just before running into her, clasping the pot and its precious contents to my chest. If I spill, I'll have nothing to enter into the contest.

"Hey, idioti!" Lorenzo turns and shouts when he sees the boys blocking Nonna's way. He lays into them, gesturing angrily, and after a moment of being scolded by a large, angry white-haired man bristling with righteous indignation, the young men meekly plaster themselves against a wall of the narrow street and let us pass. Lorenzo sweeps his arm in an invitation for Nonna, and she moves through the open space he's made, clutching her purse to her chest, head held high. The more I see them together, the more I suspect that I am right about Lorenzo's feelings for Nonna. I just don't have any idea if she's aware of them, and she doesn't seem to reciprocate them as far as I can tell. The dynamics of their relationship are a mystery to me. We parade down the narrow cobblestone street, Lorenzo clearing the way and the rest of us following.

"Buongiorno," a familiar voice says close to my ear. I jump, shriek, and clutch the pot. It's Nicolo. He chuckles and steadies me with a hand on my elbow.

"I didn't meet to startle you," he tells me, his dark eyes merry. He greets everyone in our group and falls into step next to me, casually using his body to block anyone who would get too close to me.

"Are you ready for the contest?" Nicolo asks, matching my stride. Today he's wearing pale beige slim-cut trousers, a light blue button-down shirt rolled up to his elbows and unbuttoned one button lower than American men dare to wear, and he's got a lightweight navy blazer thrown over one shoulder. His shoes are a gorgeous caramel leather loafer, pointy toed. Combined with gold sunglasses, he looks like a movie star or some sort of minor Italian royalty. I'd forgotten how gorgeous Italian men can be when they're dressed to go out. On an American, the outfit would look almost ridiculous, but Nicolo pulls it off with an effortless confidence, comfortable in his own skin. It's quite a change from the earnest young man with a hint of a mustache who gave me my first awkward kiss under the olive trees. Now he's grown fully into a very attractive, very confident man. I glance at Nicolo and stumble on an uneven cobblestone in my impractical but super cute white wedge sandals. Immediately, Nicolo is there, one strong hand clasped firmly around my upper arm, the other circling my waist. He pulls me gently upright.

"Careful," he says. "Are you okay?"

I nod. "Thanks." My cheeks flame. I'm more unsteady with his arm around me than on my own.

"May I?" He offers to take the pot, but I decline. I want to carry the heavy warmth of it myself. I glance down and concentrate on navigating the cobblestones before me. I need to pay more attention to the path and less to the man beside me, no matter how dashing he looks today.

We pass a band playing traditional music, and rows and rows of booths selling local wares. Pizza and focaccia, local honey, sausages and cheeses, a cart with gelato, handmade soaps and lotions, embroidered tea towels. The offerings seem endless. Every street is crowded with people—tourists and locals alike—jostling and laughing and yelling. It's happy chaos.

Finally, we reach the small plaza tucked away to one side of the town, overlooking the lakefront. There is a line of entrants for the cooking contest, which starts at two p.m. I check my phone. Ten minutes to spare. Nicolo suggests he take Alex to get a scoop of gelato while I check in, promising to return for me in a few minutes. Lorenzo opts to go with them. Nonna stays with me.

After I check in, I take my numbered ticket and we wander around the tables holding the other contest entries. I jot down a few ideas surreptitiously as Nonna offers a critical commentary on the various dishes on display. She would have made a great judge on one of those TV cooking shows. She's both hilarious and difficult to please.

There are some delicious local specialties from polenta with lake pike to a fragrant savory stew made with ham, potatoes, and beans. I write down the names of any dishes that I recognize, hoping that I will remember some personal connection or anecdote about some of them if I have a moment to sit and think. Nicolo and Alex reappear with gelato and we leave the contest area. The winner will be announced this evening before the free concert. Until that time we can wander around and enjoy the festival. Lorenzo peels off with Nonna to see a friend of his, a truffle hunter from the mountains, which leaves Nicolo, Alex, and me to amuse ourselves until the contest winner is announced. Sticking together, we wander down the lakefront until I spy a booth selling peach granitas.

"Oooh." I make a beeline for the booth. "Alex, you have to try this. It was my favorite thing to eat at the festival when I was younger." I get in line, excited to have her try the delicious cold treat. Even though she's just finished her gelato, Alex gamely joins me. Nicolo is right behind us. I nudge Alex excitedly. "Hey, look who's in the booth." It's the cute dark-eyed boy from the market a few weeks ago. He's taking orders and payments and I can tell he's noticed Alex. He keeps darting glances at her while he's serving other customers. It's adorable.

Alex rolls her eyes at me, but her cheeks turn a very pretty shade of pink. I think she's pleased. It's a sweet little burst of color amid her monochromatic outfit of black ripped jeans, black punk T-shirt, and thick black Doc Martens. How is she not melting in this heat?

When it's our turn, I start to translate the few menu items for her, but she cuts me off with an "I've got it, thanks." A minute later she gives her order in surprisingly passable Italian. The young man blushes bright red. I gaze at her in amazement. "When did you learn Italian? You've been holding out on us."

She shrugs, looking embarrassed. "I'm learning through one of those online apps. You mentioned it, and I thought it would be cool."

So that's what she's been doing on her phone mumbling to herself all the time! All the pieces finally click into place. I thought she was mouthing song lyrics or talking to someone back home or . . . something. But she's been learning Italian. I'm impressed.

"Your Italian is pretty good," I tell her.

"Thanks." She scuffs the toe of her Doc Martens on the dusty road. "It's not hard to learn, and I have a lot of time on my hands. I've been doing like twenty lessons a day."

Nicolo insists on paying for the granitas and steps up to the counter. The boy hands Nicolo two granitas but then reaches out and gives Alex hers personally. She murmurs her thanks in Italian.

"Mi chiamo Tommaso," he blurts out.

Nicolo and I exchange an amused look behind Alex's back.

"Mi chiamo . . . Alex," she replies. They gaze at each other for a moment, then Alex abruptly turns and hurries away from the booth. Nicolo and I follow at a more leisurely pace, grinning.

"Ah, young love," Nicolo observes with a wry smile. "Were we that awkward?"

"Probably." I scoop a big spoonful of my peach granita into my mouth. "I think it's adorable."

Made with local peaches, it is a Lake Garda delicacy, icy cold and sweet and bursting with ripe peach flavor. Why does everything taste better in Italy? Is it the water? The joy people take in eating good food? Or is it because the happiest moments of my life have all been here?

"Thank you for the granitas," I tell Nicolo, my tongue thick and clumsy with cold.

He inclines his head modestly. "My pleasure. How are you feeling about the contest?" He scoops up a spoonful of his granita as we wander closer to the marina. The day is blue and cloudless, gorgeous, and the sun sparkles on the water. The sailboats bob in a light breeze. For a moment, everything feels perfect and golden.

I shrug. "I don't think I'll win, and in a way it doesn't matter. I entered to be brave. Nonna challenged me not to let fear hold me back from taking risks that are worth it. I've spent so many years avoiding risk, afraid of failure. I entered this contest as a way to take a little risk. So being here is a win. Whatever happens, I will already have won." It's a wonderful feeling. I take another big scoop of granita and smile.

Nicolo taps his cup of granita against mine. "Here's to worthwhile risks," he says. We toast.

Chapter 33

"Fourth place!" I announce incredulously as the crowd in the square starts to disperse after the contest results are announced. "I got fourth place. I beat so many Italian nonnas!"

"Good job, Nipotina," Nonna says, patting my cheek. "I knew it. Your father would be so proud of you."

I flush pink, feeling proud and a little melancholy at the same time, wishing Dad were here to see this small victory. I've had so few since his death, it makes me sad that he is not here to celebrate this one.

"Bruna and I are going to go home," Lorenzo announces. "It's been a long day."

"The crowds have worn me out," Nonna says. "I have a headache. Do you girls want to go with us?"

"I can drive Juliana home if she wants to stay," Nicolo offers. I agree. Nonna does look worn out, but I still have to wait in a long line to retrieve my contest entry pot. Alex opts to go with Nonna and Lorenzo. She wants to stop back by the granita stand on the way back and give Tommaso her number.

"See, I told you Italy is great," I tease her. She rolls her eyes at me and follows Lorenzo and Nonna out of the square.

Now it is just Nicolo and me and about a thousand Italian revelers. The atmosphere of the festival is jolly, the crowds swelling with happy chatter and laughter. The air is thick with the savory aromas of grilling seafood and risotto from the restaurants nearby. It's just after sunset, the golden light starting to fade to gray, the lake deepening to navy and indigo, twinkling with a thousand lights reflected on the water. I'm still pleasantly in shock over the contest results.

We collect the pot, which Nicolo insists on carrying, and wind our way through the narrow streets lined with buildings hundreds of years old. They are painted in creams, sunshine yellows, and tangerine, with wooden shutters and balconies bursting with blooms and greenery. Everywhere you look there is a picturesque piazza with strings of café lights and people sitting at tables eating and drinking wine or strolling through the streets enjoying cups of gelato.

We take our time, savoring the warm evening as it gradually cools, reveling in the sense of relaxed celebration. My stomach rumbles. The granita seems so long ago. Laughing, we stand in line to buy gelato at a cheerful storefront. I get nocciola, a hazelnut flavor, which is one of my favorites. Nicolo gets stracciatella—vanilla ice cream with dark chocolate flakes. We wander around eating our gelato with tiny brightly colored spoons shaped like little paddles. I could do this all night. Italy is so good at creating these little moments of delight.

At last, as it is growing late, we reach Nicolo's car, a shiny little BMW that looks fast. I slide into the passenger seat, and he expertly navigates us through the crowded streets until we reach the main road out of town. He drives like a quintessential Italian, confident and slightly carefree, even while passing within inches of stone walls and scooters and families ambling along the side of the road. I learned long ago to trust Italian drivers to do it in their own way. The best thing is not to watch too closely, and if you arrive in one piece, consider that a success. When Aurora and I would complain about our dad's very Italian style of driving here in the summers, he would chuckle and ask cheekily, *Girls, girls. But did we die?*

As we drive, I text Aurora a photo from the festival, all of us crowded around my entry on the judging table. Lorenzo is squinting. Nonna looks a little smug. Alex is sneaking a peek at her phone. And Nicolo is standing right next to me, looking at me. I'm laughing, face so radiantly happy it momentarily stuns me. I tuck my phone back in my purse. I look up to see Nicolo watching me from the corner of his eye.

"Sorry." I gesture with the phone. "Texting Aurora about the contest."

"Ah, how is your sister?" Nicolo asks. "Is she still as bossy as she was at fifteen?" he chuckles. "I was always a little afraid of her, you know. She was so confident, so capable. I felt like she wanted to organize everything, even me." He looks relaxed while driving, one hand on the wheel, the other resting on the open car windowsill, projecting an effortless cool.

"She's living in a restored manor house in the mountains of Virginia, married to a blacksmith, has six kids, and makes her own cheese. It's her version of paradise."

"Mamma mia!" Nicolo looks impressed. "I don't know what part of that is the most surprising. So it sounds like your sister has found her right hard thing?"

I hesitate. "Yeah, I think she really has. It's not what I'd ever want in life, but she's really happy. And the kids are sweet. Their life is . . . lovely. Just not for me."

"What life is for you then?" Nicolo asks, glancing at me in the semidarkness. "What is it that you want?"

"That is the million-dollar question," I reply, blowing a breath out slowly. "I don't honestly know. I want to help people. I want to do something that has meaning. I want to give something beautiful to the world. I want to find love . . ."

"You have not yet found love?" Nicolo asks. His tone is nonchalant, but I see his gaze suddenly sharpen with interest.

I stare out the window at the shadowed houses and olive groves as they glide past. "I'm not sure I've found any of it," I reply truthfully. "My show is the only thing I've ever had that felt like it was mine, like it mattered and helped people. It's the only thing I've done well. And as for love . . ." My voice catches. "It's been a long time."

I leave it at that. I don't know his romantic history. I don't know if he's been in love once or a dozen times since we first declared our feelings for each other. It seems pathetic to admit that my first love at fifteen was the closest I've come to true love. I've been too careful, too cautious, too afraid of being hurt. It's the story of my life. Suddenly, I want to do something crazy. I'm feeling itchy and uncomfortable and eager to let loose.

We reach the driveway to the farm and Nicolo turns in, winding up the hill, gravel kicking up under the tires. I stare out at the shadowed olive trees, feeling unsettled. How long has it been since I did something spontaneous, something a little wild? I want to do something wild tonight . . .

Nicolo pulls to a stop in front of the house and I turn to him impulsively. "You want to have a drink with me? For old times' sake? I have a bottle of limoncello, the good stuff."

He looks at me for a moment, his gaze searching, then nods. "Of course. But I have a better idea. Let's go night swimming and then drink limoncello while we look at the stars."

I hesitate. He wants us to go swimming in the lake. I haven't been swimming there since Dad's death. My first instinct is to avoid the lake. It still scares me. Too many memories. But Nicolo has invited me. And maybe the only thing stronger than my aversion to the lake is my curiosity about Nicolo. He is sitting there watching me, a gleam of mischief in his eye. There are a dozen reasons to say no. I'm hungry. The water is too cold after dark. I try to avoid the lake as much as possible. But spending time with Nicolo proves too tempting; it outweighs all my objections.

In the end I agree to meet him down on the beach in twenty minutes. I jump out of the car, empty pot in hand, and hurry inside to get ready.

Chapter 34

Twenty minutes later, I walk down to the beach wearing my red bikini and a yellow linen sundress as a cover-up. I've got the bottle of local limoncello I bought at the market and two shot glasses in my bag. Nicolo is coming from the other direction. I can see him as he passes under the streetlight. He hops the stone wall and comes across the beach toward me, the crunch of his footsteps the only sound. He raises a hand in greeting. My heart speeds up a little. He has changed into casual dark blue pants and a worn white cotton shirt.

"Are you ready?" he asks when he reaches me. I nod, although I'm not, really. I try not to look at the lights reflecting off the dark water.

In one smooth motion, Nicolo shucks off his pants and shirt to reveal a tight little pair of blue swim trunks and his very eye-catching tanned, toned physique. It's not a Speedo, thankfully, but definitely not an American guy's typical swim attire. He sees me watching and grins at me.

"Do you prefer we swim like this or without clothes?"

"Skinny-dipping?" I reflexively reply, then blush furiously. "No, this is great." I stash the glasses and bottle of limoncello against the base of a large, smooth rock. Nicolo is already in the water, diving under the black surface. He comes up for air and shakes water from his eyes, calling for me to come in. I slip out of my sundress and shiver in the night air, then tiptoe gingerly to the edge of the lake and dip my toes in. It's cool and menacing looking, slick and black as an oil spill. I know there is nothing dangerous in the water. Nothing more than fish, but still . . . the opaqueness is unnerving.

"Come on," Nicolo invites, holding out a hand to me. He looks me over appreciatively. This little red bikini is my favorite. Still I hesitate. He must sense something is wrong and wades out of the water to where I am. I try not to look down at his wet swim shorts, focusing on a spot somewhere above the crown of his head.

"Jules, are you okay?" He sounds puzzled.

I take a deep breath. "Um, yeah. Sort of. It's just . . . I haven't really been swimming here since . . . since my dad."

He understands instantly. "Cavolo," he mutters, his expression sympathetic. "How could I forget? I'm sorry."

I start to tear up and try to keep it together, balling my hands into fists, fighting to gain control, but he sees my distress.

"Come here." Still dripping, he wraps his arms around me and pulls me into a tight hug. I freeze for a moment, then lean in. The warmth of his arms around me feels like safety. It's been so long. I sniff sadly, and he nestles my head under his chin, murmuring words of comfort in Italian, the water streaming from his body soaking my skin. In one way it feels like it has always felt between us, friendship and desire and his sweet care. On the other hand, we are not fifteen anymore, and these are very tiny swimsuits we are wearing. Just a little spandex on his lower half and about three triangles of bright red fabric covering my body.

"I just miss him so much," I confess, my voice muffled against his shoulder.

"Of course you do," he says, rubbing a hand over my shoulder blades in a gesture of comfort. "Tony was a good man."

We stand like that for a few moments, me sniffling and shivering, Nicolo comforting me. When I'm calm again, Nicolo lets me go gently. He sprints over to my sundress and brings it back to me. I slip into it gratefully. The night air is growing a little chilly.

"Forget the swimming," he says. "We can just sit here on the beach and drink limoncello."

For a moment I'm tempted to go into the water anyway, to prove I'm not a coward, but frankly, I simply cannot muster the courage. It's enough that I am here tonight, sitting on the shore, attempting to make a good memory in a place where my worst one happened.

"I'll race you to the limoncello," I call to Nicolo, scrambling toward the rock where I left the bottle. "Last one there's a rotten egg."

He races after me, dripping lake water and laughing. I beat him to the rock.

"I guess I am the . . . What was it? The rotting egg?" He grins at me.

I settle down more or less comfortably on the pebbled shore in my slightly damp sundress. Nicolo drops down next to me.

While he's not looking, I shamelessly admire the contours of his body, the muscled calves and trim waist, his broad chest with a dusting of dark hair. He's a beautiful man, a beautiful, kind man who makes me feel warm and safe. Nicolo uncorks the limoncello. He pours two shots, filling both glasses to the brim, and hands one to me.

"I feel sixteen again," he says with a laugh. I wonder if he's thinking of the sips of limoncello we used to sneak during that feverish summer of our forbidden teenage romance. Of our secret meeting place under the oldest olive tree in our grove. The tree was said to have already been here when my ancestors first purchased the farm. They planted an olive grove around the tree. No one really knows how old it is. Hundreds of years at least. It is believed that olive trees can live at least fifteen hundred years. Most reach five hundred. That gnarled tree may have been a tender sapling when Botticelli, Raphael, Michelangelo, and Leonardo da Vinci were painting Italy. I'm always amazed by the thought.

"I haven't drunk limoncello in years," I tell him. "Not since that summer we got in such trouble." We clink glasses.

"That was a special summer," he says lightly. We sip our shots, strong and sweet. The lemon essence makes my mouth pucker.

"Sometimes I miss those days." I sigh, gazing out over the dark, rippling water of the lake. "I don't think growing up is all it's cracked up to be."

"How so?" Nicolo rests his hands on his knees, leaning back in the sand, seemingly perfectly at ease.

"I thought it would be more fun, and I thought I'd have done more. I feel like all I did the past decade was try to survive."

"I think many people feel that way," he says.

"I know, but sometimes I feel so . . . stuck." I sip my limoncello. I know there's no way the alcohol is affecting me so quickly, but I swear it's loosening my lips. "Stuck in my career, stuck in my life, stuck in love, just stuck. Sometimes I feel like everything and everyone is moving on around me, but I'm standing still."

Nicolo regards me curiously, his expression open. "Why do you feel like this, Juliana? What have the years held for you?" he asks.

I reach over and refill my shot glass.

Fueled by limoncello courage, I tell him everything in the quiet stillness of the beach. It feels holy somehow, like I'm being purged of years of shame and grief. It feel almost as though I am in a confessional, unburdening a life filled with unexpected loss and false starts. Many years have passed since we shared confidences like this. My mind flashes back to those soft summer nights, the silky darkness alive around us, moonlight filtering through the branches of the olive trees, the planes of Nicolo's young face stark and shadowed, and the way we'd put our heads together to whisper our truest thoughts, lips pressed to the shell of an ear, bodies curved close. How long ago it seems now. But how right it feels to be doing it again.

"So now you know my story," I tell him when I'm done. I set down my shot glass and look him square in the eye, almost daring him to pity me. I realize I've consumed quite a lot of limoncello. The world is tilting ever so gently, rocking like I'm on a boat.

He says nothing for a long moment, just looks at me in the dim glow from the streetlamp up near the road behind us, those dark eyes warm on my face. I feel heated under his gaze, and glance out at the lake.

"You are not the only one who has regrets, Jules." He says it with tenderness and just the barest hint of a bitter edge. He refills his glass and tosses the shot back in one smooth motion. He could always hold his liquor better than me.

"What do you mean?" I watch him, realizing how little I know about him now. Once I knew everything, but that was fifteen years ago. What has happened in those years? What has the shape of his life been?

"Tell me one of your regrets," I say.

Chapter 35

Nicolo is quiet for a long moment. "Her name was Natalie," he says at last.

"Natalie." I taste the name and grimace. "What did she do?"

He smiles humorlessly. "She held my heart too carelessly," he replies. Then with a sigh he explains. "After law school I got a job with an international company. I had no desire to stay in Italy. To tell you the truth, I wanted to be as far away from Violetta and Alberto and this place as I could get. So I took a job in Australia. A couple of years later I met Natalie. She was an attorney too, from Sydney."

"I bet she's pretty," I blurt out. It's the limoncello loosening my lips.

He smiles ruefully. "She is, and such a sharp legal mind. I felt like the luckiest guy in the world. We fell in love, got engaged . . . I thought I was finally going to have the life I wanted." He pauses, tipping the shot glass to his lips and sipping the last drop. "And then it all fell apart."

"What happened?" I ask, still trying to picture him with the lovely Natalie. I hate the mental image. I bet she has shiny hair and endless confidence and a mind like a mousetrap.

He shrugs. "She left me. She fell out of love and I didn't. Or maybe it's more accurate to say she fell in love, just not with me. She broke our engagement a month before we were planning to fly home so she could meet my family and see the farm. Last I heard she's living with the guy somewhere on the Gold Coast. He's a professional surfer."

"Ouch." I wince. "I'm sorry. That's awful." Stupid Natalie. How could she not see what she had in Nicolo?

He shrugs philosophically. "I don't regret that we are not together anymore. I only regret that I entrusted my heart to someone who cared for it so poorly. Maybe it's for the best, though. I came home without her. I already had the ticket. And I discovered what bad shape the farm and business were really in. My grandfather had already been gone for several years when I returned, and I suspect things had been let go for a long time before he died. Everything was a mess. Nonna V. was trying her best. She's a strong woman, but it was too much for her. So I stayed . . ." He toys with the empty shot glass, his arms resting casually on his knees. He's gazing out at the lake, his profile pensive.

"Are you glad you stayed?"

"Sometimes," he says frankly. "I told you how it is with her. I'm trying to save the farm from ruin, trying to modernize all the systems, trying to get us online so we can sell to more than just tourists passing through. But my grandmother is stubborn and set in her ways. Everything is a struggle between us, and she still sees me as a little boy, not a capable man." He runs his hands through his curls in a gesture of exasperation, making them spring up. "Sometimes I'm not sure I'm making any progress at all," he admits.

"That sounds incredibly frustrating."

He rolls his eyes. "You have no idea."

"But you're still here," I observe.

He shrugs. "Of course. How could I do otherwise? It is my home and this is my family legacy. I have a responsibility to preserve it if I can."

It's an honorable sentiment, and I think of our olive farm with a pang of guilt. I'm not the right person to help, but if I do nothing, what will happen to it? It's a puzzle I can't seem to solve, and it gnaws at me constantly.

"Are you happy here?" I ask suddenly. "Do you feel you made the right choice?"

Nicolo thinks for a minute. "If you ask if I am happy, the honest answer is not really. My life is not as I once dreamed it would be." He shifts restlessly. "I'm stuck in a very frustrating situation trying to save my family's farm. I always dreamed of a family, of someone to share my life with, and yet I am still alone." He turns and looks at me seriously. "So no, I would not say that I am happy. But I know I am doing the right thing, and I am content with that." He gives a small, noncommittal shrug. "Sometimes life is hard and often we don't get what we thought we wanted, but then I ask myself, is happiness the only measure of a good life?" There's a note of challenge in his voice. "There is also duty and honor, sacrifice, commitment. Those are important too, maybe more important than happiness. I am trying to make a difference for my family, for this community, and I hope I am making the right choices. I hope happiness will come again for me, but there is no guarantee, and I have to be okay with what I have. This is enough for me."

I admire his dedication, his sacrifice, but that sentiment is incredibly sad. He deserves to be loved, to have a family, to be happy. He's wonderful.

"I wish there was a way to see what would make us happy," I muse, then freeze as a thought strikes me.

What if there is?

"Nicolo, has your grandmother ever talked about Orange Blossom Cake?"

He looks puzzled by my abrupt change of topic. "Not that I remember. Why?"

I blink and try to focus my thoughts. I've always been a lightweight when it comes to liquor. The taste of lemons is thick and sweet on my tongue, and the alcohol slowly seeps into my bloodstream. I feel more than a little lightheaded.

"Because I think that's why Nonna Bruna and Violetta hate each other."

I quickly explain about Nonna Bruna's cookbook and its purported magical properties. As it turns out, Nicolo knows already.

"Bruna is a local legend," he tells me. "People come to her from all over the area for advice and to consult the cookbook to help them sort out their troubles or desires."

I think of the young women making a recipe at the crack of dawn, seeking Nonna's help in love. This morning Nonna showed me a text she received, just a single word. *Grazie*. And a photo of the girl with the jet-black bob. Her smile is luminous as she shows off an engagement ring while a young man with a dark beard gazes adoringly at her.

"I had no idea about the cookbook," I admit. "Nonna never told us about it. She said she was waiting until we were older to explain everything to us, but then when my dad died, we never came back to Italy. I'm only learning about it now. But there's still something that's a mystery."

I tell him about the Orange Blossom Cake and its ability to show you the happiest moment of your life. I explain about the torn half of the recipe that shows up every time Nonna touches the cookbook, and about what Nonna told me about Violetta and their history with the cake recipe. Nicolo listens intently.

"I've always wondered what happened between them," he admits. "My grandmother has never mentioned the cake, though that doesn't surprise me. She's a very private woman. She could have the other half of the recipe hidden away somewhere, although I've never seen it." He picks up a pebble and throws it overhand into the lake. It sinks soundlessly, the dark water shimmering away in widening circles. The mountains on the far shore jut up against the dark purple sky, and the night air smells of lake water, sunbaked rocks, and the mouthwatering aroma of grilled fish drifting from a restaurant somewhere upwind.

"Would you do it?" Nicolo asks curiously. "If you had the whole recipe, would you want to eat the first bite of this cake and see your future happiness?"

I exhale and think about it for a moment, shivering a little in the coolness of the evening. My dress is still damp on the front, and I'm getting a little chilled. "I think so," I admit finally. "It would be nice to know that something good is coming. Right now my life feels like such a shamble. Maybe if I saw the happiest moment, I'd get some guidance on what choices I should make to get me there."

"Then let's go find it," Nicolo announces suddenly, jumping to his feet and holding out his hand to me.

I sit up straight, my head spinning a little. "Go find what?"

"The other half of the recipe." He grabs his shirt and pants and shimmies into them deftly.

"I thought you said you'd never seen it." My mind is ever so slightly fuzzy. It's been a long day, and after at least three shots of limoncello, I'm feeling a little slow and sleepy.

"I haven't, but I know where Violetta keeps everything she

treasures. In an old safe in her office. If she has the other half of the recipe, I'll bet you it's there." He grins, his expression lit with excitement. Right now, he looks like the boy I first knew. I take his hand and he pulls me easily to my feet, steadying me.

"And you know the code for the safe?" I ask, intrigued by the possibility. What if we could get the lost half of the recipe back and reunite it with the other half in the cookbook? Could we make the recipe and take that fabled first bite? Suddenly, I want very badly to see if we can make this happen.

Nicolo shrugs. "Only Violetta knows the code for the safe, but I bet I can crack it." He looks at me in the faint light from the streetlamp on the road behind us, and I can see him as he was all those years ago, dimpled and daring, the glint of mischief in his eye. "Five euros says I can get into that safe in less than ten minutes."

His mom taught him how to pick locks when he was five years old, he told me once. He stole his first bottle of wine for her when he was not much older. He probably can get into the safe.

"You're on," I tell him, excited by the adventure and the possibility.

He jams the cork back in the bottle of limoncello. "What are we waiting for?" he asks, holding out his hand to me. "Let's go find that recipe."

Chapter 36

It is surprisingly easy to break into an olive farm, especially when your accomplice lives there and knows his way around. We stash the half-empty bottle of limoncello and the shot glasses in the fork of an olive tree on the way up the Fiores' drive. The Fiore olive groves are far bigger than ours, so it's a long walk up the lane to reach the house. I'm panting by the time we get to the top, but try hard to mask it, wishing I'd done more cardio recently and wasn't quite so obviously out of shape. Nicolo doesn't seem fazed by the uphill hike. Maybe it feels like a piece of cake after hauling big rocks with Lorenzo all week.

Keeping to the shadows under the trees, we creep quietly as soon as we come in sight of the Fiores' ancestral villa. It's a tall, commanding stone structure with two long wings and an expansive view of the lake.

The front of the house has a veranda overlooking a series of terraces that nestle into the hillside, each one filled with perfectly pruned, orderly rows of citron trees. These are an especially rare and delicate variety of citron called cedro di Salò that grows well in the climate around the lake. Once, citron fruits were prized for use in medicines, liqueurs, and to make the famed local citron water, though now their popularity has waned. Citron trees have been grown here at the villa for generations and are a treasured part of the Fiore heritage. Violetta babies these trees like they are her children.

Nicolo's BMW is parked in the driveway of the house along with Violetta's older-model Mercedes. There is a light on in the main floor of the villa and a blue glow seeps through one of the windows. Someone is watching television.

"It's good timing. My grandmother is watching *Il Commissario Montalbano*, the detective show she likes. She'll be distracted," Nicolo whispers in my ear, motioning for me to follow him. We're both buzzed from the limoncello and high on adrenaline and the joy of breaking the rules. I feel like a teenager again, sneaking around with the forbidden boy from next door.

Following Nicolo's lead, I tiptoe behind him across the wide gravel driveway toward the main outbuilding. My heart is pounding with excitement and a touch of fear. We're having a caper. I don't remember the last time I had a caper. Probably when Nicolo and I were together all those years ago. What is it about this boy that gets me into mischief? I wonder. Whatever it is, I like it.

The thought of finding the recipe is thrilling. The thought of doing it together with Nicolo even more so. I want to find the recipe now more than ever. It feels crucial somehow, in a way I can't explain but sense deep in my gut. I want to see my future happiness so I know if I'm making the right choice, if I am choosing the right hard thing.

The Fiore farm is large enough to have several outbuildings with various purposes related to harvesting olives and making the oil.

Through the darkness I can see the dim outline of the infamous stable where our romance was so unceremoniously put to an end, a few sheds for machinery and equipment, and the main building that has been converted to a store where customers can purchase items from the farm.

"Violetta's office is in there, at the back," Nicolo whispers, pointing to the main building. He's standing very close to me, his breath a brush of warmth against my temple. "Follow me."

He glances around as we reach a side door, fumbling for a moment with a set of keys from his pocket before he finds the right one. We sneak inside. We appear to be in a storage room. Lots of olive-themed merchandise is stacked neatly on shelves and it smells strongly of olive oil, a rich, unctuous, peppery scent. It's dark in here, just a shaft of pale moonlight streaming through a high window and falling across the shelves. Nicolo crosses silently to the door at the other end of the room and motions to me to come. "Jules, this way." He opens the door a crack and peeks out. I scuttle over to him, peering over his shoulder into the main hallway. All is dark and silent. I'm so close to him I can feel the rise and fall of his breathing as his back presses against my rib cage. I swallow hard. My heart is pounding, although I tell myself there is no real danger. What's the worst that could happen? Violetta discovers us? Nicolo is her grandson and the heir to this entire operation. Still, sneaking around in the dark feels thrilling and illicit.

"All clear," Nicolo whispers. We tiptoe through the chilly stone hallway toward the back of the building. At a small, unassuming wooden door, Nicolo pauses and tries the handle. It's locked. "One minute," he says, searching for a different key.

After a minute he makes a sound of satisfaction. With a click the door swings open and Nicolo ushers me inside, closing the door softly behind us. He crosses the room and turns on a small desk lamp, flooding the space with warm, dim light. The office is chilly and smells of old stone and dried lavender. It is plainly furnished but elegant, very much like Violetta. A heavy, ornately carved wooden desk and chair dominate the small space, and a Persian rug covers the stone floor. Two stiff-looking armchairs sit facing the desk, as though standing at attention.

"Now for the safe," Nicolo says. He goes to a painting on the wall, a muted pastoral scene, and removes it from its place, setting it aside. Behind it is a small safe.

"Just like in the movies!" I whisper excitedly.

Nicolo grins, a flash of white teeth. "If Nonna V. has the recipe, I'm betting it will be in here."

I tiptoe over to him. "Okay, clock is ticking." I glance at the clock on the wall opposite Violetta's desk. "You bet me you could have it open in ten minutes."

It takes him a few tries and several mild swears in Italian, but exactly six minutes later we both hear the click when he finally guesses the combination correctly. The safe door swings open and Nicolo stands back and spreads his arms wide, inviting me to come see his handiwork.

"You did it!" I squeal, high-fiving him, elated.

"We did it." He grabs my hand and pulls me close, twirling me in a circle, both of us euphoric with victory. I twine my arms around his neck and hold on, suddenly dizzy. We're both laughing. Gently, he sets me down, but neither of us steps away. His hands don't leave my waist. We're standing very close together. I can feel the warmth of his skin seeping through the thin fabric of my sundress, my fingers nestling in the thick curls at the nape of his neck.

"You still had four minutes," I tell him as my heart rate rockets from more than the thrill of breaking and entering.

"You owe me five euros," he says, trying to look serious and failing. He's grinning. I'm standing so close I can smell him, something familiar in the warmth of his skin—the faintest whiff of his cologne with traces of warm amber and woody, resinous cedar and an underlying herbaceous, peppery note of olive oil that seems to be a part of his essence. I lean closer, my nose brushing his skin, and he pulls back enough to look at me incredulously. "Are you sniffing me?"

I giggle, half-embarrassed at being caught out. "Sorry, you smell delicious," I tell him a little flirtatiously.

"Oh, do I?" He watches me, intrigued. "What do I smell like?"

"Like warm honey and the sticky sap of a cedar tree. Like you," I pause and consider. "You're all grown-up but I feel like I still know you. You smell like . . . like coming home." There is a comfort in his scent, a sense of safety. It brings a lump to my throat. His eyes soften and he reaches up, tucking a wave of hair behind my ear. The rough pads of his fingers brush across my earlobe.

"It is the same for me," he says gently. "How is that possible? All these years later, and I still feel as though I know you. As though the years apart have all just melted away." He pulls me a little closer, his eyes on mine, his gaze so warm I feel like I'm the one melting.

I nestle closer to him. "You were my first love. I know we were young and naive, but I opened my heart to you, and that isn't something I can just close up quickly. I still feel so open to you." It feels vulnerable to admit that, but I find I want to be vulnerable with him.

He reaches up and traces the curve of my jaw with his thumb. "I loved you from the moment I first saw you, Jules. You got out of the car, straight from the airport, wearing a T-shirt with cupcakes on it, your hair in braids, with your mouth full of braces and those big brown eyes. You looked at me and smiled, and it felt like the sun had just come out from behind the clouds, like the world was suddenly brighter and warmer. For the first time, I didn't feel alone." He stops and meets my eyes intently. "I never forgot you, Juliana. I always hoped our paths might cross again. And now here you are. It feels like a gift."

"I . . . I feel the same way." I swallow hard, darting a look at his mouth. I remember that mouth, what it felt like caressing the tender skin of my collarbone. Nicolo doesn't answer, just pulls me closer until his body is pressed against mine. My pulse quickens. I can't seem to remember how to breathe. He lowers his head, his lips brushing the sensitive pressure point at the hinge of my jaw just below my ear. "Sei bella," he whispers huskily, the warmth of his mouth making me shiver. "Tesoro mio. La mia stellina." Beautiful. My dear. My little star. I recognize the words. He whispered them the first time he kissed me.

I turn toward him, hungry and eager and searching. And then his mouth is on mine, and a searing sense of knowing arcs between us like a current of electricity. He makes a little growl, low in his throat, his lips on mine at once tender and fierce. My knees buckle and he tightens his grip to hold me close and keep me from falling. I smile against his lips, then pull his head down more firmly toward me. Whatever this is between us, I want more.

Chapter 37

Nicolo kisses his way down the slope of my throat, and I go boneless. He lifts his head and chuckles into the shell of my ear. "You like that, yes?" He nips my earlobe. I make a little whimper.

Suddenly there is a blindingly bright light that floods the room.

"Merda! What is the meaning of this?" a strident voice cries out in Italian.

I jump back with a shriek, squinting in the harsh glare. Someone's turned the overhead light on. Nicolo stumbles back too, raising a hand to shield his eyes.

"Nonna V.?" he says in surprise.

"Violetta?" I squeak, meeting the scalpel gaze of Nicolo's grandmother, who is standing in the open doorway in her long black dress with a thunderous look of righteous indignation on her face and her hand on the light switch. A skinny white dog darts around her skirts and runs into the room barking. As soon as it sees Nicolo, the dog rushes over to him, wagging its tail and groveling.

"Nicolo! Explain yourself." Violetta speaks in rapid-fire Italian, coming into the room and gesturing angrily to the open safe. "What do you two think you are doing?" She looks furious. Immediately, I feel fifteen again. All traces of my tipsy euphoria and desire drain away, leaving me feeling rudely sober.

"We are . . . um . . ." Nicolo darts a glance at me.

"We're looking for the missing half of the recipe for Orange Blossom Cake," I say firmly, surprising myself with my courage. At those words, a peculiar look crosses Violetta's face, just a flicker of alarm but enough for me to know she knows something.

"What is this foolishness?" she demands. "You break into my office, into my safe? I should call the polizia and have you both arrested for trying to steal my personal property."

At this Nicolo seems to regain his composure. "Come on, Nonna V.," he says with an edge of amusement to his voice. "Try it. All the local police know me. They know I'm your grandson. In fact, the chief of police owes me a favor and a beer. They won't arrest me. Or Jules for that matter." He scratches the dog behind the ears, murmuring endearments to it in Italian. The dog's tongue lolls out of its mouth and its tail thumps hard against the floor.

Violetta gazes between us, scowling with annoyance. "It's always trouble with you two," she says grimly, her long lips pressed together into a thin line. She's an elegant woman, tall and slender with ramrod posture. But there's a hardness to her expression that I've always found intimidating. She perpetually looks as though she were tasting something bitter.

"You are too old for this nonsense," she scolds us. "Sneaking around. Acting like children. Nicolo, go inside. I will talk with you later. And you." She points one long finger at me. "Go home and stay away from my grandson."

"No." I surprise myself with my refusal.

She stares at me for a long moment. "What did you say?" She

looks genuinely shocked. I'm not sure anyone ever says no to Violetta Fiore.

I cross my arms, darting a quick look at Nicolo. He is watching me with a raised eyebrow and a look of respect. Even the dog is staring at me, tail wagging uncertainly. "I won't go. Not without the recipe. I know you have it. It belongs to my family. Give it back."

She rears back as though I've struck her. "Do you even know what you are asking for?" she hisses.

For a moment I waver. She's right. I don't really know what I'm asking for, not entirely. I know it's half of a torn recipe, but I don't understand the history of the recipe between Violetta and Nonna Bruna. "I know enough to know that it has value to my Nonna Bruna and that you took it," I say, lifting my chin. "It's valuable enough that she says losing it ruined her life." I'm surprising myself with my own tenacity. I can't back down now.

An astonishing change comes over Violetta at my words. She stares at me, dumbstruck for a moment. Then her expression shifts and softens to something that looks almost like regret. Quietly, she asks, "Bruna told you this?"

I hesitate, then nod. "She did."

Violetta looks up at the ceiling and mutters something. I think she's either praying or swearing; I can't tell which. "Sit down, both of you," she says, sighing heavily and pointing to the two rigid chairs facing the desk. She rounds the desk and sits down in her own chair, lifting an old black landline telephone from its cradle. The dog slinks over to her and sprawls beneath the desk, keeping a friendly but watchful eye on me. She dials a number and waits, then barks out a few phrases in rapid Italian, so fast I can't quite catch them. Then she replaces the phone in its receiver, folds her hands, and sits back motionless in the chair. She gazes up at the ceiling with a long-suffering pinched look usually reserved for saints in their moment of martyrdom.

"What's she doing?" I ask Nicolo from the side of my mouth. "Who did she call?"

"Bruna," Nicolo says softly. "She said she'd caught thieves on her property and it was a family matter. She told her to come quickly."

"Nonna is coming here?"

Nicolo nods, looking uncomfortable. "Unfortunately, yes."

"Well good, maybe we'll finally get some answers." I settle back in the stiff chair, feeling curious and a little apprehensive. Silently, we wait.

Chapter 38

"How did you know we were in here?" Nicolo asks his grandmother after we've waited like schoolchildren in the principal's office for ten minutes, all three of us sitting in complete silence.

Violetta gestures dismissively to the dog. "Argo heard you. He was going crazy and I finally came to see what all the fuss was about. I missed the ending of my show for this nonsense. Now I don't know who killed the librarian." She looks annoyed but pats Argo on the head. He licks her hand adoringly.

More long minutes pass until I hear familiar footsteps in the hall. Nonna pokes her head in the door and sees us and Violetta. Her expression is one of puzzled exasperation.

"Madonna Santa, what is going on here?" she demands in English, coming into the room. She stands in the doorway and surveys us, clutching her black leather pocketbook to her chest. She's put on fresh lipstick, I notice, and pantyhose.

"I caught these two breaking into my safe," Violetta explains stiffly in Italian.

Nonna's eyes widen. She looks between us, then clucks her

tongue and shakes her head. "Always getting into mischief, the two of you."

"We were just trying to get the other half of the Orange Blossom Cake recipe back," I protest.

Nonna looks astonished. "The recipe?" she asks. "You were breaking in to get the recipe? But why?"

"Well, because . . ." I squirm in the hideously uncomfortable chair. "Because it seems important to you, and I figured if we got the complete recipe, I could try it. I want to see the happiest moment of my life."

"The girl claims you told her your life was ruined because you only had half the recipe." Violetta's dry tone is somehow both demeaning and a touch accusing. I bristle at being called "the girl."

Nonna squares her shoulders. Violetta is head and shoulders taller than Nonna, but in a cage match, my money would be on Nonna. She's scrappy. "Juliana misunderstood me," she says coldly. "It was not the recipe that ruined my life. It was you, your betrayal when you stole Alberto from me."

Nicolo and I exchange a scandalized look. I feel like I'm watching a real live soap opera. Alberto, as in Violetta's dead husband? This is getting juicy.

Violetta scoffs. "What are you talking about?"

Nonna rears back. "Don't deny it. You stole my fiancé two months before our wedding!" she retorts hotly. "You were my best friend, like a sister to me, until you snatched the man I loved right out from under my nose."

Violetta has the grace to look discomfited. Her eyes dart away from Nonna. "You should thank me," she mutters.

Nonna huffs in outrage. She puts her hands on the desk and leans toward Violetta. "Thank you? I should thank you? You ruined my life without so much as an explanation or apology. You broke my heart twice over, first by stealing Alberto from me and again with your silence. And then I had to stand by for all these years and watch you prosper with Alberto, watch your farm flourish while Carlo and I struggled." She thumps a fist on the desk, her expression angry. "You took the things that should have been mine, the life that should have been mine. Don't deny it."

Something flickers in Violetta's eyes. I see her hesitate. "What does this have to do with the recipe?" she asks coldly, neatly changing the subject.

"You have it, don't you?" I interject.

Violetta glances briefly in my direction. "That recipe has no bearing on anything. It is a silly old family story. It means nothing."

"Then give it back to us."

"Fine." She flicks her hand dismissively, then stands and rummages in the safe for a moment. The room is quiet. Finally, she pulls out a yellowed envelope and throws it on the desk. "There, take it. I have no use for it. I never have."

"Whose fault is that?" Nonna replies quietly, her expression steely.

Violetta gives her a hard look, then sits down with a sigh.

"You understand nothing," she says, sounding suddenly weary.

Nonna straightens her shoulders. "I understand true friendship," she retorts. "And what you did was unforgivable. Do you remember, Vi, how excited we were when the cookbook showed us the recipe when we opened it one day? How we longed to see our moment of happiness? We decided to take a bite of the cake at the exact same time so we could both see what the future held for us." She glances at Nicolo and me and explains, "That's why we tore half the page out of the cookbook when it showed us the recipe. We wanted to wait and make the cake together on my eighteenth birthday. We tore the recipe in half because we did not want either of us to be tempted to cheat and make the cake too early. We made a promise to wait and make it together. That was the plan."

"Plans change," Violetta said bluntly. "By the time our birthdays rolled around, it was too late. I didn't need the cake. I could see my future laid out in front of me already, and there was no point in trying to see any future happiness. It was already too late for me."

Nonna looks puzzled. Nicolo too.

"What do you mean it was too late?" Nonna asks slowly.

Violetta looks at her, her jaw working for a moment. "I was pregnant," she says finally, bluntly. "And Alberto was the father of my baby."

Nonna gasps and puts her hand to her chest. My jaw drops. This *is* a soap opera. I glance at Nicolo, who is staring at his grandmother in complete shock. The baby Violetta is talking about would be Nicolo's mother, Alberto and Violetta's only child. I scoot forward in the chair, hanging on every word.

"No," Nonna protests. "Alberto would never have . . ."

Violetta utters a grim little laugh. "Oh, you are sadly mistaken, Bruna. Alberto did . . . with me and with many other women, before and after our wedding. I found out too late what sort of man he was. With me, it was just once. The night of the May Day festival. You stayed home with a headache and asked Alberto to take me to the festival instead. By the end of the night we'd both had too much cheap wine. We took a little drive along the lake and stopped to look at the moon. One thing led to another. We made a terrible choice." She waved a hand dismissively. "A few weeks later I found I was with child and unmarried, and the father of my baby was my best friend's fiancé. There was only one course of action. If the truth had gotten out it would have ruined me and brought immense shame upon our family, so my father did the only thing he could. He paid Alberto a large sum of money and forced him to marry me."

"You've got to be kidding," Nicolo mutters beside me. He looks stunned. So does Nonna. She's actually gone a little pale. Nicolo jumps up and ushers her to his chair, where she sits down heavily. Her feet barely reach the floor.

"You were pregnant," she says faintly. "And Alberto was the father."

Violetta presses her lips together and nods. "It is my biggest shame," she admits. "And yet I could not tell you the truth. I could not let anyone know I was pregnant before we married. My father forbade it. It was one of the conditions of the marriage, that our shameful secret never get out. I agreed to say nothing. What else could I do? I married Alberto and had his baby. I honored my father's demands in order to save our family's honor and my own reputation. I thought my heart would burst from the shame of what I had done to you, but I could not say a word. I have never said a word."

"All these years?" Nonna whispered. "Surely, you could have told me at some point?"

Violetta laughed humorlessly. "Why? So you could despise me even more? You have hated me for good reason, Bruna. How would knowing the truth change that?" She shakes her head and sighs heavily. "You should thank the Blessed Virgin that you did not end up married to Alberto. He was not a good man. He was cruel when he drank, which was often. And he had many women after me. He did not want to marry me, nor I him. The estate has prospered, you are right, but no one knew the truth of what happened behind closed doors. I suffered at his hands for many long years. I have paid dearly for my sins."

Nonna's mouth has dropped open into a round little O of shock. "He was cruel to you?" she asks. "Violetta, is that true?" Her eyes search Violetta's face earnestly.

Violetta looks down. "It's true, though I do not wish to remember it," she says dismissively. I think she's embarrassed. "Let me assure you, his death was a release for me. I did not mourn him, but I mourned you and our friendship, many times over. I grieved my failure, and what it did to you. I grieved our friendship. You were like a sister to me."

Violetta looks Nonna square in the eye. "I am sorry, Bruna. I know you cannot forgive me, but I am glad to finally be able to say the words." Her mouth is pursed tight and her bony hands are clenched together in a knot in front of her on the desk. She looks so weary.

Chapter 39

For a long minute there is only silence and the ticking of the old clock on the wall. Nonna is staring at Violetta, and Violetta's eyes are fixed on something far away and long ago. Nicolo is standing by Nonna Bruna's chair, looking from one to the other. He seems stunned.

When Nonna speaks, her tone is almost wistful. "For so long I envied you, Vi. I was eaten up with jealousy that you had everything and I had so little. You had money and power and the man I believed was rightfully mine. But now I see how foolish I was to waste so much time with such a deadly sin. Envy never leads to anything good. And it is true that I had a happy life with Carlo. He was a good man. We may not have had two lire to rub together, but we were content in our life, all the years until he passed." She pauses. "I am sorry that I wasted time in envying you, Violetta. And I am sorry for you, to be married to a cruel man. I had no idea Alberto was such a pezzo di merda. That is a heavy price to pay, no matter what you did. No woman should have to live with that."

Violetta darts a glance at Bruna. Almost imperceptibly, her

shoulders slump in relief. "Grazie," she says stiffly, inclining her head slightly in acceptance.

Nonna looks at Violetta for a long moment, then nods decisively. "What's done is done," she says briskly, clapping her hands on her knees. "Let us not dwell on the past any longer." She stands and clutches her purse. "I'm getting old," she announces. "It is time for these bones to rest."

Violetta stands too. Argo, who has been snoozing through the entire conversation, jumps up and sits at attention by Violetta. She hesitates behind her desk, then picks up the yellowed envelope and proffers it to Nonna.

"Don't forget this," she says. There is a gentleness in the set of her mouth that I've never seen before. It is no longer a thin, grim line. It looks softened by relief. She almost looks as though she might cry. I think I see her chin trembling, but it might just be a trick of the light.

Nonna takes the envelope. For a moment Violetta does not let go. "I wonder what we would have seen," Violetta says quietly, "if we had eaten the cake together."

Nonna pauses, and her expression softens too. "Maybe it's not too late," she says with a quirk of her lips. "Maybe it will still work at eighty like it was supposed to at eighteen."

Violetta gives a small, sad smile and releases the envelope to Nonna. "I'm afraid that if I ate the cake now, I might see a vision of my own passing into heaven. Perhaps when we are this old, Bruna, that is all the joy that awaits us."

Nonna scoffs and carefully slips the envelope into her stiff black purse. "Speak for yourself," she says. "I intend to have many more good memories before I take my last breath. You should do the same. It's not too late. It's never too late to live a better life."

Violeta inclines her head. "Perhaps you are right." But she sounds doubtful.

Nonna looks her in the eye. "I still cannot believe it. All these years I envied what you had—such success, money, marriage to Alberto..."

"And all these years I envied you and Carlo your happiness," Violetta admits. "What good is a big house and a fat bank account if your heart and your home are filled with such bitterness and hatred?" She looks tired all of a sudden, and sad, worn thin by regret and years of silent suffering, keeping up appearances while her life was a hollow shell of pretense.

Nonna mimes spitting on the stone floor. "Good riddance to that arrogant stronzo," she says vehemently.

"Wow," Nicolo whispers, meeting my eyes. "I had no idea Bruna knew so many swear words."

"Oh, she can curse like a sailor when she's angry," I reply. "Don't get her started."

Violetta spits too. "Good riddance. Alberto was a good for nothing pisellino."

Nonna puts her hand to her chest, looking shocked and delighted. "Violetta," she says, "no, is it true?"

Nicolo makes a little choking sound. He looks mortified. I'm confused. "Did Violetta just call your grandfather a little pea?" I whisper, struggling to translate the words in my head.

Nicolo is flushing a dull red beneath his golden olive tan. "It um... doesn't mean little pea," he murmurs, leaning close to my chair. "In Italian it is an insult for a man's private parts, calling them very small, like little peas."

My eyes widen in astonishment. At this point in the evening I'm not sure anything else could surprise me.

"It's true." Violetta sniffs and holds up her fingers several inches apart. "And his manhood, like a baby zucchina."

Nonna looks immensely satisfied by this information. "Well," she says. "Well, God bless Carlo. He was a good man and there were no baby zucchine in our house, I can tell you. Only grandi zucchine."

Nicolo clears his throat. "Your grandchildren are standing right here!" he reminds them. There are two dull spots of color high on his cheekbones. He's looking fixedly at the ceiling.

"Nicolo is right. Come, it is growing late. Argo and I are too old for such excitements," Violetta says briskly, sweeping past us and gesturing for us to follow her. Argo dutifully pads along a pace behind her.

Together we file from Violetta's office through the dark main entry hall and out the big wooden doors into the large gravel parking area. Argo comes up beside me and sniffs my hand tentatively. I scratch behind his ears and he wags his tail and leans against my leg with a happy whine. I fill my lungs with the soft evening air, which smells of the lake and tiny green olives ripening on the trees, and a hint of lavender from the lush beds bordering the parking area. When we are all outside, Violetta locks the doors and turns to us.

"No more late-night sneaking around from you two," she says sternly, wagging her finger at Nicolo and me. "You are not children now. Behave."

I nod, trying to suppress my sudden laughter at the absurdity of the evening. I feel blindsided by the revelations of the past few minutes yet also giddy with relief. Beside me Nicolo grins ruefully. "Yes, Nonna V. We'll try our best." He doesn't sound very convincing.

Violetta looks from Nicolo to me, narrows her eyes, and makes a *hmph* of disbelief.

"Juliana, do you want to come home with me?" Nonna asks, pulling the keys to the Fiat Panda from her purse. I hesitate. She is a terrifying driver. Usually, Lorenzo insists on driving her wherever she needs to go just to keep her and the other cars safe on the road.

I guess since it is just next door she can manage it. But I'm reluctant to leave Nicolo just yet. I'm not quite ready for the night to end.

I glance at Nicolo. "I need to get the glasses and the limoncello."

"I'll walk with you," he says easily.

"I'll be home soon," I tell Nonna. She doesn't protest, just hoists her purse onto her arm and nods. "Try to stay out of trouble for the rest of the night," she tells us. "I'm too old for any more surprises."

I can't see well in the pale light of the rising full moon, but I think she's smiling.

Chapter 40

"**Are you okay?**" I ask Nicolo as we pick our way slowly down the darkened lane. A few hundred feet in front of us the Fiat Panda's taillights wink red as Nonna creeps back to our farmhouse.

"That was a shock," Nicolo says slowly. "I had no idea."

"About Alberto and Violetta?"

"Yeah." He gives a dry, disbelieving laugh. "I knew they weren't happy together. I knew my grandfather could be a hard man. But no, I did not know how bad it was. And I had no idea about . . . about Nonna V. getting pregnant with my mom, or that Alberto and Bruna had once been engaged. That's crazy." He runs his fingers through his hair, a gesture of consternation, I've come to realize.

We walk side by side down the graveled driveway through the silvery olive groves alive with night sounds—the cooing of doves and the whir of insects. There is a full moon, but the night is half darkness under the cover of the trees. A light breeze is ruffling the leaves, and their papery whisper sends a shiver down my back. Somewhere an owl hoots and another answers far off. I think of the revelations from tonight. We only meant to steal back the missing half of the recipe, but instead our little caper resulted in an evening of revealed secrets and perhaps a long-standing rift now mended. I'm still a little stunned by it all.

"Do you think Nonna and Violetta could ever be friends again?" I ask.

"I hope so. They need each other, though they are both too stubborn to admit it," Nicolo says dryly.

"All those years. All those secrets..." I shake my head in wonder. "It makes me want to tell someone all my secrets immediately."

"Do you have any secrets?" Nicolo asks. He sounds curious and a little amused.

"Everyone has secrets," I tell him gravely, but then I can't think of a single one to confide.

We've reached the olive tree where we stashed the limoncello. Nicolo stops walking and just stands there for a moment, gazing at me in the light of the moon. His face is all planes and angles, but his eyes are black and intent on my face. He reaches out and brushes his thumb over my cheekbone. His expression is pained and a little hungry. "I know it's only for the summer, but I'm glad you're here," he says.

I lean into his touch. "I'm glad I'm here too." I pause, then ask playfully, "Do you have any secrets?"

He nods, then asks softly, "Do you want to know one?" His face is so close to mine I can see the inky line of his brows, the fan of dark lashes framing those deep, soulful eyes.

I nod, my heart pounding in my chest. "Yes, please," I whisper.

He leans forward until his lips brush my ear and whispers, "I watched every one of your shows."

"Every one?" I ask, dumbfounded, pulling back to look at his face. That's five years of content.

He nods solemnly. "Every single one."

"But you don't cook, do you?"

His lips quirk in a little wry smile. "I didn't watch it for the recipes," he says, his voice unexpectedly husky.

I don't know who moves first. I step forward. He meets me halfway. Our mouths find each other, picking up where we left off in Violetta's office. He pulls me closer, wrapping his arms around me, pressing us together from forehead to toes. His mouth is hungry on mine, and he makes a sound in his throat, a little desperate groan. He moves me back a few steps and pins me gently but firmly against the trunk of the olive tree.

I can't think; the darkened world spins and slips away and there is only this man against me, murmuring endearments in my ear in Italian, pressing hot kisses into the soft skin above my collarbone. The knobby trunk of the tree is wedged against my back, but all I can concentrate on is the heat of his body, his desire and mine, a potent alchemy that's making me dizzy. I can't quite catch my breath, but I can't stop touching him, kissing him. I don't want an inch of night between us. I want to stay like this forever.

And then my phone rings. I ignore it, pulling him even closer, but the ringing goes on and on. When it cuts off, it starts up again. I stiffen and he lifts his mouth from mine immediately. I murmur an apology and fumble in my purse, intending to turn the phone off, but then I see the screen. It's a giant photo of Drew looking tanned and windblown.

Instantly, I come crashing back to earth. Why is Drew calling me for the first time since he left? I check my phone record. Drew called twice in the space of a minute. Is there an emergency?

"Is everything okay?" Nicolo asks. He sounds a little winded. He glances at the screen and frowns.

I hesitate. "I'd better take this. It's my housemate Drew. I think something might be wrong." I'm still reluctant to step away. What rotten timing.

"Of course," Nicolo says reluctantly. "Do you want me to walk you back home?"

"I'll be fine. I'll call him on the way." I hold up my phone.

"Then good night, Juliana. Thank you for a very memorable evening." Nicolo presses a final kiss to my temple, then stoops and gathers the bottle of limoncello and the glasses. I take them from him and tuck the glasses in the pockets of my dress. The bottle I carry carefully. And then I walk away from him, picking my way down the dark driveway until I reach the road. I feel the heavy warmth of his eyes on me with every step.

When I turn into our own driveway, I tuck the bottle under my arm and slip my phone from my purse.

"Jules!" Drew picks up immediately. "Hey, roomie! Thanks for calling me back." I feel a rush of warmth at the sound of his voice, but also an unfamiliar hesitancy. It still stings to think of him sending the audition tape to Keith without telling me. I understand why he did it, but it still feels like a betrayal.

"What's going on?" I ask a little breathlessly. "Are you okay?"

"Yeah, everything is great," Drew assures me, but I know him too well. There's a note of hesitation in his voice. There's something he's not saying. "We're wrapping up filming in a few days, actually," Drew says. "The producers decided to just do a four-episode initial series and see how it tests with viewers." In the background I can hear a lot of noise and some sort of high-energy soundtrack. "This week we're in New Mexico, filming at this great little roadside diner that has bison burgers and these famous Hatch green chile hot dogs. You'd love the vibe." He sounds upbeat, a little too upbeat. "It's been an awesome experience to get to do this, like life-changing." It feels like there's a "but" coming, but I wait and it doesn't come.

"So how's Italy?" Drew asks. "How's the cookbook going?"

I glance back over my shoulder knowing I cannot see Nicolo

anymore through the grove of olive trees separating our two driveways. I'd bet five euros he is still there waiting, though, making sure I get home safely. Sure enough, my phone dings with a text, an Italian number.

> Let me know when you get home safely—
> Nico

My heart gives an almost painful thump. He's protective of me. It's a marvelous thought. I have to struggle to concentrate on my conversation with Drew.

"It's going pretty well," I tell Drew. "Being back in Italy has been honestly amazing and I'm making good progress on the recipes." I don't dive into the complexities of the farm and Nonna Bruna's magical cookbook, or mention Nicolo.

"Aw, that's great, Jules. Good for you," Drew enthuses. "Hey, send me some pictures, okay? I want to see what your life in Italy is like. And if you want to bounce any new ideas off me, I'm here. How's it going? Got any new ideas you might want to pitch to Keith?" His tone is studiedly casual, but I get the impression there's a reason he's asking. I wonder what it is.

"Maybe," I hedge. I don't really have any ideas at present, but I want to keep the door open in case I do.

"Oh yeah, like what?" he asks. He sounds a little too eager. I hesitate. I used to tell Drew everything, but I feel a little cautious now, like I need to be careful.

"Nothing concrete yet," I tell him truthfully.

"Well, let me know if you want to talk anything through . . ."

"Thanks, I will." Our conversation feels awkward, a little stilted. It makes me sad. We used to chat for hours, back in the pandemic lockdown days. He was my best friend.

THE SECRET OF ORANGE BLOSSOM CAKE

I come in sight of the farmhouse. The outside light is on, bathing the gravel courtyard in a warm yellow glow.

"Listen, Jules, I gotta get back to the shoot," Drew tells me. "Let's talk soon, okay?"

When we hang up, I send him a couple of photos—Alex and me at the market, a few of the dishes I've been working on, a photo of the farmhouse amid the olive groves. Then I include the @OlivesandAmore account information on TikTok, letting him know he can see more of my life in Italy there. I know Alex has been diligently posting on the site. He might enjoy the content.

Before I go into the house, I text Nicolo.

Home safe.

Then I pause, hand hovering over the screen. I want to write more, but what can I say? Thanks for the best make-out session of my life. Sorry we got interrupted. I settle for Thanks for being my partner in crime tonight.

The answer comes back quickly.

Of course. Anything for you, Jules, even petty larceny. 😏

Grinning, I slip my phone back in my purse and quietly let myself in the kitchen door. Everything is silent and dark. It appears I am the only one awake now. I go to the sink and run a glass of water from the tap, drinking deeply. I don't want to feel those shots of limoncello in the morning.

I can't stop thinking about Nicolo, about those moments under the olive tree. I brush my fingers over the tender skin of my jaw, still sensitive from the rough scratch of his beard stubble. I like him so much it's scaring me. He is a strong, intelligent, hardworking man who sacrifices for his family. He doesn't quit when it's hard. He doesn't back down from a challenge. He's funny and thoughtful and kind, and as Nonna so succinctly put it, he's such a fine piece of man.

But we are living completely different lives. How could anything work between us? He is tied to the land, to Italy and to his family's legacy. And I am heading back to Seattle at the end of the summer to keep pursuing my dream for the show. It's always been my plan, and I stick to the plan. But I can't deny how my heart is pulled toward Nicolo.

I think again of the farm, of Nonna's hope that I will stay, and immediately feel a familiar wave of panicky anxiety. If I stay, I am throwing away five years of work and giving up on my show, and for what? A Herculean task I am very likely to fail. I cannot do what Nonna wants me to do. I don't know how to save this place. But if I don't try . . . it will be lost anyway. It continues to feel like an impossible puzzle, one that makes me itchy and irritable.

I turn to head to bed, tired of going around and around in my mind. As I pass the table I spy the cookbook and beside it a familiar yellowed envelope. I pause for a moment, then pick it up. For the first time in sixty years, we have the recipe, the whole recipe, for Orange Blossom Cake. Could this be the answer to my quandary? If I make the recipe and take the first bite of cake, will I really see my future happiness? Could it help me make the right decision? Intrigued by the possibility, I head for bed. All of a sudden, I can't wait for morning to come.

Chapter 41

"**You tried to** *steal* the recipe back? And got caught? That's no fair. I always miss everything fun," Alex protests with a pout of disappointment the next morning as I fill her in on the events of the night before over pistachio biscotti and caffellattes.

"Oh, come on." I shake my head at her with a touch of amusement. "I saw you flirting with Tommaso at the festival. You're having some fun, admit it. Admit your summer is better than you thought it would be."

She crossed her arms. "I admit nothing." But she throws me a tiny smile and I know I've won. "It beats Camp Complain," she admits finally.

I knew it! It's a low bar to beat a camp whose idea of fun is a timed math-facts competition in the dining hall on Saturday nights, but still . . . Alex is officially having fun in Italy. I'll consider that a win.

"Let's see what we have here," Nonna announces to no one in particular. She has the cookbook and the yellowed envelope laid out in front of her on the table. She opens the cookbook, and true to form, the torn half of the recipe appears, plain as day. But I notice for the first time that the torn half a recipe takes up one side of a whole page of the cookbook. The other half of the page is blank.

"Why does the book show a whole page if you and Violetta tore the page in half?" I ask, puzzled.

Nonna looks at the page and shrugs. "The next time I opened the book after we divided the recipe, this is what I saw. Half the recipe, and half the page a white blank space, as though it is waiting to be filled. It has always been like this. It is useless to ask why about this book. Some things are beyond our understanding. Some things we cannot know." She carefully takes a folded half sheet of paper from the envelope and smooths it out on the table. One edge is ragged and uneven. It's the missing half of the recipe. "Ah, there it is," she says with a tender smile.

"How are you going to fix it?" I ask curiously.

"Like this." She gently presses Violetta's yellowed, folded half of the Orange Blossom Cake recipe back with its other half on the first page of the recipe book. She sits back and we all stare at the complete recipe, but nothing happens. I'm not sure what I expected. That they'd magically fuse together into one? That they'd restore justice, order, and harmony to the universe? The two halves of the recipe lie there next to each other, still torn, still separated. Nothing happens.

"I thought it might knit back together or something," I murmur, disappointed.

"Ah, the two halves have been apart a long time. This recipe might need a little help," Nonna says. She gets up and takes a small bowl from the shelves. She mixes a little flour and water with her finger, then spreads the paste thinly over the back of Violetta's half of the recipe and presses it firmly onto the blank half a page in the recipe book. "There. That should hold." She sits back and surveys her work with a look of supreme satisfaction. "Now it is whole once more."

THE SECRET OF ORANGE BLOSSOM CAKE

We all stare at the reunited recipe. Alex is the first to break the silence.

"So are we going to make the cake?" she asks.

"Do you want a chance to see your future?" Nonna asks.

Alex thinks for a moment but shakes her head. "What if there's nothing good?" she asks nervously.

"Impossible." Nonna reaches across the table and grips Alex's chin. Alex startles, but doesn't move away. "There is such greatness inside of you, nipotina mia," Nonna says firmly. "It is okay if you don't want to spoil the surprise of the happiness that lies ahead for you, but don't avoid it out of fear. Don't do anything out of fear. It will only hold you back from the fullness of what your life could be. That is a lesson for both you girls to learn, I see."

I don't miss the fact that it's the first time Nonna has referred to Alex as her granddaughter. From the brief flash of comprehension that crosses Alex's face, I see she caught the reference too. It makes me unexpectedly happy. What a difference a few weeks can make. Maybe family, like love, can grow in numbers and be strengthened, not diluted, by the increase. Maybe our family is stronger because Alex is taking her place in it.

"I want to taste the cake," I volunteer.

Nonna nods. "Let's see if the book will let you," she says sagely. "It only works if you open the book and the recipe appears. Otherwise it is not time for you to use the recipe."

"Oh, then this is probably a fool's errand," I say glumly. I have yet to open the book and see anything but a blank page. I'll give it a try, but my hopes are low. Carefully, we check to see that the paste is dry, then Nonna closes the cookbook.

"First, I must see something for myself." She opens the cookbook again as we all hold our breath, leaning in. What will be on the page?

Nonna laughs in delight and relief when she glimpses the recipe displayed on the first page. It is not Orange Blossom Cake.

"Olive oil and basil spritz," she crows. "Made with prosecco. Carlo used to love it. It's a celebratory drink. The last time I had it was with him." Her eyes get a little misty. We stare at the page in awe. It worked. For the first time in a long time, the book has given Nonna a new recipe to make. Now that the two torn halves of the cake recipe are reunited, it appears she can move on. I have a feeling that her ability to move on isn't just about her pasting the recipe back together again, but the other events of last night too. Nonna and Violetta hashing out the past, Violetta's apology and their reconciliation after such a bitter and lengthy estrangement. I'm guessing all of that has led to the cookbook's celebratory spritz today.

"I'll make us all spritzes at lunchtime," Nonna tells us, "to celebrate this success." She closes the book and hands it to me. "Now you try it, Juliana."

I close my eyes briefly, sending up a prayer to Saint Sebastian to let me see anything but a blank page. Carefully, I flip open the book and take a peek. It takes me a moment to realize that I'm staring at the familiar recipe for Orange Blossom Cake.

"No way," Alex breathes.

I can't help the huge grin that spreads across my face. "Finally!" I'm elated.

Nonna looks thoughtful. "So the book has given you a recipe? Interesting."

"Do you think this means I learned whatever lesson I was supposed to learn?" I ask. I stare at the recipe for a moment, wondering what exactly I was supposed to learn from those frustratingly blank pages.

"Only you can answer that," Nonna says. "What have you learned?"

I hesitate, thinking. "I've learned that Dad's death wasn't my fault," I say quietly. "For so long I blamed myself and blocked out anything that made me remember the pain of losing him. But now I can embrace the past again, even the memories that are tinged by grief and pain. Now when I make our family recipes, I remember all the good times that are connected to them, all the good memories, even if they also make me miss Dad. I think I've learned to open up my heart and connect to my past and our family again."

"Bene." Nonna nods in a satisfied way. Her eyes are suspiciously shiny. She clears her throat. "And now you have a new recipe to try," she says, gesturing to the Orange Blossom Cake recipe in the cookbook.

"Keep the book open to the recipe. I'll shoot a video about the cake and what we're planning to do," Alex says. She whips out her phone and narrates the video, showing the kitchen and the recipe book. She has Nonna explain about the recipe for Orange Blossom Cake, the magical properties of the cookbook, and our plan to make the cake and see the future.

Alex turns the camera to herself. "Will the cake really show us the future? Find out what happens next here @OlivesandAmore. Ciao." Then she taps her phone and ends the recording.

"You're a natural at that," I tell her. "You should be in front of the camera more." I thought she'd be awkward and shy, but she's great on-screen.

She shakes her head. "I like to be behind the scenes." She hunches over her phone and a few quick seconds later, she has edited and posted the video to TikTok.

"This is great content," Alex says, viewing the video she just posted. "TikTok eats that kind of stuff up. It could boost our followers a lot." She glances at me, offering offhandedly, "You can use any footage like this for your show if you want, since you're not shooting new segments right now."

We'd briefly discussed my show and how I was on a hiatus while my cohost was off filming in LA.

"Oh." I hadn't considered using any of the videos Alex has filmed in Italy. It's not exactly on-brand for *The Bygone Kitchen*, but I'm about to run out of content entirely. "Thanks, I'll think about it," I tell her.

"Ready, Juliana?" Nonna is starting to get ingredients out so I can make the cake. I join her in the kitchen but then I hesitate.

"Somehow it doesn't feel right for me to do this alone." I confess. "I think it should be more than just me who tastes the cake. I mean, you never got to take your first bite, right? Why don't you open the cookbook with me now and see if it will give both of us the cake recipe again?"

Nonna purses her lips and thinks about it. "I agree, but I think it should not just be the two of us," she says finally, firmly. "Violetta is a part of this too. Anyone who wants to taste this cake should do so, if the cookbook allows it." She smiles a little craftily. "Maybe Nicolo will want to join us and taste the cake too, hmm?" She raises an eyebrow meaningfully. "I wonder what he will see."

I ignore her insinuation. "I'll ask Nicolo this afternoon," I tell her. "I'm supposed to go over to the Fiores' to help with some marketing materials for their farm. I'll see if he and Violetta are interested in helping us make Orange Blossom Cake."

Chapter 42

"~~How long has~~ it been since your logo was updated?" I scoot forward in my chair next to Nicolo and squint at the slightly blurry hand-drawn olive tree logo displayed on the ancient desktop monitor on his desk. It's late afternoon and we're in his office nook, which is actually just a corner of the storage room we tiptoed through last night. It's not even an office, just a chair and desk surrounded by merchandise for the storefront and extra rolls of toilet paper and bottles of cleaning fluid. It looks different in daylight. Way more Office Max and less James Bond.

"I think Violetta's cousin drew this in the sixties, so it's been . . . a while," Nicolo admits, running his fingers through his curls. Increasingly, he has an air of exasperation as we go through all the marketing and branding materials related to the farm. It's in a sorry state.

"Oh wow, okay." I scribble "new logo" under the other items on the ever-increasing to-do list. I clear my throat and try not to think about last night. We're trying to be all business today, but it's hard to think clearly with Nicolo sitting so close our elbows are brushing.

I can feel the warmth of his skin through the thin cotton of his shirt, and I keep getting distracted thinking about those heated kisses in the darkness under the olive trees.

Nicolo peers at the list. "Thanks for helping us with this," he says. "I can handle the legal end of things, and I'm good at overhauling the business practices to maximize our efficiency, but marketing is not my strong suit." He grimaces.

"I'm happy to help. You've been incredibly kind to Nonna and Zio Lorenzo. It's the least I can do." I fiddle with the list and try to maintain a professional composure when really I just want to grab Nicolo by the collar and kiss him senseless. I clear my throat and squint hard at the desktop, trying to corral my overheated thoughts. If only he didn't smell so good. I want to lick him.

Focus, Jules, focus, I tell myself sternly. The Fiores need my help. I majored in marketing at Seattle University and minored in English. I've always been interested in marketing and branding. What draws people and creates instant brand appeal? How do you make good on what your advertising promises? I love exploring these topics. I've spent the past five years building my show's brand from scratch, so while I'm by no means a marketing professional, I can certainly improve on what the Fiore family business has now. Which is essentially nothing.

I force myself to concentrate on the marketing plan, and try to ignore Nicolo as he frowns at the screen, quirking those delicious lips and muttering to himself in Italian.

"You need a fresh logo and some basic marketing materials," I tell him briskly, scooting my chair a few inches away from him and fanning myself with an old brochure I found on the desk. It's hot this afternoon and the office is not air-conditioned. An ancient fan wheezes asthmatically in the corner but the air around us doesn't stir. "I have a few people we can ask for an estimate for those," I add.

"And I know someone who can build a website for a pretty decent price. You've got to bring your advertising into this century at least."

Nicolo groans. "I agree, but Violetta is very set in her ways. I can't promise I can get her to budge on anything." He blows a breath out in exasperation. "It took me weeks to convince her to change the brand of toilet paper in the store bathroom. The old stuff was like sandpaper." He winces. "This is what my life is now, arguing with a stubborn old woman about toilet paper." He leans back in the chair and laces his fingers behind his head, meeting my eyes with an expression of fatigue and exasperation. "Some days I'm not sure I can do this," he admits. "I don't know if I can get her to change enough to save this place."

I don't know what to say to that, but I can see the cost of what he's given up and how hard he's trying now.

"Okay, that's enough strategy for the moment. Let's go outside," I suggest. "We can brainstorm some good locations around the farm to photograph for the new website and tourism ads. I'll bet we can hire Alex to shoot them for us." I hop up and head out the side door. He follows.

It's a beautiful day, the late-afternoon sun bathing everything in a golden honey glow. The air is filled with the scent of lavender and the industrious buzzing of bees. Around the side of the villa I can just catch a glimpse of the terraces filled with tidy, glossy rows of citron trees. The unripe fruit hangs from the boughs, huge and green as limes. They will gradually turn bright yellow as they ripen through the summer until they are harvested in late fall. It looks like it will be a good crop this year; the boughs are heavy with fruit. I wonder if Violetta still makes her candied citron. We loved to sneak tastes of the special treat when we were younger.

There are a few cars parked in the wide gravel parking area between the villa and the gift shop. Through the shop window I can see a young saleswoman assisting a few middle-aged tourists wearing waist bags and floral T-shirts.

"Now picture this." We stand back from the entrance and I describe my ideas for improving curb appeal with a bigger sign sporting a new logo, a sandwich board down at the bottom of the drive to attract the attention of passing motorists, and some brochures to leave in local hotels to draw tourists. I'm halfway through my description when I hear the crunch of footsteps on gravel.

"What do you think you're doing?"

We both whirl to see Violetta striding toward us, looking imperious.

"Nonna V.," Nicolo says, forcing a smile. "Jules is helping us with some new marketing ideas for improving the business."

Violetta looks down her long nose at me suspiciously. "And what would she know of running this business?" she asks pointedly.

"I don't know the ins and outs of running an olive farm, but I can give some good suggestions about branding and marketing," I tell her calmly. "I studied marketing in college." What is it about this woman that always makes me feel like a scolded child?

She ignores me and turns to Nicolo. "We don't need to change anything," she insists. "This farm has been in our family for five generations. We stand proudly on tradition here."

Nicolo clears his throat and glances at me, then lowers his voice. "You know as well as I do that this place is no longer profitable," he says firmly. "You know we're at risk if we don't manage to increase our profit margin somehow. I've shown you the numbers and how this all plays out if we don't turn things around soon."

"And you think you know how to do this?" Violetta sniffs scornfully. "We have been doing things the same way in our family for generations. It is the way it has always been done, and yet you think you can come in here with your modern, fast ideas, and change things any way you want? You think you can improve on hundreds of years of tradition?"

I glance at Nicolo, noting his rigid posture, his jaw clenched in frustration, as he tries to reason with his grandmother. It isn't right that he has sacrificed his career, his entire life, to try to help his family, and she treats him like an incompetent child.

"He can, actually," I pipe up, surprised by my own temerity to stand up to Violetta. This is becoming a habit. "You should listen to Nicolo," I tell her, standing up straighter and meeting her shocked gaze. "He has great ideas and good business instincts. He knows how to grow a business. Farms like yours and ours are failing and being sold all over this region." I think about what Nonna and Lorenzo said the night I eavesdropped on their conversation. It's such a tragic thought it almost makes me want to cry, to think of the family farms scattered across the hillsides of Lake Garda being gobbled up by foreign investors or bigger olive-farming businesses. It cannot happen to the Fiores. It cannot happen to our family either. It's unthinkable. There must be another way.

"If you don't find a way to modernize this place, you're putting your family and legacy at risk," I tell Violetta firmly. "You have to change with the times, or you may not have anything left to pass on to the next generation of Fiores, and that would be such a loss for your family, the community, and this region. Farms like this are what makes Lake Garda so special. Don't get stuck in an old way of doing things and miss the opportunity to save your family's legacy."

I pause for breath, surprised by my own passion for this subject. Violetta is staring at me as though I've suddenly sprouted two heads. Nicolo is staring at me with a look of such astonished admiration it makes me blush.

"Sorry," I mumble. "Just giving you my thoughts." My phone vibrates in the pocket of my jeans. I want to peek at it, but Violetta's sharp eyes are trained on me. I just let it vibrate until it goes to voice mail.

"Well, next time you can keep your thoughts to yourself," Violetta retorts tartly, but I see her dart a glance at Nicolo and then at the list in my hands. She hesitates. "But perhaps a few changes would not be a terrible idea," she says finally, reluctantly. Silently, I whoop with glee. Victory! She holds up a warning hand. "But not too much. Nothing flashy. We must protect the dignity of the family name."

Nicolo glances up in surprise, then hastily agrees. "Nothing flashy," he promises her, then throws me a sly wink. "I guess we can forget that disco ball in the entrance hall to the gift shop," he says.

Violetta looks startled. "Disco ball?" she repeats in a scandalized tone.

"Joking, Nonna V.," Nicolo tells her. "I'll show you some of our ideas this evening. We'll keep it tasteful, I promise."

Chapter 43

By the time I finish up at the Fiore farm, it's growing dark. Nicolo and I worked through dinner and my stomach is growling. We sat side by side for hours, brainstorming, crammed together in the storage room office. Now we have a bare-bones marketing and branding plan laid out as well as a punch list of items for Nicolo to introduce to Violetta slowly—ideas for a website, new signs, an updated logo, and better customer interfaces. As soon as he gets her approval for the items, he can get to work. I feel satisfied that I've done a small part to help the Fiore olive farm hopefully thrive once more. At the same time, I feel a little guilty that I'm not helping my own family in this way. But the reality is that our farm does not need a marketing plan. We are not a business like the Fiores. We are a small, family-run olive farm in desperate need of a new generation to take over the care and running of the place, to carry on the legacy. And unless I'm willing to take on that role, there is not much to be done to help our farm. That's the truth, and it's a hard pill to swallow. If only I could solve our family's problem with a new logo and a glossy brochure.

Nicolo goes into the house to make us sandwiches, and I step outside to stretch my legs. Twilight is falling, that magical moment between day and night where it feels as though the world is holding its breath. Golden lights glimmer far below on the tranquil surface of the lake, spilling from the houses and hotels along the shore. From the nearby trees drifts the sleepy twittering of birds. Violetta is inside the villa, mostly likely watching her favorite detective show. I can see the dim blue light through the window. I look at my phone. I've had it on silent all afternoon and forgot to check it until now. It appears that a lot has happened in a few hours. The first text I see is from Lisa.

How r my girls? She includes a photo of her new pottery piece, which looks kind of like a bud vase shaped like a vagina. It's a mottled pink color. Unleashing my feminine power! she captions it.

I shudder but text back Everything is great. I send her a photo of Alex helping me in the kitchen, and she hearts it immediately. With Lisa, that's about all I can expect. I'm used to it by now.

Aurora has sent a two-minute audio text complete with the children's new penny whistle / flute / violin quartet playing discordantly in the background, and at the end, a few seconds of panicked yelling when Doris is discovered inside the mudroom eating Meadow's rubber rain boots. I make a note to send her a long audio text back, updating her about everything that has happened since we last spoke. She is going to be over the moon when she hears about my safecracking and make-out session with Nicolo last night.

Alex has also texted twice.

> Our video from this morning is really popular. People love this magic cake idea. We're at fifteen thousand views already, and a thousand shares.

An hour later she texted again.

Now it's got fifty thousand views and
five thousand shares. This is crazy. I think
this might be going viral.

I check the @OlivesandAmore TikTok account. Yep, Alex is right. The video is trending. Even as I'm looking at the post, people are commenting. I scroll down through the hundreds of comments—some enthusiastic, some skeptical. A few trolls. The usual mix, but so many more people than I'm used to. I see a comment from Drew.

This is awesome! Jules, call me! I need to talk to you.

I close TikTok, feeling astonished and also thoughtful. Where does all this publicity lead? We've got momentum, but what do we do with it? Is there a way we can leverage it to help the farm? But even if we did leverage it, to what end? I am leaving at the end of the summer. Who would carry on the momentum?

I see I've a missed call from Drew. He texted too.

Call me. Keith wants to talk to you.

Frowning, I reread the text. Keith wants to talk to me? Why? Is there renewed interest in our show?

I call Drew's number, heartbeat quickening with a nervous hope. He doesn't answer. Disappointed, I leave a message telling him to call me and hang up just as Nicolo comes out of the villa, laden with sandwiches and glass bottles of a fizzy yellow drink. He hands me a bottle and I recognize the Tassoni label on their famous citron-flavored soda. They once used citron from the Lake Garda region for the flavoring, but now use a different variety grown in Calabria. I learned that tidbit from Dad, who loved this beverage.

"I spoke to Nonna V. about your idea for the Orange Blossom Cake," Nicolo tells me, offering me a sandwich on thick, soft bread, "and she's agreed to come over tomorrow morning to see if the cookbook will show us the recipe. I told her if it does, the plan is that we make the cake together and then all take the first bite at the exact same time."

"She said yes? That seems suspiciously easy." I take a big bite of the sandwich, layered with peppery mortadella (heavenly Italian bologna that puts American bologna to shame), cheese, and sliced ripe tomatoes. I stifle a groan. It's so good.

Nicolo chuckles. "She was skeptical until I mentioned that Bruna was going to participate. I told her how exciting it would be that Bruna would finally get to see her happiest moment. I was banking on Nonna V. being competitive enough not to want to be left out."

"Clever you." I take a sip of the citron soda, the bubbles tickling my nose. It's refreshing and citrusy and aromatic. I'd forgotten how unique the flavor of citron truly is.

I reach out and clink my bottle to Nicolo's. "Cin cin," I say, the casual Italian version of cheers. "To second chances."

He raises his bottle in a little salute. "And to the promise of Orange Blossom Cake."

We drink.

Chapter 44

"**What are we** waiting around for?" Violetta demands impatiently. "We're not getting any younger."

It's nine a.m. the next morning and Nonna Bruna, Alex, Nicolo, Violetta, and I are gathered in Nonna's kitchen, crowded around the prep table where the cookbook lies waiting for us. The only person missing is Lorenzo, who left for Udine yesterday while I was at the Fiores'. Apparently, he's gone to help his sister with an urgent plumbing problem at her restaurant. He is due back sometime today.

"We have to open the cookbook together at the same time," Nonna reminds us. "And then we'll see if it gives us the recipe for Orange Blossom Cake."

Dutifully, all of us (except Alex, who has decided to video everything and not participate herself) lay our hands on the cookbook. My hand is next to Nicolo's and his fingers brush mine. He looks delectable today in a cream-colored linen shirt and olive trousers with leather boat shoes.

"Now we open the book together," Nonna explains. "I will count to three. Uno. Due. Tre." She opens the book slowly as we all manage to keep contact with it. I draw a quick breath. There is a recipe waiting for us.

"Mamma mia!" Nonna breathes reverently. I peer anxiously down at the cookbook. The recipe for Orange Blossom Cake is sitting there whole on the page.

"Non ci credo," Violetta gasps, looking astonished.

I don't believe it either. Apparently, it is our time to make this recipe. Alex hovers close by, recording everything.

"The cookbook is never wrong," Nonna says briskly. "Now we make the cake . . . together."

Nonna gathers the dry ingredients and puts us to work on the rest. Nicolo measures out a cup of the best olive oil from our trees, pouring out a stream of pale shimmering green. Violetta purees a whole orange, and the fragrance of the pulped peel and juice fills the kitchen. Alex circles around us, videoing our group effort. I combine sugar and eggs, beating them with Nonna's ancient electric mixer, which makes alarming grinding sounds but gets the job done eventually.

The sun is shining on the courtyard and streaming in through the open kitchen door. Nonna has the radio on, turned down low as a tenor croons ballads in Italian. All is peaceful and productive. When the sugary egg mixture is fluffy, Nicolo slowly pours in the olive oil. Violetta adds her orange juice and zest and I dump in a half cup of milk and a few tablespoons of orange liqueur. The batter gradually turns a beautiful golden color. Nonna has measured out the dry ingredients and slowly adds them next—the flour, baking powder, and salt. As a last step, I spoon a brimming tablespoon of orange blossom extract into the bowl and stir.

"This is the magic cake?" Alex asks dubiously, peering at the slightly lumpy golden batter. She is busy snapping photos and recording. I sniff the batter, savoring the sweet, delicate aroma of orange blossom extract and the unctuous aroma of good olive oil.

"You sure this is all there is to it?" I ask Nonna. "It just seems too simple."

"Simple can be just as good as complex," Nonna says serenely as she whips up a simple sugar and orange zest icing to pour over the cake when it's done. "Often it's better. Life doesn't have to be so complicated. It doesn't need to twist you into knots. Often the best choice is the simple one. Simple is beautiful."

"Okay then." I carry the cake pan to the oven and Nicolo opens the oven door for me. Alex hovers at my shoulder, recording and narrating. I slide the pan into the oven and set the timer on my phone. Now we wait.

Nonna makes caffellattes for Nicolo, Alex, and me. She and Violetta drink espresso—black and strong—served with small glasses of water to cleanse their palates. We sit on the patio under the olive trees and drink our coffee, chatting a little nervously, counting down the minutes until the timer dings. Finally, it does and we all breathe a sigh of relief. Wordlessly, we crowd into the kitchen. Nonna pulls out the cake and sets it on the prep table. We gather round eagerly.

"It just looks like a normal cake." Alex sounds slightly disappointed. It's wafting the most delicate, delectable aroma of oranges and orange blossoms, and my mouth waters. Alex lifts her camera and takes a few photos as I test the cake for doneness. I slide the knife from the center. It's ready.

"Now we will try it together," Nonna instructs.

I leave the cake on the table to cool a little and help gather small plates and forks. Nicolo and Violetta offer to set the table on the patio. I eye the cake as I pass by. Somehow the thought of taking that first bite feels daunting. What if I don't like what I see? What if it surprises me? I feel a flutter of anxious anticipation. Will the Orange Blossom Cake really show me something? Perhaps me standing in a professional soundstage kitchen filming an episode of *The Bygone Kitchen* for Netflix? Or accepting a Taste Award or a Daytime Emmy for the show's creative success? Or is it possible that it will be something else entirely? I cast a quick glance out the window at Nicolo on the patio. I'm nervous yet eager for the cake to give me some guidance, to show me if I am choosing the right hard thing.

Finally, Nonna deems everything ready. I carefully remove the cake from the pan, first putting an upside-down plate over the top of the cake pan and then flipping it over quickly. I tap the bottom of the pan gently and feel the cake release with a soundless plop onto the plate.

Almost instantly, an image flashes through my mind. I am standing in one of our olive groves, dressed in work clothes and boots. The air is crisp and the sun bright on the silvery leaves. Tarps are spread below each tree. It's harvest time, probably mid-November, just before the winter chill sets in. There is a man standing across from me, wearing gloves and operating an electric rake. He's carefully combing the higher branches of the tree while I harvest the low-hanging fruit by hand. When he turns and looks at me, the late-afternoon sunlight makes an aureole of gold around his dark curls, illuminating him clearly. It's Nicolo. He pauses combing the branches, olives falling gently down around him like fat raindrops. He smiles at me and I feel my heart leap.

"Tesoro mio," he says, his voice tender. He holds out his hand and I move toward him eagerly . . .

"Juliana?" Nonna's questioning voice jerks me rudely back to the present. I blink uncertainly and take a quick, sharp breath.

Nonna gives me an odd look. "Are you all right?" she asks.

I nod. "Sorry, my mind wandered there for a second." I glance down and lift the cake pan off the cake. It is perfect, golden and moist-looking.

"Where did you wander?" Nonna asks, searching my face.

"Nowhere," I tell her honestly. "I was right here on the farm." And it's true... but still, it felt different. It felt... satisfying. What an unexpected word, but it's the right one.

I take a quick peek at the cake. Could it be a coincidence that I had that vivid daydream just as I took the cake from the pan? Was it just my mind playing tricks on me? I shake off the prickle down my spine at the memory of Nicolo's eyes on me, the look on his face, radiant with love.

Alex wanders into the kitchen, looking at her phone. "People are going crazy over those magical cake recipe videos I posted this morning. They've gotten so many shares already." She looks gleeful. "And the viral one from yesterday is still going strong. It's been viewed over two hundred thousand times already!"

I don't completely love the idea of posting about the cookbook on social media. It feels a little too personal, sacred to our family. But Alex is excited, and the numbers are certainly impressive. I don't have the heart to quench her enthusiasm. It's good to see her excited about something.

Nicolo pokes his head in the kitchen. "All is ready out here," he says, meeting my eyes with a swift, intense look.

"One last step." Nonna pours the icing over the cake and smooths it with a knife. The icing is shiny and the palest shade of yellow with bits of orange zest giving it tiny, bright pops of color. "Now it's time," Nonna says, looking satisfied.

"Ready?" I smile at Nicolo, remembering the thrill of him holding out his hand to me in the olive grove. It was a daydream, but the sensation of contentment is still pulsing in my chest like a little ray of sunshine. I carefully pick up the cake plate and head outside.

It's time to see what happiness awaits us.

Chapter 45

"*Are we all* taking a first bite, except for Alex?" I glance around the patio table, knife poised over the cake plate. It's cooler in the shade, though the day is warming and promises to be a scorcher in a few hours. Nicolo is sitting directly across from me, looking relaxed. He meets my eyes, arches a brow, and nods. "I'm in," he says.

Nonna is sitting to my right, clutching her rosary, and Violetta—in her usual black dress—sits ramrod straight next to Nicolo, her mouth a thin line. Alex is standing back from the table, phone in her hand, documenting the occasion.

"I will try the cake," Violetta says stiffly.

"As will I," Nonna says. "It's never too late to glimpse your happiness."

"But what if our happiest moment is behind us?" Violetta asks, looking uneasy. "Do we see nothing at all?" She sips her espresso and frowns.

"The cake shows you the happiest moment of your life that is still to come," Nonna explains. "Hopefully, we have all already lived many happy moments. The cake simply shows us a glimpse of the happiness still awaiting us." She speaks calmly, but she's worrying the rosary beads between her fingers. She's nervous, I realize. We all are.

"Bene." Violetta nods, satisfied. "What are we waiting for then? Allora!"

"I'll start recording when you cut the cake," Alex tells me. With her hair slicked back in a high ponytail, and wearing a new black-and-white-striped Breton-style shirt, she looks a little more Milan and a little less NYC today. She also looks happy. She's been texting nonstop with Tommaso all morning, grinning as she does so. It's cute.

The cake sits in the middle of the table in front of me, waiting. I count my breaths for a few beats, trying to calm my nerves. Alex has her camera raised, ready to record everything.

Mustering my courage, I cut thick wedges, lift out the golden triangles, and slide each piece onto a small plate. Nonna passes the plates around and hands out forks. I gently poke my wedge of cake with my finger. It is moist with a beautiful crumb and the smell is subtle but enticing. My heart flutters with anxiety and excitement. What will I see?

"I think someone is coming up the drive," Nicolo says suddenly, cocking his head to listen.

Just then the familiar rattle of the Fiat Panda sputters up the lane and a moment later Lorenzo pops into view. We all pause as he parks the Panda and gets out. He is wearing a pair of dark blue work overalls and a fisherman's cap. He has smudges of grime on his face and looks exhausted.

"Lorenzo." Nonna calls out a greeting, waving him over. "Vieni qui. Come here. There is cake."

Lorenzo lifts his hand in greeting. "A moment," he calls. "Let me get cleaned up. Don't wait for me. Continue." He disappears into the stable, presumably heading to his apartment.

"We will save him a piece," Nonna announces, then nods to me.

"I don't think he cares about the first bite. He thinks the cookbook is all nonsense anyway. Juliana, let's get started."

"Okay." I stare down at the slice of cake in front of me. Alex presses the record button on her phone and aims it at me, stepping a little back from the table.

"Here we are, about to try the first bite of the Orange Blossom Cake," she narrates. "Is everybody ready?"

"Get on with it," Violetta mutters, giving the phone's camera a narrow, suspicious look. She stabs her fork into her cake and cuts off the tip of the wedge.

"Jules, will you count for us, from three?" Nonna asks, sharp eyes on me. She's holding a forkful of cake. So is Nicolo. I neatly slice off the tip of my cake and spear it on my fork.

"On the count of three," I tell them. "We'll taste the first bite all at the same time. Uno . . . due . . ." And then I pause before tre. "Wait, do you hear that? I think someone else is coming up the driveway." I can hear the motor purring up the hill.

"Madonna!" Violetta exclaims in exasperation. "What now? I'll be dead and gone to my eternal reward before we take this first bite."

A gleaming black sedan noses its way up the lane and into the courtyard.

"Who's that?" Alex asks. She keeps filming.

The sedan halts in the middle of the courtyard with a crunch of gravel. One of the back doors opens and a man emerges. A golden-haired man with a familiar gait.

"Drew?" I drop my forkful of cake. What in the world is he doing here?

He lifts his hand in a half wave. "Hey, Jules!" he calls, grinning and walking toward me, arms spread wide. "Surprise!"

Across the table, Nicolo sits up straight, his expression shifting from intrigued to wary in an instant.

"Your housemate Drew?" he says. "Why is he here?"

"I have no idea," I murmur to Nicolo, then say brightly to the group, "One minute, everybody. Sorry for the delay." I clatter down the uneven stone steps to the courtyard.

"What are you doing here?" I demand in astonishment as Drew grabs me in a hug.

"We came to see you, silly. Since you weren't answering your phone." He places a smacking kiss on my forehead.

I pull back quizzically. We? Who's we? Did he bring Desiree Reyes with him? I glance around, then back at Drew. He is tanned and dressed in shorts and a casual salmon colored T-shirt, wearing a straw fedora and a pair of his vintage Adidas. He smells like Drew, like Tide laundry detergent and Speed Stick with a hint of sunscreen. At that moment, Lorenzo saunters out of the stable, giving Drew a curious look as he heads up the stairs toward the patio table.

"This is Drew. A friend from back home," I call out to him in explanation.

"Ciao," he says amiably. "Welcome to Italy."

Violetta and Nonna are watching the scene unfold with identical looks of skepticism. Alex appears to still be filming. A car door slams and I peer around Drew to see Keith, hands in his pockets, looking around the farm with a dispassionate interest. What is he doing here? Has he reconsidered interest in *The Bygone Kitchen*?

Suddenly, I hear a throat clear.

"Buongiorno," Nonna announces, although it doesn't sound exactly like a welcome. More like a warning. She comes down the steps and stops at the bottom, drawing herself up to her full height, which is still pint-sized. She looks regal and stern, if diminutive. "I am Bruna Costa, and this is my home."

Keith moves toward Nonna, his hand outstretched, a professional smile plastered on his face, but Drew beats him to it. He lets go of me and grabs Nonna's hand, pressing it between his own.

"Nonna Bruna!" he says, giving her his most boyishly charming smile. "I've heard so much about you from Jules. I'm sorry we just showed up like this, but I had to come see this famous Nonna that Jules loves so much. It's a pleasure to meet you. I'm Drew."

Nonna's stony demeanor softens a little at his words, although her eyes on Drew's are sharp and searching. "You are welcome here, Drew," she says, patting his hand. "Our door is open for any friend of Juliana's."

She casts a speculative glance at me. Drew beams at her and she smiles back, a touch tight-lipped. I get the feeling she is not pleased about something. Behind me, Keith clears his throat. He approaches, hand outstretched.

"Mrs. Costa, I'm Keith Garvey. I'm a talent scout for television shows . . ." He is speaking slowly and strangely loudly, as though he assumes Nonna is hard of hearing.

Nonna does not take his hand. Her stony expression slips back instantly. "Oh yes, I know who you are," she assures him. "The man who rejected my Juliana's show." Then she turns around and motions to Drew, completely ignoring Keith and leaving him standing there with his hand outstretched.

"Sorry about that," I murmur. I don't want Nonna to alienate him in case he comes bearing good news. Keith doesn't appear to hear me.

"Come." Nonna motions to Drew. "We are about to enjoy a slice of cake. You look as though you've had a long journey. I will make you a coffee." She leaves Keith standing there in the gravel courtyard looking confused and ushers Drew up the stairs toward the patio.

"Um, can I get you an espresso?" I ask Keith.

He waves off the offer. "I'll hang back for a minute." He looks nonplussed. Alex and Nicolo are standing at the top of the stairs as we go up. Alex is filming everything with a look of avid interest on her face. Nicolo, on the other hand, has his arms crossed, his expression guarded. He steps aside to let Nonna and Drew by, but the glance he gives Drew as he brushes past is anything but friendly. Drew doesn't seem to notice.

"Lorenzo, no!" Violetta's sudden scream pierces the air. We all freeze, staring at Lorenzo, who is standing with a puzzled expression on his face, his fork raised over a slice of the Orange Blossom Cake. A slice that is now missing one big bite.

Chapter 46

"What?" Lorenzo says, his mouth full of cake. "It's delicious."

"Idiota!" Violetta chastises, hurrying over to him. "The first bite was not for you!"

Lorenzo looks down at his fork in confusion, and then the strangest thing happens. Just for a moment, his entire being goes perfectly still. His face changes ever so slightly, awash with a look of bewilderment that melts a few seconds later into an expression of tenderness and adoration.

"Lorenzo?" Nonna says sharply, clapping her hands. He does not even blink. He is staring fixedly into the distance, smiling so broadly it looks as though his heart will burst with joy.

"What's happening?" Alex whispers beside me, still filming. We stare at Lorenzo. I am teetering between intrigue and alarm.

"Do you think the cake worked?" I pause. For a few seconds, no one moves. And then Lorenzo blinks once and looks around in puzzlement.

"Che é successo?" he asks. What happened?

Nonna stands in front of him, hands on her hips, scolding him in rapid-fire Italian. She barely comes up to his shoulder, but she is brimming with exasperation. "What happened is that you ruined everything! Idiota! Can't you see we were all waiting to take the first bite? Imbecille!"

And then the most extraordinary thing occurs. Lorenzo sets down his fork, swoops Nonna up in his big, beefy arms, and gives her a firm, smacking kiss on the lips. "Bruna," he says, setting her down gently again. "You are a beautiful and amazing woman, and I am in love with you."

Nonna is so astonished she cuts off mid-tirade and just stares at him in shock. Her maroon lipstick is a little smeary and she wobbles slightly in her sensible pumps. He steadies her with one hand, looming over her with a fierce tenderness I've glimpsed before. Aha, so I *was* right! He does love her!

"I see now I've been a fool to wait this long. I have loved you since Carlo died," Lorenzo tells her earnestly in Italian. "I love you still. We don't have much time left, but what we have, I want to spend with you . . . as your husband. Bruna Costa, will you marry me?"

My jaw drops and Alex and I exchange dumbstruck looks. She is still filming the entire thing on her phone. "Did he just propose?" she whispers. I nod.

"What's happening?" Drew asks beside me, confused.

I have only ever seen Nonna at a loss for words once before, the day my father died. This is definitely a happier occasion. She puts a hand to her hair, smoothing a strand back into her tight bun. She looks dazed.

"Well," she says stiffly. "I . . . I have to think about it." She looks up at him and I swear she blushes. "Thank you, Lorenzo," she says with an air of shaken dignity, and then she carefully walks past me down the steps and disappears into the house. No one says anything for a moment.

"Cavolo!" Nicolo exclaims, looking impressed. "The cake actually works?"

Violetta gives a long-suffering sigh and puts down her fork. "Not for us, not now," she says bitterly. "The first bite is gone."

Alex looks disgruntled. "Now what?" she asks. "Since Zio Lorenzo ate the first bite of cake?"

"I think you can stop filming. I'm guessing that's all the excitement for today," I tell her. Then I turn to Violetta. "I'm sorry," I say with a sigh. "We can make another cake. We can try this again."

She waves a hand dismissively. "It is what it is," she says with resignation. "Maybe it is best we do not see our happiness in advance. Maybe it is enough just to breathe each day." She stands and motions to Nicolo. "Come, Nico," she commands. "I am tired and I want to go home now. I must rest a few minutes before we go to Verona for my appointment."

Reluctantly, Nicolo follows her, offering her an arm as she descends the stone steps. He glances back at me, his eyes straying to Drew and then away. He doesn't say anything, but his jaw clenches. I glance down at the ground, not sure where to look.

"I got all of that on film. It's going to be gold," Alex crows excitedly, coming up to me. "I bet we pick up a ton of new followers from this. People are going to love it."

"That's great," I murmur, but my eyes keep going back to Drew. What is he doing here? Lorenzo is now the only one sitting down at the table, tucking into another big slice of the cake.

"Excuse me for a minute," I tell Drew. "I'll be right back." I head over to Lorenzo.

"I'm sorry, picolina," he says as I slide into the chair next to him. "I didn't know the first bite was special."

I am aware of Alex hovering over my shoulder. I suspect she might be filming our conversation.

"It's okay." I pause. "We can try to make the cake again, if I can convince the others to give the recipe another chance." I feel a little shy asking the question on my mind. "Zio, what did you see? When you took the first bite?"

His face breaks into a smile as warm and big as the sun. "It was nothing out of the ordinary," he answers in Italian. "Bruna and I were sitting at the kitchen table having a coffee as we often do. But we were holding hands, and she was wearing a new wedding ring." He shrugs. "We are old and the years we have left may be few," he says contemplatively, "but I cannot think of life without her. After all, it is never too late to love." Then he takes another big bite of cake and chews with relish. I glance at Alex, who lowers her phone and gives me a look of pure astonishment.

"No one is going to believe the cake actually works," she murmurs with a touch of awe. "I bet this will go super viral."

I'm puzzled as to why the cake worked for Lorenzo at all. He wasn't even part of the cake preparation process. But regardless of that apparent fluke, it appears that the cake did show Lorenzo a glimpse of the future, which is more than a little astonishing. I hope we get to try the recipe again, now that we know it really works.

Leaving Lorenzo to his cake and Alex sitting across from him, fiddling with her phone, I head back to Drew. He looks a little shy. "Was that what I think it was?" he asks. "The whole cake thing?"

"If you mean did you just see an elderly Italian man accidentally take a bite of magical cake and see a vision of the happiest moment of his life, then propose to his dead cousin's wife who he's secretly been in love with for decades? Then yes."

"Wow, cool." Drew looks impressed. He glances toward the courtyard where Keith is talking on his phone.

"Hey, Keith, I'm going to hang out here with Jules for a while, talk to her about the thing," Drew calls out, giving me a little sideways look. "If that's okay?"

"Sure, of course," I say immediately. What is the thing he's going to talk to me about? My heart skips a beat. Is it good news about the show? Keith gives him a little nod and a thumbs-up. He pauses his conversation for a moment and calls back to Drew, "I'm going to head to our hotel. Text me when you're done and I'll send the driver for you." Keith disappears into the back of the sedan, and we watch it drive away.

"Want to see the farm?" I offer, gesturing toward the rutted lane leading up into the oldest part of the olive groves.

"Sure. Lead the way," Drew replies, gazing around at the picturesque scenery. I keep my eyes firmly on him. I'm determined to get some answers.

Chapter 47

"Drew, what are you doing here?" I burst out as we amble up the grassy lane among the olive trees. I can't stand not knowing any longer. We come to a stop in the oldest part of the grove, the trees planted far apart to give them breathing room. Dappled with sunlight, they are silvery and gnarled with twisted branches, each a unique shape. It is my favorite part of the farm. I pause by one of the oldest trees. The wood of the trunk beneath my hand feels warm, alive. Drew comes to a stop next to me.

"This place is amazing, Jules," he enthuses, glancing around him, taking in the sloping hillside, the glimpse of blue water down below, the cloudless azure of the sky. He whistles in appreciation. "You told me about the farm, but I had no idea it would be so cool. I feel like I'm in a movie."

"Drew, why are you here, in Italy?" I ask again.

He stops and faces me, his expression eager. "Jules," he says seriously, "I had to come tell you in person." He pauses for a beat. "We have another shot at a show."

My heart skips a beat. "What do you mean?"

"Keith wants us to cohost a show together," he explains. "Not *The Bygone Kitchen*. A different format."

I lick my lips. "What format?" I'm trying to keep up.

Drew looks excited. "I showed Keith the account you sent me, @OlivesandAmore, and he loved it," he explains. "He showed it to a couple of producers and they loved it too. Everyone is really excited about this new idea. When Keith saw the recipe video you posted yesterday about the orange flower cake, he booked us tickets to Italy immediately." He steps closer to me and puts his hands on my shoulders, peering intently into my eyes. "Jules, we have an offer already. Peacock wants us to shoot a pilot, and if they like it, they'll sign us for an entire ten-episode run for the first season with the chance to renew for more seasons. It's a dream come true for both of us." He stops, looking expectantly at me.

I stare at him in bewilderment. It's amazing news. So why am I suddenly feeling hesitant? "Orange Blossom Cake," I correct him, stepping back a little so his hands fall away from me.

"Right, whatever," he agrees distractedly. "Jules, they want us, together, to do a show. Can you believe it? It's what we planned. And yeah, it's not the old format, but Keith says vintage is out and paranormal stuff is in."

"But what about your show with Desiree?" I stammer.

Drew winces. "Um, well." He blows a breath of air out like a deflating soccer ball. "To be honest, the network decided not to pick us up when they saw the pilot. I guess it wasn't what they were hoping for." He looks disappointed. "And Desiree got a chance to be on this reality dance competition show, which is great for her . . . but . . ."

"So your show got cancelled?" I clarify.

He looks down at his feet and nods. "Yeah, it sucks. I was really hoping this was it. But hey, now we get a chance to make a show together." He grins at me, although the smile doesn't quite reach his eyes. He's making eye contact with me, but there's a hesitancy there that gives me pause. What is he not telling me? After the last time when he didn't tell me about the interview tapes, I'm a little cautious.

"It sounds like a dream come true," I murmur, trying to grasp this unexpected turn of events. Frankly, I'm stunned. "What would the new show be like? What's the format?"

I gesture for him to follow me and start walking again, this time toward the house. I don't know why, but I feel like I want to go back.

"You and I would cohost," Drew explains.

"I thought Keith didn't like my style," I interrupt. "He said my hosting style didn't set the right tone." The comment still stings.

"That was before he saw the videos of you cooking here in Italy, and before he knew about your family's mystical cookbook." Drew bounds along beside me with barely contained enthusiasm.

"My family's cookbook?" I slow, suddenly wary. "How does the cookbook factor in?"

"Keith and the producers want to do a reality cooking competition," Drew explains. "Sort of like *Chopped* with a magical twist. Imagine this—home cooks from around the country compete against one another, and the winner of the competition gets to make a recipe from the cookbook to help them solve whatever problem they're facing in life. Keith said shows about the supernatural are really hot right now, and everyone loves to root for the underdog. Picture a cooking competition where every contestant has a problem they need help with—some family issue or they're lonely and looking for love—and the cookbook helps solve the winner's problem. I'd be the host and you'd be the lead judge and cooking expert. Keith says it's an original concept. He's excited about it, and Peacock agrees."

I'm baffled by this entire notion. I have to admit I've watched my fair share of reality TV. There are weirder shows out there, but something about Drew's description of the show is making me increasingly uncomfortable.

"But it's my family's cookbook," I protest. "It's not mine. I doubt Nonna will let me borrow it for TV." The idea feels sacrilegious somehow, to use the cookbook in this way. "Where is Keith planning to film the show anyway?"

"LA of course," Drew says.

"LA?" My voice falters. Would the cookbook even work away from this place? I have no idea. I hesitate.

Drew turns and faces me. He grabs my hands and holds tight. "Jules, this is our chance! What you've been dreaming of for five years! This is it! And we get to do it together. All we need is for your nonna to lend us her book, just till we're done shooting. And if it works, if we make a great show, the sky's the limit. Think about it. The money is good. Like really good. No more working at Trader Joe's good. You won't have to worry anymore."

That part catches my attention.

"The farm is struggling," I admit. "And I've been trying to figure out how to help."

"Exactly," Drew cuts in eagerly. "If you do this show, whatever your nonna needs, whatever the farm needs, you can pay for it. All you have to do is say yes. Convince your nonna to lend us the book, and you can have what you've always wanted." He looks so earnest and excited.

I hesitate. It does sound amazing. Almost too-good-to-be-true amazing. I don't know what to think. Could this really be the solution to all our problems?

Drew reads the indecision on my face and his own expression clouds. He drops my hands.

"I thought you'd be more excited," he says quietly. "I thought this is what you wanted."

"I am excited," I hasten to reassure him. "It's just . . . a surprise. It's a lot to take in all at once, you know? I thought that dream was over, and now you're telling me we have a chance again. I just . . . need a minute to wrap my head around it all."

"Of course," Drew says instantly, his enthusiasm bouncing back. "Take your time. Keith said you can let us know tomorrow."

"Tomorrow? That's really fast." I'm taken aback. "This is a big decision."

Drew gives me an uncomprehending look. "This is what you wanted, right? What's left to decide? Things move fast in LA. If we don't jump on this, Keith has a bunch of other ideas waiting, other dreamers like us who will sign on the dotted line." He gives me a determined look. "We're being offered a once-in-a-lifetime opportunity, Jules," he urges me. "Let's go for it."

He slings an arm around my shoulders and pulls me against his side. I let him, but my mind is spinning. I should be over the moon. He's offering me the exact thing I've been working toward. It's everything I thought I wanted. So why am I so hesitant?

"Let me think about it," I tell Drew finally as we approach the farmhouse and come to a halt on the patio. It's empty now except for Alex, who has her feet propped on the table and is practicing Italian on her phone. "I'll have an answer for you by tomorrow."

"Okay. I'll tell Keith." Drew sounds disappointed, and I almost cave and hasten to reassure him that it's a brilliant idea. Of course I'm thrilled. Of course I'll do it. But something holds me back.

Drew yawns suddenly and pulls his phone out of his pocket. "I'm beat. I didn't sleep at all last night on the plane. I think I'm going to head to the hotel. We can come back tomorrow morning to get everything signed."

"Come back tomorrow." I nod, realizing he's already assuming I'm going to say yes. While Drew arranges for the car to come get him, I pull out my phone and text Nicolo to ask if he and Violetta would be up for trying to make the cake again and if so, how soon could they come over for a redo. Ideally, I'd really like to be able to taste the cake before I have to give Drew and Keith an answer tomorrow. I need all the guidance and help I can get to decide what to do.

When the gleaming black sedan pulls into the drive a few minutes later, I walk down the stone steps with Drew. He hugs me enthusiastically and kisses my cheek before hopping into the back seat. As the car disappears down the curve of the drive, he sticks his head out the window.

"Just say yes, Jules!" he yells as he disappears down the drive.

Chapter 48

"Say yes to what?"

I glance over to find Alex standing beside me, her earphones around her neck. She must have heard Drew's parting encouragement out the car window.

"It's . . . complicated," I say with a frown, staring in the direction of the departing car. My phone pings with a text. Nicolo. He has taken Violetta into Verona for an appointment, but she is willing to come tomorrow morning to try to make and taste the cake one more time. My heart flutters with hope. If we start early, I can eat that first bite of cake before I have to give my answer to Drew and Keith. Relieved, I text back a confirmation and a start time of seven a.m. tomorrow morning, then tuck my phone away. While I might have a momentous decision to make, I also have my own cookbook I need to finish. Regardless of what I decide about Drew's offer, I still need to keep cooking. I turn toward the kitchen with a sigh. I need an espresso, and then I need to make some Italian food. Wordlessly, Alex follows me.

We find Nonna in the kitchen. She is sitting in a chair, an

untouched espresso in front of her, staring into space. For an alarmed moment I think she may have suffered a stroke, but then I notice that her gaze is soft and far away, and her lips are curved into a smile. I have a hunch she's thinking about Lorenzo's proposal. I'm not the only one with a big decision to make.

She starts when I lay a hand on her shoulder. "Ciao, Nipoti," she says. "Quite a lot of excitement this morning, eh?" She rises and briskly claps her hands together. "But now we must get to work on your recipes. What are we making today?"

"Hold on," I stop her. "We can't ignore what just happened. The Orange Blossom Cake worked! It actually worked, and you just got a proposal of marriage from Zio Lorenzo!"

Nonna makes a *pfft* sound and waves away my words. "Of course it worked. The cookbook always works." She pauses thoughtfully. "Though sometimes not in the way you think it will."

"Why did it work for Zio Lorenzo when he didn't even make the cake with us?" I ask.

Nonna shrugs. "Who knows? Sometimes the cookbook does unexpected things. Always they turn out for the best, though. I've learned not to question it, but simply to trust the wisdom it contains. For instance, look at this." She pulls out her phone and shows us a photo. The young woman with long brown hair pulled into a low bun looks vaguely familiar. I think she was one of the women cooking love pasta in the kitchen that morning.

"Who's that?" Alex asks, peering over my shoulder curiously.

"A woman who consulted the cookbook for help," Nonna explains. "She liked a man who worked in the next office over, but he did not seem to notice her. So she took the gnocchi al pesto recipe she made here and shared it with the man and his coworkers. It was not the man but the owner of the company who ate the gnocchi and asked if she would like to go on a date. He took her on a boat ride to dinner in Riva del Garda. See?" Nonna points at the photo. The young woman is sitting in a chic cigarette boat with a handsome older gentleman. They are toasting with champagne. "See how happy they look? Not who she had in mind, but the cookbook knows best."

Nonna slides her phone in her pocket and looks very satisfied. "Now, what are we working on today?"

I guess we are not going to be talking about Lorenzo and his proposal after all.

I consult the list Nonna and I made a few weeks ago. "Cassata Gardesana," I tell her. It's a refreshingly sweet and creamy frozen dessert that is popular in this region.

Alex grabs a glass of milk and two biscotti and settles down with her phone at the table. It's sweet how she does not hide away in her room now. She still spends much of her time on her phone, but she's usually just hanging around the kitchen when we cook, texting Tommaso or practicing her Italian. A few days ago I found her reading a book in Italian, and although she struggled with some parts, overall she managed to follow the plot pretty well.

I grab the ricotta cheese from the refrigerator and Nonna gathers the icing sugar and honey from the cupboard.

"So, what does that Drew boy want?" Nonna asks, arching a brow suspiciously. "Why did he come all the way to Italy?"

I bite my lip, hesitant to tell her about Drew's offer, but this concerns her too, and I need her advice. "He offered me a role as cohost of a TV show," I tell her baldly.

Nonna doesn't flinch, but I hear her quick inhale, as though she is bracing herself for impact. Her hands are steady as she measures out the honey, though. "It sounds like what you hoped for," she says. "So you will say yes to him?"

"I don't know. There's a catch." I spoon the right amount of ricotta into a big mixing bowl and Nonna pours in the sugar and honey. I start to beat them smooth using Nonna's ancient handheld mixer. "It would be filmed in LA, so I'd need to be there for the filming, and then if the first season went well, there's the possibility of them renewing the show for more seasons." I have to talk loudly over the grinding whine of the ancient mixer.

"So you would go to LA?" Nonna purses her lips. She is chopping toasted almonds for the recipe, and she's handling the knife with a sort of terrifying vigor. *Chop. Chop. Chop.*

"There's something else," I admit, turning off the mixer. The silence is blissful. "They want to use our family cookbook in the show."

The knife falls still and Nonna gazes at me quizzically. "Our cookbook? But why?"

I explain the premise of the show. Partway through, I'm aware that Alex is no longer focused on her phone. She's still sitting there with her phone in her hand, but she's listening to our conversation intently.

When I'm done talking, Nonna looks troubled. "Is this what you want, this show? Is this your dream, Nipotina?"

I exhale in frustration. "It's an amazing opportunity. I'd get to cohost with Drew. And the money would be good."

Nonna frowns, opens her mouth, and then seems to reconsider and closes it. "Humph," she says, a noncommittal sound.

I dump a container of heavy cream into a separate bowl, cold from the freezer, and turn the mixer back on. The noise fills the kitchen, giving me a moment to think. When it is whipped into firm peaks, I gently fold the cream into the sweet ricotta mixture. Nonna is still wielding the knife. The almonds are in very small pieces now but she keeps chopping.

"When do you have to decide?" She adds the slivers of almond to the creamy mixture, scraping them off the cutting board with her knife blade.

I don't meet her eyes. "They asked for an answer tomorrow."

"So soon for such a big decision," Nonna says reprovingly, clicking her tongue and eyeing me.

"I guess the entertainment industry moves fast." I add raisins and candied citrus peel to the creamy mixture and stir them in by hand. There is a sliver of citrus peel on the table and I pop it in my mouth. The sugary bite is tangy and bitter on my tongue. "If the show gets picked up, I could help you out financially. You could do the repairs this place needs," I tell her.

"What this place needs is not something money alone can fix," Nonna says shortly. "It needs a new caretaker, someone who loves it and will care for it for this generation and see it into the future. Without that . . . we will be forced to sell. Already it is heading that way. That is the harsh truth. We assumed it would be your father, but . . ." She sighs. "After Tony passed, our hopes turned to you."

I look down at the bowl of airy Cassata Gardesana, feeling put on the spot, feeling the sharp squeeze of anxiety as I contemplate trying to fix something when I have no idea how. I know I'm the only one left who can do it. And yet, what do I know about running an olive farm? The thought of saying yes, of taking on the risk and responsibility, makes me panic every time I even entertain it for a moment. I never intended to take over caring for this property. What if I fail? What if I am the one who ruins it or lets our family legacy die? That's an appalling thought. "I don't know if that's me, Nonna," I murmur finally, reluctantly. "I don't think I can. I'm sorry."

At this, Alex huffs loudly and springs up from the table, grabbing her phone and glaring at me. "This is bullshit. I can't believe you," she spits out as she brushes past me and heads out the door. I stare after her in dismay. What was that all about?

Nonna looks as mystified as I feel. She watches Alex leave, then turns to me and presses her lips together firmly. "What is it you truly want, Juliana?" she asks abruptly. The use of my full name takes me aback. She sounds so weary and a touch exasperated.

"I . . ." I stop. What *do* I truly want? I think for a long moment. "I want to feel safe again," I say finally, simply. It is the truest thing I know how to say.

Nonna glances up sharply at that, her gaze probing as she scans my face slowly. "And do you think that being on this TV show will make you feel safe?" Her tone is soft.

"I don't know if it will," I admit, "But it would take care of a lot of things. I'd have money, and good potential for job growth. I'd be hosting with Drew. We've been friends for a long time, which is appealing. I think I'd enjoy hosting a show. I know how to do it and I'm good at it. Those are not small things."

"But are they the most important things?" Nonna asks, her gaze sharp on me.

I hesitate. "It seems like a smart choice."

I felt so fundamentally unsafe after the death of my father, after being yanked so abruptly from Italy and having to spend the last of my teenage years under Lisa's roof. Ever since they pulled my dad's lifeless body from the water, I've been looking for that sense of safety again. It always seems just out of reach. If I could have more job security. If I could increase the number of followers on the show. If I could land a TV deal . . . Now it feels like it might be within my grasp. I can finally reach out and touch it. But at what cost?

Nonna pulls out a stack of dessert molds and lines them up on the prep table. "Ah Nipotina, life isn't safe," she says sensibly. "Sometimes life is good and beautiful. Sometimes it is cruel and seemingly senseless. But we are never guaranteed safety. We are promised many things in this life, and chief among them is suffering and grief and loss. We are not promised a life free of pain. Anyone who tells you this is lying to you."

"Am I wrong to want to feel safe?" I protest, feeling instantly a little defensive. I take a spoon and start filling the molds with the fluffy dessert.

Nonna considers this for a moment, then shakes her head. "No, of course not. Safety is important. We all want to live in a world that feels safe for us and those we love, but safety is not the most important thing. Ask yourself this, Juliana. What if the most important thing in life is not feeling safe? What if it's to love something or someone enough that they're worth risking for?"

I freeze, full spoon poised over a half-filled mold. The thought scares me. Nonna watches me, waiting for an answer. Apparently, her question was not purely rhetorical.

"I . . . I don't know . . ." I stammer, feeling caught out.

A brief look of disappointment flashes across her face. "If we constantly look only for safety, then our fear controls us," she says quietly. "You think your fear protects you, but it holds you back from living a full life. You used to be brimming with curiosity and adventure, Juliana. You were always a quiet one, but so eager to take all of the world in your hands and taste each bite. Where is that girl now?"

"I . . ." I don't know what to say. I consider her words. Is she right? In trying to feel safe, am I focusing on the wrong thing? Have I lost myself in the process?

"That girl is gone," I say finally. "I think she disappeared at the bottom of the lake the day Dad died."

Nonna nods, her expression sympathetic. "You can find her again. It isn't too late. I know how much you miss him, mia cara. I do too. But it would break Tony's heart if he knew what his death did to you. He did not want this for you, Juliana. He wanted more than anything for you to have a life full of light, full of joy, full of love."

I glance down at the spoon in my hand, feeling ashamed, knowing she is right. My big, loving, heart-on-his-sleeve dad would have been heartbroken to see how careful I've become, how afraid of anything that might hurt me. But how can I possibly risk that pain again? I know how much it hurts to lose everything most precious to you. I felt my entire world fall apart from the inside out. I never want to feel that way again. I'll do anything to avoid it.

"I don't know how to not be afraid," I confess in a small voice. "I have no idea how to get the girl I was back. I feel like it might be too late."

Nonna shakes her head emphatically. "It is never too late," she states firmly. "Don't let fear win. Be brave enough to let what you truly love guide your choices. Then you will make the right decision from the heart." She surveys me.

"I have put too much of a burden on you," she announces abruptly. "You must be free to make your own choice. Listen to me, Juliana." She looks me in the eye, her gaze boring into mine. She reaches across the prep table and takes my chin firmly in her hand, a little too tightly, wince slightly at the pressure. She does not let go. "I release you from my hopes for your life, Nipotina, from any burden or expectation you feel. I release you to do what your heart is telling you to do, and I pray to the Blessed Virgin that when you do, you will find what your heart is truly seeking." Then she releases my chin and steps back.

I look down swiftly, blinking back sudden tears. "Thank you," I manage to squeeze out. Nonna nods but says nothing more. I fill the molds and stash them in the freezer, then head outside. I need some air, to clear my head and think.

Chapter 49

I head for the patio, looking for a place to be alone, but stop short at the top of the stairs. Alex is sitting in a chair at the table under the olive trees with her arms crossed, her expression tight and angry. I hesitate. "Hey," I offer tentatively, trying to figure out what is going on.

She turns on me, radiating disapproval. "You're going to LA?" she asks, her tone accusing.

"It's just a possibility," I tell her, approaching the table cautiously. No one has cleaned up from the cake fiasco earlier and the sweet mess is attracting bees. Nonna usually whisks plates away as soon as the last bite is consumed, but she had bigger things on her mind. I gather the dirty plates and stack them. There are some crumbs from the cake scattered around, and I brush them away with my hand. Already the ants have found them. "But don't worry," I hasten to assure her. "It wouldn't be until the end of the summer. We'll stay until you go back to school, like we planned."

"You think that's what I'm worried about?" Alex scoffs. "Staying here until the end of summer?"

"Um . . . no?" I'm really feeling at a loss here. I gather forks, not sure what else to do.

It seems I've touched a nerve. She levels a hard stare at me. "Fine, whatever. You're right. I'm leaving anyway. Do whatever you want." She stands and grabs a few empty espresso cups and saucers, the porcelain clanking together alarmingly. She doesn't seem to notice.

I'm genuinely puzzled. "Why does it matter what I do after the summer is over?" I ask, trying to adopt a reasonable tone. "This was only ever supposed to be for the summer, right?"

She stiffens, not looking at me. "Right. Of course." She grabs the stack of plates and stomps down the stone steps. "Tell that to Bruna, okay?"

"Hey, what do you mean by that?" I demand, following her. I'm carrying the remains of the cake, a fistful of forks, and a teetering stack of plates, which, in hindsight, was a little ambitious.

She whirls on me at the kitchen door. "I know the farm is in deep shit financially, okay?" she hisses. "I hear everything, by the way. None of you are quiet and sound carries in this house. I know Bruna was hoping you were going to come and save the farm, that you could save the family legacy. And I know you have zero interest in doing that." She pushes open the door and goes in.

"Alex, wait." I trail her inside, carefully balancing the dishes and the leftover cake. Thankfully, the kitchen is empty. Nonna must have gone upstairs. I don't know what to say. "That was never the deal," I stammer. "I came for the summer, that's it. I'm not the right person to take on this place. That was never even on the table." I gently deposit the forks and dishes in the sink.

Alex slams the saucers down on the counter hard enough that I am afraid she'll shatter them. "So you're just going to let this whole place go?" she challenges. "What's going to happen to Bruna and Lorenzo?"

"I mean . . . I'll send them money and help as much as I can." I carefully set the cake on the kitchen table.

"Oh, that's big of you," she says sarcastically, rolling her eyes.

"Hey, that isn't fair," I protest, growing annoyed. "And frankly, I don't think it is any of your business what I do or what happens to the farm."

"Why, because I'm not really a Costa?" she asks. There's a hard edge to her voice. I feel ambushed. I can't tell what's riling her up, and I feel like she's catching me up with her words.

"I didn't mean it like that," I say, trying for a conciliatory tone. I just want to escape to a quiet place where I can think. Having a provoking row with my half sister is not high on my to-do list today.

"Yes, you did," Alex says quietly. There is something in her face that gives me pause, a challenge I don't know how to counter. I wait silently. "Do you ever think about anyone but yourself?" she asks, her tone conversational, the words brutal. When I don't respond she continues. "Do you realize this is the most normal family life I've had in my entire life? You know what it's like with Mom and Dad. There's not a whole lot of parenting going on in our house. But here . . ." She pauses, sounding a little wistful. "I was beginning to like this place. It feels good to be part of something for the first time. I know I'm not a real part of the family." She rolls her eyes. "I know I'll never be a Costa, but I felt like here it didn't matter so much what my last name was." She falls silent for a moment, then says softly, "Nonna Bruna called me her granddaughter. For the first time, I feel like I might belong somewhere, like I'm wanted, like I have a family who cares about me." Her face clouds with anger as she stares hard at me. "And now you have to go and ruin it all with this stupid TV show no one is going to like or watch." Her mouth is pinched tight with anger. "Good to know that all that talk about family sticking together wasn't real. At least next time I'll know not to believe you."

Quickly, she turns on her heel and rushes from the kitchen, but not before I catch a glimpse of her face crumpling with hurt.

"Alex!" I call in exasperation, but she is gone. I hear her feet pounding up the stairs, and then a moment later the door to her room slams hard. I start to follow her, but stop. I'm at a loss for words. I've never seen her so vulnerable. What she's saying isn't fair or true, but I can sense the emotions underneath those harsh words. She finally found a place to belong and she's scared it's going to be taken away again. I understand that feeling. I've had to live for years with the loss of my safe place. The problem is that even if she loves this place, Alex is going back to Manhattan in a few weeks, and I am going to . . . well, I have to figure that out and fast. Drew is coming in the morning, and I have to have an answer by then.

I cast one last glance at the ceiling. I hate quarreling, and having her mad at me feels awful. We were just starting to connect. I don't want to lose that, I realize in surprise. I will miss her when she's back home in New York. With a sigh of frustration, I cover the remnants of the cake with a clean cotton towel to help it stay moist, then head outside. Maybe stretching my legs will bring me clarity. I'll go up and talk to Alex when I get back.

I head up the lane through the olive groves at a brisk pace. Surprisingly, when I reach my favorite olive tree, I see the green patch of grass underneath it is already occupied. Nicolo is sitting propped against the trunk of the tree, shirtless and wearing work pants and suspenders, drinking a bottle of Peroni. He looks a little dusty. He takes a swig of beer, sees me, and inclines his head to the side in tacit invitation. I hesitate briefly, unsure, then drop down beside him. From here I can see the pile of rocks sitting along the broken bit of wall has shrunk and the new wall has grown. Apparently, Nicolo has been busy lifting heavy things.

"That kind of day, huh?" I ask, gesturing to the beer. I'm not sure it's even noon yet.

"That kind of day," he says and offers me a sip. I accept. The beer is cold and crisp with a bitter, citrus note. I hand the bottle back. We sit in silence for a long moment, listening to the hum of insects. I take a deep breath, trying to quell the panic I can feel roiling just under my breastbone.

"What are you doing out here?" I ask quietly.

"Trying to see the future without the aid of a magical cake," he says, a dry note of irony in his tone. "And contemplating all those bad sonnets I wrote you when we were young."

I smile despite myself. What is it about this man that makes me feel instantly reassured and calm? My world is in turmoil, but here with Nicolo I've entered a little pocket of peace. "I still have them," I tell him. "No one else in my life has ever written me a sonnet."

He tilts his head and gazes at me. "If you were mine, I'd write you a sonnet for every day of the year."

"Sounds labor-intensive," I gently tease, reaching for the beer again. I put my mouth where his just was on the rim. "Can you write me a bad sonnet about a magical cake accidentally prompting an eighty-year-old to propose marriage?" I ask wryly.

"I may not be able to do that surprising turn of events justice," he retorts, his eyes crinkling at the corners with amusement. "I admit, I didn't know what would happen this morning, but I did not expect that."

"This entire day has been unexpected." I hand the bottle back to him.

He glances sideways at me, raising an eyebrow. "This entire summer has been unexpected," he parries.

"True."

We fall silent.

"So that was Drew," he says at last.

I blow out a breath. "That was Drew," I confirm.

"I recognized him from your show."

"Oh, right."

Nicolo waits a beat. I can sense he's curious but not going to pry.

"He wants me to host a new show with him, in LA," I blurt out. I still can't believe this is happening. I haven't even finished my cookbook, and the thing I was working so hard to achieve has literally fallen into my lap. Why am I not delirious with joy right now?

"So your dream comes true then?" Nicolo says lightly. "Lucky for you." There's a tight set to his jaw and he takes a big swig of the beer.

"Yeah, I guess so." I nod uncertainly. "I just wish I could know for sure that saying yes to Drew is the right thing. I wish I'd gotten to eat that bite of cake. Maybe it would give me some peace of mind, you know, shed some light on what is really going to make me happiest."

"Jules." Nicolo's tone is faintly chiding. I turn my head and look at him. His eyes are dark and intent on my face. "You don't need a bite of cake to decide your happiness," he says. "Just be honest with yourself. What do you want?"

I shake my head. "I don't know."

He narrows his eyes. "Not true."

I feel a flash of annoyance. "How do you know what I want?" I ask. Why is everyone challenging me today?

He doesn't take his eyes from my face. "Because I know you," he murmurs, and the words make me shiver. "I know the essence of you, Juliana. All those nights we lay here trading kisses and secrets. I know the real you, deep down, and I know you're hiding."

"Hiding from what?" I demand, piqued by his insinuation that he knows so much. Everyone seems to know what's best for me but me.

"From yourself. From your life. From all the things that scare you." His tone is a challenge. He looks a little irritated and my temper rises. Why should he be annoyed with me about this? He has no claim on me.

"You knew me once upon a time," I counter, my voice tight. "When I was fifteen. You knew me before the really bad stuff happened. You knew that version of me, the Jules with pretty dreams and big aspirations, the Jules who still trusted that the world was good and kind and right somehow." I lean toward him insistently.

"But you don't know me now, Nicolo. Don't fool yourself and think that you do. You don't know the me that's spent the past fifteen years trying to rebuild my life, rebuild a sense of safety and home and hope. I am not that girl anymore. I wish I was, but I'm not. She's gone, and I'll never get her back. She vanished that day in the lake. And there will never be another day where I get to be that girl again."

I stop abruptly, realizing I'm crying. There are fat tears rolling down my cheeks. I sniff and look away, but then Nicolo's hand is there caressing my jaw, turning me to face him. His thumb brushes away the tears tenderly. I glance at him, expecting to see understanding or compassion, and it is there, but he looks disappointed and a little sad and angry too.

"She's not gone," he says softly. "That girl is not gone. You're just afraid to let her have a voice, afraid that if you do, you might start to trust that you can be happy again, that you might start to hope . . . and dream . . . and that feels dangerous, doesn't it, Juliana? Because hopes and dreams are fragile things, easily shattered." He leans closer, so close I can smell the sun-warmed skin of his neck, feel the raspy stubble of his cheek as he presses his face to mine and whispers, his breath warm in my ear, "You think it's better to build thick walls around that tender heart of yours so you don't get hurt again.

You'd rather go without than risk losing something you care about. You're rejecting what you care most about, your right hard thing, because you'd rather fail from the start than give it a try. You're a coward."

I jerk away from him, scrambling to my feet in outrage. He stands too. We face each other, locking eyes warily. His jaw ticks.

"You know nothing," I inform him icily.

He crosses his arms and arches a brow maddeningly, a challenge. "Prove me wrong then," he says. "Tell me what you really want. What is in your heart, Juliana Costa?"

"None of your business," I huff, brushing bits of leaf and grass from my skirt.

He sits back down with a smile that is at once both disappointed and infuriating. "I thought so," he says, and drains his bottle of beer.

As I march back toward the house, huffing in frustration, I feel his eyes following me until I'm out of sight.

Chapter 50

I skip lunch, spending the time in my room alternately sulking and contemplating my decision. I video call Aurora to fill her in on all the newest developments. There's a lot to say.

"You'll make the right choice," Aurora tells me encouragingly as she helps the kids hand-dip their own bayberry beeswax candles. "Look at it this way. You have two good choices. Host your own TV show or stay in Italy running a historic olive farm and making lots of shiny brown-eyed babies with your Italian hottie. It's like one of those books where you can choose your own adventure. Both options are great." She winks at me. I roll my eyes.

"That's not helpful," I tell her.

"Just keep things in perspective," she tells me sunnily. "You'll know what to do when the time comes." I have a sense she wants to say more but is holding back by sheer force of will, trying to let her baby sister make her own decisions. Adulting is hard. I just wish someone would walk by carrying a big sign with an arrow that says THIS WAY.

After I hang up from the call with Aurora, I check my email and find a message from Michelle. Last week I sent her several more recipes, photos, and additional content, and she's giving me feedback.

> Claire LOVES this! Epicure is very happy with this direction! Keep up the good work! Can't wait to see the finished collection of recipes!

All exclamation points is good news. My editor is happy, my agent is happy, and I'm on track to generate enough recipes to finish the cookbook by the deadline if I can stay focused and disciplined for the rest of my time in Italy. So that's a relief. Regardless of what I decide, I will have a cookbook of delicious recipes with my name on it. At least that's something.

I answer a text from Sandra informing me that one of our windows in the apartment is broken. At the same time I get a text from Solomon that contains the words

> An unfortunate cricket bat incident while Method acting . . .

I just forward them the maintenance man's number again.

I hear the door to Alex's room open and shut once in the early afternoon, but other than that, the house is quiet. Outside, Lorenzo is working in the courtyard and I can hear his distant sonorous baritone warbling along to an Italian ballad on his ancient black radio. I haven't seen or heard Nonna in a while. I wonder where she is.

I busy myself online. Reluctantly, I check the comments from the final post of *The Bygone Kitchen* episodes, the one for Sunshine Salad. I posted it a few evenings ago, saddened that it was the last one Drew and I may ever make. It felt like the end of an era.

In an unexpected twist, it turns out that Jell-O salad is surprisingly controversial. Ethel has declared it "a trip back in time" with a string of pineapples, suns wearing sunglasses, and flower emojis. Marv says it's the most disgusting thing he's ever made. Another woman says her children ate the entire salad while she was taking a nap. A mom in Minnesota states that Jell-O contributes to diabetes and includes links to articles on the dangers of sugar.

I click on the post and watch the episode in its entirety, wishing I had some Jell-O salad. I could use the boost. I watch Drew's little goofy dance number, the fedora tilted at a rakish angle on his head, and my obvious joy as I show viewers how to make the gelatin salad and pour it into a mold. It seems like a lifetime ago, and yet it feels so comfortable and familiar too. I'm good at this. I love this. Under the eye of the camera, I feel shiny and happy, productive and . . . safe. The show gave me a creative outlet and a sense of joy and safety. But it is over now. The thought makes me sad. I poured my heart and soul into that show for five years and now it's just . . . done. It feels so anticlimactic, so disappointing.

On impulse, I make a final post for *The Bygone Kitchen* profile using a video Alex shared with me. It is Nonna, Alex, and me making the pizza together. Nothing fancy, just having fun in the kitchen and making something tasty.

My life has taken a slight change of direction, I write under the post. **Currently, I'm in Italy with my nonna and my sister. I'll be taking some time off for personal reasons but hope to be back with you soon! Until then, enjoy some pizza for me!** I quickly type up the recipe for the pizza and add it to the links in my profile in case viewers want to make it.

Then I close my computer and take a deep breath. *The Bygone Kitchen* might be over, at least for the foreseeable future, but now I'm being offered a new opportunity—bigger stakes, more money, exponentially more viewers. I could become a household name, like Ina, like Giada. It's so tempting. It's the safe option, the obvious choice.

I have been working toward this for so long. Sure, it's not *The Bygone Kitchen*, but it's a great next step. I'd be with Drew. The money would be a relief. It would be fun and it could actually help people. It's everything I said I wanted. But that would mean leaving Italy, leaving the farm and Nonna, leaving Nicolo.

Tiring of the endless loop of questions with no answers, I decide to go try to patch things up with Alex. I knock on her door but there's no answer. I try the handle and peer into the room. The bed is neatly made. There's a sweatshirt lying over the back of a chair. But she is not there.

I send a text: Where are you? Can we talk?

No answer. She always has her phone with her, so she's probably ignoring me. I decide to call instead, but her phone is turned off. That's strange. I've never seen Alex turn off her phone. I start to get an uneasy feeling in my gut.

I head down to the kitchen, which is also empty. The Fiat Panda is gone from the courtyard. Maybe Alex went somewhere with Nonna? Now there's a scary thought. Alex riding along as Nonna navigates the twisty narrow roads with more confidence than aptitude.

Lorenzo looks up when I step out into the courtyard. He's pounding nails into a plank but stops when he sees me.

"Have you seen Alex?" I ask. "Or Nonna?"

He wipes his brow with a crumpled, stained handkerchief. "Bruna went to the bank in Garda Town about an hour ago," he says. "and I saw Alex walk down the drive soon after. Maybe she's going for a swim? It's a hot day," he observes.

My concern ratchets up another notch. Alex has been gone almost an hour. Did she go into the water by herself? Or try to hitchhike somewhere? Surely, she wouldn't be so foolish.

"If you see her, tell her to text me." I'm already headed down the lane, hurrying as fast as I can. My sandals slip a little on the gravel and I almost lose my footing. By the bottom of the driveway, I'm panting. I pause for a moment, scanning the road for any sign of Alex. I'm growing more uneasy by the second. It's the heat of the day and a few insects are buzzing lazily around me. I can smell the lake and the chalky scent of sunbaked rocks. Maybe she hitchhiked to one of the little towns? Or maybe she texted Tommaso to pick her up? I'm trying not to panic. She's my responsibility and I've lost track of her.

Across the street and down a few hundred feet is the beach. I decide to check it first. There is a narrow path between a few buildings that allows access to the lakeshore. I take a deep breath and call, "Alex?" No answer. I head down the path.

In the sunlight the water is a vivid sparkling blue-aqua in the shallows and deepening to turquoise in the center. Across the vast expanse of the lake, tall green mountains rear up from the western shore, their ridges and folds shadowed beneath a cloudless blue sky. The effect is breathtaking. Even in my alarm it catches me off guard. I never quite remember how truly stunning this place is.

I reach the few steps down to the beach and pause at the top, scanning the shoreline. The last time I was here it was dark and I was drinking limoncello and preparing for some mild larceny with Nicolo. Today the beach is empty, just a wide swath of white pebbles cascading down to the shore. But there's something in the water. My heart stops. There, right where the color deepens from aqua to turquoise, a familiar little figure clad all in black is floating face down, motionless.

In an instant the bottom drops out of my world.

Chapter 51

"Alex!" A scream rips from my throat. Panicked, I stumble down the stairs, missing the last step and twisting my ankle in my haste. I force myself up with a gasp. I can't get to her fast enough.

"Alex!" I yell again. Ignoring the sharp stabs of pain, I hobble across the pebbled beach, kick off my sandals and drop my phone, and wade into the water frantically, heedless of my orange mod print dress, which instantly plasters itself to my body and slows my progress. "Alex?" I yell again. Alex isn't moving. She's still face down in the water. My heart is pounding so hard in my ears I can hardly hear my own voice. I'm straining against the water, thrashing, trying to get to her as fast as I can.

"Oh God, please don't let it be too late." I plunge forward, lunge the last few steps and grab her around the waist, hauling her up with a grunt of effort. She's surprisingly heavy.

And surprisingly conscious. When my arms close around her, her entire body reacts as though she's being electrified. She comes up out of the water with a shriek so loud it could raise the dead, flailing around and almost hitting me in the face. I rear back instinctively. "Alex, it's me," I yell, my feet scrabbling for a foothold on the loose pebbles at the bottom of the lake. My sprained ankle throbs in agony at the movement.

Alex claws her way free from my grasp and turns on me, eyes wide and wild. We stand chest deep in the water, facing each other, dripping and gasping for air.

"What the hell are you doing?" I demand at the same moment she cries, "Why did you grab me?"

I stare at her in shock. "I thought you were drowning!" I retort, my panic slowly melting to a righteous sort of indignation. I put my hands on my hips.

Alex crosses her arms and looks sulky. "I was watching the little silver fish," she says, her tone unapologetic. "You scared them away." She actually sounds sort of accusing, which is galling.

"I was trying to save you!" My tone is sharp with exasperation.

"I don't need saving," she replies, her expression mutinous.

"Well I didn't know that. And why in the world are you still wearing your clothes to go swimming?"

And all of a sudden I am crying. I don't even feel the tears come. I thought I'd cried all my tears for my dad years ago, but suddenly, it's overwhelming. The panic melts into a deep sense of grief. I'm wet and shivering and crying. Not delicate crying either, but big, ugly sobs that wrack my entire body. I wrap my arms around myself, trying to draw comfort, but there is none to be had. Alex looks at me, alarmed.

"What are you doing?" she asks hesitantly.

I don't answer her, just keep sobbing uncontrollably. She looks increasingly uncomfortable and unsure. "Sorry," she mutters finally. "I didn't mean to scare you."

"It's not you," I tell her after a few minutes, through the tears and the snot. "I mean, I was scared you'd drowned. You were face down and just floating there. You weren't moving!" I sniff and wipe my nose with the back of my hand, calming a little.

Alex hesitates. "Is this about . . . your dad?" she asks finally. I just nod.

"Was this where he . . ." She doesn't finish the sentence and I'm grateful. I nod again.

"They found him in the water, out a little farther than this. He died when he was swimming." I can feel my heartbeat starting to slow now. I take a big, shuddering breath. I feel completely wrung out. "It's why I haven't come back to Italy for so long. It's why I avoid the lake. It hurts too much to remember what happened to him here."

Alex glanced behind her, out over the water. "That sucks," she says.

"Yeah, it does." I chuckle a little, a dry rasp. Her words are not eloquent but they are true.

We face each other for a long minute.

"So this is where your dad drowned, and you jumped in the lake and swam out here to save me anyway?" she asks tentatively. There's something I can't quite decipher in her tone of voice. She sounds . . . touched. I nod.

"Of course. You're my half sister." I think of Nonna's disapproving voice telling me there are no half sisters. "We're family," I amend.

Alex glances up at me quickly, startled and a little skeptical. "Really?" she asks. "I always thought you kind of wished I'd never been born."

I wince. It's not entirely untrue, but it sounds so ugly coming from her. I think of her angry words on the patio earlier, her confession about being so lonely and feeling so unwanted. And I am ashamed for my part in that. I've blamed her unfairly and kept my distance without thinking how she might feel, how she might need a sister for solidarity. I've always had Dad and Aurora and Nonna. Through no fault of her own, Alex has had no one. She's always been alone.

"I'm sorry," I tell her.

She looks surprised. "For what?"

"For not making you feel like you are part of the family." I meet her eyes, knowing these are things I need to say. "You know stuff with Lisa and my dad was . . . really complicated. It was hard for us when Lisa left, and I think I just lumped you in there with everything messy that happened, but that isn't fair to you. I'm sorry." It feels good to say the words, and even better to realize I mean them. "I'm sorry I didn't try harder before," I tell her. "I should have cared more for you."

Alex shuffles her feet over the rocks at the bottom of the lake, looking down almost shyly at her toes in the clear aqua water. "I've always wanted a sister," she admits. "I used to make up pretend sisters when I was little, imagining what it would feel like to not be the only one. I always envied you and Aurora because you had each other."

"Well, now you have real sisters," I tell her. "And you're an aunt too, you know. Wait till you meet Aurora's kids. They're so much fun. Maybe I could take you down there when you have a school break sometime?"

It's the only gift I have to give her, and I wait to see if she will accept the olive branch. I'm nowhere near as close to Alex as I am to Aurora, at least not yet, but Alex and I have built something in the weeks we've been together. She feels like a friend now, and that's a good start. She cocks her head and considers. Her hair snakes over her shoulders in wet strands. She looks so tiny in her heavy, drenched black clothes. She nods. "I'd like that."

She hesitates a long moment. "Thanks for coming in after me," she says finally. "I've never had anyone try to rescue me before. Even if I wasn't drowning." Her lips quirk a little at the irony.

I nod. "Anytime," I tell her with a relieved smile. I feel a little giddy now that the adrenaline is fading. "Can we start over?" I ask, holding out my hand.

She nods, then clasps my hand in a firm handshake. Impulsively, I pull her in for a hug. Unfortunately, I forget momentarily about my injured ankle, lose my balance, and end up dunking us both in the lake. We come up spluttering and laughing.

"Wow." Alex wipes the hair from her eyes. "That was an epic fail."

"Yeah, another epic fail." I giggle. She smiles and rolls her eyes, then instead of wading back to shore, she swims off a few yards and treads water. I hesitate. I'm cold and soaked and starting to shiver. It's getting toward late afternoon and the air is cooling. But there's something in her smile, an invitation or a dare. I follow her out farther from the shore.

Chapter 52

The lake is cool and so clear I can see all the stones at the bottom. I can't touch now, and I kick my legs, treading water like Dad taught me. It's hard with the sodden dress dragging me down, but I manage to keep afloat.

It feels strange to be here, swimming once more. I've tried so hard not to think about this place, attempting to blot out the terrible memory it holds. Losing my dad was the worst day of my life. He was the most loving, constant presence I had growing up, and now I am reminded of how cold and alone I felt with his death. But as I swim out a little farther, I'm also reminded of so many other memories. Not just that awful day, but the hundreds of good and beautiful days that preceded that terrible one.

Dad went swimming right here at this beach almost every day of our vacation, and most days I joined him. He taught me the backstroke and breaststroke and how to tread water for twenty minutes. After we worked hard at a lesson, we'd lie on our backs and watch clouds, looking for familiar shapes of animals and vegetables and shouting out the names of them in Italian. Il gatto. L'elefante. La carota. La patata.

I'd forgotten those silly, carefree moments. Some of the happiest memories of my life are tied to this place. The saddest memories are too. I've spent years avoiding the sadness here, but I see now that this has robbed me of the joy too. I've been trying to avoid pain, but in doing so I've also avoided so much of the good. No more, I vow. I'm going to embrace all of it, the hard and the happy, the sour and the sweet.

I flip onto my back and float spread-eagled, staring at the clouds. "La tartaruga!" I call out, spying a cloud shaped like a turtle.

Alex looks startled. She translates the word in her head and looks around excitedly. "A turtle? Where?"

"There, that cloud right above us. It's a game I used to play with my dad. Name all the cloud shapes in Italian that look like animals or vegetables."

Hesitantly, she floats on her back too, staring up at the clouds. "Zucca," she calls out, pointing to a cloud that does indeed resemble a pumpkin. I laugh and she joins me, chuckling wryly. The game is ridiculous and cute and funny. We spend a few more minutes identifying a cabbage, a rabbit, and a bunch of grapes. I spy one that looks like a jellyfish. "La medusa!" I shout. Then we fall silent for a few minutes, floating.

"So what are you going to do?" she asks.

"About?"

"Are you going to LA?"

I blow out a breath and flip over, treading water once more. That is the million-dollar question. "I don't know yet."

She nods and we float in silence for a few minutes, lost in our own thoughts. Alex is on her back, drifting gently away from me, watching the clouds. I catch sight of the farmhouse on the hill far above us, the white plaster walls shining bright in the sunshine. The sight of it steals my breath, and a wave of tenderness washes over me. It represents the embrace of love, home, and family. How often has that place beckoned me back to its warmth? It has been waiting patiently for so many years while I was running away.

"Here I am . . . finally," I murmur. I stare long and hard at the farmhouse, nestled like a sugar cube amid waves of silver olive trees spreading out over the gently rolling hills. A lump rises in my throat at the thought of it ceasing to be a place that beckons us home. Who would I be if not for this place? Who would I be without the love and embrace of the family within those walls? What would I have left if all this were gone? The thought makes me shiver. The world would feel unbearably cold and lonely.

The farm is special not just because of the history and the olives or the magical cookbook, but because it is a gathering place for us. Those who are lonely find it a place of love and acceptance. Those who are wounded find a place to be made whole. It isn't in the stones or the olive wood or the dirt of the hills. It is in the long history of family meals, births, deaths, marriages, and heartbreak, love lost and found. The coffees and pasta, the dreams we dream there safe in our beds at night. It is the life that happens on that patch of land, within those stone walls. What a precious gift. Looking at it now, I realize this place means everything to me. It always has.

And not just me. All of us. My dad while he was alive. Lorenzo and Nonna and now Alex. I think of my family. Nonna Bruna, who has only ever shown me such wisdom, devotion, and acceptance. And Lorenzo, who laid aside his own life when Carlo died to take up the load and care for his cousin's family. And Alex, smart, lonely Alex, who is desperately seeking a family and a place to belong. Alex's harsh words from earlier echo in my mind, demanding to know if I ever think of anyone but myself. Harsh, but true. I have been thinking only of my own grief and loss and fear and need for safety. But now I see this question is much bigger than me. What does it mean for them if I say no to taking on the responsibility of running the farm and instead move to LA? What would it mean for all of us to lose this place? What would it mean for the community around Lake Garda? Nicolo said farms like ours are being sold all over the area. The loss is gutting the region as big olive farms and foreign corporations gobble up small places like ours, erasing generations of family legacy. If I say no, ours will be the next.

I think of Nonna Bruna's words in the kitchen earlier, releasing me from obligation. It is my choice. Truly my choice. Her words come back to me now.

Ask yourself this, Juliana. What if the most important thing in life is not feeling safe? What if it's to love something or someone enough that they're worth risking for?

Gazing up at the farmhouse, treading water in the liminal space between my past and my future, I realize this is the only question that matters. And between one breath and the next, in a moment of illumination, I realize I know my answer.

"Yes," I whisper aloud, softly, then louder. "Yes."

I love this place enough to take the risk. I love my family and our home more than anything in the world. I cannot let it be lost, not while there is breath in my body. I must find a way to save it. I have no idea how. I have no money, little knowledge of running an olive farm, and probably even less skill. But I will do whatever it takes. I am choosing my right hard thing.

Slowly, I let the gravity of my choice sift through me, down through my blood and bones and into every crevice of my heart. I am making a commitment, no matter the cost. It is sobering and thrilling and feels so right.

Decision made, I feel a rush of relief followed swiftly by determination. How am I going to make this work? And what do I tell Drew? In the light of my decision, I consider Drew's offer again. If I say yes to the show, I am assuring the farm's financial security. We can afford to do all the repairs, pay the taxes, whatever it needs. The idea is appealing. Maybe going to LA is not running away. Maybe it's provision—just for a time, a season of taping the show, or a few seasons if it gets renewed. Maybe me saying yes to LA is the best thing for our family. But I also know that Nonna and Lorenzo are at the end of their capacity to keep things running. They're not spring chickens. They are tired and aging. They need someone to be physically present on the farm, to lift the burden from them as soon as possible. But if I say no to LA, where in the world will we find the money to keep things running? How can we possibly survive?

The options feel like a Gordian knot. I don't know which is best. How can I choose? I think of the Orange Blossom Cake we'll taste tomorrow morning if all goes well. Maybe that bite of cake will help me. When I see the happiest moment of my life, perhaps I'll find it contains an answer for the choice before me. Suddenly, tomorrow morning can't come soon enough.

Chapter 53

"Okay, are we ready to try this again?" I look around the kitchen expectantly as I tie an apron around my waist.

It's early, barely seven a.m., and we are gathered once more in Nonna's kitchen. Nicolo stands across the prep table from me, gazing at me searchingly with those dark eyes as though trying to read my mind. I offer him a brief smile but avoid his gaze. I'm not ready to tell anyone the path I've chosen, not until I taste that first bite of cake. I'm hoping against hope that what I see will reveal the best choice to me.

"Let's get on with it," Violetta grumbles. "No need to delay."

Alex and I exchange a glance. Things are definitely warmer between us after yesterday. After our unexpected swim, she ran up the hill to the house and brought Lorenzo back with the Panda to transport me home since I couldn't put weight on my ankle. After an evening spent keeping ice on the sprain, it's feeling much better this morning with just a twinge if I put my full weight on it. I feel a rush of affection for Alex as I watch her fiddling with her phone, getting ready to record. I tried to rescue her, and ironically she ended up rescuing me. I have a feeling we've rescued each other in ways we do not even understand yet.

"Let's see what recipe the cookbook gives us. All together now." I hold the cookbook and everyone except Alex puts our hands on it. I flip open to a page, catching my breath.

"Yes!" Alex cries jubilantly, peering over my shoulder. It's the recipe for Orange Blossom Cake. I let out a gusty sigh of relief.

"Let's start baking," Nonna commands.

Just like the last time, we all help make the cake. Nonna handles the dry ingredients, Violetta purees the orange, and Nicolo measures the olive oil. He uses the best olive oil, the one that includes olives from the oldest tree in our groves. I dip my finger in the oil and taste it. It is a clear, slightly green color, light and fruity with the slight aftertaste of almond. It is as precious as gold in these parts and used only for special occasions. This is as special as it gets.

Alex records everything on her phone while Nonna greases the cake pan. I add the orange blossom extract last and stir it into the batter. Then we put it in the oven, set the timer, and wait.

When we pull the cake from the oven, I breathe in the fragrant aroma, then cross myself and say a little prayer for clarity and courage.

"Are we ready?" Nonna asks when the cake has cooled and she's spread the icing over the top. She seems resigned since our conversation yesterday afternoon, at peace and yet a little sad. I want to reassure her that I'm trying my best, that I'll do everything I can to save this place, but this is not the time. Later I will tell her, after I've seen what the cake has to show me. There are no easy solutions, but at least I know I am making a decision for the right reason, for our family home and the people I love. Now I just need some guidance as to how to do it best.

※

We file out to the patio. Nonna is carrying the cookbook so Alex can get some good shots of the finished cake with the recipe. In the excitement of our first attempt, she didn't get as much content for TikTok as she wanted to. Nicolo brings out a stack of plates and Violetta follows him with napkins. Alex, still filming, distributes forks, and I bring out the cake and set it on the table, wincing slightly as my ankle protests the steep climb up the steps. Lorenzo is there too, just to observe. He is sipping an espresso and eyeing Nonna with unabashed appreciation. She appears to be ignoring him, but her color is higher than normal. I think she's aware of his gaze on her.

The morning is slightly overcast. There is a thunderstorm brewing, and a cool wind is whipping the leaves on the trees. It blows strands of my hair—still a little damp from my morning shower—from my thick yellow fabric headband into my eyes. I tuck each strand back into the headband, but they just come loose again. I give up and focus on the task at hand.

I'm just about to slice the cake when we hear the crunch of gravel in the driveway.

"You've got to be kidding me." Violetta rolls her eyes just as Nicolo nods his head toward the car nosing into the courtyard and says, "Look who's back."

I get a sense of déjà vu as I see the big black sedan come to a halt. Drew and Keith are early. I texted Drew last night and told him that I was redoing the cake this morning and I'd have an answer for him by eleven. It's barely nine. What are they doing here? They park close to the house and alight from the car with looks of anticipation when they see us all gathered.

Drew takes the steps two at a time, Keith following behind.

"Sorry to interrupt, folks," Keith says with a smooth smile. "We thought we'd get an early start this morning." He sees the cake and the cookbook and his eyes widen in anticipation. I wonder if Drew told him what we were doing this morning. I wonder if they intentionally joined us early so they could see the cookbook in action. I can't say I blame them, but it makes me uneasy. This is a family affair and I don't like almost-strangers like Keith being a part of it. Drew comes up close to me and squeezes my shoulder. "Have you made a decision yet?" he asks me in an undertone.

"I'll let you know at eleven, like I said in my text," I whisper back with a frown. I'm not saying anything until I take that first bite.

I cut the cake and slide the wedges onto plates. The delicate floral essence is mouthwatering. I pass cake to Violetta and Nonna, then set a slice in front of Nicolo and serve myself a piece. In a repeat of yesterday, Nicolo is sitting across from me. His arms are crossed, his eyes fixed on Drew in what can only be described as polite, steely animosity.

"Everyone ready?" I ask, cutting the tip off my wedge of cake and holding it aloft with my fork. The wind is really picking up, whipping olive leaves and kicking up dust swirls around the patio. I hope we have time to finish before it starts raining.

"Now remember," Nonna instructs. "We take the first bite at the exact same time. After that, everyone can enjoy the cake and coffee. Even our unexpected guests." She gestures toward Keith and Drew with a slightly reproving air.

Everyone nods. I see Keith whip out his phone and start filming, walking slowly around the table so he can get the whole group. It feels wrong somehow, that he would be filming such a personal moment. I want to protect us and these sacred few seconds.

"Do you mind turning your phone off, please?" I request politely. Keith lowers the phone in surprise.

"Why?" he asks. "This is great footage. It shows the cookbook in action."

"This has nothing to do with the show you've offered me," I tell him firmly. "This is a private family moment."

He looks annoyed but lowers his phone. I'm not convinced he's actually stopped recording, though. The first raindrops patter on the leaves above us and the sky is a weird purplish color.

"Okay, on three . . . Nonna, will you count for us?" I ask.

She nods. "Of course. It would be my honor."

I lift my fork with the bite of cake and look around the circle. How is it that in the space of a few weeks so much has changed in my life? How have my priorities rearranged so drastically? I look at Nonna's lined face, at the shadows of exhaustion but also the pride in her eyes as she gazes at us around the table. How many years has she waited for someone to lift the burden of our family legacy from her? Now I am taking up the mantle, though she does not know it yet. Somehow I must be ready to bear the heavy weight of responsibility.

"Uno," Nonna calls loudly. My eyes skip to Lorenzo, faithful Lorenzo who has loved Nonna for so long and cared for her so selflessly. What will happen now that he has declared his love? And what will Nonna see when she finally takes her first bite of the cake?

"Due."

My eyes pass over Alex. We've spent years as strangers. Now we are sisters. She is a part of this legacy, a part of our family and our future, no matter what happens. Nonna was right. There is no such thing as half family. I know that now. I hope Alex does too.

And then just as Nonna takes a deep breath to say the final number, my gaze snags on Nicolo. He holds his fork poised, the bite of cake speared there. He's not looking at Nonna or the cake. His dark eyes are fixed on me, and I see in his gaze all the longing and loneliness, the burden of the years we've been apart. He is so changed. He is exactly the same. He gives me a look of such piercing tenderness, such hope and apprehension. And suddenly, my mouth goes dry. I want . . . I want . . .

"Tre," Nonna calls. Out of the corner of my eye I see Violetta and Nonna pop the cake into their mouths, but Nicolo and I do not move. We are frozen, staring at each other with a shared look filled with questions and longing, his gaze torn, mine confused. Neither of us takes a bite.

There is a long moment of silence. It feels as though the world is holding its breath. Even the wind has died down, and there is a strange hush over the landscape. I glance at Nonna, who has her eyes closed. She looks beatific.

Just then Alex points. "Um, guys. Look at Violetta."

Nicolo and I turn toward the old woman. She is sitting there like a statue in her chair, her hand on her heart, her eyes widened and fixed on some point on the cloudy horizon with a look of radiant joy stamped on her severe features. For a heart-stopping moment I think she may have suffered some sort of heart attack or stroke and breathed her last, but just then she blinks and gives a little gasp. She turns, her expression a bit confused, and sees all of us gaping at her.

"What are you staring at?" she demands crossly. Nope, she's obviously fine.

"Nonna V." Nicolo touches her arm gently. "What did you see?"

Violetta lifts one trembling hand and smooths her gray hair into her tight bun. "It was so beautiful," she says, looking from Nicolo to me and smiling. "I could die this minute and be at peace."

"Well, let's no one die quite yet," Nonna quips practically. Her eyes have popped open and she appears unfazed by whatever she experienced. "You want to live to see the vision come true, don't you?"

"I do," Lorenzo interjects cheerfully.

A peculiar look comes over Nonna's face at his words. She turns and looks at Lorenzo long and hard for a moment, then nods her head decisively as though making up her mind about something. She stands and goes to him, cups his big, tanned faced in her hands, and gives him a quick peck on the lips. "Maybe you will, you big idiota," she says crisply, turning away immediately.

He looks gobsmacked for a moment, then a satisfied smile creeps over his face. "Maybe I will," he repeats, giving us a sly wink. Nonna sits down and quickly sips her espresso, her cheeks a dull red. She's blushing! It makes her look like a young woman. I think perhaps Lorenzo isn't the only one in love.

"What did you see, Bruna?" Violetta asks.

"None of your business, any of you," Nonna replies tartly. Then she notices Nicolo and me, still holding forks with a bite of cake on them.

"You didn't take the bite?" Nonna exclaims, looking scandalized. "Nicolo, Juliana, why did you not take a bite?" She presses her hand to her heart in dismay.

I shoot a wild glance at Nicolo, feeling disappointment and dismay. "I don't know . . ." I stare down at the bite of cake. "I meant to, and then when you counted to three I just . . . didn't."

I'm not even close to understanding why I did what I did. I glance up to find Nicolo watching me curiously.

"Still afraid to take a risk for what you want?" he asks softly.

My temper flares instantly. "I know what I want," I tell him hotly. "I want to be the next caretaker of this farm, I want to carry on the legacy. It feels impossible right now, but I'll figure out a way. I don't need a bite of cake to show me that. I was just hoping the cake could give me a clue as to how I do it, so I don't fail miserably." My voice trails away as my anger dissipates. I'm left feeling a little shaken. But in that moment the strangest thing happens. Nicolo's face clears instantly and he breaks into the biggest grin. It's like looking at a sunrise after a storm. He sets down his bite of cake and applauds, his gaze still fixed on me.

"Brava, Jules," he says. "That took courage. It seems you have chosen your right hard thing."

I flush and look around. Nonna is beaming at me, hands clasped over her breast like a saint receiving a holy vision. "I am so glad," she whispers.

Lorenzo slaps his hand on his knee in glee. Even Alex shoots me a look of quiet relief. Only Violetta is looking at me sourly. "Oh, so you're staying?" she says.

I laugh. "Sorry to disappoint you, but yes. You can't get rid of me that easily," I tell her.

She *humphs*, but a reluctant smile tugs up one corner of her mouth.

"You can always make the cake and try again," Nonna say comfortingly. She slides the cookbook over to me. I pick it up and open it, expecting to see the familiar cake recipe, but instead to my surprise there is a recipe for a risotto dish with truffles on the page. No Orange Blossom Cake in sight. I shut the book quickly, dismayed. I missed my chance to see the happiest moment of my life and to hopefully get some answers. Now I'm going to have to figure things out on my own. What an intimidating thought.

"What did you see?" Nonna peers across the table, sees my expression, and frowns. "No cake recipe?" She reaches over and pats my hand. "Trust the book," she says. "It always knows exactly what we need."

Chapter 54

In all the excitement, I've lost track of Keith.

"So this is the famous cookbook?" he asks. I turn to find him standing by my shoulder. He reaches out and picks up the cookbook. I don't like seeing it in his hands. For some reason, I don't want him touching it. He flips it open and riffles through the pages. "What's the trick with this thing?"

I stiffen. "Sorry. Family heirloom. We have to be really careful with it." I take the book from him and gently place it on the table.

"Well, you better get used to other people touching it if it's going to be on the show," Keith says. He looks annoyed. A few more raindrops hit the leaves of the olive tree above us with small, sharp popping sounds. I take the cookbook and tuck it in my apron pocket to protect it.

Keith narrows his eyes at me, then glances around to find Drew. "Can I talk to you a minute?" he asks tightly. Drew nods and they head down the stairs and walk to their car. Everyone else is sitting at the table eating cake and chatting, sheltered from the rain by the ancient spreading olive branches above them. I have no appetite. I feel buzzy, like there is a swarm of bees in my blood, and a little shaky too. Being courageous takes a lot of energy. A little at a loss, I take the cookbook into the kitchen. I have the sense that I need to keep it safe somehow. As I slide it into its place in the drawer, I realize I can hear tense voices outside the open kitchen window. It's Drew and Keith. The wind is carrying their raised voices right to me. I tiptoe closer to the window. I can hear their conversation clearly.

"I thought you told me you could handle her." It's Keith's voice, tight with anger. "She wouldn't even let me touch the damn book."

"I'll take care of it." Drew's voice, placating and a little worried. "Just give me a minute. I'll talk to her, convince her. She'll listen to me."

My ears perk up. It sounds like they're talking about me.

"We need that book. That's the entire point of the show, Drew. Not Juliana. Girls like her are a dime a dozen." Keith's voice is dismissive. "We don't need her. We need that book. Do you understand? No book means no show. And you're skating on thin ice right now, pal. After Desiree left us on the hook to do *Dance Off*, we need a fresh idea. This is it. So either you get her to sign a contract giving us access to that cookbook or the entire deal is off, got it? I've got plenty of options other than you. I don't need you. You need me, remember that."

I listen for Drew's reply, but it's too faint and mumbled for me to hear it clearly. My heart drops with dismay. They don't really want me. They only want the cookbook. I'm just the inconvenience Keith has to put up with to get what he wants. This feels like the last time all over again. What a rotten realization.

"I thought you said she'd do anything you want her to do." Keith's voice is filled with scorn.

"She will!" Drew's panicked reply is loud and clear. "I can get Jules to agree. Just give me a chance. I can convince her."

I gasp. Drew is using me, using our friendship. I swallow hard, tasting bitter dregs of my earlier espresso. I am being betrayed a second time by the man I thought was my closest friend.

They move away and their voices grow distant and indistinct. I hear a car door slam, but I'm rooted to the spot. All the blood seems to have rushed to my head. I feel dizzy and unmoored. If I don't go back out there, someone is going to come looking for me, and I have a sinking feeling that it will be Drew. I want to see him out in the open, not alone in here. I head out the door and across the gravel courtyard, trying to reach the patio where everyone is still eating cake and drinking espresso despite the gathering storm. Sure enough, Drew stops me before I reach the stairs.

"Hey, Jules!" His tone is light, as though he hasn't just bartered our friendship for his career.

I ignore him. The clouds are black over the lake now and racing fast across the sky. I think we may get really wet soon. A few raindrops splatter on the crown of my head.

"Jules." He catches me by the wrist as I put one foot on the steps. He gently tugs me back to face him. "Wait a sec. I want to talk to you."

I whirl on him, temper flaring. "Well, I don't want to talk to you."

He looks genuinely puzzled.

"I heard what you said to Keith," I confront him. "I think you need to leave." I'm so disappointed I feel sick.

"Hey, hey. I don't know what you've heard, but let me explain," Drew says, drawing me toward him. He reaches up and brushes a wisp of hair back from my eyes and tucks it in my headband. The tender gesture feels insincere. I jerk back. How can he use me like this? It's so manipulative.

"I know what I heard," I mutter. "Keith doesn't want me. You're just using me to get the cookbook."

He shakes his head, his blue eyes wide and pleading. "No, you've got it all wrong. Keith wants the cookbook. I'm just using the cookbook so we can do a show together. Just like we planned. Come on, Jules. We can still do this. Isn't this what we've always wanted?"

For an instant, I'm tempted. Even after all I just heard, it's hard to look into those earnest blue eyes and not believe him. He's been a good friend to me for a long time. He's saying what I want to hear. Too bad I know it's all false.

I glance over my shoulder, up to the patio table where my family is chatting and enjoying one another. Violetta says something and Lorenzo roars with laughter. Even Alex is smiling as she pokes at her slice of cake. This is the end of our friendship, I realize miserably. Even if what Drew says is true, even if he does want to do a show with me, he's using me. He has not been honest with me. He's putting himself first, just like he has before.

It's a pattern with him. I see it now, the slightest hint of trickery, the whiff of selfish interest. Drew takes care of Drew first. I know he probably cares for me as a friend, but he cares for himself more. I see him now for what he really is, charming and fickle, sweet but self-centered at the core. He is not a man. He is still a boy.

"Jules, everything okay?" I look up and see Nicolo standing at the top of the stone steps, watching us, his dark eyes hooded and fixed on Drew. There's something protective in the way he says my name. I feel an instant rush of relief.

I hesitate, then nod, glancing between Nicolo and Drew. Nicolo doesn't lie or deceive. There is nothing self-serving about him. He has given up everything to come to aid Violetta, and he has stuck with it despite her difficult attitude and lack of appreciation for his efforts. He has cared for Nonna and Lorenzo too, without seeking any reward for his duty and generosity. The difference between the two men is starkly clear.

I turn back to Drew.

"It's too late," I tell him. "Go home. The answer is no." I start to turn away and head for the stairs, but he grabs my wrist. I whirl on him, wincing as my ankle twinges sharply.

"Let go of me," I demand. Raindrops splatter on the gravel at our feet, on our joined hands. I blink as grit flies in my eyes, picked up by the wind.

"No, Jules, wait. I can explain." His expression slides toward panic and desperation.

"Ouch. You're hurting me." I struggle in his grasp, trying to get away. My wrist aches where he's pressing the bones too tightly.

"Hey, bastardo!" Suddenly, Nicolo is there at my side. Quick as lightening he lunges for Drew, twisting my wrist out of Drew's grip in one smooth motion and punching him hard in the solar plexus. Drew reels back with a grunt, clutching his abdomen with a look of astonishment. His mouth opens and closes like a goldfish but no sound comes out.

Nicolo draws me behind him, shielding me with his body. "She said let go," he growls through gritted teeth. He glances back at me. "Jules, are you okay?"

I nod, clasping my tender wrist, feeling perilously close to tears. This is all terrible, but the solid weight of Nicolo standing in front of me is reassuring. He's come to my aid and now it looks like he's prepared to fight for me. His whole body is tensed, on guard.

Drew gasps for air and stares at Nicolo, holding his midsection. "Why did you do that, man?" he wheezes. "We were just talking."

"No, you weren't," Nicolo says bluntly. He starts to roll up his shirtsleeves in a calm, calculated way. I'm aware the entire patio table has fallen silent and is watching us in fascination, like we are one of the episodes of the Italian soap operas Nonna likes to watch in the front parlor when she thinks no one can hear the TV.

"Let's ask Jules," Nicolo says conversationally. He turns to me, his eyes scanning my face, a faint line of concern creasing his brow. "Jules, do you want to continue talking to this pezzo di merda?" Nicolo asks me politely. There is a crack of lightning from across the lake and the deep boom of thunder. I jump, then glance at Drew. He gives me a pleading look. He doesn't know any Italian and so therefore misses the fact that Nicolo just called him a derogatory name.

I shake my head sadly, trying to keep my voice from wobbling. "No. I don't want to see him ever again."

There is nothing more to say. Maybe Drew is telling the truth about his motivations, at least as he understands them. But I cannot be sure he will be honest with me, that he will put me first. And if I cannot trust him, really, what more is there to say? He is no true friend, and it breaks my heart.

"Jules!" Drew tries again, pitifully.

"I think it's time for you to leave," Nicolo says conversationally, but he takes a firm step toward Drew, who flinches and stumbles back a couple of feet.

Just then Keith hops out of the sedan, talking on his phone. He stops short when he sees the confrontation in the courtyard. He swears and hangs up the phone mid-sentence, then comes striding over to Drew and gives us an exasperated look. "This is you handling it?" he barks at Drew, grabbing him by the shoulder and pointing him to the sedan. "Get in the car. I'll take it from here."

I almost feel sorry for Drew as he slinks dejectedly toward the car like a scolded child. Almost but not quite.

Chapter 55

"I apologize for that unpleasant scene," Keith says smoothly as he draws out a checkbook from the pocket of his jacket. "I was hoping it wouldn't come to this." He sighs. "Okay, how much?"

"What do you mean?" I stare at him in confusion.

Keith looks at me. His eyes are hard. "How much for the cookbook? Do you have any idea what a great hook that is? This show is guaranteed to be one of the most talked about programs on whatever network is lucky enough to pick it up." He licks his lips like he can already see the money pouring in. "Look, Jules, you're a great girl. People like you. I'll tell you what. How would you like to do a show without a cohost, just you? Or we can replace him if you want to find someone else." He gestures toward Drew, who is climbing into the back of the sedan, still clutching his midsection and wheezing slightly. Then Keith looks speculatively at Nicolo. "Have you ever thought about being on TV?" he asks.

Nicolo crosses his arms and snorts. "No."

Keith shrugs. "Okay, so what's it going to be, Jules? Do you still want to do the show with a nice hefty advance? Or do you want to just sell me the cookbook instead? Name your price."

My jaw drops open. "For the cookbook? It's not for sale."

Keith laughs humorlessly. "Everything's for sale," he says flatly. "It's just about negotiating the right price."

I glance back at the patio. Nonna is sitting there watching us. She has given me the freedom to choose my path. This is my decision to make. I look at the farmhouse, at the stucco falling in chunks off the wall, at the paint peeling from the shutters. It would be so easy. I can name the price, do the show or not, and save this place.

I think of leaving here, leaving Nonna and Lorenzo, leaving Nicolo, and trying to find my way in LA. The thought makes me feel desolate, even if it is for a good purpose. There is no spark of joy in it. Do I sell the cookbook then? I recoil at the thought of the book in Keith's hands. That book is the heart of our family, a book of blessing, of hospitality and care. It symbolizes all that is right and good about the Costa name. It is our history and legacy. It would be like selling the heartbeat of who we are.

"The cookbook is not for sale," I say flatly, loudly so everyone can hear. "And neither am I. You should go. There's nothing for you here."

As I say it, I realize that I am throwing away all our financial opportunities. But I cannot agree to what he wants. It is terrifying to say the words, but it feels so right. Still, my heart quails a little. I know I am making the right decision, but it is hard to see the money go. Above me Alex whistles and claps. Keith looks like he is growing annoyed.

"How about two hundred thousand," he offers. "I can't go higher than that." He actually starts to write the check. Fat raindrops splatters on his checkbook. We are about to get really wet.

"No," I say firmly. "Not for any price." I turn away, heading back to the patio. We should clear the table and get inside before the rain really starts. "Have a nice flight."

Lorenzo lumbers down the stairs like a big, protective bear. He brushes past me and stands shoulder to shoulder with Nicolo, their bodies forming a barrier between me and Keith, a living wall of suspicious Italian protective manliness standing guard over our family. I love it. Keith starts to step toward me, but Nicolo and Lorenzo block his way.

"You heard her. It's time for you to go," Lorenzo says in heavily accented English. He slaps one fist into his meaty palm. He sounds like the Godfather. I almost laugh at Keith's shocked expression.

"And if we see your face here again, please know that I am friends with every judge and policeman in this region. You will be arrested, and I will personally make it my goal to guarantee that your stay in Italian jail is as miserable as possible," Nicolo says conversationally. "And that goes for your cowardly little Ken doll friend too." He nods toward the sedan.

I'm pretty sure he's bluffing, but Keith seems convinced.

"Fine." Keith flinches and holds up his hands, a placating gesture. He's not a fool. He knows when he is beat. He turns toward the car. "What a waste of a trip," he says loudly in disgust. Getting into the back of the sedan with Drew, he slams the door hard. A moment later, the driver starts the engine and the car pulls away in a spray of gravel. Silently, we watch the sedan disappear down the drive fast. I see them go, feeling strangely hollow. Slowly, I trudge up the steps to the patio, wincing slightly. I feel sick with apprehension as the magnitude of my hasty actions sinks in. What in the world am I going to do now?

"You did the right thing," Nonna tells me as I approach the table. Her eyes are soft with sympathy and suspiciously shiny. Is she . . . crying?

Alex eyes me with a grudging respect. "That was so hardcore," she tells me. "Ruth Bader Ginsburg–level cool."

Even Violetta looks impressed. "You are a strong woman," she says reluctantly. "Just like your Nonna Bruna."

I nod wearily and sit down with a thump, ignoring the impending rainstorm. My wrist and ankle are both aching. I don't feel strong or hardcore. I feel scared and tired and a little heartsick. For so many years I wanted what Drew and Keith just offered me—a hit show with my best friend, a sense of safety and security that all that would bring. But now I've traded safety and security for the unknown, for a chance to save what really matters to me. And despite my fears and misgivings, I know I have chosen correctly. This is my right hard thing. I have found the things in my life that are worth taking risks for—this place and those who are sitting at this table right now. I am determined not to let fear win. I'm practicing courage and trying to let what I truly love guide my choices. I cross myself and kiss my thumb for luck. I need all the help Saint Sebastian can give me.

"I think I need some cake." I hungrily eye the fat wedge sitting on my plate. "But shouldn't we get inside before it really starts pouring?" No one seems concerned.

"The storm is passing us by," Nonna says, sliding a mostly cold cup of espresso in front of me. I glance up in surprise. She's right. A few olive leaves skitter across the table, driven by the wind, but inexplicably, it looks as though the brewing storm is blowing right past us. I can see blue sky over the lake and a pale beam of sunlight on the water. The rain has stopped. I take a bite of the cake, closing my eyes and savoring the delicate flavor and the sudden calm with a sense of relief. I'll worry about how I'm going to save the farm later. Right now I want to enjoy my cake and the satisfaction of having made my decision, having chosen my right hard thing. I take another bite of cake, and another. Every one tastes like olive oil and orange blossoms, earthy and honest and a little bittersweet.

Chapter 56

"So are you staying in Italy?" Alex asks tentatively. I look up from my half-eaten slice of cake to see all eyes on me. I swallow a forkful down with a gulp of cold espresso. Bolstered by sugar and caffeine, I nod slowly.

"I'm staying," I say firmly although my stomach is clenched in a hard little knot of anxiety. "I'll do the best I can. I can't promise I'll succeed, but I'll try my hardest."

Lorenzo whoops with glee. Nonna nods with a small, satisfied smile. Nicolo lets out a breath I didn't know he was holding. Violetta looks long-suffering, but there's a tiny quirk to her mouth that looks almost . . . pleased. Alex looks contemplative.

"But my biggest potential source of income just drove away in that sedan," I say soberly. "Now I need a new plan."

I stare down at my plate with a sinking heart. How in the world are we going to make this work? The reality of what I just committed to starts to sink in, and my anxiety ratchets up, a sharp squeezing in my chest. I press my hand to my breastbone, trying to ease the pressure.

"You mean *we* need a new plan, right?" Alex says with a reproving note in her voice.

I look at her quizzically.

She rolls her eyes. "You're acting like you have to be Superwoman or something and figure this all out on your own, but we all love this place. We can figure it out together. I mean, I'm not an expert, but isn't that what it means to be a family? We do things together?"

"But of course." Lorenzo looks astonished. "You cannot do this alone, Juliana. No one can."

Nonna nods vigorously. "Certamente. We do it together. You are not alone, Juliana." She reaches for my hand and squeezes it. "Thank you for saying yes, Nipotina. I am so deeply glad. We will help you, all of us."

I'm touched, looking around the table at their eager faces. They mean it. I am not alone. They will help me, stand by me, whatever comes. It has been many years since I felt so supported. It brings tears to my eyes. I draw a shaky breath, feeling steadied by their care and commitment. Over the lake, the dark clouds of the thunderstorm have passed by completely and a golden light streams down over the hills and on the water, limning everything in a radiant glow.

"Grazie mille," I murmur. I am not alone. The warmth of that realization seeps slowly into my lonely heart like a balm.

Violetta gives a prim little nod. "You are right to help your family," she says. She reaches out and pats Nicolo's hand stiffly. "Like my Nicolo," she says. "You honor us all. There is nothing more valuable. We are grateful to you both."

I glance at Nicolo. He is looking at his grandmother in shock. I don't think I've ever heard her say a complimentary word about anyone. Whatever she saw with that first bite of cake must have been a doozy. Nicolo glances over at me and meets my eyes. He looks like he might be getting a little choked up. I slide my sandaled foot over to his side of the table and find his loafer, resting my foot against his. His gaze flickers up in surprise and then he relaxes and gives me the sweetest smile and a nudge with his shoe. The barest hint of pressure, but it brings a warmth to my chest. Whatever this is that is blooming between us, now that I'm staying, there is a chance for us to let it grow. The thought makes me feel radiant with anticipation and joy.

"I'm staying, but I have no idea what I'm doing," I say, clearing my throat and trying to keep on task, even though Nicolo is still foot cuddling with me. "*We* need a new plan."

"First we eat," Nonna says firmly. "No one can think on an empty stomach. First we make pasta, then we make a plan."

An hour later, we are all seated around the patio again, tucking into bowls of Trofie al pesto, a chewy slightly spiraled pasta drenched in freshly made pesto. It's simple and utterly decadent, one of my favorite recipes. It's going to be a great addition to my cookbook. I used to beg Nonna to make it every summer because I loved to help shape the spiral noodles. Today it was fun to make them again. Alex gets a few good shots of the pasta glistening with fresh pesto, and then Nonna says a quick grace over the meal. The sun is out again, the air fresh and clean. The world looks newly made. I am feeling a little more hopeful. How can you not on a sun-drenched day in Italy eating homemade pasta?

"Mangiate, mangiate," Nonna urges us, spooning generous portions onto our plates. Eat. Eat. We do, enjoying the food and sipping glasses of light, dry local red wine. The day has turned sunny and warm. There are insects buzzing under the rustle of the olive trees, and from far below us, we can hear the faint road noise and see the flash of blue water, smooth and calm. We don't linger, though. We have big work to do.

"How bad is it?" Nonna asks, doling out early-afternoon espressos to Lorenzo and me. Nicolo left to take Violetta home after lunch and is handling a few business matters at the farm. He's due back at any moment. Alex took a break and is finishing her third Italian lesson of the day and no doubt texting Tommaso.

"It's not terrible, but it's not great." I sigh and massage my neck where it's cramping from being bent over the numbers for too long. We've spent the past two hours since lunch trying to piece together a complete financial picture for the farm, and the patio table is covered with ledgers, receipts, and official letters in Italian. The first step, we agreed, was to understand how much it costs to run the farm before we can start brainstorming how to meet those costs.

I show her the numbers. The yearly operating budget for the farm isn't really a huge sum, but it might as well cost the moon since we have no viable way to pay for it. Plus the needed repairs are well over six figures. Lorenzo and Nonna both have a small pension that covers their personal expenses with a little left over to chip in for utilities and gas for the car, that sort of thing. Still, that leaves my personal expenses, the farm operating costs, and the huge backlog of repairs. How in the world are we going to raise the money? I take a swallow of espresso and try to calm my racing thoughts.

Nicolo comes back as we are sitting around glumly staring at the numbers. He zooms up the drive on a vintage red Vespa, which he parks at the bottom of the stairs.

"What happened?" he asks, taking off his helmet and coming up the steps to the patio. "This feels like a funeral."

I tell him the numbers and he whistles. "Okay, so what's the plan?" He takes a seat.

"There isn't one," I admit. "Doing the show was the plan."

"Good riddance." Nonna spits on the ground, her mouth puckered like she's tasted something sour.

Lorenzo nods. "It was a bad plan," he says solemnly.

"Obviously, we need a new plan," Nicolo says firmly. "So let's think of something."

We all are silent for a moment.

"What about letting people stay on the farm?" Alex pipes up, looking up from her phone.

"What do you mean?" I ask her.

"Like a bed-and-breakfast but with farm stuff," she explains.

"They call it an agriturismo here," Nicolo says. "It's sort of like a rural bed-and-breakfast. Guests come spend a few days on a local farm. They pick vegetables and eat foods grown in the area. It's very popular here."

"We have those two extra bedrooms no one is using," Nonna muses. "We could clean them out and make them into guest rooms."

"How much do people pay to stay in one of these places?" I ask.

Alex shrugs. "Let's look it up." She pulls up Google on her phone and shows us a few listings for nearby agriturismos. The farms look similar to ours and the money is good. Surprisingly good. This might not be a bad idea.

"This farm near Garda Town offers wine and olive oil tastings," I say slowly. "We could do that too."

Nicolo runs his fingers through his curls and they spring up excitedly. "Bruna, you could offer cooking classes. A lawyer friend of mine took a class in Provence last year in a private home. She paid two hundred euros for a couple of hours."

"So much money for a few hours? I can do that with no trouble," Nonna agrees.

"Authentic Italian cooking classes with a real nonna," I muse. "Like real-life Pasta Grannies."

"I know better recipes than those women on the YouTube," Nonna says with a sniff.

"They don't have a magic cookbook, so cut them some slack," I tell her dryly. I drum my fingers on the table, thinking through the idea. "But where would we get people who want to stay?" I ask. "How would we advertise the agriturismo and Nonna's cooking classes?"

Alex looks surprised. "Oh, that's easy. Social media. I'm getting more and more messages from people asking if we host guests, if they can use our patio for a wedding, if they can come open Nonna's magic cookbook. At least a few a day now are sending me messages asking about stuff like that."

"Really? That many?" I stare at her. I had no idea.

Alex shows me some of the messages. From Alabama, California, Canada, Brazil, Malaysia, South Africa—all from people asking to come stay with us, wanting to meet Nonna, wanting to see the cookbook, wanting to come learn the recipes we are making.

My mind races with the possibilities. It is a surprisingly good idea. As Nonna pointed out, we have those two unused bedrooms next to Nonna's room upstairs. We could empty out the junk and spruce them up with a little elbow grease and some new décor. I do some quick calculations. Even if we have reservations only part of the year, it would bring in a fair amount of income. Not enough to cover everything we need, but it would certainly go a long way toward helping us stay afloat.

Chapter 57

"This is a good start, but we need something else." I tap my pen on the notebook in front of me. "I don't think hosting people in our two extra bedrooms and offering cooking classes is going to generate enough income. We need big money for things like roof repairs. This place needs a lot of work."

"What about your cookbook?" Nonna asks. "Could that help us?"

I shake my head. "I already got the advance. I mean, if the cookbook sells really well, then yes, the royalties could help a little bit. But I don't think we can depend on it for income."

"Maybe not for money," Nonna says thoughtfully, "but these are our family recipes; this is the place you learned to cook. Could you use the cookbook to let people know about the farm?"

"You mean use the cookbook to market what we offer at the farm?" I ask, thinking about the possibilities.

"We could do the same thing on social media," Alex interrupts excitedly. "We could run a contest for a free farm stay. We could do more promotional videos." She looks ready to take on the world. Her enthusiasm is infectious.

"We could build a brand around the farm," I say, mind whirring with the germ of an idea. Now I'm getting excited too. It probably isn't enough to dig us out of the hole financially, but there's growth potential. How much potential I don't know yet.

"I can handle the guest bookings and their stays with us." I am warming to this idea. "Nonna, are you sure you can handle the cooking classes? It's a lot of work."

She waves away my concerns. "I'll work until my last breath," she tells me. "If it means we can keep this place and our legacy."

"Zio Lorenzo, if we got you some help, could you continue to oversee the grounds and olive groves?" I ask. Lorenzo readily agrees.

"I'll help him too," Nicolo volunteers abruptly. "As much as I can."

"Hey, what about me?" Alex interrupts. "Why am I not included in this?"

I stare at her in surprise. "Because in a few weeks school starts, and you have to be back in New York."

Her jaw juts out stubbornly and she shakes her head. "I don't want to go," she says.

"Alex, you knew this was only for the summer," I tell her, confused. "It was never supposed to be more than that."

"Too late," she says, her tone insistent. "I don't want to go back to New York. I want to stay here. I can run all the social media for the farm. I can be useful. You need me to help you do this."

I glance at Nonna for moral support but she only shrugs. "She has many useful skills," she points out unhelpfully.

Nonna isn't wrong. Alex would be an amazing asset, but she's a high school student. She can't just up and move to Italy with no parents. "What about Ted and Lisa?" I ask. "And school?"

"They have schools here, don't they?" she points out mulishly. "I could finish school here."

"You have to be fluent in Italian," I protest.

"Try me," she challenges. "I've been practicing a lot." And then she rattles off a long string of pretty decent Italian. Lorenzo whistles. Nonna looks surprised and delighted. I don't know what to say.

"Wow, that online language course has really been paying off," Nicolo says admiringly.

Alex shrugs modestly. "I told you, I'm good with languages."

"She really got you there," Lorenzo tells me. I shoot him a dirty look, which he cheerfully ignores.

"At least ask Mom?" Alex asks, her tone pleading. I see the expression on her face, the defiance mixed with longing. It softens me. "Please?" she asks again.

"Are you sure you want to stay here and finish school?" I ask. "This will not be easy. You'll have to adjust to the culture. And we're going to get on each other's nerves. There will be hard days working together as a family. Are you sure this is what you want?"

She lifts her chin, determined. "Yeah. I'm sure."

I glance at Nonna, who shoots me a guileless smile. Still, I get the feeling that this may be an outcome she's been angling for all along. "She's your sister, Nipotina," Nonna says. "How can we say no? She needs us and we need her."

I sigh, sensing a losing battle. When I agreed to chaperone her for the summer, I had no idea how quickly things would change. How much I would come to care about Alex. "Okay, I'll ask Lisa. But she and Ted get the final say."

"They'll say yes," Alex predicts, looking a little smug. I have a feeling she's right. I can't imagine Lisa not jumping at the chance to be unencumbered by her teenager. Most likely I just have to say how well Alex is doing, how she's making friends and seems so happy, and Lisa will readily agree to Alex staying with us in Italy.

Surprisingly, the thought of Alex staying makes *me* happy. I don't want her to leave. We started the summer as strangers and now we are ending as sisters. As family. I look around the table, realizing with a sweet sense of relief that I won't ever feel alone again. My family is here to help me. We will stand together, shoulder to shoulder. The thought is warming. It feels so right.

I pull out my phone and text Solomon and Sandra.

> Change of plans. I'll be staying in Italy after the summer. Do you want to take over my half of the lease or should I look for someone to sublet my room?

A few seconds later a text pops up on my screen. It's from Sandra.

> We will take over the whole lease. With Drew staying in LA permanently, Ophelia can have her own room.

Drew is staying in LA? That's news to me, not that it really affects me now. I heave a sigh of relief. At least the apartment situation is sorted. I add "alert landlord re: Solomon and Sandra taking over lease" to my to-do list on my phone, right under "let Trader Joe's know I'm not coming back." I'll have to fly back to Seattle and clean my stuff out of the apartment. I could ship my belongings to Italy, but I'm thinking I might just fill a few suitcases and donate the rest of it to Goodwill. I don't have that much I'm attached to, and I like the idea of a fresh start in the place that feels most like home.

"Hey Jules, people really like that video you posted on your profile." Alex interrupts my thoughts. She holds out her phone to show me. It's the pizza-making segment I posted on *The Bygone Kitchen*. She's right. People are liking and sharing and commenting on it. While I'm sitting there, a few new comments pop up.

> **More pasta please!**
> **Ur grandma is a hottie!**
> **EEEK! I LOVE ITALY!!!**

I look at the number of comments and shares. Wow, this is unexpected. This video is more popular than any I've shared in . . . well . . . maybe ever. I narrow my eyes, a notion niggling at the corner of my brain. What if I take *The Bygone Kitchen* and rebrand it as @OlivesandAmore? Alex only uses that name on TikTok. We could expand to all the other social media channels and build one integrated brand. It would be based here in Italy and focus on introducing readers to Italian recipes from our region. There are so many amazing recipes that go far beyond pizza and spaghetti Bolognese. Could I still give something good to my followers, something they'd enjoy, but connect it to Italy, the farm, Nonna, and my heritage? Maybe I could tie in the cooking classes and farm stays we're talking about too.

I don't have to lose the show, I realize with a little fizz of excitement. I can simply transform it into something that still gives me and my followers joy, but fits my life now. A fledgling idea starts to take form.

Chapter 58

"~~How do you~~ feel?" Nicolo asks, helping me gather up all the financial papers and empty espresso cups.

It's late afternoon and we're all exhilarated and exhausted from planning and brainstorming and mapping out a possible future. Nonna is inside lying down. Lorenzo is in the stable tinkering with machinery. Alex has gone inside to get ready. Tommaso and a few friends are coming to pick her up and take her to the best gelato place in Bardolino. He texted her earlier to invite her. I took one look at her excited face and agreed, as long as she keeps her phone on and is back by eight.

That leaves Nicolo and me.

"My head is spinning, and I think there's a decent chance I'm going to mess this all up and lose the farm that's been in my family for generations, but also after today I feel sort of weirdly hopeful. We might just make this work." We reach for a cup at the same time, our fingers brushing. Neither of us pull our hands away.

"You're really staying," Nicolo says, meeting my eyes. It is not a question. He says it like he's testing it, deciding if he can put weight on it.

"That's my plan."

"Good," he says, and his eyes crinkle at the corners. His smile is pure joy. "I'm so glad."

I nod. "Me too."

"Are you still afraid?" he asks, his gaze searching.

I nod again. "I'm terrified. But someone wise once told me that the secret to life is not in staying safe, but in finding something worth taking a risk for." I look out at the olive groves, at the lake sparkling in the afternoon sun, back at the farmhouse where love and warmth are spilling from the open door. "I think she's right. So here I am."

Nicolo's eyes are warm and heavy on me. "And is it only this place that calls you back?" he asks with a touch of hesitation. "Only your family?"

There's a note of vulnerability in his voice that reminds me of Nicolo when I first met him, the tenderness of his heart. I think I know what he's asking.

"If I'm honest," I tell him, leaning closer, "it's not just the land and my family. It's the neighbors too. I think they're pretty amazing. One in particular." I smile at him, meeting his eyes, mine alight with joyful anticipation.

His face breaks into a boyish grin and I see flashes of young Nicolo once again. How extraordinary that our lives have come full circle. How improbable, yet how marvelous.

"I'm still scared," I admit. "But I want this so, so much." I don't explain what the "this" is. I'm not sure I fully know yet. It's family and place and a sense of belonging. It's Nicolo and the possibility of a future together.

"You are not alone in the wanting," he says simply.

I put down the papers and cups and his arms come around me, encircling me snugly. He presses his cheek to my hair. "I am here," he whispers. "I want you too, so much." I feel him brush a kiss across my forehead, my temple, the hinge of my jaw.

I think of the start of our love story, that sweet, doomed summer. Sneaking out to meet under the oldest olive tree, high on pheromones and forbidden love. The moment everything was wrenched away from me. Now we are older, steadier. We know who we are, what we value in life. We're friends who are once again turning into so much more. I could not have predicted this. It feels like the best kind of surprise.

"Will you write me another sonnet?" I ask, my voice muffled against the worn cotton of his work shirt. For some reason I'm thinking of the sonnets we wrote each other and left in the fork of the olive tree, so poorly done, but so earnest. We were so besotted with each other. I have a feeling we might still be.

He laughs, a deep, warm rumble against my cheek. "I'll write you a sonnet for every day we were apart," he says softly, his voice a velvet rasp in the shell of my ear. "For what I felt then is still true today. Juliana Costa, my heart is yours. I think somehow it always has been." He nips my earlobe and I squeak in surprise.

I press my cheek against his chest, squeezing my arms around him, hearing the steady beat of his faithful heart. He nudges my cheek and I lift my face to his, our noses brushing, then lips, and as the kiss deepens, I lean into him. The road ahead is shrouded with uncertainty, risk, and the very real possibility of ruin. But I am taking the chance because I have finally found something worth fighting for.

※

"Mamma mia!" Nonna's exclamation bursts our bubble and we break off the kiss abruptly. I have no idea how much time has passed, but now Nonna is standing at the top of the steps, hand on her heart, beaming at us. Well, that ratchets things up a notch. We break apart, feeling a little self-conscious.

She motions to us. "Come, there is one more thing I think you need to do. You too, Nicolo."

Curious, we follow her into the kitchen. The cookbook is lying on the prep table. Nonna motions us over.

"In all our plans today we neglected one thing," she says solemnly. "We did not consult the cookbook. We did not ask if it had any help to give us."

Nicolo and I exchange a look. I am not sure how any recipe is going to help us solve our financial issues, but Nonna seems insistent, and what could it hurt? We humor her and both put our hands on the cookbook. This time Nicolo flips the pages open. There is something written there.

"It's a recipe for agrumato," he says, sounding surprised.

I roll the unfamiliar name in Italian around on my tongue. "Agrumato? What's that?"

Nicolo's brow is furrowed. "I don't exactly know," he admits. "I've heard Violetta use the word." We turn expectantly to Nonna.

She explains, "It's the term for olive oil that is combined with other things," she says. "When the olives are crushed, sometimes whole fresh fruits, herbs, or vegetables are crushed alongside the olives. It gives the oil the rich flavor of whatever is crushed with it, more so than infusing the oil with other things after it is pressed."

I scan the page with interest. "What does the recipe call for?"

Nicolo reads silently. "It uses Casaliva olives," he says.

"That's the type we grow," I exclaim.

Nonna leans between us and peers at the recipe. "And cedro di Salò citron," she says.

Nicolo and I exchange an astonished glance. "That's the citron we grow on our terraces," he says slowly. "It's extremely rare."

"Violetta's prized citron and our olives," I reply. A recipe that combines the fruits of both our lands. Interesting.

Nonna clicks her tongue. "I have had this agrumato once before, many years ago," she says. "The flavor was divine, as if from heaven. I have never forgotten it. If you made this, the value would be high. It would be a prized item for those who want the highest quality and rarest ingredients."

I bite my lip, thinking. It's a risk to make something so niche. What if there is no market for it? But then again, what if the cookbook is trying to give us a solution to part of our problem?

"Want to give it a try?" I ask Nicolo. "Would Violetta let us use some of the citron from her trees?"

Nicolo nods. "I think she'd be happy to see it put to good use. She doesn't do anything with it now, and she hates to see it go to waste." A slow grin breaks over his face. "Let's see what happens."

"Trust the cookbook," Nonna tells us wisely, looking decidedly pleased with this turn of events. "It is always right."

Three Years Later

My afternoon is erupting in beautiful, exhilarating chaos. I'm running late and nothing is going quite to plan. My cell phone keeps ringing as I attempt to do five things at once. I'm texting, answering calls, trying to dry my hair and slick on some lipstick, and find my good leather Mary Janes. A TV station from Milan is coming to do an interview about the farm and our most famous product, our Cedro di Salò Oro, in twenty minutes and I'm not even close to being ready.

The baby is crying. At a year old, he's teething, his face red and his dark eyes wet with tears. Aurora's face keeps popping into my screen as she calls me repeatedly. She's started a new project making baby swaddling blankets by weaving wool from her sheep and using natural dyes from vegetables in her garden, and she wants to send me a blanket to try. I send her a hurried text with my thanks and race to the bathroom, trying to apply makeup with one hand while jiggling a fussy baby Antonio—we call him Tony after my dad—on my hip. Finally managing to get my face and hair in order, I shimmy into my goldenrod-colored mod print dress and find my shoes under the bed.

Too late I notice the hefty squish of Tony's soggy diaper, decide there's no time to change him, and hurry down to the kitchen, where Nonna is teaching a cooking class. She looks up as I come in, pausing her instruction. There are three chicly thin Upper Manhattan women clustered around a pan of Nodo d'Amore, devouring the delicious love knot shapes with ravenous, slightly guilty looks. They glance up at me, forks poised.

"Sorry to interrupt, it's just the film crew will be here any minute and I can't get him to stop crying..."

"Come here, my sweet bambolotto." Without missing a beat, Nonna swipes the baby from my hands and pops the tip of a whole, unpeeled carrot in his mouth. Instantly, the crying stops. Tony looks startled, then cautiously curious. He grabs the carrot in his chubby little hand and starts to gum it with enthusiasm.

"Thank you!" I mouth to Nonna, blowing her and my now happy, gurgling baby a kiss as I hurry out the door. I need to make sure the patio is in order and ready to be filmed. The film crew from Milan is coming today, and then tomorrow a food writer from the *New York Times* is flying in to interview us. Since the Barefoot Contessa Ina Garten herself recommended our agrumato last month in *People* magazine, things have gone absolutely nuts. She named Cedro di Salò Oro, our citron and Casaliva olive oil agrumato, as her must-have new ingredient of the fall. "The name translates to citron gold," she explained under the photo of one of our bottles. "It's subtle yet alluring with the zing of the citron zest and the bright herbaceous notes of the olives. It's simply sublime."

The Barefoot Contessa called our citron olive oil sublime.

I can now die happy.

Nonna continues her instruction as I fly out the door. She loves what she does, teaching these cooking classes to guests who travel from all over the world to stay with us on the farm for a week or two.

They swim in the lake, sunbathe, work in the garden, sample the local olive, citrus, and wine harvests, and take classes in local cooking from Nonna. And they pay a lot, leaving happy and full and suntanned.

And occasionally, for a special guest who has a hungry, searching look, Nonna will pull out the cookbook and have them open to a recipe just for them. She picks and chooses who she thinks the book will help, continuing the legacy of hospitality, assistance, and welcome that is the backbone of our family. I am proud of her, proud to be a Costa.

Surprisingly, Lisa was our first guest. She took one bite of Nonna's pasta her first night staying with us and almost swooned. True, she only took that one bite since she doesn't eat carbs, but it was enough. As soon as she got home, she started spreading the word, and suddenly, we were swarming with wealthy Upper East Side women eager to taste "a little bite of heaven," as Lisa labeled Nonna's tagliatelle. We have her to thank for helping us get started. Now we attract visitors from all over the world. It has been a hard three years filled with long hours, setbacks, and often just barely scraping by. But now it is finally all starting to pay off.

As of this year we are one of the ten top places to stay in the Lake Garda region. I credit Alex's social media savvy for most of it. A few other things have helped too. Two years ago, I got Nonna on Pasta Grannies and she rocked her segment on Tortellini nodo d'amore. Turns out everyone loves the idea of love-knot tortellini. And my cookbook, which I barely managed to finish on time with a lick and a prayer, surprised everyone by doing pretty well. It wasn't a *New York Times* bestseller, but the publisher was happy enough with the sales numbers that they offered me another cookbook deal. And I was happy enough with the advance they offered that I said yes. The advance paid for some much-needed repairs around the farm and a good used car with room for the baby.

Now I am collaborating with Nonna on a new cookbook, an exploration of family and tradition through the favorite recipes of local families around Lake Garda. I adore what I do, and although it often means a lot of work and little sleep, there's a new roof on the farmhouse and our bank account has a fat little cushion in it that makes me sleep easier at night.

This frenzy of media attention for the agrumato recipe has taken us by surprise, however. I just got an email this morning from Gordon Ramsay's personal assistant letting us know that Gordon would love to sample a bottle of our Cedro di Salò Oro and is considering featuring it on *Gordon Ramsay: Uncharted*. It's amazing news, and I'm feeling overwhelmed and grateful and a little anxious about it all. Things are moving so fast these days. It's making me a little dizzy.

I climb the stone steps to the patio, glancing over the silvery olive groves and down to the lake. Nicolo and Lorenzo are somewhere out in the groves, getting ready for the harvest. It won't be for a few more weeks. The sunshine is still warm and golden in mid-October, but I can feel the chill in the air. Soon we will enter a quieter period after the bustle of the summer and the long days of the olive and citron harvest. As if summoned by me thinking about him, Nicolo pops out of the tree line and comes over to the table where I am tidying up. He is sweaty and dirty. He has never looked happier. He drops a kiss on the top of my head, and I close my eyes and press my lips to the warm stubble of his cheek, savoring him for a moment. He smells like amber and cedar overlaid by sun-warmed soil and almost-ripe olives. In a word, delicious.

"What are you doing out here, amorino mio? Aren't the television people coming soon?" he says with a chuckle. I nod, leaning into him, eager for his touch but not wanting to muss my camera-ready hair.

"They'll be here any minute." I wipe away a few stray olive leaves from the table.

A car crunches up the lane, but it is only Tommaso in his disreputable old Dacia, dropping off Alex after school. As Alex predicted, Lisa was more than happy to have Alex finish out high school with us. She enrolled in the local high school and discovered to her delight that Tommaso was in her class. Now she is in her fifth and final year of Italian high school, studying at a classical and linguistically focused school. She's doing amazingly. She's made a nice group of friends, speaks Italian like a local, and wants to either go to law school or be an interpreter for the UN. She's planning to study linguistics at university in Milan next year. We love that she won't be too far away.

"Ciao, Jules, ciao, Nicolo." Tommaso rolls down the window and waves to us, and Alex hops out of the car and grabs her heavy book bag, all long ash-brown hair and dark slim pants, chattering and laughing with Tommaso. Gone are the baggy, angsty clothes and the guarded demeanor. She has blossomed in Italy. I feel a lump in my throat as I watch her. When she leaves for university, we will all miss her terribly. But to see who she is becoming is a gift and a great joy.

Tommaso drives away and Alex turns and sees us, calling over her shoulder, "Be right there to get footage for the socials. Just let me drop my books."

"Take your time," I call back.

"How's our bambino?" Nicolo asks, straightening a chair.

"Cranky and cute as ever." I stand back and survey the patio. There, all is ready.

"Good," Nicolo says approvingly. "He may be named for your father, but he is my son for sure."

"Because he's cranky and cute?" I tease.

Nicolo grins. "Exactly."

He wraps his arms around my waist, nuzzling my neck for a moment. I melt. We took it slow at first, finding our footing as business partners and friends and gradually more. Then a year to the day I'd decided to stay in Italy, Nicolo led me to our tree, the oldest olive tree in the grove, and recited a sonnet he'd written. It wasn't very good poetry, but I didn't care. When he got down on one knee, I said yes immediately. I knew without a doubt who I wanted by my side for the rest of my life. Our wedding was a couple of months later—simple and small and perfect. We got married on the patio, surrounded by our loved ones and the olive trees. Aurora officiated after getting ordained online a week before the wedding. Nonna made the cake—not Orange Blossom but still delicious.

Tony arrived a year later, an unplanned surprise that has upended our lives in the best possible way. Violetta and Nonna are both besotted with the baby and engage in a good-natured competition to see who can spoil him more. So far I think Violetta is winning. I caught her feeding him sugar cubes straight from the bowl last week.

I hear the crunch of tires and see the film crew's white van turn into the courtyard. My pulse speeds up a bit and I feel a flutter of the old anxiety. I still get nervous before the cameras turn on, but I've learned how to manage it well here. I don't panic as often. I've learned to hold the tension of the unknown more lightly, to let myself rest secure in the love of my family.

For some reason I think of Drew, of the day three years ago when I said no to everything I thought I wanted and yes to all that really mattered. Saving the farm and building this business has been hard and frustrating, scary and exhilarating, but I've never regretted my choice. Last I heard, Drew was working as a backup dancer on a cruise ship show out of Florida. I guess he got the entertainment life he wanted after all. And me? I'm right where I belong.

Nonna sticks her head out the door as the film crew van pulls to a stop. A quiet Tony is perched on her hip, happily gnawing his carrot. "Lorenzo!" she yells. "You gnocco! Come have some pasta."

Slowly in the past few years her insults have softened to far more complimentary nicknames.

"Did she just call Zio Lorenzo a hunk?" I giggle. Nicolo and I exchange a knowing look. While on the surface nothing about Nonna and Lorenzo's relationship seems to have changed, more often than not now, when we head to our bedroom late at night, we see a sliver of light underneath the unused front parlor's door and the sound of muted laughter and endearments murmured in Italian. Often in the morning there are two little glasses with the dregs of grappa sitting by the sink. We don't talk about it, but I see the way he looks at her and the knowing smile she gives as she pretends not to notice. Whatever they're doing, it seems to make both of them happy.

I stand and wave to the film crew as they pile out of the van, then smooth my bob nervously, and cross myself and kiss my thumb for luck. I take a deep breath and try to relax. Out of the corner of my eye I spot Alex sprinting out the kitchen door, her phone in her hand, ready to capture footage for our social media accounts, which have each now surpassed 120,000 followers. Alex and I have painstakingly built up Olives and Amore as our family's brand. Now under the name @OlivesandAmore on Instagram, I demonstrate how to make local Italian recipes on my weekly segments and Alex shares all sorts of glimpses of our life on the farm through the @OlivesandAmore account on TikTok. Nonna often appears in my weekly segments to help me cook, and our followers adore her.

Often I think back to that day three years ago when I did not take the bite of the Orange Blossom Cake. Sometimes I regret that I missed my chance to see the happiest moment of my life, but mostly I just feel grateful that I found the courage to take a risk for my right hard things. Now I try to live as though each day may indeed contain the best moment of my life. One day it will, but I won't know it until I look back on my life from beyond the grave, with the wisdom and perspective of eternity. So I embrace each day as fully as I can, trying to infuse each hour with purpose, meaning, love, and joy. I think this is the most important lesson of the cookbook. This is the true secret of Orange Blossom Cake.

I call out a greeting in Italian, welcoming the news crew to the farm, to our life and family. Then I stand at the top of the stairs waiting for them to come up to me. Whatever this day holds, and the next and the next, I am here with open arms, eager to embrace it all. I am courageous and unafraid. I am ready.

Orange Blossom Cake Recipe

This recipe makes one 9-inch (nonmagical) orange blossom cake that is irresistibly rich, aromatic, and delicious! Don't skip the icing! It adds a zesty citrus punch that makes it the true star of this recipe.

- 2 cups flour
- 1 Tablespoon baking powder
- ¼ teaspoon salt
- 1 cup sugar
- 3 eggs
- 1 whole navel orange (You'll need a total of two navel oranges for this recipe. One for the batter plus one for the icing.)
- 1 cup olive oil
- ½ cup milk
- 3 Tablespoons orange liqueur (triple sec or Gran Marnier works well)
- 1 Tablespoon orange blossom extract

Note: Orange blossom extract is a delicious but uncommon ingredient. You can find it on Amazon or other online stores easily and it is not expensive.

Caution: This recipe calls for orange blossom extract, *not* orange blossom water or orange extract. If you cannot find orange blossom extract, you can substitute with an extra teaspoon of orange zest and a teaspoon of vanilla extract in the batter to achieve a slightly similar flavor. To substitute for orange blossom extract in the icing, add a teaspoon of vanilla but do not add extra orange zest as it is zesty enough!

1. Preheat oven to 325°F.

2. In a medium bowl, whisk together flour, baking powder, and salt.

3. In a larger bowl, whisk together the sugar and eggs.

4. Cut the navel orange into quarters, removing any hard stem parts, and puree the entire orange (peel and segments) until no distinct pieces of peel remain and the mixture is fairly uniform. It will be pulpy, which is normal.

5. Whisk the olive oil, milk, pureed navel orange, orange liqueur, and orange blossom extract into the sugar-egg mixture.

6. Add the dry ingredients and combine. The batter will be runny, which is normal.

7. Pour the batter into a round 9-inch cake pan or other similar sized cake pan.

8. Bake at 325°F for approximately 40–45 minutes until a cake tester inserted into the center of the cake comes out clean. Remove the cake from the oven and cool completely.

Icing

1 cup powdered sugar
1 teaspoon orange blossom extract
Zest from 1 navel orange
Juice from ½ navel orange

While the cake cools, make the icing.

1. Combine powdered sugar and orange blossom extract in a small bowl.

2. Zest whole navel orange and then squeeze the juice from half the orange.

3. Add zest and orange juice to sugar and orange blossom extract. Whisk until smooth.

4. When the cake is completely cool, pour the icing over the cake. Enjoy!

Acknowledgments

Grazie mille to the following wonderful folks who each in their own way helped make this story better and brighter. My fantastic agent, Kevan Lyon, who is simply a dream. My delightful and insightful editor, Kate Seaver, who strengthens every story with wisdom and kindness. The clever and capable Amanda Maurer and the rest of the wonderful team at Berkley—true professionals and lovely humans to boot. The kind and canny Ashley Hayes of Uplit Reads. My best book buddies—bestselling authors Marie Bostwick and Katherine Reay. These ladies are great literary sounding boards, and supportive and smart cohosts of our weekly author interview show @The10minutebooktalk (check us out on Instagram, Facebook, and YouTube). My generous and talented author community, including the lively PNW author lunch crew and the wonderfully supportive brunch bunch, especially Debbie Macomber and Sheila Roberts. The delightful Bookstagram community—true book lovers with kind hearts and amazing creativity! All my incredible independent bookstore friends including but not limited to Away with Words, Watermark Book Co., Invitation Bookshop, Island Books, Magnolia's Bookstore, Liberty Bay Books, Edmonds Bookshop, and Brick & Mortar Books, among other amazing Puget Sound bookshops. A million thanks for supporting local authors. You are the best!

Special thanks to the following: Book maven Brandy Bowen for being an awesome early reader with a keen editorial eye; Alessandra Casella, my Italian translator and now friend, who so warmly and generously corrected my Italian language in the story and gave me tips on Italian life. Any remaining errors are mine! Valentina and Agriturismo Costadoro for a wonderful stay in Lake Garda and delicious wine and olive oil tastings! Sweet and thoughtful Tracy Wall for the yummy orange olive oil cake recipes. My talented baking mom, Adelle, for being a good sport and helping me create an orange blossom cake recipe that would make Nonna Bruna proud. A and B, who bring such joy to my life. It's the greatest privilege to be your mom as you grow. And Y for joining me in delicious book research—driving me around Lake Garda, tasting olive oil with me, and being my adventure buddy and constant loving support for eighteen years! And for every reader who chooses not to let fear hold them back and instead courageously says yes to the right hard things in life. This story is for you.

The Secret of Orange Blossom Cake

RACHEL LINDEN

READERS GUIDE

Questions for Discussion

1. Why is Jules's show, *The Bygone Kitchen*, so important to her? What does the show represent in her life?

2. At the beginning of the story, why do you think Jules is unable to cook any recipes that feel personal to her? What changes for her as the story progresses?

3. Jules's family is filled with strong women. In what ways do Nonna Bruna, Alex, Aurora, and Lisa impact Jules's life? Are there strong women that have impacted your own life?

4. The connection between food and family is a major theme in this story. What is one recipe that is special to you or your family? Share what it means to you.

5. Loss, grief, and fear are major themes in this story. How does Jules wrestle with each of these emotions, and how does she grow by the end of the book?

6. Lake Garda and the Costa family's olive farm in Italy have been special yet complicated places in Jules's life. How have these places shaped her life?

7. How does the recipe for Orange Blossom Cake influence the lives of the Costa and Fiore family members, both in the past and the present?

8. How does fear of failure affect Jules as she struggles to make a decision about her future? Do you think fear often holds people back from what they want in life? Why or why not?

9. Nicolo tells Jules, "You have to pick the hard that means the most to you. The right hard thing." Do you agree? Why or why not? Is there a time in your own life where you have had to choose your right hard thing?

10. Nonna Bruna's cookbook acts as a catalyst to help change lives in unexpected ways. How does the cookbook influence the characters in the story? Is anyone left untouched by its magical abilities?

11. What important lessons does Jules learn by the end of the book? Which of those lessons most resonates with you and why?

12. If you could try a bite of Orange Blossom Cake and see the happiest moment of your life, would you choose to do it? Why or why not?

Photo by Mallory MacDonald

Rachel Linden is a novelist and international aid worker whose adventures in more than fifty countries around the world provide excellent grist for her writing. She is the author of *Recipe for a Charmed Life*, *The Magic of Lemon Drop Pie*, *Ascension of Larks*, *Becoming the Talbot Sisters*, and *The Enlightenment of Bees*. Currently, Rachel lives with her family on a sweet little island in the Pacific Northwest, where she enjoys creating stories about hope, courage, and connection, with a hint of romance and a touch of whimsy.

Ready to find
your next great read?

Let us help.

Visit prh.com/nextread

Penguin
Random
House